Under the Dog Star

Also by
Joseph Caldwell

In Such Dark Places
The Deer at the River

Joseph Caldwell

Viking

Under the Dog Star

VIKING
Viking Penguin Inc., 40 West 23rd Street, New York, New York 10010, U.S.A.
Penguin Books Ltd, Harmondsworth, Middlesex, England
Penguin Books Australia Ltd, Ringwood, Victoria, Australia
Penguin Books Canada Limited, 2801 John Street, Markham, Ontario, Canada L3R 1B4
Penguin Books (N.Z.) Ltd, 182–190 Wairau Road, Auckland 10, New Zealand

First published in 1987 by Viking Penguin Inc.
Published simultaneously in Canada

LIBRARY OF CONGRESS CATALOGING IN PUBLICATION DATA
Caldwell, Joseph, 1928–
    Under the dog star.
    I. Title.
PS3553.A396U5   1987   813'.54   86–40320
ISBN 0–670–81108–4

Printed in the United States of America by
The Book Press, Brattleboro, Vermont
Set in Avanta and Wolf Antiqua
Designed by Amy Hill

To Don Ettlinger

The author wishes to thank the Alfred
University Summer Place, the Corporation
of Yaddo, the Virginia Center for the
Creative Arts, and his friend Katrina
Ettlinger for their help and their
hospice during the time in which
this novel was written.

The title of this novel is taken from a
poem by Molly Peacock and is used here
with the kind permission of the poet.

Under the
Dog Star

1

When Grady Durant's husband, Andy, was killed holding up a gas station, he was wearing a mask made from the stockings Grady bought to go with the black dress she wore when she sang in the Christmas Cantata at Holy Apostles Church. The stockings, too, were black, but because it was Christmas and because Grady herself did not tend toward the severe, she'd added a random pattern of tiny red stars cross-stitched into the nylon. They would show only to the knee, but she worked the pattern all the way up because anything less would have been a half measure and she didn't like half measures.

When one of the stockings was made into the mask, it must have seemed that the wearer had taken on, along with his anonymity, a bad case of the chicken pox. The red stitchings were, in a way, prophetic, since they marked on Andy Durant's cheeks and forehead and chin with almost complete accuracy the places where the exploded glass would strike his face.

Andy Durant was not killed by a bullet. The way it was reported to Grady—and to the police—he'd already completed the hold-up and was on his way out to the car. The gas-station attendant, a kid really, who'd been on the job less than a week, called out to him, "Wait! There's more!" Andy had turned around just as the young man fired his hunting rifle through the station's window. The bullet missed, but one shard of the thrown glass hit Andy in the neck, effectively slitting his throat. Other pieces of the shattered window struck at various parts of his body, wounding him all over, especially in the face, chest, and arms, with one piece even nicking his left ear.

It hadn't been necessary for Grady herself to identify the body. Once the stocking mask was removed, both the police and the doctor at the hospital recognized him. He was Andrew Durant, associate editor of the local newspaper, the *Coble Tribune*. He'd come several times before to the police station in Schuylerville, where his final robbery occurred, but those other times it had been to cover a story. (It was of some interest later to realize that Andy himself had dutifully covered several of the hold-ups in the surrounding counties committed by the "Chicken-pox Bandit.")

By the time Grady saw him he'd been washed and it did seem indeed that he'd died of some peculiar disease or that the red stitchings of her black stocking had run their colors and left this imprint on his handsome face. He'd been stripped of the bloody clothes, and Grady could see that the body wounds were larger, as if he'd been shot, like Saint Sebastian, with arrows and had died a martyr's death.

Five robberies were attributed to Andy, all of them at filling stations within a fifty-mile radius of Coble. The total take was said to be $7,342, but none of the money was recovered. Grady accounted for every penny that had passed into and out of the family economy, discovering in the process that she'd paid twice for her son Peter's skis. A search of the house and Andy's desk at the paper turned up no money at all. There was talk of gambling and "another woman," market speculations and blackmail. But there were no answers.

As for Grady herself, it was as if the gunshot had been a starting pistol, sending her off at an accelerated pace that left her little or no time for reflection. She shed tears induced more by shock and perplexity than anguish and grief; buried her husband; and consoled, to the degree that she was able, her three children. She accepted sympathies and ignored stares, telling herself that all she had to do for the moment was go through the motions; she could add the emotional content when there would be more time. She felt, in a way, as though she were handing out promissory notes that would be called in sooner or later, but she never doubted that the funds could be found if and when they were needed. She knew she was a resourceful and intelligent woman, and her adequacy was never in question, especially to herself. The only noticeable effect of this response was that she felt pursued; she had the impression that she was in constant danger of being gained on, overtaken. Whether these were her emotional creditors who would eventually demand full or possibly usurious payment, she had no way of knowing. It could even be a rescue party or Andy himself, masked, trying to catch up with her, eager to explain everything. But Grady didn't care. She wouldn't look back. She merely set herself a goodly gallop and moved ahead.

Her major decision was to return to the farm that had come to her through her grandparents, her mother's parents who'd raised her since the age of three, after the car crash that had killed her mother and father. The move back, her friends told her, was absurd, even insane. Farm foreclosures were epidemic in the territory and even if she started out free of debt the banks were there, waiting. She should go back, she was told, to being a singing teacher. But Grady didn't want to go back to being a singing teacher; she wanted to go back to the farm. For her, the extravagance of Andy's death seemed to require an extravagant response. If he'd died in his sleep, she would have gone back to teaching; if he'd died of a stroke or a heart attack, she would have considered the farm but then gone back to her teaching. Andy killed, masked, in a hold-up, required nothing less than a return to the farm. She could be as stupid and as daring as he.

In the days and weeks that followed, she sold the house in Coble, paid off the mortgage, secretly returned to each of the filling stations the amount stolen, reclaimed the leased acreage on the farm, took stock of her pastures and outbuildings and machinery, hired an extra hand, gathered her children, the six hens and one rooster she'd kept even as a town dweller, and took off.

But now the pickup truck she'd bought secondhand stalled at the foot of the hill leading up to the farmhouse and wouldn't budge. Grady stared through the windshield at the tall grass, not even looking up. She would ignore the delay and, withered by her indifference, it would go quietly away.

Peter, Grady's fifteen-year-old son, felt otherwise. He'd never driven a pickup before and he was worried that the truck's refusal to move was a reflection on his inexperience. He pumped the clutch, shifted gears, turned the ignition off, then on, and kept trying to surprise the motor with sudden pedalings of the accelerator. He got nothing for his efforts but a low throaty growl, the truck's warning that it intended to stay exactly where it was. Peter tried the left- and right-turn signals and even the windshield wipers, hoping that one functioning part might inspire the others into action through good example. It didn't work.

"Stay here. It'll only take me a minute," he said. Then got out, raised the hood, and ducked his head inside like an innocent child curious about the tonsils of a crocodile.

"It won't go," said Martha, Grady's five-year-old, certain that this was a needed summary of their situation. Martha sat next to her mother in the middle of the seat, clasping a heap of her brother's clothes as if she'd been holding him in her arms but now he'd gone, leaving her nothing but this empty bunching of shirts and pants and jackets. She, too, stared ahead at the raised hood, quietly bewildered, wondering what had happened to the previous landscape.

Grady looked another moment at the unbending grass on the slope of the hill, then raised her feet from the cardboard carton jammed under the dashboard. She opened the door and shifted her legs sideways. The avocado plant lodged between a swollen suitcase and the sewing machine in the well behind the seat brushed her cheek. She looked at it, a warning to watch its step. All during the trip from town it had been nodding its floppy leaves right next to her head. Twice Grady had slapped her neck, thinking it was a bug. If the plant hadn't been a survivor of Peter's fourth-grade botany experiment, she would have chucked it out the window the minute they'd turned onto the country roads. Grady glared at it. Knowing what was good for it, it didn't move.

She got out and slammed the door. A deadweight clunk came from inside the hollows of the door, the sound of something knocked unconscious. "Easy on the truck, Mom," Peter said. He pulled his head out from under the hood and pressed his right ear as if it had just been punched.

"Sorry," Grady said. She put a hand on the door, a touch of apology if not of healing. But when she stepped back and looked at the truck, she thought of flogging it. They should beat it until it moved. It had it coming. That it was stalled was the least of it. Why had it allowed itself to be so put upon to begin with? Anything that submissive deserved to be flogged. Piled in back were a chest of drawers complete with mirror, an overstuffed chair, a hallway coat tree, a hump-topped trunk that looked as if it dated back to pirate days, a rocker, boxes of food and stereo records, a brand new plastic garbage can packed with dishes and, tied to the very top, a kitchen table flat on its back, it four legs sticking straight up in the air like those of a dead deer.

On the roof of the cab, Anne, Grady's seventeen-year-old daughter, sat backed by the crate of hens, presiding over the heap like a pageant queen enthroned on her float. The hens clucked away like maiden aunts giving conflicting solutions to the present difficulty. "Oh, shut up," Grady said. Offended, they fell silent, but stretched their necks to the limit and, with quick jerks of the head, pretended to be evaluating the view. Anne looked at them over her shoulder, then faced front again, contemptuous that they'd been so easily subdued. One hen clucked a seeming complaint at such a harsh judgment.

Anne began picking a scab on her right elbow, quietly, purposefully. Grady wondered if she wasn't ridding herself of this last vestige of childhood before completing her move to the farm. In the time since her father's death, Anne had changed from a pudgy duckling into a swan. Grady thought at first that her daughter had merely done what she'd been told to do for the past five years: stand up straight and pull in her stomach. Then she thought the girl's neck had lengthened, drawing the bulky body upward, shaping it to a perfect form with each proportion pleasantly related to the others. Grady finally decided she just hadn't been watching closely enough, that it wasn't until she'd seen her daughter mourning at the side of her father's grave that she realized she'd become a woman, and a beautiful one at that.

So that she wouldn't see again her daughter praying at her father's grave, Grady looked over toward Peter, bent down under the hood. The motor was a greasy crawl of tubes and blocks and cylinders, a stomach blackened and bloated by the plague. She took a cigarette from the pack in her sweater pocket and lit it. She'd started smoking again three days after Andy's death and had promised herself she'd quit once they'd arrived at the farm. The farm was at the top of the hill. She was at the bottom.

Grady drew in on the cigarette and let the smoke out slowly, a curling cloud weaving upward in front of her. When it cleared, she raised her head, cocked it a little to the left and looked up at the house on top of the hill. Its paint weathered away, it was the color of ash, as if it had been burned and this was the moment just before it would fall into a light gray dust. There was, Grady conceded, a certain rightness to this. One suggestion she'd heard recently was to burn the empty house and the unused outbuildings, plow it all under, and lease the cleared acreage—some of the best on the whole farm—for additional income. Looking at the house now, Grady was relieved that she hadn't listened.

Of course there was work to be done. The sag in the porch that ran the front length of the house had gotten worse, and Grady could see the black pockmarks on the green roofing left by the hail storm twelve years before, when her grandparents were still alive and working the farm. Under the dining-room bay at the side of the house spindly stalks of woundwart had replaced the irises; a few surviving hollyhocks at the far end of the porch struggled up out of a patch of horseweed. Grady was surprised to see horseweed growing so close to the house. It belonged near the pasture fence or even in the field itself. But then the house had been untenanted for seven years, since her grandfather's death, so it was really no wonder that the horseweed had felt bold enough to advance almost to the front door.

Grady considered climbing the hill and letting the pickup either follow or stay where it was and rot—along with all the junk heaped onto its useless carcass. Then she felt, no, she'd rather make her formal return to the house of her childhood accompanied by the furniture she'd taken with her at her marriage and by her three children, and armored (somewhat) by the recalcitrant truck. Also she didn't think she should go ahead without the hens. They were the descendants of the small brood she'd brought with her into town, a wedding present from her grandmother accompanied by the injunction that she not forget her proud origins as a farmer.

Grady took one last puff on her cigarette, dropped it onto the gravel and ground it with the sole of her shoe. "Martha," she called, "do you want to get out? Peter has to fix the truck. Wouldn't you like to pick some flowers?"

Martha reached over and opened the door on her mother's side, then crawled out over the clothes, trailing Peter's pants and jackets onto the driveway after her. She kicked a sweater away, sending it under the front wheel, then slammed the door, catching the sleeve of a shirt she'd been holding with such concern only a moment before.

"Pick Mother a pretty bouquet," Grady said, leaning against the side of the truck and lighting another cigarette. Martha dutifully made for the dandelions, fleabane, and gentians that grew in the tall grass along the rutted road. What had been the front lawn had deteriorated into almost perfect hay. The hillside abounded in alfalfa, clover, and timothy, but it should be mowed before it topped off and before the next rain. Automatically, Grady checked the sky. A few cumulus high in the west, but no threat of rain that she could see. Peter was staring down at the motor, his fists clenched at his hips as if he were getting ready to challenge it to a fight. "You'd better get Royal," she said.

Peter looked at his mother, then toward the top of the hill. He put his open hands to the sides of his mouth and yelled, "Royal!" There was no answer. Peter called again, and started up the slope, bending into the high grass.

Around the side of the house came a young man, a boy really, tall and skinny, an old stained gray fedora shading his pale face. His loose chinos were held up by brown suspenders and he was wearing an unironed white shirt with sleeves that came to about three inches above his wrist bones. It was Royal Provo, the extra help she'd taken on, but, with the hat, the suspenders, the shirt, and the pants, he could have been one of the hired hands Grady'd seen in photographs taken during threshing time, long before she had come to live on the farm, a photograph taken when oats were still grown, and wheat. The current teenage dress code required that everything look discarded, preferably by someone a different size, as if everyone between the ages of twelve and twenty wanted to disclaim vanity and assert independence from the tyrannies of exact measurement. Royal Provo, apparently, was no exception.

Royal was Peter's friend. They'd met about two months ago, when Peter had worked after school at the checkout counter of the Dawson Mall Grand Union. Royal had been a full-time cashier and Peter had bagged groceries for him. When Grady announced the return to the farm, Peter proposed that Royal come along to live there, to help, since Anne would be away most of the summer working as a swimming instructor again at Camp Kennedy. Grady did not think so. There was no extra money to pay a hired hand and she didn't want to take on the burden of another human being in her life.

But Royal was not really a cashier, Peter explained, he was a mechanic; he knew all about motors. Grady began to be interested. Her interest, however, faltered again when Peter, overplaying his hand, mentioned that his friend had recently been sent out into the world from what was locally called The Home, an industrial school for orphans; that he lived alone in a rooming house on Larkin Street; and that he was very quiet.

To Grady, Royal sounded far too frail, far too waiflike. But Peter had the good sense to repeat his praise for Royal's genius as a mechanic. Grady knew that the first thing a farmer should be was his own mechanic. If he couldn't take care of and repair his own machinery, he was at the mercy of charlatans and incompetents, to say nothing of delays. For want of a tightened bolt, a baler was lost, for want of a baler a day was lost, for want of a day—right on to a lost crop, a foreclosed farm, and a ruined life, probably unto the third generation.

She asked Royal the day she met him what he could do with

a tractor that hadn't been used for seven years. He said he could make it go. So Grady had brought him to the farm when she and Peter came to take the boards off the windows. He made the tractor go. He was taken on, and moved himself to the farm that night so he could begin work on the disker, the baler, and even an old wheelbarrow. His only request was that he be allowed to fix up what had been something of a bunkhouse in the old, old days of hired help and itinerant workers. Grady had said there was plenty of room in the house and that he would be more than welcome to be one of the family, but Peter had taken up the cause, including himself in the arrangement, citing it as an adventure, and Grady had consented.

She'd thought since that Royal might have wanted to be alone, especially after his years of enforced communality at The Home, that it was privacy he wanted, not adventure, and that Peter was an intrusion. But Royal had said nothing, nor had he even looked as if he might object—and besides, Peter deserved some reward for being uprooted, to say nothing of a recompense for the loss of his father—so Grady gave her permission to them both.

Looking at Royal's clothes, it occurred to Grady that these might well be genuine hand-me-downs, that the boy had nothing of his own except what had been bequeathed by others, and she was somewhat ashamed for having judged him a conformist when he was probably the uncomplaining recipient of whatever came his way. Seeing him there at the top of the hill, in front of the old house, waiting, wearing the old gray fedora he'd found on a nail in the tractor shed, Grady couldn't help feeling that she'd come on the wrong day, in the wrong time. The young man seemed puzzled by their arrival, bewildered that these strangers should have summoned him from his chores, interrupting the harnessing of a horse or the honing of a plow. Why was he being asked to welcome and accept them, especially when they had come to take his place, to usurp his stewardship, to make of him no more than a ghost, an unnamed youth caught in a fading photograph.

The boy took off his hat and ran his sleeve across his nose. Immediately the hired hand vanished not in a puff of smoke but in a burst of flame. A great shock of orange-red hair had been sucked up from the boy's scalp by the hat's removal, chunks and clumps tossed and leaning against each other, a conflagration the hat had only momentarily extinguished but that could now rage unchecked. This was not the first time she'd seen the hair, but she wished he wouldn't surprise her with it. No sooner had she adapted herself to his general lack of color than he'd spring this on her, a joke and a reproof. Except that the boy obviously intended nothing of the kind. All he did was take off his hat, and since it was likely that this action would repeat itself quite frequently during their association, Grady recognized that she might have to adjust her susceptibilities.

"What's the matter?" Royal asked, his voice low and solemn without being gruff.

"We're stuck," Peter said. Royal nodded, put his hat back on, and started down, not through the grass, but along the curve of the roadway.

Peter watched him as if to identify the proper route for his own descent, then moved out onto the gravel and followed at a respectful three paces behind.

As Royal got closer, Grady could see again how pale he was. No wonder that with the hat on he would suggest a ghost. He was grub-white, as if he'd lived his whole life under a stone. His blue eyes were practically the only color on his face, since even his lips were only the palest pink and he didn't have a freckle or even a pimple to his name.

"If it's the carburetor, are we dead for good?" Peter asked. From the tone of his voice, part casual, part serious, Grady could tell that his concern was not for the carburetor; he only wanted to hear himself say the words, proving himself an initiate into the mysteries of motors—which he wasn't, or hadn't been until Royal had introduced him.

Royal, however, took him seriously. "Is that what it looks like?" To Grady's relief, Peter answered, "I don't know." They put their heads under the hood. Grady turned away. If the hood came slamming down it would halve them at the waist and she'd just as soon not see it. "Will it be very long?" she asked.

"Two seconds," Peter said.

"Is there anything I can do to help?"

"You can tell Martha to get away and stop telling us what to do," he said.

"Martha, did you pick your flowers?" Grady asked.

Martha stepped away from the truck and shifted her eyes a little, the way she always did when she was about to tell a lie. "They don't want me to," she said.

"Yes, they do. Tell them they're for Mother."

"I did."

"Well, tell them again."

"But they—"

"Never mind what 'they.' Just go pick Mother some flowers."

Martha climbed back into the cab of the truck and looked out again at the raised hood. It was Grady's guess that she'd sit there a few minutes, then get out and do what she'd been told. Whether these intervening moments were given over to interior persuasion or were a necessary show of independence, Grady could never tell. All she knew was that Martha required a brief interim between being given a command and carrying it out.

Right now, however, Grady wished Martha would look a little less independent. It made her seem isolated, almost forlorn. Grady considered being insistent about the flowers, not because she felt it necessary to win so petty a struggle, but because she'd found long ago that adamancy, or even outright anger, was her best defense against heartbreak. It seemed to her that, in the wisdom of things, mothers had been given the gift of exasperation because, without it, their children, with all their earnest goodwill, their high-minded sulks, their brave shows of integrity, would break their hearts ten times a day.

Anne had climbed down from her perch and was collecting the clothes Martha had strewn in the roadway. She shook them out, one at a time, and placed them carefully across her arm. The path of the clothes led her to the door of the cab. Grady watched her lean in and say something to Martha. Martha seemed impressed. Anne leaned in again. This time Martha turned and looked at her, not sure she wasn't being tricked out of her sullenness. Anne simply tilted her head to one side, a way of underscoring whatever suggestion she might have made.

Martha slipped down from the seat, jumped onto the gravel, and marched self-importantly toward the grass, pretending to ignore her mother on the way. Grady realized that Anne had hit upon a new and workable strategy for getting Martha to do what she wanted her to do: present it as a conspiracy, a plot shared only by Martha and the co-conspirator. Grady must add this to her repertory of persuasions for future use.

Anne smoothed the clothes out on the seat of the cab. This was the first time since her father's death that Grady had seen Anne return to her habit of doing things, without thought, without comment, for her younger brother. It seemed that from the day of Peter's birth Anne had not only watched over him but enjoyed him. As a baby, as a child, Peter had been a prime source of wonder and amusement. When the two of them got older, they developed an enthusiasm for each other's achievements, a belief in each other's merits (visible at times only to themselves). But since their father was killed, they seemed to have gone off separately, the death too private to be shared. Maybe that period was ending now. Grady hoped so. Each could use the encouragements that only the other could give.

Anne left the door open and went to watch Peter and Royal.

First she watched their hands at work under the hood, then she bent down to watch their faces, then the motor itself.

When Royal straightened up to rub his nose, Anne too straightened up, waited until he'd finished, then walked away as if her assigned task had been to see how Royal Provo rubbed his nose.

Grady decided to have another cigarette. There were four more in the pack. She lit one, inhaled, inspected the tip, then dropped the cigarette and mashed it with her shoe. She pulled out the remaining three and, one by one, tore the paper apart and released the tobacco to the wind. The hens clucked their horror at the waste and Grady, twisting the empty pack, was reminded of wringing a hen's neck. She twisted it again in full view of the protesting fowls, then crumpled it and jammed it back into her pocket.

Peter and Royal were bent well under the hood, speaking in low voices like two surgeons working away at the innards of an anesthetized patient. From the movement of their arms and the flex of their muscles, it seemed they must be dealing with nerves, veins, something intricate. Peter emerged with a small chunk of metal. He turned it over in his hand, examining it. A liver? A left ventricle? The small intestine? A lung blackened by pollution? He ducked back under, twitching with excitement and purpose. Royal, too, had become more animated.

Now not only their arms, but their legs were in motion, their entire bodies. A crucial moment had been reached. Their feet stepped sideways, backwards, and forwards; their heads came together and parted; they brushed against each other's ears, each other's hair. They were consulting, exchanging information, necessary data, hushed, intense.

Slower now, more deliberate, they knocked elbows, rubbed forearms, the muscles moving under the skin like sleek and supple animals. Hips and thighs came together, parted, then came together again. Royal was saying something, but Grady couldn't hear. Peter then rushed around to the driver's seat, jumped inside, and turned on the ignition. The motor turned over, once, twice, then caught.

He jumped out and went back to where Royal was watching the motor, alert to a possible relapse. Peter studied Royal's face as if he might read there the actual reasons for the truck's recovery. Royal looked at him a moment; then they both stared blankly at the throbbing motor as if they'd forgotten completely what their relationship to it had been.

"Come on," Grady called, "before it stops again. Martha? Come get in the middle." Martha and Anne came down the hill, looking thoughtfully at the flowers in their hands as if counting them. "Come on. We're ready!" Grady said.

She turned to get into the truck just as it drove right past her. Royal was at the wheel. Peter was in the middle of the seat with his arm stretched across Royal's shoulders. They didn't even seem to see her; their eyes were on the bend of the drive ahead.

Anne and Martha stopped at the edge of the roadway to let the truck go by. The horn honked and, at the sound, Martha threw her flowers up into the air. Anne shrugged, then tossed her own flowers at the truck. The horn honked again, the truck reached the top of the hill, turned at the side of the house, and was gone.

Anne had taken Martha's hand and the two of them were trudging up ahead. Grady watched as they too rounded the house and were gone. She stood there, not sure if she wanted to make the climb after all. She heard one door of the truck slam, then the other. Still she waited. Then there was the slam of the screen door leading to the back hall, sounding far away, as if it were already evening. Grady waited another moment, then, putting one foot in front of the other and drawing her body forward with each step, she started up the hill.

2

It was not Anne's habit to take out the money and count it over and over again as if it were a miser's hoard, but she had very specific plans for it, and the idea had come into her head that morning, when she was watching the truck being fixed, that the plans might be affected by Royal Provo. Rather than just sit down and think the idea through, she decided that an intimate session with the money might enlighten her, might clarify what were only the first stirrings of a suggestion. She figured she'd count the money and by the time she was finished, she'd know what was on her mind.

She'd have to hurry. Royal had surprised them all by having cut and baled the hay in the field just beyond the barn—a testing of the tractor and the cutter bar and baler he'd repaired in the week and a half he'd been staying alone at the farm. Now she was supposed to drive the pickup through the field (he hadn't gotten around to fixing the axle of the old hay rick yet) while Royal and her brother loaded the bales. Ordinarily she would have refused. She was not there to do farm work. She was very specifically a temporary guest and unavailable for any chores whatsoever. But she did want to take another look at Royal Provo, and driving the pickup would be her chance to do it.

Before taking the money out of the bottom of the garment bag where she kept her winter coat and woolen skirts, Anne looked around her room. She knew no one was there, but she felt the gesture was required, a ceremonial offering to secrecy. She'd pulled back the bedspread, a covering in the design of a Raggedy Ann doll that dated back to her mother's childhood. The money now would show itself more clearly against the pale blue sheet. And besides, she had some vague sense of not wanting to corrupt Raggedy Ann by putting all that money into her embrace.

Anne looked over toward the window. The white cotton curtains blew in lightly, then were pulled onto the screen. If she were going to stay here on the farm one of the first things she'd get rid of, after Raggedy Ann, would be the curtains. They were limp and dingy even after washing and ironing. They too were from the time when this had been her mother's room. The wallpaper had been there for years, the bed, the dresser, the chair, the same.

It had surprised her mother to realize that this would be her daughter's room and that she, as head of the house, was expected to move into her grandparents' room down the hall near the bathroom. Anne had come with her before the move to scrub floors and wash windows and rehang the curtains. Her mother had brought along some clothes, and when she'd headed for her old room Anne had asked, "Isn't that going to be mine?" Her mother had looked at her as if not sure what her daughter was doing there, then examined the clothes thrown over her arm. She seemed for a moment not to know whose they were. Then she'd headed for the larger bedroom with the larger bed, walking slowly, thoughtfully, not quite sure she was doing the right thing.

Anne, her hand fumbling around in the bottom of the garment bag, looked at the wallpaper. After the curtains, the wallpaper would have to go. Strawberries on a vine bordered by bands of silver and cream were not her idea of decor. The bed and the dresser could stay, but a coat of fresh paint would definitely be called for to cover the varnished baseboard, the door, and the window frame.

Then Anne remembered again that she would not be staying. Tomorrow she would be leaving for her summer job. And after that she'd start to carry out her plan. She drew out the money, packets the size of bricks, and tossed them onto the bed. The rubber band on one of the stacks snapped and the bills fell away from each other like leaves in an opening book, as if to reveal something on a particular page. It showed, finally, a twenty-dollar bill on one side and a five-dollar bill on the other.

There should be $7,142 in all, mostly tens, twenties and singles. One time she'd counted $7,082; another time, $6,977, but $7,142 was the most consistent count and the fourth time around she accepted it as official. It was two hundred less than the tally given by the police and published in the papers, but her father might have used that much for ready cash. Or the police could be wrong, or the gas-station attendants could have lied. In any event, she had enough for her purposes.

She'd found the money in a carton labeled EXTRA CHRISTMAS TREE LIGHTS when she was helping pack for the move. It was her job to go through the basement storeroom, and when she'd lifted the carton down from the top shelf, it seemed too heavy for lights. When she looked inside, there was the money.

Her first thought was to yell upstairs to her mother, but before the thought could become a genuine impulse—much less a decision—she began prodding and probing another idea. That the money wasn't hers was quickly struck from her mind. Finders keepers losers weepers would be good enough for her.

As she began to count now, on the bed, she realized she couldn't think about her plan and keep accurate track of the money at the same time, so she decided to separate the bills into stacks of ones, fives, tens, and twenties, the few fifties, and the three one hundreds, while keeping some thought of Royal Provo in her mind. If the thought of him persisted even in the face of a natural distraction like all that money staring right at her, then she'd know she was supposed to give him a more serious and thorough consideration.

The plan itself had its origins in Anne's experience during her father's wake, the night after he'd been killed. At the funeral parlor, something peculiar happened to her. She wanted desperately to have sex. Before that particular evening, sex had been a possibility, an event that would take place all in good time. It was an interest, a fascination, but hardly an obsession. That night it became an unbearable need, a craving she'd never had before.

As she stood near her father's casket, school friends, boys to whom she'd been indifferent, suddenly presented possibilities she hadn't been able to see before. Acne and glasses were no longer a deterrent. They even took on a sexuality she hadn't sensed before. For the first time, she became aware of hands, the size of them, the shape and length of fingers, the corded veins on their backs. Eyes and lips didn't count for much anymore. She'd always been aware of them. Now she was looking for the secret signs. A neck, a nose, feet, an Adam's apple, ears—the cast rather then the color of the eyes, slightly crossed or vaguely out of alignment, suggesting the aftermath of lovemaking, a near insensate condition where the eyes had been knocked out of focus by all that slamming and banging.

And she realized for the first time that her nominal boyfriend,

Bob Burton, had on his head not merely coarse and unruly hair but a rampage of wild confusions that invited contest. (During the wake, he had stood nearby, far enough so as not to claim kinship with the family, but close enough to indicate a more than ordinary degree of sympathy.)

Looking at his hair, Anne began to feel wet and wondered if she might have started to smell. After fending off a disturbing appreciation of Steven Curry's walleye, she excused herself and went into the alcove off the main parlor. Bob followed her. If she'd had her way, she would have drawn the drapes and started in with him right then and there.

And all the time, she couldn't believe that this was how she was feeling. This was not who she was. And her father had just been killed. He was dead; he was there in that coffin. And all she could think about was sex. Making love. Fucking.

This was, she told herself, panic over her father's death, the wild reach for a diversion strong enough to distract her from the truth of what had happened. Or it could be a cry for compensation, for a reassurance in its most primitive form that she was loved. It could be revenge, it could be the first step on a journey toward new comfortings, new allegiances; it could be the eruption of a new freedom, the release from an unspoken constraint that her father's presence had imposed.

What surfaced finally was the notion that, through some error in evolutionary time, she'd been thrust back into a primal state long since discarded by her species, where death demanded immediate procreation, where a loss, in reflex, activated with implacable force every impulse toward sexual union, guaranteeing without delay the continuation of the race. She'd been thrown back to a time before grief had been invented, before respect and reverence had even been thought of. There was no moment allotted to sorrow and obsequies, no time of mourning and loss. Fuck. Nothing but fuck.

Anne protested that a mistake had been made; this was worse than a case of mistaken identity, it was a cosmic blunder that canceled the civilizing advances of years upon years, of generation upon generation. And even if this primal practice were still in operation, it had chosen the wrong proponent. She was not—the phrase would allow no substitute—"that kind of girl."

Protest, argue, and quarrel as she might; rationalize, theorize, and analyze as she did, it affected nothing. All she could rely on to disguise or control her present state was habit. She had her native reticence, her pride, even a certain stinginess that might be counted on to rescue her. But when Bob Burton offered to drive her home later and she said yes with quiet thanks, she decided, within the moment of acceptance, what she'd do. And she did it.

When they'd stopped in front of her house, she leaned over and kissed his cheek. As was their custom, he turned and kissed her on the lips. Then, to continue the ritual, she reached her hands toward his shoulders. He shifted toward her and she shifted toward him and they embraced.

It was here that the set ceremony was disrupted. She pressed her face into his and began rubbing herself against him. When he drew back a little, probably more to get air than to collect his senses, she said, "Don't. Don't." She pulled him toward her, but before she could begin kissing him again, he said, "I think what you need is a good night's sleep."

When, after the funeral, Anne and Bob stopped seeing each other, it was assumed that the manner of her father's death was the cause: Bob Burton didn't have the guts to stand by her. Because he was an eighteen-year-old with honor, Bob said nothing to change the general thinking, and Anne, because she was too confused to tell one motive from another, made no comment either for or against him.

Besides, she had decided she'd better get married, and Bob was too young. Marriage was the only solution to the relentless condition, which failed to end after the funeral. It persisted, a chronic state for which there was only one known remedy. Married, she'd be taken care of. What she'd do then wouldn't count. All she had to do was find someone who'd reveal himself to be as possessed as she was, someone who shared the same necessity to "settle down"—and as soon as possible.

But a further complication had entered her life. As the daughter of Andrew Durant, as a child of tragedy and crime, she experienced a certain local celebrity. Wherever she went, people were aware of her. She was spoken of in tones not employed for just anyone. She found that, in a store, it was best not to look around because everyone was looking at her and she wasn't supposed to notice.

She began to walk with a certain dignity; she began to be more than usually polite; she began to speak with a clearer diction and to use more grammatical sentences. Her improved walk was interpreted as reform; her politeness as reparation for her father's crimes; and her diction and grammar as amends for the crudity of the family scandal. Again the interpretation was preferable to the truth. Anne had, in fact, taken on the role of a celebrity and was acting out, with her walk, pride; with her diction, condescension; and with her grammar, disdain—all characteristics she deemed essential to her newly bestowed status.

Her celebrity, however, interfered with her plan to marry. She did not want to marry beneath herself. It would have to be someone who, first of all, appreciated her singularity, and was himself somewhat out of the ordinary. No one in the town of Coble seemed to qualify. She also suspected that marriage would put an end to her distinction, that she would be retired from notoriety, that the stares would stop, that the tone of voice would lose its hush. No longer a Durant, she would have to surrender all the perquisites that attached to her father's name. She wasn't sure she'd like that.

At the same time, of course, she mourned for her father. She pitied her family. But none of this superseded or cancelled her other urges. She hadn't known that one could be sexually rapacious and still faithful to family feelings. She'd thought that sexual ravenings would gobble up sympathy and affection and pity, and leave her free to follow a single-minded pursuit. She had also assumed that selfishness, greed and vanity would replace her life-long instincts for generosity and concern and that she'd be relieved by the substitution. But it hadn't worked out that way, not at all. The fabric of her character was apparently still loose enough to accommodate these new and gaudy strands and to weave them easily into the general pattern. It altered the design—radically—but it was still the same cloth. Her arousals were looped in and out of her pity; her grief was interwoven with her vanity, her love was cast into stunning relief by her deceits.

When she found the money, she wasn't sure at first whether this was an added complication or the means of resolving the conflicts that had been harrying her. Almost immediately, she decided it was a solution. She knew what she'd do with it. She'd run away. She also knew where she'd wind up. But she was too ashamed by the obviousness of her idea to let it present itself in just so many words.

She took into account her need for sexual experience; she also considered her recent addiction to celebrity. Only one place that she could think of would take care of both. It could even bring the two elements together in a congenial mix. She had decided to run away to Los Angeles and be, of all things, a television actress.

(That she had no talent, that the money would not last very long, were given quick consideration and swift dismissal. Once in California she would be in a position, she believed, to receive both. She had the notion that if she were in the right place at the right time, doing the right thing, talent or some workable equivalent would be given and her money supply would be replenished.

This notion was accompanied by a vision of herself sitting in an outdoor café sipping something from a frosted glass.)

Even as she made the decision, even as she embraced it as the perfect resolution of all the contending elements—sex, celebrity, money—she rebelled against it. She thought it unfair that such a clichéd notion, available to any unthinking teenager, should be the one presented—and accepted—by a young woman of her intelligence. More than that, it seemed insulting that the whirlwind that had caught her up—her family's tragedy, her sudden sexuality, her grief for her father, her discovery of the money—should set her down in a place no more imaginative than Hollywood. Surely she, Anne Durant, should be able to come up with something more exotic, even more outrageous, than television acting. But she couldn't.

She figured autumn would be the time to do it. She would indeed have to "run away." She could hardly explain where the money had come from. And besides, she liked the idea of a fresh start. She would be a new and different person, a young woman no longer bound to kindness and generosity, to easy affection and unharried sexuality. She would be what she had already become.

"Anne!" Royal called from outside. "We need you."

Anne went to the window. There was Royal Provo, kicking the tires of the pickup. Her brother, next to him, was jumping up and down, yelling, "The cows are coming! The cows are coming!"— a refrain he'd started when their mother had announced earlier that the herd would arrive in three days and they'd better be ready.

"Right out," she called. When she turned back to the bed, she realized she'd gone to the window holding a fistful of tens in her right hand and a fistful of twenties in her left. There was no problem, however. Neither Royal nor Peter had been looking up at the window. Royal was looking at the tire and Peter was looking at Royal.

Carefully she stacked the money again in the bottom of the garment bag.

"Anne!" Peter called again. "The cows are coming."

"Anne!" Royal yelled.

Anne zipped the bag shut and hung it on a hook at the back of the closet.

Driving the pickup truck over a bumpy field with small inclines and hidden rocks was not easy, and Anne had to move at the pace Peter and Royal required to throw and stack the bales. The usual lurchings and slidings, the bouncings and tossings that one could expect on a rutted and stony road were transformed now into slow rollings and pulls, easy tilts and smooth recoveries, dream motions, except that they required a control beyond Anne's abilities.

When the truck stalled for the fourth time and Royal was waiting up ahead holding an already lifted bale, Anne started the motor, shifted into third, and drove off as fast as she could go. She passed Royal, dumbfounded, made a sharp left at the edge of the field and cut back, steering in and out of the bales on the ground, running an obstacle course. Peter, in the bed of the truck, was pounding on the roof of the cab, shouting, "What are you doing? Where you going? Slow down!"

Anne bounced up and down on the seat, twice hitting the roof with the top of her head, once swinging way to the right but keeping her hold on the wheel. When she'd completely circled the field, she pulled to a quick stop in front of Royal. Before she could spit out the words "I quit!" Royal said quietly, "You're a good driver."

Peter jumped down, dusting from his arms and shoulders the hay that had stuck when he had been thrown against the stacked bales in the bed of the truck. He was laughing; he was happy. "Do it again," he said. "Only let Royal ride in back too so he gets to know what it's like."

"No!" Royal said. "We've got to finish." Still holding the lifted bale, he stared at Anne.

As far as Anne could see, Royal Provo had the face of a catfish. His thick lips looked as though they'd been rolled outward and up, exposing parts on each lip that should have been left inside his mouth. His snub nose was turned up just enough so you could see how pink it was inside his nostrils, and his pale blue eyes were rimmed with a light red line as if he had a perpetual cold. She knew that under his hat was the carrot-colored hair, but the face itself—as a matter of fact his whole body, from what she could see and what she could guess—was like something in a coloring book before the crayons had been applied.

And yet she was curious. Was he really as scrawny as he seemed? That he was efficient, even gifted, counted for something too. He was out of the ordinary, that was certain. He'd be like no one else—whatever that might prove to be. He seemed to challenge her imagination. Maybe he didn't look so much like a catfish after all. And his eyes, she noticed for the first time, were ever so slightly crossed.

"Peter," Royal said, "you can throw and Anne can stack."

Peter's mouth immediately went slack with disappointment. "But I like it the way we work together," he said. "When you throw and I'm up back."

"But I don't think Anne wants to drive."

"Sure she does. She never drove a pickup before and now's her chance." He turned to his sister. "You want to drive, don't you? At least give it another try. You can do it, Anna Banana. Let's see you go for it."

There was no way for Anne to refuse. Her brother wanted too much to preserve the present arrangement. And besides, it was the first time since their father's death he'd called her by the name permitted to him alone, Anna Banana. His exuberance had returned and she was touched by her brother's willingness to be cheerful. "Okay," she said. "I'll see what I can do, but don't blame me if you get knocked around."

"I like it," Peter said and jumped up onto the truck. "Come on, Royal, throw!"

Anne started the motor and began the slow, controlled movement forward. She felt the thump of the thrown bale and the thud when Peter lifted it into place on the stack. "Okay," Peter yelled again. "Throw!" And the thump came again, Royal's response to Peter's call.

Holding the steering wheel in an easy grip, her foot touching as lightly as possible on the accelerator, Anne began to sense the feel of the truck, not so much a mastery as a kinship. She found herself rolling with the tilts, rising and falling with the bounces, liking them, liking the long draw of the shared movement.

She had come to a decision. Tomorrow she would leave for camp and there she'd continue her search. Royal Provo came nowhere near her specifications, in spite of his gifts and his slightly crossed eyes. Also, he was her brother's friend. Peter obviously enjoyed his attentions and might be jealous if anyone intervened. She'd seen it just now. Peter wanted to work with Royal, not with her. Well, she would be the last to interfere. Peter could use a friend, especially since she herself was going away, and not just for the summer.

There was the thump and the thud of the bales being thrown and stacked. Anne, listing with the truck to a near twenty-degree angle, began to feel sorry for Peter. It seemed to her a sad thing that her brother should be so desperate for a companion that he would even consider Royal Provo. Surely he could do better. But then, she told herself, Peter hardly had to worry about anyone trying to compete for Royal's friendship. Peter might think Royal was extraordinary, but no one else ever would.

With that, Anne began to feel better, then worse, then better again.

3

To get the platter down from the top shelf in the pantry, Grady pulled open the lowest of the built-in drawers, stood on its lip and reached up. She grabbed the platter, stepped off the open drawer, and tried to shove it shut with the side of her right foot. It wouldn't close. Her weight had tilted it down.

She put the platter on the counter that topped the drawers, pulled the drawer farther out, raised it a little, then shoved again. The bent metal lid of a stew pot, the size of a small shield, was in the way. She tried to set it straight, but the handle of the meat grinder was sticking up too far, pushed there by a cabbage shredder on one side and a tangle of measuring spoons on the other.

Grady stooped down and with both hands rattled everything in the drawer, trying to settle it all down. Now the lid was lower but an egg-beater had been heaved to the surface by the cover of the huge cast-iron frying pan. Grady tried to burrow the egg-beater down behind the cover, but there was no give because of a water dipper and a flour sifter.

Grady did not become impatient even though the hamburgers were overcooking on the stove and Anne and Peter and Martha and Royal were already waiting at the table for their first meal in their new home. Accepting this as a standard requirement for getting the platter, a simple continuation of her reach up to the shelf, she rattled and shifted the contents of the drawer again, moving both her hands as if she were idly playing a keyboard instrument, appreciative almost of the cacophony she was producing. A cupcake pan surfaced, a pancake griddle disappeared; the lid to a blue and white porcelain coffee pot fixed itself snugly against the curve of a tea strainer and the top to the popcorn popper clamped itself down over a nest of measuring cups as if it had finally caught its prey. Because the knob handle on top of the popcorn lid was missing, the sought-for level had been achieved. Grady could tell as much by touch as by sight. After one quick jerk upward to correct the tilt without disturbing the contents, Grady closed the drawer.

Few things in the house had changed, certainly not the pantry. It was, in its own way, like an attic. It had cupboards and drawers and bins and shelves, but it also had hidden corners, places seldom seen. It even had a window looking out over the kitchen garden and the rock-strewn pasture that sloped down to the cow pond. Grady remembered measuring her growth by how many opened drawers she'd have to climb before she could reach the top shelf: three, then two, then one.

Never had she dreamed of needing no drawer at all. No one she knew could reach that high, not her grandfather, not even Andy. Ceilings were loftier in her great-grandfather's time when the house was built, and it was taken for granted that certain things were out of reach. As far as Grady was concerned, that was one of the reasons why the drawers and bins had been built, why the counters between the lower cupboards and the upper shelves were so sturdy. They were meant to be climbed on. She could remember balancing herself on the edge of the flour bin to reach a jar of the green tomato pickles lined up along one of the upper shelves; she'd knelt on the top of the lower cupboards to bring down one of the larger serving bowls; her bare feet had spanned the dividers of the silverware drawer so she might explore among the more exotic treasures on the topmost shelf: a pair of glass candlesticks, the huge enameled roasting pan used only for Thanksgiving and Christmas turkeys, and, best of all, the big brass bell that, in the days before everyone owned a wristwatch, had hung on the back porch to summon the men to meals.

Even though Grady could hear from the kitchen the popped explosions of grease reminding her again that the hamburgers had been frying too long, she opened one of the bins, the one that had been for flour. With the slightest tug of the handle, it came toward her, a whole panel tilted away from the cupboard. It had always been a marvel to her that it could lean out this way and never fall. There were four bins in all, deep triangular chutes that lent a fascination to whatever they stored because of their shape and the oddity of their engineering. Flour, potatoes, onions, and oatmeal gained an interest beyond themselves. Of course, once out of the bin a potato quickly became no more than a potato, an onion no more than an onion.

In the kitchen Anne was telling Royal that once they'd built up their flock she could come home on a weekend and kill a chicken if that's what they wanted for supper. Royal assured her that he liked hamburger too; Peter stated his preference for pizza, and Martha added, with a shudder of pleased revulsion, "with anchovies."

Grady closed the bin with her hip. She was already at the door when she remembered to go back and pull the string to turn off the light, pleased that she no longer had to climb to the second drawer to reach it.

The peas and potatoes were already on the table, and when Grady set down the hamburgers and onions, Peter made a reach for the potatoes, Anne for the peas. Without warning, Grady stayed their hands by making the sign of the cross, bowing her head, and saying, "Bless us, O Lord, and these thy gifts which we have received from thy bounty through Christ Our Lord"— Before she was halfway through, they'd all joined her, except Royal, who'd simply bowed his head toward his empty plate. But they became confused when she continued ". . . and may the souls of the faithful departed through the mercy of God rest in peace. Amen." When they saw her make the sign of the cross again, they fumbled their way through the motions and stared at her, waiting to see if there were any more surprises.

Grady shrugged and sat down. "Don't ask me," she said. "My grandmother always said it just that way and since this is her kitchen, I guess we'd better keep it up. I think it was the hamburger made me think of it. For her, hamburger was the meal of first resort. Well, at least it isn't Chinese the first night." She took a hamburger and put some onions on top.

"It wasn't for Daddy?" Peter asked.

Grady hadn't thought of that. But now she knew that the prayer was indeed for Andy, that she wished him God's peace and God's mercy, especially since she herself seemed to have none of her own to offer, at least not yet. There was still the resentment at his stupidity and the exhaustion of her own bewilderment. But this reminder that mercy existed, that peace might possibly be bestowed, made her feel that both peace and mercy were given to her instead of to Andy and that the decision to pass them on was hers and only hers.

She hesitated. She knew that if she gave assent, if she were to become the instrument of this blessing, she would be possessed at last by the mourning and the grief that had eluded her since the day of Andy's death. She might have to give her body over to tears and all her strength would be taken from her. She might have to hide her face, dismiss her children, refuse all consolation. Tears were already threatening her eyes; her legs and arms had weakened.

She wouldn't do it. Not now. Supper was on the table, her family was ready to eat. They would be frightened. She was not willing to surrender herself to this possession. The blessing was withheld. It would have to come another time, in another place. She couldn't take any chances right now.

The prayer was safely restored to its original intent, a tribute to her grandmother's piety. Strength returned to her legs and arms and her tears receded to some place behind her nose, which would probably begin to run before supper was over.

There was a silence, then Anne said, "I like the word 'bounty.' It makes me see a pair of big old-fashioned bloomers on a clothesline with the wind blowing."

"Because *Bounty*'s a ship," Royal said. "You're thinking of the sails."

Both Anne and Peter looked at Royal, surprised at this perspicacity from an orphan. Now Royal was the one who shrugged, a halfhearted effort to shake from his shoulders the mantle of wisdom. It seemed he didn't like being conspicuous.

Martha came to his rescue, drawing all attention to herself by spilling her milk. It ran in a narrow river toward Peter's plate, then formed a pond just above his knife. Without making any reference to it, Anne got the dishrag and mopped up the spill and Grady poured more milk into Martha's glass from the same big-bellied pitcher that had supplied Grady herself with nourishment from the day, beyond her remembering, when she'd come here after the car accident that had killed her parents—and which she alone had survived.

The pitcher, like the rest of the house, meant nothing special to Grady. Time had not endowed it with any properties beyond its essential clay, paint, and glaze. It had no power to summon the past. She had not found something she'd lost; she had merely picked up again something she'd set down, a gray pitcher with a blue stripe around its girth and another stripe near its mouth.

In addition to the lengthened prayer before meals, Grady made two more concessions to her grandparents' ways. One was a reversion to calling the midday meal dinner and the evening meal supper. The other was her decision to wear only dresses and skirts, never slacks or jeans. This had been her grandmother's custom and Grady adopted it as her own. Because she worked in the fields and the barns, because she cut wood and shoveled manure and drove a tractor, because she did what some considered man's work, her grandmother was expected to wear overalls and dungarees. She didn't. She wouldn't. And neither would Grady. There was a stubbornness in this decision, a quality she was going to need in some abundance. The dresses might be considered a form of practice, an exercise, for other, more important challenges that lay ahead. Which was fine with Grady.

Royal was talking about the tractor and the hay baler that still needed more work. There was no boast in his voice; the words fell easily. Peter interrupted with something about a "drive shaft" and a "main frame." The implied familiarity was so hopeful, so innocently anticipatory of the day when he might actually know what he was talking about, that it embarrassed Grady. She wanted to smack him.

To shut him up, she said, "Next thing we do is fix the fence along the road by the far pasture." Fence mending, she was sure would allow for no arcane terminology. Post holes and barbed wire could be discussed without resort to a private nomenclature or a privileged vocabulary. "And the fence between the pasture and the alfalfa."

There was a confusion of objections, especially from Peter. He

had been begging her to let him and Royal mow the hill in front
of the house with the tractor and now he renewed his plea with
added fervor. The incline, she said, was too steep. The tractor
could tip over; they could be hurt; worse, the tractor could be
wrecked.

Royal joined in; they wanted to try. It was the challenge that
attracted them, the danger. Grady made a deal with them. If
they'd repair the fence on the roadside, she'd let them mow the
hill. Fence repair was boring and this particular fence would need
some brush cleared away before the actual work could be done.
They agreed, then haggled: first the mowing, then the fence. No,
she said. First the fence, then the mowing: First the work, then
the reward. But it did occur to her that if they did the fence first
they'd rush the posts, it would be a sloppy job, and the herd would
be out in the road by the next afternoon. She gave in. They could
mow the hill as soon as they had bought the posts at the lumber
mill the other side of Schuylerville.

Royal became quiet. Moments before, he'd been enthusiastic
about the bargaining. Now he looked thoughtful, even worried.
He told her what the trouble was. "I don't think I can go to the
mill," he said. "I think my father works there."

Grady's impulse was to ask him, not how he knew his father
worked there, but how he knew who his father was. It had been
presumed that not even his mother had been sure. She kept the
question general. "How do you know?"

He shrugged. "I just know, is all." He thought a moment. "But
I guess I can go anyway if you want me to. I don't think he'd
recognize me."

"But you'd recognize him?" Peter asked.

"Sure. Of course." He shrugged. "He's got a big nose."

Peter searched Royal's face, then asked the question Grady
herself was tempted to ask. "How can your father have a big
nose?"

"He just does. I'll show you. Tomorrow. He's got a big nose."

Grady was surprised, but it wasn't at this unexpected news about Royal's possible father. She was surprised by the sexual twinge she'd felt the moment he'd mentioned that he had a known father. Even the big nose figured into it. A possibility suggested itself. She couldn't stop it from happening; there it was, before she could do anything about it. She dismissed it and it went away, obediently, immediately. She'd forgotten all about it a few seconds later when she said, "Never mind, I'll go. They'll load for me because I'm a woman. We'll get more for our money."

With that, discussion would have ended except that Martha finally found an opening for the statement she'd been preparing throughout the negotiations. "Momma said you're an orphan. She said orphans don't have a father and they don't have a mother either."

"Martha!" Anne said, managing to make it a three-syllable word.

"Momma said you grew up at The Home, didn't you?"

"Martha!" Anne made a face and shook her head.

Still not looking up, Royal said, "Yes, I grew up at The Home. But I guess I've still got a father."

"If Momma dies," Martha continued, "then I get to go live in The Home, don't I?"

"No, you don't get to go live in The Home!" Anne said.

"Why not?" Martha asked.

"Because Momma's not going to die," Grady said. "And stop playing with your hamburger and eat it."

"I could live in The Home if I wanted to."

"Well, I'll tell you one thing," said Grady. "They don't take little girls who play with their hamburger and who don't eat what's on their plate."

"I don't care," Martha said. "I can go there if I want to." She turned to Anne. "And you can't stop me."

Anne reached over, picked up a chunk of hamburger from Martha's plate and put it into her mouth. "Hmmmm," she said, "is this ever good. Hurry up and finish, then you can go live in The Home." She took another piece, put it into her mouth and began an exaggerated chewing accompanied by *hmmmm* sounds as if she were tasting some great delicacy. "Hurry. They're waiting for you."

Martha began to cry.

"What're you crying for?" Anne asked.

"I don't want to go live at The Home." Martha put her face in her hands.

With an annoyed look at Anne, Grady reached out to touch Martha's arm. Instead, it was Royal's shoulder she touched. He'd come around from his side of the table and was hunched down next to Martha. There were tears on his cheek, blue against his pale skin as if they had taken their coloring not from his flesh but from his eyes. What, thought Grady, was *he* crying about?

"You don't have to go to The Home," he said quietly, as if he and Martha were the only people in the room and he was bringing her news of a decision that had been made in some distant and important place. "Anne was only spoofing, to make you laugh."

Martha swung away, and punched Anne's arm.

Royal wiped the tears from his cheek. "You can stay here with us, with your mother and Peter." He hesitated, then added, "And with me."

Martha was staring down into her lap. Royal watched her for a moment, then went back to his chair and began to eat his peas.

Grady got up to put more hamburger on the platter. Now Anne was crying. She shoved her chair back from the table, scraping it loudly along the floor. "Why don't people just leave me alone!" She bumped against Grady as she made for the door and her feet could be heard coming down as heavily as possible as she stomped up the stairs. A door was slammed. Grady was almost sure she heard the give of the mattress where Anne had no doubt flung herself.

With the old wooden-handled spatula, Grady lifted the hamburgers from the grease on the bottom of the frying pan, let them drip a moment, then put them on the platter. She shoved it toward Peter. "More?" she asked. Without looking up, he shook his head. Before she could move the platter toward Royal he, too, shook his head and went on eating his peas.

Watching him, Grady wondered if she should have allowed this strange and pallid boy to step into the midst of her family's bewilderment. Without his knowing it, he had become a part of the extravagance that had brought them to the farm, the peculiar death of Andy Durant and the determined foolishness of her own response. Maybe he should be warned, maybe he should be told outright that she and her children were, at best, in an uncertain state; that he must pay as little attention as possible, that he must keep clear of their confusions and avoid, at all cost, being drawn into the absurdities of their present conduct.

Royal pushed his fork down into the peas on his plate, squashing them against the tines, then brought the mash stuck to the bottom of the fork to his mouth. Grady watched him do this a second time, and decided he didn't deserve a warning.

She went back to the stove and listened for sounds from upstairs. She heard nothing. She listened for sounds from the table behind her, but from there, too, nothing. As if suddenly in need of nourishment, she carried the frying pan to her own place and gave herself the rest of the onions.

Royal was busy eating and Peter was watching him as if to see how it was done. After a moment, he went back to his own food, then said, more with bewilderment than with conviction, "You'd look funny with a big nose." Royal shrugged.

By the time the rhubarb was served for dessert, Anne had returned, her face washed and her hair combed back as if that had been the sole reason for going up to her room. Martha had eaten most of her hamburger and Peter was expanding on the repairs that had put the tractor in operation, praising Royal's expertise. Nobody praised the rhubarb, but then, nobody complained. Their first meal, Grady decided, had been a success.

4

Peter began edging toward the car, eager to get back to the farm. The hill was ready to be mowed. The tractor could tip because of the incline. He couldn't wait to see if that was what would happen.

Martha was causing the delay. She'd not only put her shoes on the wrong feet, she'd forced her way into the left one with the strings tied in an unyielding knot. She'd also put the halter of her sunsuit on backward so she'd have quicker access to the buttons. The peaked parts of the design intended to cover her five-year-old breasts were in back where, with unintentional practicality, they protected her pointy shoulder blades, leaving her chest bare and a simple straight band of cloth to conceal her upper belly. All this was now being corrected.

They'd come to Camp Kennedy to deliver Anne to her summer job. Peter had promised Martha she could carry the suitcase, and it was when she stumbled on the first step leading to the porch of the cabin that Anne and Royal noticed the shoes. This led to the overall scrutiny that revealed the halter's displaced function and the shoe's obstinate knot. Peter watched, wishing they'd hurry.

Probably because she was a woman, Anne went to work on the halter while Royal picked away at the knot. Anne finished first and was using the wait to give her sister an affectionate farewell, disguised as a thoroughgoing readjustment. She tugged at the halter and smoothed it as if it needed molding around the contours of Martha's bony little body. She rubbed Martha's cheeks with the heel of her hand, even though there seemed to be no tears forthcoming, and brushed her palms over Martha's forehead and hair, then ran them over her shoulders and down her arms. It was as if she wanted to make sure her sister was sturdy enough to withstand the rigors of her absence. Martha passed the test: she was given a kiss on the forehead, a seal of approval.

The knot had been untied and Royal helped Martha put on her shoes. Then he, too, rubbed her cheeks, smoothed her hair, braced her shoulders, and kissed her forehead, tracing, if a bit more awkwardly, the route just traveled by Anne.

"Come on, Martha," Peter said. "We've got to get back." Martha didn't seem to mind having his impatience aimed at her, even though she had done nothing more for the past five minutes than submit passively to the ministrations of others. She skipped toward the car as if she'd been waiting only for her brother's command. Royal followed.

Farewells were called; promises of postcards made; hands waved. But before Royal got to the car he stopped, thought a moment, and went back to the porch steps. He stood in front of Anne and, without looking at her, took off his hat. Peter could see her blink at the sudden flame of hair. Just loud enough so Peter could hear, he said, "I meant to tell you before. I'm sorry about your dad." He looked up at her quickly, just long enough to see her nod and say a bewildered "Thank you"; then he put his hat back on, extinguishing the flame. He slid in behind the steering wheel, slammed the door shut, and started the motor. He seemed angry, as if he'd asked Anne for something and had been rudely refused. Peter was tempted to ask what was the matter, but was afraid that the question might make *him* the target of Royal's displeasure, so he kept his mouth shut.

Once they were off the campgrounds and on the highway, Royal seemed to relax and the anger—if it had been anger— disappeared. He even turned to Martha and said in tones of mock weariness, "Well, when we get back, I guess Martha has to mow the hill. She has to drive the tractor and I sure hope she doesn't break it."

Martha considered this for a moment, then said in a pleased hush, "I'm going to break it."

"If you break it," Royal said, "you have to fix it."

In the same near-whisper, Martha confided, "I can fix it."

Now Peter, too, relaxed. But he was still perplexed. Royal had never said anything to *him* about his father's death, and he was Royal's friend—or at least his co-worker when the shooting had taken place. But Peter remembered that he himself might have fended off any reference, the way he'd acted when he'd returned to work two days after the funeral. Until then, he'd been reticent with Royal because Royal was older by at least two years, and might resent or dismiss too bold a bid for friendship. But his father's death, Peter felt, earned him a fund of Royal's interest, and he didn't hesitate to draw on it. He even found himself grateful for his family's tragedy because it might increase his importance in Royal Provo's eyes. He now became openly, aggressively, friendly. The drama of the incident allowed him to claim attentions and assume initiatives not available to the supernumerary he'd been before.

When his mother told Peter about the shooting, he'd been, quite literally, thrilled. A fluttering, giddy sensation ran through his entire body as if alerting him to a near calamity that had yet to take place. It was as though he had been told not that his father was dead but that he should prepare himself for some imminent devastation. But the actual defense never materialized, and the truth was allowed to touch him. His father was dead.

Peter's father had been different from the fathers of his friends. For one thing, other people's fathers were of no interest to Andrew Durant. He was never rude; he was even reasonably amiable, but opinions, jokes, comments were never exchanged. His enthusiasm for his children tended to be erratic. For an extended period, Peter would be pretty much ignored. Then he and Anne would be taken ice skating or swimming or fishing.

Once, before Martha was born, they were all hauled off at a moment's notice, on a camping trip in the mountains for a week. His father, to Peter's surprise, knew how to do everything from pitch a tent to cook outside. He knew the names of all the trees and all the stones. It was only then that Peter learned his father had studied botany and geology in college and hadn't always intended to have, in turn, the several careers Peter could remember: newspaperman, insurance salesman, real-estate broker, freezer salesman, and finally newspaperman again. It astonished Peter to realize his father knew about something like this; Peter had never been happier. He began to believe that his father knew everything. But after the camping trip Andrew Durant reverted to keeping mostly to himself. Once they were home he took up his book-reading again and listened to the records in his study that no one else wanted to hear: string quartets and the music of someone he called Scarface who later turned out to be Scarlatti.

When Anne and Peter were very young their father had a beard. It was soft and silky, unlike the hair on his head, which was rough and coarse. Peter thought for a while that this was because his father stroked and pulled on his beard so much, but he later came to think of it as a reversal that typified his father's singularity, another proof that he was like no one else.

It was his father's beard that Peter had liked best about him. In those days, their father would let first Anne, then Peter, sit on his lap; like ventriloquists, they were allowed to pull on his beard —to open his mouth; out came a word; then they'd push up on the beard and close his mouth again. Questions were answered, permissions given, opinions and judgments offered. The beard was tugged and shoved; the mouth obediently opened and closed.

The game came to an end possibly because they were getting too heavy to sit on their father's lap. More likely, however, it was because Anne, one evening, pulled down on the beard to open her father's mouth wide, and decided not to wait for his own words, but to try out some new ones she'd heard that afternoon on the school playground. With two quick pulls and shoves she had their father say "Fuck you"; he seemed to think the game had seen its season. The beard was shaved off the next day and never grown again.

When Peter got older and began growing pubic hair, he wondered if the peculiar reversal that had softened his father's beard also applied to his crotch. It never occured to Peter until his father was dead and in his grave that he might have asked him a direct question and received a direct answer, but now it was too late. Peter might, someday, ask his mother, but the day did not seem to lie in the near future. His own pubic hair, he was pleased to notice, was coarse and dark and wild. Whether this was a challenge, a goad, or a permission he could never decide, but Peter was sure it was trying to tell him something.

The car was slowing down. Royal had been quizzing Martha on how she'd make her tractor repairs and she'd been giving considered solutions that involved hatchets, hammers, and a zipper.

Royal stopped in mid-question. They had turned off the highway a mile back and now there was a bull blocking the narrow road.

Royal eased the car to a stop and honked the horn. The bull took its attention from the short grass growing alongside the road and jerked back its head as if to flick the sound off with a quick twitch. Then it lowered its head and began feeding again—docile, almost tender nibblings. How, Peter thought, can it satisfy that huge body with such tiny bites? A steak would seem more fitting, but he immediately realized he was proposing cannibalism and decided the bull knew what was good for it. "What do we do now?" he asked.

"We wait."

"You mean we just sit here?"

"It can't feed too long. There's not that much grass."

"Doesn't it know it's got a whole pasture the other side of the fence?" Both Royal and Peter looked at the breach in the field-stone wall where the bull had broken through.

"The grass out here is shorter, sweeter. That's their favorite," Royal said.

Martha leaned forward to get a better view out the windshield. "He's not supposed to be in the road," she declared.

"What if you eased the car up to it, real slow," asked Peter, "just a little push—maybe then it would—"

"I don't know. It might and it might not. They sort of make their own rules."

"But it wouldn't just stand there and let itself be run over. I mean, not that we could run it over, but—"

"And then," said Royal, "then it kicks hell out of your mom's car?"

"But we can't just sit here." Peter leaned forward, sat back, then leaned forward again for a closer look at the bull. It seemed to be tickling its snout against the grass, not even eating it. Smelling it, savoring it. Peter expected it to close its eyes, the better to take in the aroma. But the eyes didn't close, or at least the left one, which Peter could see. It seemed very much aware of the metal hulk aimed at its side.

Peter recognized the bull. It was, his mother had told him, an ancient, almost feeble animal that their neighbor, Ned Ryerson, had put to pasture rather than send in for slaughter, a sentimentality, he'd been assured, most unusual in a farmer. But apparently the bull had done long and faithful service and Mr. Ryerson had devised this final reward. Thinking the animal might be a little hard of hearing, Peter said, "Give it another blast."

"Are you sure?" Royal asked.

Peter nodded. "Who wants to just sit here? We've got things to do."

Royal gave the metal rim the pressure of a downward tilt. It was not a harsh sound—somewhere between a request and a complaint. Nothing about it suggested either command or threat. The bull raised its head, straining it back toward its shoulderblades, then shook it as though trying to clear its ear of an annoying insect. It looked toward the car, not with suspicion, but with curiosity, and lowered its head again to the feast.

"I guess he wasn't impressed," Royal said.

"He'll move." Peter was opening the door next to him. Royal reached his hand over to Peter's arm. "We can wait."

"Why should we?" Peter was out of the truck, leaving the door open.

"What're you going to do?" Royal asked.

"Get him back into the field so we don't have to sit here all day."

"I can turn around. We'll go the orchard road."

"Too narrow to turn."

"I can back us up until we get to the crossing."

Peter closed the car door halfway so he could get past. He hoped it looked like he was surrendering a shield, inviting the bull to mortal combat. Royal would be impressed.

"The cow isn't supposed to eat the grass over there," said

Martha, preparing an excuse for whatever brutality her brother might practice on a defenseless bull.

Peter went to the side of the road and began kicking the underbrush. Finally he found what he wanted, a stick about three feet long. He snapped off the few twigs still sprouting and whisked it a few times through the air like a swordsman testing the heft and balance of his weapon. Satisfied, he walked over to the bull and gave it a whack on the rump, then stepped back, hoping the bull would chase him.

The bull, still munching, flicked its tail, not really interested in brushing off whatever pest had tried to light on its backside. Peter came down harder, and this time the bull lifted its head and strained its eyes to the side to see what was behind it. Peter stood still. The bull returned to its meal. When Peter brought the stick down on its spine, half the branch went flying through the air, landing next to the bull's head. It sniffed the stick, nosed it aside, and ate the grass it had landed on, consuming the territory the stick had come to claim.

Royal rolled down his window. "Maybe we can edge him away with the car after all. He doesn't seem to care what happens to him."

"I'll get him back into the field. Don't worry." Peter was kicking the underbrush again. He found a thicker, more menacing stick, and peeled away the small branches that might make it seem less severe. He saw Royal lean forward and put his arms over the steering wheel. He was watching. Peter took a firm grip on the stick and went to the far side of the bull, away from the protection of the car, cutting off the path to his own easy retreat.

"Peter wants us to close the door," Martha said.

"We have to leave it open so he can get back in."

"He doesn't want to get back in."

"He will."

Peter brought the stick down just above the bull's snout, between the nostrils and the eyes, then backed away, ready to run. The bull raised its head, stretching it back again toward its shoulder bones, slowly heaving the head from side to side as though it had taken the blow on its neck and was trying to ease the pain. It didn't return to the grass but held the head straight forward, blinking its eyes, trying to figure something out.

The next blow came quickly, sharply, right on the snout. Again Peter backed away, ready for a possible charge. Raising its head skyward, the bull let out a bellow, a summons for someone to rid it of this petty annoyance. Peter poked again at the flank, twice, then started toward the breach in the wall, shouting a long "Aaaaah" and brandishing the stick.

Slowly the bull swayed where it stood, gathering momentum. The right front hoof pawed the earth, then there rose toward the sky a great bellow protesting that it had borne all with patience, but that endurance was at an end. With a slow heave, ponderous and graceful, it began the inexorable turn toward Peter. About fifteen feet away, Peter raised both his arms, the stick held firmly in his right hand. He started to repeat his war cry, the guttural "Aaaaah," but cut it short when it began to sound, even to himself, as if he'd already been trampled under.

Now facing him, the bull scraped its left hoof three times along the gravel, mocking the restraint that was about to explode.

"Forget it! Get back in the car!" Royal yelled.

Martha, sitting back comfortably in the seat, said, "He wants us to close the door."

Peter looked toward Royal, raised the stick in salute, then began his dash toward the breach in the fieldstone wall. The bull charged, brushing against the car, rocking it like a rowboat caught in the wake of a steamer. Pleased by the success of his taunts, Peter bounded through the breach, the stick held aloft, a reminder of the pokes and beatings that had finally teased the beast into action.

Running swift and sure, he started up the pasture slope, then turned not so much to see if the bull was any threat as to wave again to Royal. Royal waved back, feebly.

Free of the wall itself, the bull was charging up the hill. Peter ran a wide arc along the slope and headed back toward the wall. The bull, ignorant of geometry and the usefulness of the straight line, followed in the arc already traced. Now Peter ran toward the car, ready to clear the wall away from the breach. Royal had jumped out to help him over.

On the downslope, the bull seemed to be gaining. Peter began running a broken field, up the slope and down, but some of the principle of the straight line had begun to reach the bull's consciousness. Peter ran almost straight uphill, where he thought his lighter weight might be an advantage.

"Come back!" Martha called, leaning out the window. "You're supposed to come back!"

Peter turned to face the bull just before reaching the top of the pasture. It suddenly occurred to him that a few more feet and his last advantage would be gone. Somewhere in his mind he had the idea that he might explain to the bull that it had all been in fun, that he hadn't meant any of it. But he realized that truce or compromise was unacceptable, to the bull and to him. Royal, after all, was watching. Flinging out both arms, the stick still in his hand, Peter made a few threatening steps in the bull's direction. In the momentary break in the animal's gallop, he began a wide-end run. He hoped the bull would play fair and follow exactly his path. It did, and he found himself admiring the bull's sportsmanship.

Peter's fear now was that he would lose control of his stride and stumble on his way down the hill. "Over here!" he heard Royal yell. Royal was there, clear of the car, waving his arms, shouting as if *he* were the one in need of rescue.

Peter reached the wall and pitched himself over. Royal quickly reached out and rolled him into the road. The bull swerved off to the right just before the wall, then ran alongside and up the hill again.

Peter lay on his back, panting, the cavity of his stomach heaving up and down, his pulse an even faster rhythm thumping in the hollow just above his stomach. He could feel the sweat running off his face and neck. A small pool filled the cavity at the base of his throat. His shirt was sucked onto his skin, drawing water out of his body and into itself, clinging even closer, as though the more it drank the more it thirsted. He tried to close his eyes, but the lids fluttered. He couldn't hold them still. His open mouth seemed to expel more air than it breathed in, as if his lungs weren't ready yet for the oxygen they so desperately needed.

Royal backed away, pulling the toes of his shoes out from under the weight of Peter's left arm. Peter raised his head a little. Up the slope, almost at the top, the bull stood watching them, its right front hoof patting down the turf as if to calm the ground after all the disturbance it had endured. Royal went to the breach and, carefully, quietly, as if afraid to wake a slumbering child, put the stones back in place. The bull stopped patting the turf. Peter lowered his head and managed to close his eyes.

Martha nudged her brother with her foot, tentative little forays, testing to see if he was still alive. "Get back in the car, Martha. We're going to go now," Royal said. Martha gave one more nudge, laughed nervously at her own daring, then did as she was told.

Royal knelt down next to Peter. Peter's breathing had slowed but his heart was still thumping. He felt Royal reach over to take the branch still clutched in his right hand. He tightened his grip, looked up at Royal, laughed, and then relaxed his hand so Royal could take the stick. Peter immediately bounded to his feet as though a spell had been lifted and he were restored to his friend, refreshed and ready for anything.

He put his hand on Royal's shoulder not because he needed

support, but to celebrate his survival and his triumph. Between breaths, he said, "We can go now, can't we." He pressed his hand more firmly on Royal's shoulder and let himself be led back toward the car.

Once they were moving, Royal asked, without looking over toward Peter, "Does Anne ever come home on weekends or anything?"

Peter was surprised at the question. It ignored the whole episode of the bull, which had not yet been given the commentary it deserved. It was as if they had just left the campgrounds and the recent demonstration of his courage had yet to take place. Still, he answered. "I don't think so. I don't really know."

"I wanted to ask her myself just before we left, but I was afraid she'd think it was none of my business. So I said that stupid thing about your dad instead. I was just wondering though. I mean, if she ever needed me—us—to come and get her. That's what I wanted to ask."

"Oh," Peter said. Then, knowing he couldn't just say that and nothing else, added, "No, I don't really know." Then he kept quiet, expecting that the silence would give Royal a chance to say something about the bull. But he said nothing at all. Peter began to think that the bull should have trampled him after all. Then Royal would *have* to say something. As it was, Royal said nothing.

5

Grady moved backward along the opened trench, not much deeper than a snake track after a good rain, slowly rubbing her thumb against her fingers, letting the seeds sift down into the little gully as if she were lightly salting the earth. She dipped into the stiff paper sack she held in her other hand, pinched up more seeds, and continued along the row that ran from the wire fence of the chicken yard, past the back of the barn to the edge of the near pasture.

She liked the hard feel of the seeds. These were carrot. She rubbed them before letting them fall, as though reassuring herself of each one's individual worth before trusting it to the ground.

She had planned to help put in the fenceposts, but with the excuse of keeping Martha out of the way, she decided to plant the vegetable garden instead. There was Martha, coming slowly down the row toward her, doing her assigned job with her usual solemnity. Carefully bringing her hands together, she covered the seeds with earth as if she were burying pet bugs. She was even humming, a wordless melody that could easily do the service of a dirge.

Grady was relieved that it took Martha longer to cover the seeds than it took her to sow them. She wanted to be as alone as she could manage and still keep Martha occupied. The planting, for her purposes, was working very well. She recognized, not without amusement, that she'd chosen a task she could do bowed low, like a penitent.

That morning, when she'd gone to the lumber mill to buy the fenceposts, she had, for the first time in her life, made love to a man other than her husband. And it was the man Royal Provo had said might be his father. His name was Guy Duskin, and where Royal had gotten the idea that he was his father was anybody's guess. There was certainly no genetic evidence. The man was like a bear, hairy, with swarthy skin.

But at least part of what Royal had said proved to be true. He had a big nose. He immediately told Grady to call him by his first name, Guy, as if he anticipated everyone's inclination to call him Dusky. Then, to reassure her that the name was not as indistinctive as she might think, he said, "It means 'leader,' like in guide. You know. 'Leader.' 'Guide.' "

Because she knew now, even if she hadn't before, Grady nodded and repeated the word, "Guy."

It was Guy who loaded the posts onto the bed of the pickup. When she'd backed up to the loading door, there he was, the order form in his hand, waiting to confirm that this was the truck that would haul away twenty posts of number-one locust. When she got out of the cab, he looked up from the order, at first dumbfounded, then amazed, then what Grady could only interpret as thrilled. Maybe no woman had ever ordered fenceposts before. Then it became clear. He was thrilled because Grady was a woman.

Each time he slid an armful of posts onto the truck, he'd look at her and smile, the smile of a man who hoped he was giving pleasure by the task he was performing and the way he was performing it. When Grady nodded her appreciation, the smile became slightly embarrassed, as if Guy didn't want her to think he was working at the peak of his powers, but still wanted credit for what was, after all, not a negligible display. Then he would study her face: first her left eye, then her right, her hairline and her mouth, her ears, her cheeks, making sure he'd collected every indication of her regard. Completely satisfied, he went back to the shed for the next load.

With each successive return—four posts, then five, then six, then only five because that completed the order—Grady found herself more and more pleased by this man's attentions. He seemed to find such joy just at the sight of her, as if he couldn't quite believe his good fortune that this extraordinary creature— Grady Durant—was standing in front of him. There was no invitation in the smile, no request, no suggestion of anything beyond itself. It was, quite literally, "pure pleasure." He was like a boy newly aware of the female of the species, conscious only now that something so incredible as a woman had been included in the great plan of creation.

By the time he'd carried out the load of six posts, Grady was aware of more than just his nose. True, it was ample, but hardly a deformity. It was fleshy, but just the right size to carry its share of the pockmarks that distinguished rather than disfigured his face. And the wide nostrils suggested great healthy breaths, consistent with the expansiveness and well-being so evident before her. His lips were as generous as his nose, and his brown eyes— which Grady had always thought proper for a man (blue was for girls)—were set wide, making his broad face seem sufficiently inhabited. On his last trip with the final five posts, Grady thought she saw, deep in the waved folds of his dark hair, the slightest touch of a red that might have asserted itself in the gene that brought to Royal's head its distinguishing flame. But no, the red in Guy Duskin's hair was too close to maroon. There was no relationship possible between this exuberant, bearlike man and Royal Provo.

Their lovemaking happened easily enough. The battery of the pickup was dead when Grady tried to start the motor. Guy Duskin pulled up in his own car, a dark blue Galaxy, attached the cables, and made the jump. He then suggested that he follow her part of the way in case there was any further trouble. If there was, she should make the turnoff just before the bridge that crossed the Battenkill. She would be on a short stretch of the old dead-end road that had been abandoned when the new highway was built.

Grady thought she knew what he was talking about but she was sure she'd never go through with it. She drove off and made the turn onto the highway. After a few moments, she checked the rearview mirror. He was following at about fifty feet. She felt a pleasant relaxation inside of her as if all her organs, especially those in her stomach, had suddenly loosened from their usual moorings and had gone calling on each other in an extremely agitated but agreeable way. This was accompanied by an equally pleasant tingling along the outermost layer of her flesh. Whether it was to ward off or to lure, to protect or to invite, she wasn't sure.

The Galaxy had come no nearer. She was almost at the bridge. She knew she wouldn't make the turnoff. She was not a promiscuous woman. She had a moral code and it did not include side-road shenanigans, or any other kind of shenanigans for that matter. She had too many other things to do: a farm to organize, children to care for, a life to remake, a soul to save, a reputation to uphold —though she hoped it was not in that particular order. Peter and Royal would be waiting. There was the porch to repair, the fields to mow, the fences to mend, the northern wall of the barn to rebuild. The house needed her. Wallpaper to be peeled, linoleum to be lifted, the attic—

She made the turnoff. She shouldn't have listed so many tasks. She should have contented herself with the porch to repair or the reputation to uphold. Now she was feeling so burdened that she felt a desperate need for some respite before all these chores would begin to flatten her out like a penny on a railroad track. She wanted to lie down, and here was her chance. She'd think about it later.

When she pulled up, the truck brushed against the young oak that had begun to encroach on the old road. She got out on the passenger side and realized, too late, that she'd closed the door quietly so no one would hear. Guy Duskin drove past and parked in front of the truck. When he got out, he too closed his door with the quietest possible click.

Grady looked at his forehead as he walked toward her. The creases, two of them, seemed kind and comfortable. She meant to look next at his eyes but she was looking instead at the license plate of his car. She read 576 and a dash, then said out loud, "It seems to be running all right, but"— Before she could read the last two numbers and add "I wanted to thank you," he had taken her in his arms, wrapping them all the way around her. He pulled her whole body against him and began a slow and growing kiss.

For a moment, Andy Durant had come back. Grady was about to slump deeper into his arms with relief, the single second of repose she'd allow herself before she'd pull away to look into this man's eyes and know he wasn't really her husband. She felt a release of her old longings, a flow that enclosed the man holding her, shielding him from all harm, protecting him from any hurt. Then his lips were moving against hers as if saying something, a swelling and fluttering that spoke a message new to her and strange, a message that asked for a reply.

She wanted to pull away, to reassemble her bones into their proper structure, locking and joining them until they became again what they'd been before this moment, not the loose and rubbery jumble they were now. She wanted to reorder her organs so they'd stop free-floating inside her. But it was too late. What she felt was an urge to relieve herself of this heaviness, to surrender to this giddiness. And only the man holding her could make it happen, only he could draw the two urges into one, only he could recall her to herself. She had to trust him now. She was lost and he must find her. He must look everywhere, daring everything, never stopping, searching, calling out for her, bringing her with a great struggle back to herself, finding her at last, huddled in his arms behind the sapling oak.

The man was smiling at her, a soft amazed smile as if she'd just performed a feat of magic. Grady, too, tried to smile but failed, a trial response that was obviously not the right one. She tried again, but so quickly that it must have seemed more like a twitch.

The man spoke. "You like to do it as much as I do, don't you?"

The tone of his voice struck a blunt thud against Grady's ear. It was a tone she recognized, but from where? It had in it a kind of satisfied pride, not about his lovemaking but about his ability to have recognized in her a woman who shared his interests. It was as if this act of his intelligence pleased him more than anything else that had happened between them, as if part of his pleasure was this triumph of the mind, this proof of his deductive powers. "Sometimes I'm wrong," the man confessed, "but with you I was right, wasn't I?"

Grady didn't answer. She was studying the smile, the eyes, the face, the set of the lips, the meaning behind the gaze.

"Wasn't I?" he asked again. "I was right, wasn't I."

"Yes," Grady said. She knew now where she'd heard that tone before, seen that pleased smile of accomplishment that related not so much to what had happened to as to the understanding of what had happened. It was a child's.

To ward off the dread she felt was about to come over her, Grady told herself the man couldn't possibly be retarded. She would have noticed it. Then she acknowledged that she had noticed very little beyond his face and his body, that she hadn't listened to his manner of speaking or even to what he'd said. He seemed willing to help her with the battery, which was all she had had on her mind. Or, perhaps, what she had on her mind prevented her from guessing at I.Q.s.

Then she decided that this was just his manner at a time like this. Perhaps he became momentarily stupid after lovemaking, as if he had just spent his intelligence instead of his ardor. Any moment now he'd snap out of it; they would have a brief discussion about the unreliability of batteries, then a mature parting, not with a formal handshake, but surely with a friendly wave and the honk of a knowing horn.

"I knew I was right all along, before the battery."

He would snap out of nothing. His mind was moving at the same persistent pace and along the same set path that described a child's journey from one experience to the other, from one event to the next. But the expected dread, the shame she felt she deserved, never arrived. Instead she found herself able to smile. "Yes," she said. "You were right."

"I knew I was."

She reached over and rubbed his pitted cheek, then straightened the collar of his workshirt. She checked to see if any curiosity or bewilderment had come into his eyes. None had. Lying next to him, she buttoned a pocket button on his shirt as if making a final adjustment before sending him out into the world. Then she brushed back the hair on the left side of his head so he would be presentable to anyone he might encounter on the roads ahead.

Grady thought now of all the children she had sent out and

away from her; how, one by one, she had let them go, unprepared, unprotected, alone without her. She thought not only of Anne and Peter and Martha, but of Andy, as if it were she who had sent him away into some solitary exile where he would have to wander forever, alone, without her. And now the time had come to send this man away, to leave him to live as best he could.

She looked again at his eyes. Already they showed the loss; already she could see the dumb, wondering sorrow. He was staring at her breast. He had not even touched her there, but now, he slowly parted his lips. Grady looked for a moment at the bent head, then unbuttoned her dress and brought out her breast. The man watched closely and waited for Grady to take her hand away. He then cupped the breast gently, brought forward his parted lips and began to suckle. He brought his knees up, brushing them against her stomach, then bent his head more closely into the breast, all very slow, all very tender.

Grady put one hand on his neck just behind his left ear, then reached the other down to the top of his head. She lay quiet, feeling the gentle tugs, the light pressure of his nose on the soft flesh. There was a name she wanted to whisper but she wasn't sure whose it was. She felt a great yearning being drawn out of her as if for want of milk, her body was yielding up instead some terrible tenderness. Because she didn't know what name to say, she moaned lightly and brought her head forward until her chin rested in the man's hair.

He didn't move. He had stopped. He was heavy against her, breathing evenly. She had suckled him to sleep. Slowly she pulled herself away, turned onto her back, and looked up at the sky. A bank of clouds, one heaped on the other, was crossing the sun, a massive gathering of held thunder that seemed to shield his sleep and mute all the sounds of the sky, so that even the crow was quiet and the sun-drugged insects were brought, in mid-labor, to a languorous halt. Grady stood up, adjusted her skirt, and brushed the dried leaves and fresh grass from her clothes, from her arms and legs. She shook her head to free the grass and leaves and pine needles from her hair, but when it occurred to her that she was shaking her head in a violent *no,* she stopped and simply combed her fingers through the tangled strands that reached down to her shoulders. She looked at the sleeping man, still curled up in the cropped grass. She would not say no to what had happened here.

She started the motor, but didn't look over to see if the noise had awakened him. She hoped it hadn't. Before making the turnoff, she was tempted to look back, but decided not to. She didn't want to see him watch her go. She wanted to be gone so that, perhaps, it would all seem to him, as it did to her, a late-morning dream in the summer of the year when everyone who'd gone away returned, a child, to suckle himself to sleep.

Grady let more carrot seed sift down from her fingers. She had come to the end of the row. There were still some seeds left in the paper sack but she thought the one row would be enough. For good measure she dropped one more seed into the furrow. It landed between two crumbs of ground. It had bounced a little before settling in and it seemed to Grady a little surprised to find itself where it was. To give it an immediate explanation of the whys and wherefores of its situation, Grady preempted Martha's job and folded it over with earth.

She did not stand up. She stayed where she was. She missed her husband. It was the tenderness that had done it. As if it were his grave, Grady gently touched the crumbled earth with her hand. The time had come to give Andy his mercy and his peace. It was then that she noticed that Martha wasn't ahead of her along the opened row. She turned around just in time to see her fling the carrot seeds from the pack into the chickenyard.

The unsuspecting hens protested the sudden shower, then,

with Martha looking on as if evaluating the results of an important experiment, they began pecking the seeds off the ground, puzzled but not unimpressed by this unexpected feast.

"Martha!" Grady got up, went to her, and gave her a hard whack on the behind.

"They were left!" Martha cried.

"They were not—" Grady's voice broke and to hide her face from her daughter, she turned and pressed herself against the fence, curling her fingers through the wire and holding on. Because she had hit Martha, whose father had died, because she'd yelled at her, Grady began to cry.

6

Royal let the suction claw slip itself up onto Myrtle's teat, then reached for the next and the next until all four claws were in position, tugging noiselessly away, the milk spurting down into the stainless-steel bucket placed carefully between the curve of Myrtle's belly and the swollen udder. The cows had arrived and, at Martha's pleading, they'd all been given names beginning with *M*. Royal patted Myrtle's left flank, thanking her for her contribution, and moved on to Maud, here too patting the flank. "Attagirl, Maud."

He placed the stool just forward of Maud's right hind leg and sat down. He washed the udder with soapy water, wiped it clean with a rinsed rag, and pulled lightly, straight down, on each of the teats to make sure none of them was hardening. He also watched to see if this caused the cow any discomfort, if she was sore. Maud was fine.

Royal flattened his left hand against her flank, his arm crossing in front of his face to keep her tail out of his eyes if she decided to swish it. It was when Mrs. Durant had showed him this last trick—how to keep the cow's dung-flecked tail away from his face —that Royal felt he had become a true farmer. She'd taught him and Peter everything—how to approach the cow, where to put the stool, how to apply the milking apparatus—but when she introduced him to this particular part of the procedure, he was certain he was being given a special piece of knowledge known only to the insider. It was a sophistication that elevated the entire operation beyond mere instruction. Gestures unknown to town dwellers had passed between them. He'd been advanced into a secret society, an order with its own signs and symbols; and he could now lay legitimate claim to all the smugness and scorn that are the first satisfactions of any special sect. It thrilled him to know what he knew; it pleased him to pity his former self, the ignorant boy who had lived his whole life without knowing how to keep a cow's tail from whisking across his face while he was washing and tugging her teats.

Mrs. Durant walked past to empty her bucket into the five-gallon pail at the end of the aisle. He liked the easy way she braced the bottom rim of the bucket just above her right knee, then bent her leg, tipping the milk into the pail. No stooping, just a little leg action and it was done. Without saying anything, Mrs. Durant passed him again and he could hear the scrape of her metal stool as she moved on to the next cow. There were sixteen cows on her side, twelve on his, a herd of twenty-eight.

Peter dropped another scoopful of feed pellets in front of Maud, then moved on to Myrtle. "You're a good girl, Mandy," Royal heard Mrs. Durant say. He didn't catch the sound of the friendly pats meant to assure Mandy that she was known and valued. Aside from the rain of pellets onto the cement floor there was little sound now in the barn, and even that was stifled when Peter let some of the feed fall onto the hay bedding.

This was the evening milking. This was the fulfillment of all their labors. Everything they did—planting, mowing, repairing, fence-mending, storing, feeding, rising in the morning, and resting at night—all of it had no purpose beyond this: getting the milk. Which was why, so far at least, there was always a certain excitement at milking time.

The barn had already been cleaned; the old manure shoveled and squeegeed out; the floor swept with a hard broom; the new bedding laid down; the feed set out. No dinner party had ever been given a more detailed preparation. When Mrs. Durant opened the door at the far end of the barn, in came the cows, stately but gracious, nodding, approving. They stepped across the drain ditch, each into her chosen stall, and nosed toward the feed placed cleverly so that it could be reached only if the cow stuck her head through the metal stanchions that would encourage and support her docility during the milking.

Then the servants—Royal himself and Peter and Mrs. Durant —swung into action. Washing buckets were clumped down, milking claws rattled, milk pails clanked, stools scraped on cement. The concern and courtesy of those accommodating the "guests" could leave no doubt in the mind of the least self-respecting cow as to who was the master (mistress?) of whom. Urinations into the litter aisle were almost immediately covered with hay, flops that missed the drain ditch were disposed of at the first opportunity, and the food supply was constantly replenished with an implied exhortation to eat, eat!

There were also the tender fondlings, the impulsive squeezings, the gentle tuggings, drawing the cows down into a drowsy satiation; rest was obviously the best statement of gratitude toward those who had obliged them so efficiently.

Royal got up to see if Minnie had completed her contribution to the evening festivities. She hadn't. "You're a splendid specimen, Minnie, no matter what Madge and Mandy say." He gave her three soft slaps as proof of his sincerity. Minnie, taking it all as her due, continued the munchings, the even-measured mastications and ruminations that had first claim on her concentration, and Royal headed back toward the slandered Madge.

Peter had finished meting out the feed pellets and was preparing the solution for dipping the teats, more or less the final service to be offered. A plain plastic cup filled with an iodine concoction would be brought up to the udder, and each teat immersed separately, a hedge against any infection that might have been introduced by these less than perfect menials. It was also the obvious equivalent of finger bowls, a sure sign that this had indeed been a classy affair.

Mrs. Durant was far down the other side, taking the claws off Marna. Royal wondered if this would be the right time to ask her about the old threshing machine. He wanted to see if he could make it go. He knew it no longer served any purpose. Oats and wheat were no longer grown. Still, he wanted to see if he could fix it, an urge he'd had ever since he'd first seen it off in the weeds behind the pump house. To him, its rusty orange suggested that it was slowly turning into gold. Its size, its complexity, its promise of gargantuan power had exacted from him on first sight an oath of fidelity, a vow to restore to it its lost supremacy, to make amends for its humbled pride. He would allow it again to belch and growl and grind as it had in the days of its great labor.

Royal gave Madge's udder a gentle squeeze. She was milking nicely. The claws were secure, the milk spurting into the bucket. It was all made to seem so businesslike, so matter-of-fact, but for Royal it was still anything but. He'd watched Mrs. Durant—and Peter too—when she was teaching them how to do the milking. It was supposedly no different from learning how to drive a tractor. You put this here, turn that on, watch out for this, then do that, and what more could it be about? Royal pretended to take it on exactly those terms, but he couldn't, not really. He didn't see how Mrs. Durant and Peter could either. The cow had four penises and they were all being sucked off. That was all there was to it and to pretend otherwise was a deception. At the same time, he liked the pretension. He liked the idea that he was above sexual connotation, that he was so incredibly mature that he could do this and it would mean absolutely nothing to him beyond milking a cow. At the same time he knew that if the opening weren't so small, he'd like to stick his prick into one of the suction claws and let it do its job.

He also felt embarrassed by a cow's udder. It was an enormous breast, and if the teats didn't look so much like penises and if there were only one of them, not four, he knew he'd be down there, his mouth pulling away. Cows, to him, were pure sex. And he knew that someday he was going to fuck one of them. It was destined. He couldn't help it. It was what they were made for. He'd even started getting specific about it, wondering which one it was going to be, casting an appraising eye over the herd, evaluating their individual qualities. He was tending, at the moment, toward Madge, but Maud was not yet out of contention.

Which reminded him. He started back toward Minnie, certain that she was milked out. He saw Mrs. Durant soaping Mabel's udder, pulling the teats. She could be washing Martha's ears, she seemed that unconcerned, that unaware. He wanted to ask if she was faking it too, if she, too, was merely pretending to ignore the implications of her actions. But he didn't want to involve Mrs. Durant in this kind of thinking. She was separate, inviolable. None of this had anything to do with her. And besides, he was sure she *was* above and beyond it all. Unlike him, she wasn't faking it. To her, this was business, no more, no less. He decided he'd ask her about working on the threshing machine. Then he'd check on Minnie.

Before he could get to her there was a sudden stomping behind him. Something was distressing the cows. Royal thought at first that a woodchuck had come into the barn. But it was a puppy. Wagging its behind, it went sniffing first one cow's leg, then another's, a milk bucket and a heap of bedding, a cowpie, then Mrs. Durant's left shoe.

"Who's that? What is it?" she yelled, sticking her head out into the litter alley just in time to see the puppy try to climb up Peter's leg. Peter clapped his hands to call it back when it ran to the five-gallon pail at the end of the alley. It tried to scratch its way up to the rim, to put its paws over the top and look inside, but the stainless steel made it impossible. Registering no disappointment whatsoever, it raced over to Minnie and began sniffing its way through the bedding toward the feed pellets under the raised water bowls.

"Get it out of here!" Mrs. Durant was making shooing motions with both her hands as if the puppy were a fly. Peter clapped his hands again but by now the puppy must have heard it as applause. Having disdained Minnie's feed, it wagged its way to the feet of a boy about Peter's age standing just inside the barn door.

"Can I help you?" Mrs. Durant called.

"Grady?" the boy said.

"Yes?"

The boy bent down and scooped the puppy into his arms, then took a few steps toward Mrs. Durant. Royal still couldn't see his face because the puppy was licking the boy's eyes, his forehead, his cheeks, his mouth as if it had been told to get everything clean, and right away.

"I thought maybe you didn't have yourself a dog yet," the boy said. His voice was pitched a little high, but with some sand or gravel mixed in. He walked past Royal, the puppy now struggling to get down. It wasn't a boy Peter's age; it was a man Royal guessed to be close to forty. His close-cut hair, the small features of his face, his medium height, and his sturdy, compact body— even his voice—were those of a teenager. But now Royal could see the lines radiating from his eyes and the two faint folds starting just above his nostrils, forming parentheses around his mouth. His skin, lightly freckled, was dry, and his hair slightly coarse, as though he had sand in his blood as well as in his voice.

"Your long hair, what'd do with it?" Royal heard Mrs. Durant ask. "Ned! Your beard! It's gone!"

"Long, long time ago." The man spoke shyly as if he didn't really deserve credit for so interesting an act as cutting his long hair and shaving his beard. "I figured it was time to come clean." He made a quick attempt at a laugh but didn't get very far.

This, then, was Ned Ryerson, the man on the next farm and a childhood friend of Mrs. Durant. She'd mentioned him. She hadn't gone to see him yet because she was going to ask him to lease back to her the twenty acres she'd sold him a long time ago. It had been her best pastureland and, according to all the careful calculations she'd made when she'd bought the herd, she was going to need it badly. She'd even intimated that the farm couldn't make it without it. A smaller herd wasn't the answer. She had to produce enough milk to make the place pay—and to feed the cows that gave the milk she needed the pasture.

"Come to the house," Mrs. Durant said. "The boys can finish."

"Thanks, but I can't."

"For a few minutes?"

"No, I really can't. I just thought—well—you need yourself a dog? Last of the litter, but she's had her shots and all."

Royal watched as Mrs. Durant reached out and took the puppy. Immediately it licked her face as if this were its first duty whenever it was picked up. "You look good without the beard. I always thought it made you look like one of Santa's helpers."

"Well," he said, looking down at the floor, "you can't stay a kid forever, can you?"

"I should hope not," Mrs. Durant answered. "Uu-uu. Never again!"

"Yeah, I guess so." With his foot he drew some hay from the

edge of the drain ditch and spread it over some urine Mandy had sent out into the alley. "You'll take the dog?"

"Of course I'll take the dog. She's exactly what I need for Martha, to keep her busy."

"Her name's Raggles, but you can change it if you want to. She's only six weeks."

"Raggles?"

"Claire's idea. Because it always raggles its tail." He made sure the urine was completely covered by the absorbent hay, then looked up at Mrs. Durant. "Claire kind of liked that."

Mrs. Durant held the squirming puppy away from her and shook her head at it. "Raggles!" she said in a voice Royal had never heard her use before, the one some people take on when they ask a baby silly questions, the words all in the mouth, not in the throat. "Is your name Raggles?" she asked. *"Is your name Raggles?* Yes, it is. It's Raggles. Your name is Raggles. Did you know that? Did you? Did you know your name was Raggles? Did —you—know—your—name—was—Raggles?" The puppy, incited to a joy beyond endurance, leapt at Mrs. Durant's face, trying to eat it but not knowing where to start. Mrs. Durant let out a half-scream, half-laugh, closed her eyes, and let the puppy continue its nips at her nose, her chin, her cheeks.

The man looked on, smiling expectantly as if it might be his turn next to be nipped and licked. "You need anything else?" he asked.

"Oh. Oh. Oh. Raggles! Don't! Somebody—somebody take her. Oh, Raggles! Don't!"

"You . . . you sure she's okay?"

"Of course she's okay. I wouldn't give her back for a bundle of hay with a fence around it."

The puppy squirmed free and leapt to the floor. It sniffed its way down the alley as if it were on the trail of something momentous, leaving Mrs. Durant and Ned Ryerson with nothing in particular to occupy them. The man chuckled slightly. Mrs. Durant smiled, then brushed the hair back from her forehead to let him know that she was not otherwise occupied and that he was free to speak.

"I can see all the work you've done," he said. "The place looks nice." He looked around the barn, nodding first to Peter, then to Royal. Peter nodded back, but before Royal could follow his example, Mrs. Durant, as if suddenly aware that they were there, introduced them. The man was indeed Ned Ryerson; he and Mrs. Durant had known each other as children. Then the new information began. Mr. Ryerson was the best dairyman in Washington County; Mrs. Durant was smart as a whip; Mr. Ryerson had gone to SUNY in Albany for two years; Mrs. Durant had made the captain of the football team cry when she sang Handel's Largo in Italian at high-school graduation.

Was he sure he couldn't stay? No, he couldn't. Mrs. Durant would walk him to his car. He hadn't driven, he'd walked through the fields; the old stile was still there to climb over. He praised the new fences. He said they were smart to use locust. Peter nodded in agreement as if the choice had been his. Mrs. Durant would come visit soon; she wanted to see Claire. Claire was the reason Mr. Ryerson hadn't come before; she'd been ill; she was fine now; she'd be happy as anything to see Mrs. Durant. Mrs. Durant couldn't wait.

The man hesitated, wondering if this needed a response, then decided it didn't. He turned and walked out of the barn without saying goodbye or giving a final nod to either Peter or Royal. When the puppy started toward the door, Mrs. Durant clapped her hands and called, "Raggles! Here, Raggles. Come here, Raggles."

The dog wagged its way toward her. Mrs. Durant sat down on the stool next to Mabel and leaned forward. Tickling the dog behind the ears, she asked, in her dog-voice, "Is he going to give me the twenty acres? Is he? Is he going to let me have them back? Yes, he is. Isn't he?" The puppy only whimpered, but Mrs. Durant seemed to find this an acceptable answer. She leaned down farther and closed her eyes so the puppy could have its way with her entire face.

Royal liked Mrs. Durant. He felt comfortable around her. She was almost homely, but not quite. As a matter of fact, she was close to being a horse-face. It was the narrowing jaw that did it, the long, slightly flattened nose, fleshy at the nostrils. She also had a good-sized mouth. But then she had dark brown eyes, round, and long brown hair. This helped. Nature had at least been fair, giving her some of the horse's better features along with the worst.

What puzzled Royal was that Mrs. Durant didn't seem to know she was so close to being homely. She held her head with all the assured pride of a great beauty; she moved her body gracefully as if it could afford to attract attention to itself. More than once, watching her, the way she walked, the way she held her head, Royal had to wonder if he could be wrong. Maybe she *was* beautiful and he, not she, was the one who'd gotten it all wrong. But then he'd look again and be reassured. She was a horse-face. But what was wrong with that? Nothing that he could see.

He decided he wouldn't ask her about the thrasher. He'd fix it and surprise her. It would be the ultimate wonder and she would be amazed. He would do it secretly. He wondered if he would even let Peter know, but it would be impossible to keep it from him. He'd swear him to secrecy. Peter would like that. Royal's mind was made up. He'd start that evening.

Royal became both tremulous and calm, as if he'd already made the thrasher go. Then he realized it wasn't really the thrasher; it was another prompting entirely. All his life, for as long as he could remember, he had expected to be "sent for." It was the idea that

had given support to his existence: to be sent for. He waited for
it, he dreamed of it, he never doubted it. Even as year piled on
year and the summons never arrived, he was steadfast in his belief:
he would leave The Home, he would go to the place prepared for
him. All errors would be corrected; all perplexities explained.
Royal had never abandoned this faith even in his most rational
moments, even when he adjusted himself to the harshest realities.
He watched Peter raise the teat-dipping cup to Maud, worried
that he might spill some of the fluid or that Maud might not find
his offering to her liking.

Peter worshiped him, and Royal liked being worshiped. He'd
even come to think of it as right and proper. It was as though
Peter was the first person to recognize him for what he really was,
flawless and extraordinary. Even Royal himself hadn't been aware
of it until now, until Peter, with his devotion and his discipleship,
had made it unmistakable.

Only once had Peter disappointed him. On the afternoon the
bull had chased Peter, Royal had hoped Peter would be killed.
After all, Peter, in getting the bull to chase him so Royal could
drive on, was performing an act of worship. But it seemed incom-
plete without a sacrifice. Not that Royal scorned what Peter had
done; it had been exciting and frightening but, in the end, unsatis-
fying. So brave an act should have had a greater consequence.
Clearing the roadway didn't seem to be enough.

Royal knew he shouldn't have felt that way, but he couldn't
help it. Now that the moment was past, he was quite content with
the display and the outcome. The only improvement in his present state would be the adulation of Anne Durant, equal, if
possible, to her brother's. That would be best of all, but it was
nothing he felt he could aspire to right now. For the time being,
Mrs. Durant's acceptance, Martha's allegiance, and Peter's abjec-
tion were surely enough.

Royal looked down the line of cow flanks, Minnie's idly swishing tail, the drop of Margot's indifferent flop. He looked up at one of the bare lightbulbs, the one farthest down the alley, near the door, a steady if insufficient glow. Minnie's tail brushed across his face, his eyes, his mouth. He caught the scent of urine and manure in the harsh hair. Before she could offer him a second whiff, Royal put his left hand gently into the hollow between her flank and her belly, bringing his arm up again to cross against his eyes.

He had been sent for. And had arrived.

7

Grady brushed the grain from her skirt. Some had seeped through the burlap sacks and she could feel the siftings on her arms and legs. Never before had she made love in a barn. It was not the most romantic place in the world. The feed bags had been an uneven bed at best; the barn was dark and smelled of stale breakfast cereal. But the wide doors were open to the southwest, which always brought the breezes in summer, and the mid-afternoon light had already honeyed the hard ground in the barnyard. It even mellowed the mud-covered wheelbarrow propped against the wall of the cow barn and struck gold into the weathered pine of the broad barn doors.

Ned Ryerson didn't turn away to pull up his pants and zip his zipper, but kept looking at her with an approving smile. There was nothing triumphant or smug in his gaze and for that she was grateful. At least he didn't seem more pleased with himself than with her. But he did have a right to feel some sense of vindication. When they were children, he was forever saying, "Let me see you."

"You can see me," she'd answer. "All you have to do is look."

"No, I mean *see* you."

She liked it the way he'd never said "yours" or "it," always "you," making her crotch and her buttocks the repositories of her identity. But, no, he couldn't "see her," and—lying through her teeth—she said she didn't want to "see him." Seeing him would have put her in his debt and she instinctively knew with what currency she'd have to pay. Seeing would not be enough. She knew it would be a fair trade but felt at the same time an inclination to imply that he'd be getting by far the better part of the bargain and that she was therefore not interested.

To Ned's credit, he never tried to supplement his side of the deal with gifts or bribes or promises; apparently he felt that it was even steven and he had no intention of admitting to an inferiority of product or a deficiency of design. This kept their negotations brief so that, once concluded, they could get on with their search for woodchuck holes, their berry-picking, or their discussion about the relative merits of Holsteins and Brown Swiss. Holsteins always won because the herds of both their farms were Holsteins while the Dempseys on the far side of the river, who let their machinery rust in the rain, kept Brown Swiss.

Now that she had brushed the seed dust from her skirt and Ned had smoothed down his Hawaiian shirt, Grady wondered if it would be all right to begin the conversation she'd come here to have. She wanted Ned to lease her the fields—twenty acres in all —that she and Andy had sold him when they were buying their house in Coble. She couldn't afford to buy them back without a loan from the bank and she knew that in this day and age a bank loan was the first step into a sinkhole. She had no loans, no mortgage, and she intended to keep it that way.

So that it wouldn't seem that their having been together on the feed sacks was just one phase of the business at hand, Grady put her hand on Ned's cheek. He obligingly moved his head so that he could kiss the tip of her thumb.

"You want to take a look at the place?" he asked. His voice was lower than usual, and quiet, as if he were inviting her to watch a sunset or observe the rising of the moon. Still, it was the right response to what she'd said just before they lay down on the sacks. She'd come to the place looking for him and had found him in the barn stacking feed. He'd seemed pleased to see her. He'd held on to her hand and had commented almost sadly that it obviously wasn't the hand of a farm woman but that now all that would change. She'd said she didn't mind. He asked her how it felt, to be back after so many years. She told him it was a necessity, that she didn't mind, that it would keep her busy.

Instead of his mentioning Andy and the reasons for her return, Ned had simply drawn her down to sit next to him. Grady asked him how the farm was doing. He answered fine, then asked her if she wanted to borrow any equipment. Apparently Andy was a subject he either wanted to avoid or considered negligible. He began a slow inventory of his machinery, taking her hand, not looking at her, counting her fingers. He looked tired, as if naming the machines recalled all the work he'd done with them. She thanked him for the offer and, instead of just going ahead and saying that she might sooner or later need something, she said, "You were always so good. Even when you were little, you were good."

She'd meant this as a calculated preamble to asking about the fields but found that she really meant it. She'd always been touched by his goodness and his kindness; she remembered how awkward he'd always been, but how well intentioned. As a boy he'd had an almost painful yearning to be of service. A fence repaired and nothing said; a stray cow returned; the way he sat with her on the school bus, a girl and from a grade lower at that, despite the taunts of his classmates; his willingness to wash jars for canning; his gift of the root beer he made the summer he was seven. She'd forgotten most of this, but she remembered it now as if these were the incidents he'd been counting out on her fingers.

"I wish you'd never left the farm," he'd said. "It got so lonesome. Your dog, barking. It was funny not hearing your dog bark. That made it lonesomest of all."

Grady considered saying she'd missed him when she'd made the move to town after marrying Andy Durant, but the truth was that she hadn't given him a thought, and she didn't want to mar his sincerity with a lie. "I didn't know that," she'd said.

"Well, it's not much to know."

Grady had turned and looked at him. He was thinking of something, remembering something, smiling a little. Had he done all those deeds, she wondered, partly out of this same kind of loneliness, hoping for some moment of recognition that no one had the time or the inclination to give? She didn't know, but he didn't seem to have minded the lack of reward then and he didn't seem to mind it now.

She had leaned over and kissed his cheek. He'd turned and looked at her. Grady realized she shouldn't have kissed him, but it was too late. To dismiss it would have meant that she hadn't felt this surge of belated gratitude, that she hadn't acknowledged at last all of the old, forgotten kindness. She could have pretended the kiss was of no consequence, a familiarity that she should be allowed as an old friend. It obviously meant more to him and she decided that she too had meant more, a sort of retroactive application of a deeper intent.

When he'd reached over and put his hand on the back of her

neck and then, with the pressure of his kiss on her mouth, forced her gently down onto the feed sacks, she'd put her arms around him as though this was what she'd had in mind all along, and her being there had nothing to do with her need for the fields. He worked her over like a puppy crazed with joy and she couldn't help wondering if his lovemaking had been unduly influenced by Raggles. He whimpered with pleasure, uncertain as to which part of her to enjoy first, which part to lick or nuzzle or nip—or which part of himself he wanted appeased first. Grady, with time out for a few appropriate responses, tried to think the situation through.

Had she really come for this, or to ask about the fields? The answer was immediate: to ask about the fields. Then how had this happened? She'd made a gesture that had been misinterpreted. Then why hadn't she explained herself? Because it would have negated the gesture and she hadn't wanted to do that. But hadn't she done this same thing—with the same ease—at the lumber mill? Not exactly the same thing. Guy Duskin had been less needful, more aware of what he was giving. But what about her lack of resistance or even consideration? There had been, in both instances she had to admit, very little. None at all, really. What did this mean; what was she becoming? She'd been too annoyed at the question to offer herself an answer.

Still, a thought did occur to her. She had an appointment with Clive Colwick—better known as Cowlick—about insurance next Thursday; was this going to happen there too—in his office, on his desk? With Clive Colwick? Never! But doesn't it seem to be what's called "an emerging pattern"? Twice is not an "emerging pattern." No? No. And was she sure about next Thursday? Of course. Positive? Ask me another question, she'd said to herself. What's going to happen next Thursday was the question. I'm going to discuss insurance with Clive Colwick was the answer.

After a pause only long enough for her to gasp at something Ned Ryerson was doing to her neck, the question came: hadn't her husband been the only man she'd made love to before Guy Duskin? Yes. Well? Well what? Well, explain. Acknowledge. Oh, leave me alone. No. All right, then—you asked for it: I like it.

Ned Ryerson had seemed, for just a moment, startled by how active she'd suddenly become. Then he responded in kind, whimpering even louder than before.

Grady agreed to look around the farm but wasn't sure if she'd talk about the fields. It might seem a payment for services rendered. In a way, she wanted the fields badly enough to have considered exactly this kind of bargain, but she didn't want Ned Ryerson to know how crass she could be. Besides, she could ask Ned another time, or maybe entice him into making the offer, thinking the idea was his own. He'd been kind before, why not again? With a hint planted here and a comment there, she'd get him to make the offer before the month was over. Pleased with herself that she'd agreed to be devious, she followed Ned out of the barn.

Across the yard, a young woman with just a few wisps of blond hair blowing up from her balding head stood near the tractor shed examining the edge of an ordinary garden hoe as if she was uncertain about its intended use. She was wearing a short-sleeved white cotton dress and a pair of low-heeled white shoes that laced up the front like the kind older nurses wore. She also had white ankle socks and white gloves. Hanging from a strap at the crook of her elbow was a white patent leather purse with a big gold clasp shaped like an arrowhead. The clasp caught the sun and reflected it in a bright patch onto the underside of the wheelbarrow. Except for her lack of a hat she could have been dressed for a trip to town forty years ago.

"Claire!" Ned sounded more awed than surprised to see her there. "You're all dressed up." He went over and kissed her forehead.

Claire laughed as though the kiss had tickled her. "I was going to sit on the porch," she said, "but I got restless and thought I'd hoe the beans and be of some use for a change. It looks like we're growing Indian tobacco back there and not much else except for some ragweed that's just starting to come up." She turned and started toward Grady, using the hoe as a staff, leaning her weight on it as she walked across the yard. Grady could see now that her skin, including her nearly bare scalp, was a pale tan. Her face was both gaunt and puffy, drawn, but with the cheeks swollen so that the eyes, a bright clear blue, were narrowed, reminding Grady, against her will, of the eyes of a pig. She smelled of old, unstirred dust.

"Grady!" she said. "I was wondering when I'd see you." She held out the hoe. Quickly she pulled it back and held out the other hand so that the purse slid down her arm and slipped into the notch of their held hands.

This was Claire Pickering. She'd married Ned Ryerson. Grady remembered her singing Ado Annie in the school production of *Oklahoma!* She'd had long blond hair halfway down to her waist and freckles on her forehead. The freckles, Grady saw, were still there, but almost invisible now, absorbed into the tan flesh.

"Oh, Claire—" Grady had started to reach her face toward Claire's to offer a kiss, but she stopped when Claire began brushing something from the shoulder of her white dress, the movement bouncing the purse between them.

"I wish I'd known you were going to come over," Claire said cheerfully. "I'd have gotten dressed and come out sooner."

Ned took a big crumpled red handkerchief from his back pocket and tied a knot in each of its four corners. "Grady came especially to see you. And the place. It's been a long time."

The handkerchief had become a big skull cap. Still talking, he put it on Claire's head, tugging down the back two knots so that it wouldn't fall too low over her forehead. "Fifteen years on the farm," he said, "and she still forgets to keep off the sun."

Claire adjusted the handkerchief, bringing it low to one side. It covered one ear and exposed the other, an attempt, perhaps, at style. "We were just going to take a look around," he said. "Would you want to come along? I can hoe the beans after supper."

"The hay isn't so good this year," Claire said, turning away from them both and starting toward the far side of the barnyard. "Ned says not the right amount of rain, but I think the field needed liming and he was too lazy to do it."

"Maybe," said Ned.

The three of them set off down the tractor lane that ran between the unweeded bean patch and the cow pond, then between fields of alfalfa, then through the corn on an upland field that led to the edge of the woods. Along the way Ned mentioned that his old bull, Solomon, had been found dead in his pasture, just plain keeled over as if he'd had a heart attack. By the look of the turf someone might have been teasing him or chasing him. Did her son Peter or maybe the other fellow ever say anything about it? Grady told him no, then assured him that Peter and Royal couldn't possibly have had anything to do with it. They were far too busy to play around. And much too devoted to whatever chores she might give them. They'd become like brothers, a team that seemed never to tire. Ned didn't seem all that convinced, but before he could pursue it, Claire asked Grady if she still sang. Grady explained she hadn't, not for a long time.

"But you've got to!" Claire said. "You mustn't stop." She sounded alarmed, as if Grady had stopped eating or had given up prayer. "I could never stop my singing, even if it's only to myself. If I didn't have that, I wouldn't have anything. I'd be nothing. And you, without your singing, you'll be nothing. Nothing at all. We mustn't stop. We can't. It's all we have!"

To calm her, Grady promised she'd take up singing again as soon as she had the chance. Claire became silent, walking at

Grady's left, helping herself along with just the slightest reliance on the hoe.

Claire, Grady guessed, was dying. Grady knew about chemotherapy and how it made you bald. The dark skin was almost bloodless, a mock suntan sent to taunt with its suggestion of easy health. The full cheeks that puffed the eyes to slits were no doubt the effect of a drug, distorting the once-lovely face into a clown version of itself. It retained just enough of its beauty to make the emaciations and the bloatings a cruel parody of what had been the pleasing curve of a cheek, the delicate mound of a chin, the blue eyes wide with ignorance and hope.

Walking along, Grady could catch, if only for a moment, a scent of fresh water as if a breeze were coming to them from the shore of a nearby lake. It mingled with the smell of mud and made Grady think of the clay-banked brook on the far side of Ned's orchard where, as a child, on hot summer days, in the glare of the sun, she would bake the best mud pies ever shaped by human hands. How they'd managed not to turn into plump gingerbread cookies was always more of a mystery than a disappointment.

When they reached the top of the rise they could see, on the downslope, the old acres Grady hoped to lease. There had obviously been too much sun after a long series of spring rains, the right amount of water and light but in the wrong combination, and the grass was a little dry for this time of year—but in no real danger. Grady could see that the drainage was good, that the incline of the slope wasn't too difficult for the cows to maneuver.

To the south was pastureland, too rocky and gullied for cultivation, where her own herd was grazing in the afternoon sun. To her, the cows seemed the same as always: with the great rounded masses of black and white spotting their hides, they looked like gigantic pieces of a jigsaw puzzle that she wanted someday to put together. It was a handsome herd and she felt she had every right to be standing next to Ned Ryerson, one of the better dairymen in all the counties around.

The three of them stood still for a moment, not so much to take in the view as to give Claire a rest. Past the field to the east, the land lay flat, given mostly to orchard and, beyond that, corn; then a wooded hill topped by the low Vermont mountains on the horizon. Grady would not ask for the pastureland, not today. She wanted to give the lovemaking in the barn a generosity it didn't have at the time, to free it of all claims, to relieve it of any motive other than the impulse to be passionate and tender. The ideas she'd had earlier now became a resolve. She would, retroactively, bestow a virtue on her act by not completing its purpose. She would have come to see Ned and Claire just to be neighborly, with no business matters in mind. She would become what, until now, she had only pretended to be.

Just as Grady set herself on this road to altruism, Claire said, "I hope you're not going to ask for these acres back, Grady. We're building up the herd and we need all the pasture we can get. As a matter of fact, if you can let that other pasture go, we'll be able to use that too. Of course, not right away. This is two years from now I'm talking about, building up the herd, I mean."

Without turning to look at his wife or at Grady, Ned said, "Grady didn't come to talk about business."

Grady's moment had come. She would calmly agree with Ned and at the same time tell Claire she'd think about letting them have the other pastures too, though it made her a little uneasy to support the two-year plan of a woman who couldn't possibly live more than a few months. It seemed an insult to Claire, a deliberate lie about her condition, a willingness to ignore what she was going through.

"I'll think about it, Claire," Grady said—and as she said it a new thought slammed itself smack into the middle of her brain. Claire would die and Grady would marry Ned. She'd get the acreage that way, and more besides.

Grady felt exhilarated. The feeling derived not just from the perfection of her idea but from the knowledge of her newly revealed ruthlessness. She had discarded the petty manipulations that might have induced Ned Ryerson to give up the fields, and had brought forward in their place a grand design that included the entire farm. She'd come in the hope of gaining a few acres; she was leaving with a determination to get the whole works— and Ned besides. Devious she'd still have to be, but now there was more dimension to her plan. It was clean, without complication, free of reserve. It dispensed with niggling. Her realization that she had only to wait for the death of her friend Claire to get what she wanted elevated her from the posture of supplicant to the status of schemer. She liked the height. The air was crisper, clearer—and the view most pleasing.

Grady was able now to look at Claire and say, "I really came today just to see you and Ned, and to say hello."

8

Peter knew he wasn't going to fall asleep again and he sensed that Royal in the bunk above him was wide awake too. It was still dark outside, but he had already heard the call of a phoebe in the pines beyond the farmhouse. It had been a windless night, the kind that brought the smell of dried hay rather than the scent of fresh pine into the room.

Peter was tempted to whisper to Royal, to ask if he was awake, but what would he say if Royal answered yes? He could ask him why he hadn't appreciated the Swiss Army knife Peter had showed him earlier that evening, but that hardly seemed a question pressing enough to be asked in the predawn hours after a restless, almost sleepless night. Still, it had bothered Peter that Royal hadn't been interested and, more important, hadn't expressed his appreciation in the usual way. Until now, whenever Peter had shown Royal something he might enjoy, Royal displayed his enthusiasm by asking "Can I have it?" The leather belt with the White House on the buckle; an athletic jacket with felt letters spelling out WISCONSIN on the back; most of Peter's tape collection; a book about whales; and a souvenir from the Battlefield Monument just outside Schuylerville.

At first Peter was puzzled by Royal's policy of never wearing or using any of his acquisitions. He didn't even play the tapes. He simply put everything into the suitcase he'd brought his clothes in, as if they were either treasures too precious for use or artifacts too ordinary for further attention. Sometimes it seemed that the object had fulfilled its function by entering Royal's possession and could now be put into everlasting retirement.

Peter finally convinced himself that this was not miserly or even selfish; it was simply one more proof of Royal's individuality and depth of character. Royal was a mystery, far beyond Peter's powers of understanding. This pleased Peter as much as it enticed him. Royal was unattainable, inaccessible, and Peter no longer required that he understand. He wanted only to observe and, occasionally, to participate. Giving Royal these possessions was a form of that participation. They had been his and now they were Royal's; they had given Royal pleasure and Peter was the source of that pleasure. They were a bond between them. This was the purpose of Peter's generosity and its satisfaction.

But that evening when Peter had demonstrated the intricacies of the Swiss Army knife he'd been given for his birthday, Royal had watched the blades and the tools emerge, then asked for a closer look. Carefully he tested each one, pulling it out, snapping it back, examining each blade, scraping its edge against his thumb, pressing the mound of his finger against the tip of the corkscrew. Then he had handed it back to Peter and said, "Here. Don't lose it."

Peter was confused. Was the knife unworthy? Was it insignificant? Peter began showing the blades all over again, intensifying his enthusiasm, but Royal interrupted him, calling to Martha, asking her if she and Raggles wanted to see the nest of a song sparrow he'd found in the high grass that afternoon. Raggles barked, Martha yelled, and off they went. Peter followed.

Peter heard Royal turn in the bunk above. Then he was still. Peter threw off his blanket. He inhaled deeply, trying to draw the blunted scent of hay down into his lungs. The phoebe called again, two long notes, one descending from the other; the answer came, slightly off key, two notes of equal length. Four times the call went back and forth, as though the birds were trying to agree on a common pitch but couldn't manage.

Peter let his legs hang over the side of the bunk. He stood up and turned toward Royal. He saw two kinds of dark; the dark surrounding the bed, and then the shape of the bunk, the blanket covering Royal, a range of mounds, black hills seen on a night when there are no stars, no moon.

Peter slid his arm under the blanket until his open hand rested on Royal's stomach. With his little finger he could feel the beginning of the hair below the navel. He kept his hand there, not moving it, letting Royal's breathing slowly raise and lower it.

He was ready to make an outright offer of the Swiss Army knife, but Royal spoke first. His voice stepped into the stillness so naturally that it seemed it had always been there. "When I broke my arm that time I told you about in the seventh grade?" Peter said nothing, did nothing.

"They took me to the hospital alone in the school bus," Royal said, "and when they got me there they called some man where he works." His voice was quiet, but matter-of-fact, as though he were continuing a story or a conversation that had been interrupted only a minute before. "I told them not to telephone anyone, there wasn't anyone, but they called him anyway. I wasn't even crying or anything. They didn't have to call anybody, but they went right ahead, and then they told me when they finished taking the x-ray of my arm where it was broken that he was coming to see me. I told them I had to go back to The Home, but they'd telephoned him anyway and he was coming."

A note of amazement had come into the quiet voice as if Royal himself was finding his story difficult to believe. "What you should understand is that this man, my dad maybe, isn't a cutter at the mill. He's a loader, I think, so he doesn't get the lumber dust all over him, into his hair or anything.

"There were all kinds of people waiting around," he continued. "Some of them had bandages, on their hands or their feet, and this one woman with one on her eye. The nurse made me sit on a chair where you could look down the hall to where people came in, so my dad—so this man—could see me when he got there."

Peter imagined Royal on a chair at the far end of a long corridor. He saw himself coming in the door and Royal watching him as he came closer down the long hallway. Royal kept talking. Nothing in his voice acknowledged Peter's hand, still rising and falling with each breath Royal took.

"He looked like he was gold all over," Royal said. "His arms were gold, his clothes were gold, his face was gold, even his shoes. They were all gold and everyone sitting on the chairs along the walls, they were all looking at him. It was the man who might be my dad, all covered with lumber dust from the mill even if he's a loader. He just stood there, looking at one person, then another, quick, like he'd come running all the way up to the door. He looked like a lion, all the lumber dust, all the gold. Then he walked toward me fast, bumping into a nurse, sending lumber dust onto the floor. I looked the other way, afraid he'd come for someone else."

Slowly Peter's open hand rose and slowly fell, not moving on its own, but still resting where the hair began.

"I waited for him to say something so it would be all right to turn and look at him, but he didn't say anything. I waited for him to touch my shoulder or maybe my head, but he didn't. He didn't say anything and I didn't turn. And he didn't touch me. I waited and then I turned anyway. Lumber dust was in his eyebrows and his eyelashes, covering his whole face, even his lips. He opened his mouth and licked in some of the dust. Then he just turned around and went back out the door. I guess he saw me and decided he didn't want me to be his son. All that was left was this trail of sawdust, and a pile of it next to my chair where I was sitting down. I could taste the gold in my mouth, the dust."

Peter waited to hear more, but Royal said nothing. The slow move of his hand up and down was like the riding in a boat, peaceful, safe, as though it could go on forever.

Slowly he drew it back toward himself, feeling the bone of Royal's hip. When he was about to pull the hand from under the blanket, Royal put his own hand on top of it, and held it where it was. With one swift move, he shoved it down until it touched his penis, already erect. Before Peter could make a move of his own, Royal threw back the blanket and shifted onto his side. He reached down under Peter's arms and helped lift him up onto the bunk. With his arms he clamped Peter against his stomach and began an upward heaving with his hips. Peter, trembling, began his own downward thrusts.

9

As far as Grady was concerned, Claire Ryerson—born Pickering —didn't need imminent death to stay her pace. Claire had always been a slowpoke. On the days that Grady brought her to the clinic, she would steer her from the car to the hospital steps, from the steps up to the door, and from the door into the waiting room with an impatience accumulated since childhood.

If Grady weren't using this kindness as part of her plot to get Ned for herself, she wouldn't have put up with her friend's pokiness for a single minute. But her determination to marry Ned gave Grady the control she needed to keep herself from tugging, pushing, and threatening Claire the way she used to when they were girls growing up.

Grady was, of course, shamed by this disgusting fraud. But it wasn't so much the hypocrisy that shamed her; it was the need for hypocrisy. The idea that she, Grady Durant—born Conroy— had to connive to get a husband, even at thirty-seven, was a far greater source of distress than the connivance itself. She'd lived her life feeling she could pick and choose—which was exactly what she'd done when she'd met Andy Durant and forgotten Ned Ryerson.

Grady kept a firm hold on Claire's arm as she guided her up to the second of three steps that led to the side door of the hospital. When she applied the light pressure that meant Claire should try for the top step, Claire relaxed her arm and drew it away. She was looking at the sign on the door giving the days and hours the clinic was open, not to make sure she'd come to the right place at the right time, but more to take thoughtful note of the lettering, the spacing, and the general design.

She'd already stopped twice since leaving the car; once to look at her right foot as if she'd forgotten the word for shoe, then to stare into the branches of a maple tree, seeming to search for one particular leaf it was her duty to find. It had always been like this. As a child she'd stop dead in her tracks to examine something no more exotic than the head of a wind-blown dandelion, or she'd hesitate at a discarded beer can long enough to read the small print. Often, when walking, she'd stop and look back as if she could better locate herself by knowing how far she'd come rather than by how far she had yet to go. She'd speeded up only when, at twenty, she noticed that Ned Ryerson seemed to have forgotten Grady and had started after her. Her speed, of course, was in Ned's direction, and the acceleration was sufficient to propel her at a decent pace during the years of her marriage—until last winter, when her illness and the treatment restored to her her lost hesitations, her forgotten pauses, her forsaken interest in detail.

After Claire had given the hospital sign the scrutiny only she could give it, Grady took her elbow again and they went inside.

The waiting room was like a courtroom or the chapel of a very severe religious sect. Facing the receptionist's desk were five rows of polished high-backed wooden benches, pews stretching from wall to wall with only a narrow aisle cutting down the middle. Arched windows lined each of the side walls, their shades half drawn to cut off at least some of the beauty burgeoning outside. Above the receptionist's head was an oval-framed portrait of Wendell Loftsgard, a stiff-collared elder, one of the hospital founders and a man remembered as much for his righteousness as for his philanthropy. His eyes, modestly cast downward, seemed to be looking into the hairdo of the receptionist, certain that at any moment, fleas would be seen crawling along the trough of its wave.

The first time Grady had come here with Claire she was amazed. She'd expected soft chairs, rugs, area lighting, coffee tables with magazines, the usual living-room replica that was meant to put the patient at ease, a room that spoke welcome, even sympathy.

Nothing of the kind. It was sit up straight and no nonsense. During the first visit Grady reasoned that it was a want of funds that kept this room in the previous century, that all available money had been spent on equipment rather than furniture. Then, eventually, she came to regard its decor as proper and just. The room, with an unyielding honesty, spoke the severity of the patients' situation. A harsh sentence had already been passed and these continuing attempts at appeal—called treatment—were subject to an uncertain ruling at best. No pretense to the contrary was being made, no diversionary hope was being offered.

That such consistency was cruel occurred to Grady, but she still wouldn't have had it any other way. The illness was cruel, the treatment was cruel. It would have been a greater outrage to claim otherwise in any aspect of the situation. The room was right: pitiless, uncaring, implacable, and dumb.

As usual, Claire went to the third row of benches, moving a little more than halfway in toward the wall. Even though the room discouraged conversation, Claire looked upon these moments as a truly social time of day. In contrast to her distracted behavior in the car and outside the hospital, she would now become an out-and-out chatterbox. This would be the first of her two talkative periods. Here in the room she would chronicle her complaints. Later, in the car, smoking the marijuana meant to counteract the after-effects of the treatment, she would give, for Grady's benefit, a graphic presentation of her sex life with Ned, a life revitalized, she claimed, since her illness.

Now, however, sitting upright against the uncushioned back of the wooden bench, she began the day's litany of grievances, not whining, but truly angered. "The soup Ned made for supper last night he said was corn chowder. He used old potatoes. It was mush. I don't understand. I really don't. And after supper, he said we don't get Channel Seven. I know we get Channel Seven. There are satellites up there to make sure. I told him, but he said we still don't get Channel Seven. Try it, he said, but I knew it wouldn't do any good. I don't understand. I really don't."

And so the chronicle began and so it continued—from a denunciation of Ned's decision to put the near pasture to corn when the drainage wasn't right and hay was enough anyway, on through the ugly brown bricks being used to build the bank where the old hotel used to be in town, and finishing with the herbicide she could taste in her morning coffee, probably from some Central American miscalculation.

Grady contradicted and opposed whatever Claire said, an old tactic briefly abandoned but recently reemployed. On the first few trips, whenever Claire complained, Grady would try to offer some explanation, some excuse, some consideration of the other side of the coin. At times she was the voice of reason, at other times the advocate of those who weren't there to defend themselves. She

considered it part of her job to keep Claire from getting too
excited. It hadn't worked.

When Claire had expressed her disgust at the ranch-style
houses in the development just outside town, Grady thought it
would help to remind Claire that they were certainly better than
the hovels built for the mill hands in the last century. This only
excited Claire to a condemnation of houses without an upstairs.
Grady countered with the practicalities of heating, of oil costs and
insulation problems. This led Claire to the position that no building could lay claim to being a home unless it had not only an
upstairs, but an attic.

To argue against this Grady made a few remarks about attic
clutter. For once Claire agreed, but only because it led to a greater
complaint. Ned had let their attic collect too much junk. Three
generations of it. She'd begged him to clear it out, but he
wouldn't do it. "No wonder," Claire said. "No wonder we never
had any children. Ned never made any room for them. He gave
it all to *his* side of the family. I don't understand it. I really don't."

After those first few trips to the hospital, Grady decided she
wouldn't contradict Claire. Opposing her had done nothing to
calm her. She'd agree with whatever she'd say. Maybe that would
help.

Claire led off with "Can you read magazines any more? The
print comes off all over you. Not just your hands. It gets on your
clothes, all over your face."

"It's the cheap ink," Grady said, duplicating as best she could
Claire's accusatory tone. "They could do something about it, but
they don't. It gets all over everything."

"Are you crazy?" Claire said before she realized that Grady had
agreed with her. Then the words caught up with her. She blinked
a few times, thought, then said, though not too harshly, "It's the
cheap ink." She paused, repeated Grady's word, "everything,"
and finally found herself back on the course she'd set for herself.

"Ned came in yesterday and accused me of gardening when I was supposed to be resting. I hadn't been gardening. I'd been reading *Time* magazine. You could tell. It was all over me. I don't understand it. I really don't."

"They should give us gloves," Grady said.

"Are you crazy? They—" Again Claire paused and, after a moment's consideration continued. "They should give us gloves," she said, as if that had been her own thought all along. Grady had calmed her. She turned toward Claire. There she sat, pulling in her lower lip, holding it between her teeth. She had become reflective. It was a triumph for Grady and she was pleased.

But then Claire said "gloves" again. She pulled herself up even straighter and licked her lips. "Gloves," she repeated, more adamant than before. "Who wears gloves anymore? Nobody's worn gloves for years except in winter. And then it should be mittens. Gloves separate your fingers. How can they keep warm when they're all separated from each other?"

"Mittens," Grady said. "You're right. Gloves can't do it."

For a long moment, Claire said nothing. Then she whispered the word *never* and fell silent. Grady worried that a new assault was building steam, but no, Claire continued to say nothing.

Grady turned again and looked at her. Claire was shaking her head, little sideways jerks. She'd stop, then shake again. She seemed caught in some interior dispute, trying to grab on to some particular idea that kept eluding her. She'd consider a possibility, find it wanting, then shake it from her mind. She was off course, bewildered as to how she'd got there and unable, for the moment, to get a hold on anything—a word, a thought, a realization—that might show her the way back to the path she'd charted for herself.

Grady should not have agreed with her. She had appropriated attitudes that Claire had wanted to be exclusively her own. Grady had crossed into a territory over which Claire had staked sole sovereignty. Grady's presence had confused the landscape, unmoored the compass. No wonder Claire seemed lost. Grady had wronged her. Why shouldn't Claire complain? She was feeling lousy and in a little while, after the treatment, she was going to feel even worse. She was young. She'd been beautiful. She was dying. She had every right to complain. But she could hardly keep saying over and over again, "I feel lousy" or "I'm dying." She was only trying to be less boring than she had a right to be. And she'd found her own way to give voice to her anger and her bewilderment. To stifle that voice or try to silence it was unjust. It robbed her of what was, in fairness, hers. Grady had been a thief, and a sneaky one at that.

With this jab of self-accusation, Grady was willing to let the subject drop, but another thought asserted itself. In Claire's defeated state, complaining was the easiest form of superiority. The complainer, by the nature of things, is assumed superior to the object of complaint. Another person, dying, might be able to rise higher, to heights of transcendence. Perhaps Claire had made the try but couldn't get that far. Maybe this was an exhausted attempt to reach above her situation, an ascent stalled in the lower regions. She might yet get the strength to resume the flight, but for the time being she had to settle for the poisoned and polluted airs that held her where she was, no higher than her contempt and her scorn could carry her.

Grady, to make restitution, to restore the landscape, turned her gaze upward to the oval-framed portrait of Wendell Loftsgard and made the most antagonistic statement she could think of. "What dignity. A real gentleman."

Claire stopped shaking her head and looked up at the picture. "He was an asshole."

Then, to Grady's relief, she substantiated her statement. Mr. Loftsgard's history included adultery, desertion, usury, bestiality, theft, and tertiary syphilis. To keep her going, Grady protested: Wendell Loftsgard had been a town elder, a benefactor, a pillar of the community. This brought Claire to what seemed her most scathing accusation. "Oh yeah? He probably wore baggy long underwear. All year round. Look at him. Just look at him. Baggy."

From then on Grady would counter Claire's complaints as forcefully as she could and Claire, for her part, would find— heaven knows where—the energy needed to press her case to the point where she could, with defiant resignation, say "I don't understand. I really don't."

But now, after the comments about herbicide in her morning coffee, Claire had become silent. And she was staying that way. Grady wondered if she should give her an easy goad, a mention perhaps of the weather, which, by the way, was beautiful. But she hesitated. Maybe Claire had finally gone beyond complaint, one more sign of the end. Grady was about to consider that the dying woman might have reached her transcendent state, that she had risen above the petty contempt that had trapped her for the past weeks; but then Claire whispered, her mouth twisted so that she was talking out of the side nearest Grady, "I don't have any grass for after. I smoked it all before you came to pick me up. You always complain so much. I felt I needed it to get myself through it all. Do you think they'll give me some more for the way home?"

Before Grady could say anything, the door to the side of the receptionist's desk opened and Elly Kerwin, in a white nylon dress, stepped into the room and came toward them. "Claire?" she asked. "Are you ready?" As if Claire might possibly say no she wasn't. Claire stared down at the floor, then looked out the window. It seemed she was looking for further instructions in and among the lower branches of a birch tree. Then she faced front for a few seconds, got up and let Elly lead her through the door. It was Claire who reached back and closed it behind them.

Claire leaned sideways against the car door and pulled the smoke deeper into her throat, down into her lungs. They'd given her a generous supply of marijuana and she seemed eager to work her way through it as quickly as possible. She sucked in one more breath, swallowed, then exhaled. Very little smoke came out. She'd gotten good at it during these past few weeks.

At first, smoke had completely clouded the car in spite of the opened windows. Grady was sure she'd gotten a contact high because she hadn't seemed to mind, at that time, the catalogue of sexual exploits and intimacies that Claire would list on the homeward journeys. As a matter of fact, she'd rather enjoyed it all, the two of them beginning to giggle when, for instance, Claire confessed that Ned liked sometimes to gnaw at her kneecap and chew on her instep.

By last week, however, Claire had become expert; very little smoke escaped into the car. Ned's exploits amused Grady not quite so much. She'd always questioned, in her own mind, the truth of what Claire was saying, but by now she'd declared them out-and-out fabrications. They'd begun to annoy her. She'd known from the start, from that first day when Claire, pulling at her joint, had chronicled Ned's nightly revels, she'd known Claire was only trying to make her jealous. She'd put up with it until one day the previous week when, to challenge the reality of what Claire was saying, she asked sweetly, "And what did *you* do? I mean, when he did *that?*" Claire simply ignored her. That annoyed Grady even more. That she was jealous was true. After all, Claire was talking about her future husband.

Today, as they turned off Lake Street onto the highway that led to the Ryerson farm, Claire settled back onto the seat and, as if she were talking about something astonishing she'd read in the morning paper, began describing, with a vividness an anatomist would envy, the network of veins revealed in the foreskin of Ned's penis during erection. Grady was tempted to say, "Oh, really? I hadn't noticed." But she kept her mouth shut.

As they were driving past the shopping mall Claire insisted on duplicating the sounds Ned made during his ministrations—all of them obviously borrowed from the barnyard. Grady considered saying "Yes, I know, I know. Terrible, aren't they." But again she said nothing.

As they drove through Wilton, Grady got a diagrammatic presentation of several positions devised by Ned himself, all of them firsts in the history of human copulation. As they went by the Colbert orchard, Claire began a tale involving a hassock. This carried them up the Ryerson drive, out of the car and into the house. When Claire sank exhausted into a living-room chair it seemed surely that her weariness derived not from the medical treatment she'd just sustained but from the sexual experiments she'd just endured.

Grady left her sitting there, the remote control for the television near at hand, along with two more joints, a roach clip, matches, and an ashtray. Outside, before getting into the car, Grady looked off beyond the cow pasture where Ned was disking an already plowed hill field. His dark blue fishing hat with the narrow brim was pulled low over his forehead so it would keep the sun off his face as far as the tip of his nose. He was wearing, as usual, a silk Hawaiian shirt, this one a clash of orange and blue. His bare arms lay at ease on the tractor steering wheel and he was more or less riding sidesaddle so he could look both behind and ahead. An able farmer, good at what he did.

But was he also the man whose explorations had discovered— according to Claire—erotic regions nested in the shoulderblades and who'd found in his wife's armpits an excitement that had almost crazed him? Could this patient man now making the crawl along a dun-colored field be the same one who'd made bedside staples of honey and chocolate sauce and had devised a strategy against his wife's ear that had thrilled him into ecstasy?

Grady broke off her questions. Consistently the answer had been yes. Watching his unhurried move along the field, sensing the restraint that checked the tractor's pull, she believed that he was, in actuality, slowly accumulating the passions that would erupt later with Claire. He wasn't harrowing a field; he was, with droning restraint, teasing his passions, holding them back while goading them into further vigor, creating greater accumulations, assuring them their time would come, they mustn't stop now, they must go on, droning, gathering, growing.

Grady slid inside the car and gave the door as hard a slam as she could. With the brake still on, she started through the gate, spewing gravel back toward the window where Claire was no doubt smoking away, imagining further feats for their next homeward ride. Claire, she told herself again, had been making it all up. Just as she herself had been making it up just now, watching Ned on the tractor. It had been at Claire's prompting that she'd imagined what she had. After all, she wasn't ignorant of Ned. There *had* been that afternoon in the barn on the feed sacks. He didn't have the control for all that Claire had claimed. He didn't have the discipline. He didn't have the imagination. He didn't have the dexterity.

Grady made a sharp right onto the road, not slowing down. With a quick back spin of the steering wheel she skirted a ditch, then a stand of sumac, and escaped back onto the road with a branch of syringa broken off and lying on the seat where Claire had been sitting. Grady's impulse was to throw it back out the window but there were a few quick turns ahead so she thought she'd better keep her hands on the wheel and her eyes on the road.

After the first turn, Grady began to consider that, quite possibly, Claire hadn't been trying to make her jealous after all. That would have been too simple, too ordinary. Claire wasn't the ignoramus Grady sometimes thought she was. She had a mind. She had an instinct. And God knows, she had an imagination. She must have guessed what Grady was up to. She must know Grady was offering her help just to put Ned under an obligation, to create a debt she'd collect the minute Claire was cold in the ground. And what Claire was doing now would have its true effect then, after her death.

She was creating in Grady's mind an expectation that Ned would never satisfy. She was attributing to him exploits and exercises that were completely beyond his competence, but that Grady would wait for, expect, demand, and never get. Claire had been preparing Grady for future frustrations that would distress the very sheets she'd lie on. When none of the chronicled deeds would duplicate themselves, when Ned would never reach the promised dementia, when none of the specified skills would be put into practice, Grady would think it was her own inadequacy that had blunted his ardor.

Grady had to hand it to Claire. She was far more clever than Grady had ever given her credit for. A feeling of respect, even affection was applied now to her image of Claire, back in her living-room chair, pulling and sucking smugly on her joint. They were sisters, they were equals. Each knew how to betray the other. A bond had been forged that Grady valued as a treasured possession. She could love Claire now, and care for her. She could listen to her and bear whatever had to be borne.

Grady heard Claire's words again, not an incitement to jealousy now, but a last desperate offering to Ned, each anatomical detail singled out and presented to him, a plea that each be infused again with life, that his passion rescue her, that he retrieve this ear, this mouth, this belly, this breast, that he bestow new health on this neck, this knee, this thigh, that he rouse the bones and blood, that he summon it all to himself, that he pass into it his strength, his need, his love.

When Grady made the last sharp turn onto the road that led to her drive, the torn twig slid down toward her along the seat and touched her elbow. She nudged it away without taking her hand from the wheel, but it swung right back. "All right, Claire," she said out loud. "Don't shove. I know you're there."

And now Claire spoke to her for the last time that day. No longer pleading, the words were an extended listing again of the parts of the body, even the seemingly insignificant ones. Each was given its moment of intensified life, the brief instant of aching affection and deepened recognition that will always characterize a fond farewell. It was a final inventory of all the places of pleasure and yearning. They were summoned one last time and told that they had done good service, that they had given a reasonable joy. It was a rite of dismissal and Grady had been given the role of acolyte. So be it. She would be a faithful attendant and a patient witness. She would give the prescribed responses. She would pronounce, when the time came, the needed amen.

And then, to fulfill the bond between herself and Claire, to prove its immutability, she would marry Claire's husband.

10

When Royal's "new" car made the turn and pulled up in front of the cabin, Anne saw that it was the sorriest-looking heap ever seen this side of a junkyard. The chrome bands along the sides had been stripped away like bandages removed before a wound had healed, exposing a rim of gritty rust pocked with black holes. The rust motif was repeated on the front and back fenders, both of which were crumpled, looking like sculpture made from brown-paper bags. A starburst of cracked glass decorated the windshield so that whoever sat next to the driver would seem to have an unformed, ever-shifting face. The bumpers, front and back, had acne. The grille in front, with its gaps and gapes, was obviously the handiwork of a dentist who had withdrawn from the case midway through treatment.

They were early, which made her uneasy. She was hoping that Ray, the archery instructor, might come looking for her before her brother and Royal got there. Her second night at camp she'd slept with Ray and a few nights since then and one afternoon they'd made love behind the archery range. These were her first real sexual experiences and they'd left her a little bewildered, somewhat ashamed, and constantly giddy.

After the first night she was ready to tell Ray about the money and ask him if he wanted to be included in her plans. He was very handsome and would fit nicely into the Hollywood café where she so often imagined herself. She wasn't sure she loved him, but she knew she wanted him around all the time and maybe that was supposed to be enough. Still, she thought she'd better get away for a day or so to think about it before doing anything definite.

To give Ray as much time as possible to come and say goodbye, Anne continued to sit on the top step leading to the cabin and went right on braiding her wet hair.

Royal was first out of the car. And apparently he too had priorities that were beyond revision. Without a wave or a greeting of any kind he went to the hood of the car, raised it, ducked his head inside, hat and all, withdrew it, wiped his left hand on his pants leg, and slammed the hood down. He got back into the car, started the motor, listened to it, turned it off, then got out and started toward her, still without any greeting.

He walked with a deliberate lope, spending extra time on the balls of his feet before coming down on his heels. His arms he held out a little from his sides, gorilla-fashion, trying to make his shoulders seem broader. His blue denim shirt bloused out around him and it seemed now that his suspenders were needed not to hold up his pants but to keep the shirt from bellying in the wind and lifting him up to the heavens. He'd obviously been in the sun; his face was pink and his nose was peeling, but this only made his lips even paler, as if he was allowed a limited supply of color and the beating sun had effected no more than a redistribution.

Halfway to the porch he made clear his reason for being there. "You got any water?" he asked.

Anne let him wait a few seconds before answering. "Well, there's a lake in back and a row of showers inside that shed over there with some sinks and some toilets."

"Thanks. Is there a pail or anything around?"

". . . and," she continued, "there's an outdoor faucet for washing sand and dirt off your feet just around the corner of the cabin." She moved her fingers even slower in her hair.

"Is there a pail or anything I can use to carry water?"

By this time Martha and Peter had gotten out of the car and were standing next to Royal, lined up at his side, looking dumbly at her, not as though she was their sister but a stranger on who's help they depended. This was not the kind of meeting she'd expected. She thought they would have missed her, that they would be almost jubilant to see her again.

Martha in particular was a disappointment, the way she just stood there, waiting with the others for an answer to Royal's question. One of Anne's reasons for deciding to go to the farm on her day and a half off—aside from Ray and her present giddiness—was because she'd missed Martha. She'd gotten the notion that Martha felt forlorn and abandoned without her older sister. Her fear that Martha was forlorn made *her* forlorn, Ray or no Ray. Anne had even worried that she might cry when she'd first see Martha.

She needn't have worried. Martha was doing fine. Anne was tempted to give her a good slap for not being lonesome.

"Well," Anne said to Royal, twisting her fingers in and out of the strands of hair, "if you need something to carry water in, there's a drinking glass next to my cot, and a pitcher on my shelf except it has some honeysuckle in it, and there's a bucket with some sand in you can't use on a nail just inside the door and—oh, yes—there's a hose attached to the outside faucet if that'd be any help."

All three of them turned and headed toward the side of the cabin as if they'd been given orders by a drill sergeant. Anne slowly unbraided one of the braids, then the other. Slowly she started over again, determined not to finish until she'd been given a proper greeting. It even occurred to her to change her mind: to stay at the camp for her time off, to punish their rudeness with her absence, which, she quickly had to admit, they probably wouldn't notice.

Royal, Peter, and Martha were now spaced along the line of the hose with Martha at the faucet—her insistence—Peter correcting any tangles in its unwinding, and Royal, nozzle in hand, at the car's radiator. Aware that neither Peter nor Martha would allow any assistance, Anne went over to Royal as if putting water in the radiator of a car was an instruction she had wanted for a long, long time.

"Okay! Turn it off!" Royal called as soon as Anne had reached his side. The water burbled to a stop and Royal flung the hose off to the side to show that he had no more need of it. Denied the instruction she'd come for, Anne contented herself with watching him put the radiator cap back on.

"I like your new car," she said, hoping she'd managed just a slight note of sarcasm.

Royal, who had raised his hat a few inches above his head so he could rub a streak of grease across his forehead, looked at Anne as if by pronouncing the word *car* she had suddenly materialized at his side. He immediately clamped his hat down over his hair and took his hand from his forehead. Anne got the feeling she wasn't supposed to have seen his hair, that something immodest had taken place, but she kept looking right at him to show that she was indifferent to such prudery.

"You like it?" he asked. His mouth began to stretch toward a smile, then pull back, then stretch again, ready to go all the way once the right words were spoken.

Anne was tempted to contradict herself, annoyed that he didn't take her word for it the first time. But he would, she knew, be devastated, and her inclination, when she found herself with so much power, was not to use it.

"I like it," she said.

His mouth still couldn't accept what his ears had heard. His lips kept struggling to lift at the corners. To give them a final push, she added, "It's like nothing else."

That did it. Not only did the lifted corners of his mouth shove back his cheeks but the eyes widened as if to take in a larger view of whoever had spoken so knowingly. "I figured you'd want a ride in it," he said. "That's why I told your mother we wouldn't need her car to come get you." He beamed at her and even raised his hat a little so that he could rub the streak on his forehead deeper into his skin and give her, at the same time, just a glimpse of his hair. She wondered if he was becoming addicted to her approval and might demand an endless succession of assurances that she liked the car. She might even have to increase the dosage to the point where what had started as minimal courtesy would end up as blatant hypocrisy.

To fend off a fourth inquiry, she poked her head through the window on the driver's side. What she saw she could only describe as Gypsy Caravan Seedy. A Persian rug of faded red, gold, and green was draped over the front seat, covering it completely from the back down to the floorboards. There was a slight hollow on the driver's side suggesting a poor man's version of the contour seat. Sofa pillows and scatter cushions of varying sizes and colors buried the backseat, not quite concealing the brown cotton stuffing sticking up through the holes in the original gray plush. Anne couldn't help wondering if Royal really considered himself such a voluptuary or whether this was a carry-over from the previous owner. The decor suggested that the car wasn't intended for transportation only. Maybe Royal depended on the car's interior to make a statement he himself was too shy to make. This seemed unlikely, but she thought she'd better give him a closer look. She hadn't thought of him since coming to the camp and wanted to see if he was still as unprepossessing as he'd been the last time she'd seen him.

Royal was pretending to adjust the outside rearview mirror. "It's all fixed up in there," she said, hoping she'd devised a statement neutral enough to be taken as a compliment if that's what he needed to hear. He continued to adjust the mirror. "Some of the pillows are old," he said. "I'm going to get some new ones."

"They look comfortable," Anne said.

Royal shrugged to let her know that he respected her standards even if they weren't his own. "Of course there are a few other things I want to do too," he said, angling the mirror so that he could see his face. He examined first his left profile, then his right; he tilted his head up, down, and sideways. He stuck out his jaw then lowered it to give prominence to the brim of his fedora. After one final look at his right profile, eyes narrowed, jaw set, he went back to adjusting the mirror as if it hadn't yet given him a view that would satisfy.

For Anne this display was all she needed. Royal Provo was an absurdity. His vanity was laughable, his capacity for self-delusion —whether induced by himself or by his "new" car—was almost without limit. With his peeling nose and red ears, his oversize pants and his pretentious suspenders, he was actually repellent, and Anne wished now that she hadn't said what she'd said about the car. His enthusiasms should be discouraged, his pretensions deflated, his delusions corrected. And Anne decided to make the task her own. She'd begin by casually asking if he'd really intended the inside of his car to look like an adolescent idea of a whorehouse, then go on to say something about bleached beige being her favorite color in a car, especially with a rust trim.

But before she could get her smile in place, a spray of water from the hose hit her on the arm and, when she turned to see what was happening, it got her right in the face. It had hit Royal too and had gone right through the window into the car, onto the Persian rug. "What's going on?" Royal yelled.

The spray was diverted so that this time it could go through the back window onto the pillows. "Turn it off!" he yelled.

The water went off. At first Peter seemed to be the guilty one. He was standing there, coiling the hose, with the nozzle aimed directly at the car. But he turned and focused his gaze behind him. Martha had moved a few feet away from the faucet and was looking to the side of it as if she didn't know it was there.

"Martha!" Peter yelled.

"I was turning it off," Martha said.

"It *was* off." Peter dropped the hose and came over to the car. Royal was already brushing his arm against the carpet to squeeze out what water he could. Peter, from the passenger side, did the same; then they both began rearranging the cushions in back so that the wet parts wouldn't show. That Anne was soaked down the front of her blouse and her jeans didn't seem to matter.

When Royal began rubbing the rust on the hood dry with his shirt tail, she went into the cabin, brought out her shoulder bag and garment bag and started toward the car. Before she was down the porch steps, Royal, Peter, and Martha had crowded into the front seat and Peter was wiping the inside of the windshield with what Anne recognized as her swimming towel, which had been hung out to dry.

Left with no choice, she went dutifully to the backseat and tried to push the garment bag and the shoulder bag in ahead of her. They met with resistance from the cushions, and it was only after a few unruly shoves that she herself could get in. Before she'd been able to clear a space on the seat, the car lurched forward and began turning around toward the road. Anne was thrown against the door, then brought back down on top of the garment bag. When she got up, she was dumped sideways onto some pillows. She yanked out the one pressed against the small of her back and tried to straighten herself on the seat. There was no room for her arms until she elbowed three other cushions away, and the damp from those on her left was making sure her dry side didn't stay that way for very long. Finally, she made a nest for herself and settled into it, her shoulder bag a cushion at her feet, the garment bag supine on the lumpy pillows that crowded the rest of the seat. Anne pulled her hair back behind her ears. A fresh trickle of water went down her neck.

In the front seat, her brother, sister, and Royal were looking intently through the windshield, even through the distorting cracks in the glass, as if a world seen through this particular windshield were like none other and they mustn't miss it. Anne leaned back and put a pillow under her head. She felt not only relieved, she felt released. Just now, she had been wonderfully ignored. During her time away, she hadn't been missed. Her brother and her sister did very nicely without her. When the time came, she could run away, and without a worry in the world.

A few miles later, Royal called over his shoulder, "Comfortable back there?"

"Very," Anne answered.

Royal nodded. She'd given the right response. Her only disturbance, if there was one, was a mild curiosity to see again, uncovered, Royal Provo's carrot-colored hair.

11

Grady stopped the car about a half mile before the turnoff. Guy Duskin's letter—it had come with a gift—had told her this would be the signal that she'd agreed to meet him where they'd met before. Grady reached into her purse, took out his gift—a pink plastic teddy bear—and pinned it on her blouse. She looked into the rearview mirror to check her hair, as if putting on the pin might had displaced a few strands. It hadn't.

Guy had pulled up a few hundred feet behind her. She snapped her purse shut, started the car, and went the last half mile, then made the turnoff. He followed, still at the same few hundred feet. Grady imagined she'd begin the conversation by saying that she was there to thank him for the lovely present. Then she thought she'd skip that part of it. She wasn't there to be coy. She was there for one thing and one thing only—a repeat of their previous performance—and she wasn't going to pretend otherwise. If he wanted reticence and protestation, she'd tell him to forget the whole thing. Her fund of deceit and manipulation was kept in strict reserve for Ned Ryerson and she had no intention of dipping into it now. She was there for an open declaration of need and she wanted neither herself nor Guy Duskin to make any bones about it.

Grady had come to this decision the night before, when she returned home from Ned Ryerson's, walking through the fields with nothing to show for the evening's trouble but some outdated magazines and a jar of watermelon pickles. To be more precise, yesterday evening's determination had its origins in the experiences of yesterday afternoon. When she'd brought Claire into the house after a session at the clinic the unmistakable feel of steam was in the air. It could mean only one thing: someone was canning. The scent of simmering spices made her think first of apple butter, but then, because it wasn't the right season, she guessed watermelon pickles.

She'd followed Claire into the kitchen and there was Ned, his Hawaiian shirt completely soaked down the front, looking into a boiling pot. Without acknowledging their presence, he picked up a fork, snagged a cheesecloth sack of spices and lifted it away. He looked around for a place to put it and finally settled for the left front burner.

Claire eased herself into a chair. "I decided this year I'd do watermelon pickles," she said. Ned had lifted another pot from a back burner and was tipping its contents, the cooked watermelon rinds, into the syrup the spices had made. Three times he flinched from the splashes and the steam, but went right on pouring.

"I was going to do rhubarb," Claire said, "but I just couldn't find the time. But I did manage the watermelon and thank God for that."

It was at this moment that Grady got the picture: Claire would decide to do something—hoe the beans, put up pickles—Ned would do it, Claire would take credit for the accomplishment, and both of them would be convinced that it was Claire who'd actually done it.

When Grady started out the back door, Ned seemed to notice her for the first time. "Come back tonight," he called. "After supper. I'll give you a jar." Grady nodded. "If I'm not here, I'll be up in the barn," he said. Grady nodded again.

She'd been almost certain that this was actually an invitation, a not too subtle indication that they should now begin the conjugal activity that would eventually lead to marriage. Grady looked forward to the evening's event, and not just because it assured her that her plan was progressing. Claire's sexual chronicle on the drive home had aroused more than her curiosity. After all, she wasn't made of stone.

When she came back that night, Ned was alone in the kitchen reading *Hoard's Dairyman,* a magazine her grandparents had subscribed to. It suggested a continuity between that time and this, additional support to her claim on Ned. They had things in common.

Grady asked about Claire. Claire was upstairs asleep. Ned asked about Raggles. Raggles was fine; Martha could tell him to sit and he'd sit. Sometimes. Ned marveled at how quickly she'd put the farm into operation. She praised Royal and commended Peter, then boasted at how well they got along. He asked about her herd and she gave knowledgeable answers. She asked about his herd and was told there might be a difficult calving in the next few weeks or so. Then he gave her a jar of watermelon pickles and they said goodnight.

On the way home, Grady figured out what had just happened —and it was very much to her satisfaction. Ned had arranged the evening to reassure himself that they were still good companions, that, sex aside, they got along together. He'd wanted a domestic evening but was, at the same time, testing his deeper feelings toward her. And it was Grady's conviction that she'd passed the test. The evening had been a milestone, and an important one, on their road to the inevitable.

But then, after she'd gone up the stile and down and was walking along the edge of her own alfalfa, she acknowledged again that she'd gone there to be made love to. She had wanted the whimperings, the whisperings she'd heard before. She wanted to hold and to be held. An image of Ned with Claire, a clear and well-lit demonstration of what Claire had described that afternoon, flashed through Grady's mind. She dismissed it as nothing more than pornography. But just before she reached the open pasture that would lead to her barnyard, she stopped and folded her arms across her breasts. Slowly she rubbed her upper arms with her hands. She held herself a moment, squeezed gently, then rubbed herself again, feeling the brush, up and down, against her breasts.

She lowered her hands, letting them move over her stomach, passing her groin, down along her thighs. For another moment or two, she stood there. Then she picked up the flashlight, the pickles, and the magazines and continued on home.

Before getting out of the car, Grady checked the teddy bear to make sure it was pinned securely. Touching it, looking down at it, she wondered if the pin could become a secret signal, that it could do for her the service of Marguerite Gautier's camellias: the pink teddy bear and she was there for the taking. Or, perhaps, it could be considered a mutation of the Scarlet Letter.

She was already out of her car when Guy pulled up. She wished she had a cigarette so she could be seen smoking. She didn't like just standing there. Maybe she was going to want a few moments of pretense after all. Maybe a few preliminaries weren't such a bad idea. Maybe she should start out with "I only wanted to thank you for the lovely . . . etc., etc."

"What did you do to your hand?" These, as it happened, were

the first words she spoke to him. His right hand was wrapped in white gauze, a mitten that turned it into a paw.

"I got it caught," he said. He didn't say what in, and Grady didn't ask. He was beaming at her again as if getting his hand caught was the crowning achievement of his life.

"It doesn't hurt?" she asked.

"No. They bandaged it."

From this, Grady deduced that the bandage had cured the pain. He held up the hand for her to admire. "Looks like they did a thorough job," she said.

"I had seventeen stitches once on my foot." His tone implied that Grady had missed the really important event and was being treated now to a spectacle of decidedly lesser import.

"That must have hurt."

This time he seemed puzzled by her inability to understand. "No," he explained. "They took stitches."

"Oh," Grady said, nodding her head to indicate that she finally understood: stitches were as anesthetic as a bandage. Guy immediately broadened his smile. He was pleased by her ability to process information. He was also pleased by his effectiveness as instructor.

"You like the jewelry I sent you, huh?" Without waiting for Grady to answer he said, "I knew you would. I know what you like."

Grady checked these last words to see if there was innuendo or possible insult in them, but no, they were completely without mockery, suffused instead with a genuine appreciation for his own gifts of divination.

"It's important I know what a woman likes." A breathiness in his voice gave it the qualities of a whisper. "If I don't, how'm I supposed to make her happy?" And there was also in his voice a humbleness, a gratitude that this great charge had been laid upon him and no other: to make a woman happy.

The man's sincerity was beginning to make Grady ashamed. She had come to take easy advantage of him, to use his attraction to satisfy a need rather than fulfill a desire. It was like some of her moments with Andy when they had used each other to cancel rather than satisfy a sexual urge so that one or the other could get on with some other chore, a good night's sleep or a book to be read or a moment alone. She began to feel that she should raise her own desires to the level of his, aware at the same time that she really didn't want to. She didn't consider him worth the trouble.

Guy Duskin, she told herself, was stupid, if not retarded. But then she would be doubly wrong to take advantage of his incapacities. He could even be deranged. She could be in danger. She hadn't thought of this before. Now she wasn't sure what she should do. She'd changed her mind; she'd come to her senses. She should go home. "Yes, the . . . the jewelry"—she had started to say pin—"it's lovely. Delightful." She fingered it a moment, then raised her hand and pulled on her earlobe, pretending to adjust an earring even though she never wore them.

"It's very beautiful," Guy said solemnly, correcting her choice of word.

"Yes. Beautiful."

"Of course. And you know how to appreciate beautiful things. I knew that right away I saw you."

"Thank you."

"That's why I followed you last time. Because I knew right away. I knew all about you. Everything. Otherwise I could never have sent you jewelry like that."

"Yes. Thank you." She started to finger the pin again, then quickly brought her hand down. "That—that's really why I stopped," she said. "So I could thank you. It—it *is* beautiful. And I . . . well . . . thank you." Grady almost reached out so they could shake hands, but felt it was a little too formal. "It was very thoughtful," she said. "And I wanted—well . . . as I said, to say thanks."

As she spoke, Guy Duskin's smile changed to an expression of deepest sorrow. "I know," he said. "I know that too. I know you didn't come except to say thanks. That's how much I know about you."

A moment ago, she'd been afraid of him. Now, because of his mournful willingness to let her go after no more than a thank you —and an insincere one at that—she realized she'd slandered him. He was anything but dangerous. Just a little stupid. A stupidity, she told herself, that could be measured by the distance between what he *thought* she was and what she *actually* was. Which meant he was stupid indeed not to see her more clearly and be angered or disappointed by what he saw.

Now she had to go. He'd given her no choice. To stay she would have to admit her first intention; she would have to make some sexual advance. And Grady knew she was not sufficiently schooled in the methods of seduction to devise one that would disguise her role as instigator. He'd see it immediately for what it was. He'd realize that he had not known her after all. And it was to this correction of his certainties that she did not want to give consent. "You were very kind," Grady said, her voice low and quiet. "And I'm very grateful."

He nodded his head to let her know she'd said the right words, the ones he'd known she'd say.

And for Grady too they had been the right words. For the first time since she'd gotten out of her car, she'd spoken the truth, and with honest feeling. Now she could, with a sincere heart, take him in her arms and bring the hurt hand to her cheek, now she could lower his face to her breast and offer him the swelling nipple.

But she didn't. She, too, nodded her head, then went to her car and got in. Still, she couldn't just drive off. It had all happened too quickly. Surely there was more that must be said. She'd just gotten out of the car, now she was back in. Had she come for only this brief exchange? Of course she hadn't, but it seemed to have turned out this way and it seemed, as well, that there was nothing she could do about it. Nothing, at least, that she was willing to do.

She drove off. She didn't want to look into the rearview mirror, but she did. He was standing there, looking down into his injured hand as if the wrapped bandage were a nest and he was gravely counting the eggs inside.

He had been honest with her; she had not been honest with him. She wished now that she had been. She wished she had told him that he was wanted. She wished she'd told him that he had softened the harshness of her original reason for being there, that his words and his feelings had changed her need into desire and her determination into longing.

The sudden high whir made by the tires as she drove over the bridge spanning the Battenkill challenged her thinking. Her thoughts had been tuned to the sounds and rhythms of solid pavement. Now the tires were subjected to an unexpected sensation, rubber on metal mesh. And Grady, as if startled in mid-phrase, halted her own refrain and, almost in a panic, searched for a note that would bring her back in tune. Before she could find it, she'd come to the far side of the bridge. The shock was over, but the original pitch was gone for good.

Instead of returning to her former refrain, she had thoughts altogether new. She'd been tricked. Guy Duskin had arranged it all. He had assigned her her part and dictated her lines. And it had all gone very nicely. She'd never been given the least chance to say why she was there. He'd been in control the entire time. It was his way of getting rid of her. She'd been given the brushoff —and with no more to show for it than a plastic teddy bear that looked like it was made of glazed bubble gum. She, Grady Durant. Dumped. And by a near imbecile. No, not an imbecile. Far from it. Very clever was what he was. More clever than she. And she was Grady Durant. She was Grady Conroy. "Conroy," she repeated to herself. "Grady Durant, born Conroy."

Then she laughed. Out loud. Being Grady Durant born Conroy was apparently no guarantee of preferential treatment. Like everyone else, she'd gotten what she'd deserved. Maybe Guy Duskin, along with his other insights, had seen her for what she was after all. He'd dismissed her lineage, he'd ignored her status. He'd tricked her. He'd dumped her. So appreciative was Grady of the rightness of this that she laughed again. Out loud. She, Grady Durant, laughed. Again. Out loud.

12

"Who are those people there?" Anne asked, pointing to the photograph.

"I don't know. They were just standing there." Royal turned the page of the album. Anne shifted her knees under her and leaned forward, away from the bunk, hoping that if she showed more interest, the pictures themselves would become more interesting.

That was the fourth time she had asked the same question—"Who are those people there?"—and the fourth time Royal had given the same answer. First it was the picture of an elderly couple near some flowers outside the United Nations, then a teenage girl smiling as she posed near the Central Park carousel, then two small boys with a young man and a young woman who looked like their parents standing on some steps that covered the whole background, and now three Japanese men in raincoats boarding a tourist bus.

"When you talked to them, didn't they tell you their names or anything?"

"I never talked to them."

It was a relief for Anne to see now the steps of St. Patrick's Cathedral with no one posing, only a scattering of people going in and coming out, sitting on the steps, none of them looking at the camera. "This is the one I wanted you to see," Royal was saying, but Anne was really quite ready to move on. The entire evening had been something of a trial.

He was, she knew, trying to compensate for his behavior that afternoon when the two of them and Peter had climbed to the top of the gorge, but it was a sorry compensation at best. Still, he was trying and she must be patient, even indulgent.

They'd gone first to the waterfall where, Anne had to admit, they'd all been a little idiotic. Royal and Peter had gone on ahead and Anne, her shoes in her hand, was making her way upstream in her bare feet. When she rounded the bend just before the falls, there was Royal, alone, the water splashing down on him. His hat he'd put on the bank of the stream and his head was tilted now as far back as it could go. The water ran off his upheld face, spraying down onto his shoulders, coursing off his body through rivers made by the creasings in his clothes.

She'd headed toward him, a little wobbly among the rocks. Royal had seen her. He pretended he was taking a shower, showing off for her benefit. "Come on in," he called. Anne waved her shoes at him, then pulled her elbows in toward her body, shivering to let him know it would be too cold.

Royal came toward her, purposely falling, getting up, falling again and rising, pretending that he was being sent crashing toward her by the fierce current of the smooth-flowing stream.

When he got close enough, he held out a hand as if he needed her to steady him. Anne reached toward him and he took hold of her shoes, tangling his fingers with hers in the laces. Royal worked his way through the tangle so that he was the one finally holding the shoes. He tossed them onto the bank then held out his hand again.

"Come take a shower."

"No!" Anne cried as she let him lead her under the falls. The water wasn't as cold as she'd expected nor was the water coming down on her head as forcefully as she'd hoped. She'd kept a scream ready and was a little disappointed that it wasn't really needed.

Royal had begun to scrub his sides again, rubbing his wet clothing against his ribs. Then he reached over and gave Anne's ribs a quick scrub with his knuckles. Anne pulled back because it genuinely tickled.

On the bank, Peter stood watching them. He'd been ahead of both of them but had come back. "You coming in?" Anne called, louder than she had to. The falls weren't that noisy. Peter hesitated, then jumped into the stream. With another leap he was under the falls, scrubbing himself frantically as if to catch up with the number of movements Anne and Royal had already completed. In the guise of washing her arms, Anne poked him four times with her elbow and he slowed down.

Just as she was about to step out from under the falls, Royal reached over and started rubbing her back. "I'm going to scrub your back," he announced as if he hadn't already begun. Anne didn't like him doing it, especially with her brother there. And Peter didn't help when he himself said, "Yeah, we'll scrub each other's backs." He went past Anne, almost stumbling on the rocks, steadying himself by putting a hand on Royal's arm. He began rubbing up and down Royal's back, hard, and Anne could feel Royal being pushed toward her.

She stepped out from under the falls, then up onto the bank of the stream. She put on her shoes and headed up the path.

It was near the top of the gorge that the day's trouble took place. Anne had stepped out along the narrow ledge that would be the last level ground before they'd reach the top. She'd sat down and dangled her feet over the side. The drop immediately below was steep, almost straight down, the ledge a perfect look-out. Below them the countryside, three towns, two lakes, and the river were spread out as far as the hills way off to the east.

It was quiet and Anne wondered if she should point out some places of interest to Royal or just let him take it all in. When she turned to look at him, he was standing away from the edge. He had backed himself against the rocks that rose behind and was staring ahead, not into the distance, but at a point just in front of him. His arms were rising from his sides, his fingers slowly climbing the rocks at his back, each hand trying to clutch the stones. He was holding his breath and his pale face had become a bloodless white.

Peter, too, had seen him. "You all right?" he asked. Royal became even more still. Peter went to him. "You won't fall," he said. He reached for Royal's hand. Royal gave a quick whimper. Anne got up and went to his other side. "Look over here at me," she said. She knew it was the height and she knew she had to do something about it. "Don't look down and don't close your eyes. Just look over here at me." When Royal continued his stare, she took his hand.

"No!" Royal cried. With a quick jerk of his head he looked at Anne, terrified, as if she had just taken hold of him to pitch him over the edge.

Anne looked at Peter. "We have to get him down from here. You stay on that side, I'll be here. We've got to move slow so we don't scare him more."

Royal closed his eyes, then opened them immediately as if some shock had raced through his entire body telling him that this was not allowed. He began to shiver.

"I'll stand in front of him so there'll be something between him and the drop," Anne said.

"What if he pushes? You'll go over."

Anne thought a moment, then said, "I'll do it from here then. I'll ease him toward you. You lead toward the path. But gently." With that, Anne gave Royal's body a slight pressure in the direction of Peter. "Look at me," she said softly. "You won't fall. I won't let you fall." Her voice was almost a mumble. "Just look at me. You'll be all right. You're going to be all right."

Peter took up the refrain, pulling Royal gently toward him. "Look at me. You won't fall. I won't let you fall. Just look at me. You'll be all right."

Their words joined, barely audible, like a droning prayer. With Royal between them they continued the sounds, easing toward the path, their feet shuffling slowly as they went.

As they neared the end of the ledge Royal suddenly thrust Peter against the rock wall, broke free from Anne's hold and leaped onto the path. Without looking back, he went crashing down through the trees, through the bramble, running, stumbling, sometimes on the path, sometimes not. Stones bounded ahead of him as if they too were in flight.

Anne and Peter caught up with him at the waterfall. Royal was waiting for them. "I came to get your shoes but you already have them on." Nothing more was said until, on the drive home, he told them, "I want to go back up there sometime, take some pictures."

And after supper, just as Anne was going upstairs to make her weekly count of the money, he'd said, "Before you go back tomorrow, can I show you some pictures I took? New York. Tonight maybe. A trip I took there. You'll like 'em. They'll make you feel like you're right there. Honest."

Anne had wanted to tell him that what had happened at the gorge was nothing he had to be ashamed of, that it meant nothing. Of course she felt quite differently. It had been creepy. It disturbed her to know that there was a whole secret, unpredictable part of Royal Provo, that, without warning, he could become something else. Anne liked surprises—as long as they were revelations. If they weren't—if they were mystifications—she'd just as soon do without them. But rather than say this, and to help him believe that the afternoon had affected her in no way whatsoever, she agreed to look at the pictures.

A final hesitation came when she learned that Royal had let Peter take his car—a most surprising concession—to drive all the way to the Pyramid Mall near Saratoga, where it was known for certain he could get batteries for his transistor. But this, she told herself, meant nothing to her one way or the other. All she intended to do was go through the album with what patience she could summon.

Next to the photograph of St. Patrick's was one showing a middle-aged man and woman standing next to a statue of a soldier on a horse. The woman was wearing a corsage near her left shoulder. Instead of asking him the usual question about who they might be, she tried another tack. "How'd you get them to pose for you?"

Royal looked closely at the picture to make sure he knew which one she was talking about. "Oh," he said, "they weren't posing for me. They were doing it for someone else, so I went ahead too."

Anne took the pillow from Peter's bunk and put it under her. "Oh," she said, trying to sound as if she were grateful for the enlightenment. What could be more natural, more economical in the commerce of human relations than to photograph people already posing for someone else? How could she possibly have known that if he hadn't told her just now? To demonstrate that she wasn't as ignorant as she might seem to be, she pointed to the picture of St. Patrick's and said, "St. Patrick's."

"The cathedral," Royal added. "That's the one I especially
wanted you to see. After a pause he continued, "Where the
cardinal lives."

Anne waited for a further elucidation of why this particular
picture was one he was so eager for her to see, but when he said
nothing, she felt obliged to pick up the unraveling strands of their
conversation before the weave disintegrated entirely. "Look at the
door," she said. "Big."

"I told you you'd like it."

Anne, of course, was monumentally indifferent to it. She'd seen
it too often on postcards and in newspapers and magazines and
on television. But she knew Royal was struggling to offer her some
specific and individual point of pleasure, so she said, "It's a good
picture too." She regretted this immediately.

"I used a Canon AE-1 with an automatic exposure," he said,
not so much giving credit to technology as boasting, in the off-
hand manner true boasting requires, of his easy familiarity with
it, implying that it was nothing out of the ordinary, relying on the
auditor to come to the opposite conclusion. "I used VR-100 film
on all of them."

Anne kept having to remind herself that he really knew what
he was talking about, that he was an extremely competent young
man with a real gift for anything mechanical or technological.
Peter claimed he was a genius. He might well be. But he didn't
seem to trust her to know this and it was his pushing the point
that caused her to doubt. If he didn't trust himself, why should
she?

She was shown a picture of a traffic jam at the mouth of the
Lincoln Tunnel, some ships at the South Street Seaport, the
World Trade Center, a fountain in Central Park, one photograph
as impersonal as the other, all of them near duplicates of postcards
she'd seen before, postcards she'd even received. Where was the
evidence of glory that Royal had seemed to promise?

When he showed her a picture of a woman looking out from

the observation deck of the Empire State Building, Anne didn't ask who the woman was. Royal had known no one while he was there, had spoken to no one.

Anne wished she hadn't realized this. She didn't want to know how alone he'd been. To ward off any concern, she began to praise each new picture. "Look at that man there, the way you got him perfect!" She took a desperate interest in details: she became excited about the world suggested by what she saw.

She wanted to stop, but she couldn't. She was participating in the trip with him. She was transforming it from what it had actually been into what he had claimed it was, an adventure rich with revelations and incident, crowded with human company. Anne made herself part of that company and gave back to Royal, by exclamation and by comment, by question and by response, what she knew he'd hoped for—a drama in which he was an important character.

In her effort to convince him, she convinced herself. By the time she saw the picture of Macy's main entrance taken from across the street, she believed without question that Royal Provo was a hero, that the photographs were trophies of conquest. He was never seen in the pictures; he could therefore be imagined. And what she imagined could, in turn, be invested in the young man sprawled out next to her.

The last picture, of course, was of the Greyhound bus that had brought him home as far as Schuylerville, taken in the dungeon dark of the Port Authority Bus Terminal. The driver was taking a ticket from a woman burdened with a clinging child, a suitcase, a diaper bag, a purse, and a balloon. Behind her a line of faces was discernible in the gloom, mostly by the shine of the eyes. Across the upper left corner was a slant of bright pink.

"That's my arm," Royal said. "Someone gave me a shove at just the same minute and my arm flew out in front. But I got the picture anyway, don't you think?" He sounded slightly embarrassed for the intrusion, but Anne thought it only right that he had finally made it into one of the pictures, even if it was only the lower part of his left arm. By a process of mental cloning she was able to take this fraction of his body and reconstruct from it an entire Royal. The picture became not a picture of a Greyhound bus but of Royal wearing what he was wearing now: stained khakis, a blue workshirt buttoned at the neck with the sleeves rolled down, brown suspenders, and the pair of heavy work shoes her mother had bought for him and for Peter because running shoes gave them no protection. His carrot hair was slicked straight back as if he'd combed it with water. Two blemishes, the remains of squeezed pimples, marked his chin and gave promise that someday a beard might grow. Pale lips, pale skin, the snub nose, blue eyes the blue of dragonflies.

Anne closed the album and spread her hand over the padded cover, moving it along the leathery surface. Her impulse was to go sit in the chair near the window, but she stayed where she was. Royal hadn't moved. He was staring at the cover of the album on Anne's lap.

Anne raised herself to a kneeling position and the album slid to the floor. They both let it lie there between them for a moment, then they both reached for it.

They were on their knees, and when Anne began kissing him, she could tell that the pages of the album, still on the floor, were being torn and pulled from the binding as she struggled to get even closer to him. Her right knee slipped along a picture until it was stopped by the thick metal coils of the album's spine. The rings pressed through her jeans into her kneebone. It made her gasp as she kissed his neck, his ear, the lids of his eyes. She managed to get the album out from under her right calf and shifted Royal's head so that it wouldn't be crushed against a post of the bunkbeds.

This put her own head under the bed, however, and left Royal with a choice of kissing the side of the mattress or the bed support. He chose neither, burying his face instead between her breasts, digging into her with his nose and chin. Anne stared at the slats under the bed, at the edges and corners of the sheets and blankets poking down through the springs, until Royal's eagerness for another kiss rescued her. He reached under the bed, placed his open palm against her right ear, and more or less plowed her head out from under the bed. With a series of gyrations and other body maneuvers that became without her willing it the throes of passion, Anne was finally able to lie out flat with only the rug beneath her. She wondered when she had reached the decision to do what she was doing but there was no time now to give it much consideration.

When Peter came in, Anne was collecting unglued photographs from under the bunk, then one propped against the table leg. Royal sat in the rocker, trying to match the torn edges of the pages that had been pulled from the album. "I got the batteries," Peter said, "but I had to buy four because that's how they sell them." He tossed a ring of keys to Royal, but Royal didn't reach for them and they landed on the floor next to the album. The coiled spine was flattened and bent and more of the pages were half torn away. "What happened to the picture book?"

"I was looking at it," Anne said.

"My trip to New York I showed you," Royal said.

"Oh. Those." Peter picked up the album. A triangle of paper stuck out and what looked like the design of a shoe sole was stamped onto the cover with thick black lines. "How did—" he started to ask, but stopped. He put the album on the bottom bunk. He picked up the car keys and started to hand them to Royal, but put them, too, on the bottom bunk. He saw a picture pinned under the leg of a chair near the door. He went over, lifted the chair, and picked up the picture. After hesitating a moment, as if not sure to whom he should give it, he slipped it into the album, then began changing the batteries in the transistor. "I hope I got the right ones," he said.

Royal got up from the rocker. "Anne decided she had to get back to her job at camp tonight so I'm going to drive her."

Peter turned. "Oh? Are we going now?"

"Mama's at the Ryersons'," Anne said, "so you have to stay here with Martha." She picked up the album and shuffled the pages and the pictures together as best she could. Royal took the keys and started toward the door.

"Tomorrow we get to cut wood," he said. "With the chain saw."

Peter, carefully putting the new batteries in place, nodded.

"I'm going to show you how. We'll do it together."

Again Peter nodded.

Outside, just as they were getting into the car, there was a great blare from the transistor, a blasting from a rock station. Immediately, the sound was lowered until Anne heard nothing at all.

13

The Ryersons' wide-plank picnic table had been there under the locust trees since Grady was a girl. Now it was covered with a bright blue cloth and three places set at one end. As Grady opened the car door on Claire's side, Ned came down the steps of the back porch. In one hand he held a small wicker bread basket heaped with something wrapped in a white cloth napkin. In the other he carried a pitcher of milk.

Without even looking in her direction, he put the pitcher and the basket on the table and headed back inside. By the time Grady got Claire out of the car, Ned was coming down the back steps again, this time with a steaming bowl of green beans and a platter of fried chicken. He set them on the table, examined his handiwork, moved the bowl of green beans a little farther from the chicken, then went inside again. Grady wondered if she should offer some help, but since there'd been no indication that this had anything to do with her, she thought she'd better keep out of it. Claire seemed to be aware of none of it and was studying the delicate whitish flowers on a sprig of shepherd's purse sprouting at the edge of the driveway.

Now Ned was out again, a platter of sliced tomatoes balanced on his arm, a plate of sausages in his left hand, and a bowl of what might be boiled onions in his right. He moved even faster than before, his Hawaiian shirt suggesting, with each successive trip, a bad abstract painting trying to escape from itself.

Claire had abandoned the shepherd's purse and was obviously preparing to go into the house. She'd become puzzled by the handle of the screen door and was advancing toward it to give it greater scrutiny, a sure sign that she would eventually employ it and get herself inside.

"Where's everybody going?" Ned called.

Claire stopped. She gave herself a moment to take it all in— the table, the food, Ned, the trunks of the locust trees. She turned to Grady. "I forgot. Since it was a morning appointment at the hospital, I thought I'd fix us some dinner. I meant to tell you before."

She started toward the table but, after about four steps, stopped and looked around her. Grady knew she needed something to grab on to. She went to her side, took her elbow and waited for her to make the next move. Claire let her gaze wander over the platters and plates and bowls on the table. "Good," she said. "I was afraid I'd forgotten the onions."

Claire took a few more steps, then gave an apologetic laugh. "I guess I overdid it at the hospital. You two go ahead. I think I'll step inside for a while." Her turn was a little unsteady, but when Grady reached out for her, she pulled her arm in toward her side. "I know the way." She laughed again, steadied herself and then headed toward the front door. "Go ahead and start. I'll be out later and I don't want to see it all still sitting there. Go on, Grady. You've got to be hungry by now. It's been such a terrible morning." She'd reached the steps. "And don't keep watching me. If I tip over backward, you'll hear it. Go sit down."

Grady obeyed, listening for the thump and bump that meant Claire was now in a heap at the bottom of the steps. But she heard the screen door slam—surprisingly soon—and Grady wished now that she'd watched after all, just to have seen Claire move that fast.

"If you don't have time," Ned said, "it's okay. She meant to tell you but I guess she forgot. She does that sometimes."

Grady knew she was supposed to agree, and with a certain amount of understanding and sympathy, but she wasn't about to go through a "poor Claire" routine. "Forgets *sometimes?* She *always* forgets. You mean you're just beginning to notice? Ned, where have you *been?*"

Ned, a little ashamed that he found this amusing, smiled down at his empty plate. When he lifted his head, the smile was gone. He handed Grady the wicker bread basket. "You still like corn muffins?" he asked.

"Yes," Grady answered. And they began to eat.

No time was wasted. Whatever the social lures of the occasion, they were both still farmers and the noonday meal was not meant for lollygagging. As a matter of fact, Grady was only too aware of how unusual it was for one farmer to have dinner with another. Or even supper. Food was usually plentiful, but time was not. It was either work or calamity that brought two farmers together at mealtime. Grady couldn't help making the connection: the calamity of Claire's illness had prompted the feast; nothing else.

Yet if this weren't giving her a chance to be with Ned, she would have begged off and made her excuses. She'd wanted to get home early. For the past few days, Peter and Royal, their usual chores aside, had been cutting most of the wood they'd need for the winter, not only to ease the oil bills but to assure their survival if, as often happened, there was a power failure or the furnace failed or the delivery trucks couldn't make it through the snow.

Today they expected to finish cutting up the great cottonwood that had grown on the far side of her vegetable garden—and for years had been taking up more than its share of moisture from the ground. It had been a gigantic tree and a gigantic job and today was to be the day of praise and amazement. What made her particularly eager to be there when the task was done was Peter. Lately, he'd become quiet, almost mournful. He still did his work, dutifully, he and Royal, but it wasn't with the old verve. Now it was Royal instead of Peter who would try to generate a little extra energy while still respecting Peter's mood. Royal was almost gentle with him, and it touched Grady to see him so considerate. Peter would rally at times, his old insufferable enthusiasm rising to the surface and bubbling over. But then it would subside, he would become quiet again and Royal would become more than usually kind.

Peter, of course, was grieving for his father. Grady knew only too well that the real time of mourning could come after an appreciable delay. There was, however, little she could do about it beyond extra shows of affection and special appreciations expressed. And today would have been an occasion for both. Still, she had this chance to be with Ned and she'd have other opportunities to help her son. She'd had to make a choice and she'd made it. Besides, her praise for Peter was merely delayed, not withdrawn.

As she and Ned talked and ate, it crossed Grady's mind that she might be taken, after lunch, for a quickie on the feed sacks. She was not uninterested.

To end this line of thinking, however—especially after the disappointed expectations on the night of the watermelon pickles

—Grady told herself that no ulterior motive was involved in the present situation. It was a kindness in return for a kindness. She took Claire for her treatments; now she was being given a rather elaborate meal. To support this reasoning, Grady also told herself that she'd been attributing her own deviousness to Ned. Just because she couldn't do something free of manipulation and self-interest didn't mean that Ned was a schemer too. She warned herself to be wary of attributing to others the characteristics she'd so recently acquired herself.

At her own insistence she now took an increased interest in the conversation. Ned was talking about retained placenta after a calving. One of his cows had had difficulty in late May. After treatment, Aïda had made a complete expulsion within seventeen hours. (Claire named all their cows after opera heroines.) Grady, cutting some meat loose from a chicken leg, muttered her relief for Aïda and her enthusiasm for prostaglandins.

Now it was her turn to introduce a topic of conversation. In a mild panic she ran down her list. She knew this was what she should have been doing instead of thinking about deviousness and manipulation, but there was no time now for self-criticism. She wanted something that would serve her cause, something that would prompt Ned to ponder the excellence of Grady Durant. Corn, alfalfa, hay. Her cow Maud's bent teat, which resisted the milking machine. Childhood. Her grandparents. His parents. Her children. His health. The chicken she was eating, the beans, the onions, the sausage. The design on the plates. The color of the blue tablecloth. The splendor of a locust tree. The color of the blue sky.

Even the heavens mocked and betrayed her. Directly behind Ned, rising slowly into the sky, was a succession of white clouds shaped like the speech balloons of cartoon characters—but they were blank. They gave her no clue, no hint. Grady had nothing to say. Not that that had always stopped her, but in the present circumstance she was not willing to say just anything. It had to be pertinent. It had to be significant. Her time was running out. Her turn was almost over.

"You're good company, Grady. You don't feel like you have to be talking all the time. And you make me feel like I can just shut up if that's what I want to do. I like that. We still get along, don't we?" He gave his mouth a hesitant twitch, and his steady gaze that told her she wasn't supposed to look away. When he reached over and put his hand on hers, Grady twitched back, hoping that was all that was expected for the moment.

Now she understood. It was barn time, it was feed-sack time. Which was more or less fine with her. And, as it turned out, if she'd diverted him with idle chatter they would never have arrived at this present situation. Part of her said, "If silence isn't golden, it at least pays off." But another part kept trying to evaluate the prospect before her. Would this suit her purpose? Was this the recommendation she wanted to give Ned on her behalf? She had to think fast, but the only thought that came to her was that she had to think fast.

"Do you understand what I'm saying?" he asked quietly.

Grady twitched her mouth again and realized, by going through the motion herself, that this was meant to be the smile of someone bashful. She twitched once more and this confirmed her first impression. She was being bashful. Maybe she'd come upon a whole new approach to understanding other people: mimic their motions and see what feeling they might suggest. Maybe it was her own body, her own gestures, performed in accurate imitation of others, that would communicate to her brain what had remained an uncertainty to the unassisted eye. There were drawbacks, of course. It would slow things down. And there was the danger that the person being mirrored might think he was being made fun of. There could be resentments, retaliations. Grady finally decided this was a method of insight to be reserved only for those occasions when it could be interpreted as a gesture of agreement, sympathy, or support.

Ned tightened his hold on her hand, then relaxed it. "Sometimes we feel things we don't know how to talk about," he said.

"You understand?" he asked, then withdrew his hand as if he thought it unfair to try to influence her answer. Grady wanted to reach over to him, but before she could move her hand the screen door slammed behind her. Ned lifted his head and Grady looked up just as Claire brushed past and dropped herself into the chair at the head of the table. She was wearing a yellow silk bathrobe tied closed at the waist with a light green sash. She had taken off her wig, and the wisps of blond hair stuck out from her bald head too thin, too spare to be a tangle. Her unlined face looked as though it had been set in white tallow, her lips cracked because their movements had broken through the waxen casing.

"I'm so *hungry,*" she said. She sounded as if her exhaustion was from want of food. "I didn't eat any breakfast." She leaned forward, almost a lurch, grabbed a corn muffin, and began crumbling it against her mouth. "I've got to *eat* something," she mumbled. "I mustn't stop *eating.* I'll get *sick* if I don't eat." She tried to force the muffin into her mouth but her lips refused to open far enough. She began to make snorting sounds as if trying to inhale the crumbs. Then the sounds became a cry of protest, a complaint that she was being fed against her will. But even as she was trying to stuff the muffin into her mouth or up her nose, the gagging began.

She dropped her hand from her lips and stood up, tipping her chair behind her. She turned away from the table and bent over as the great heavings gripped her body. She gagged again and opened her mouth but nothing came out. Only a few crumbs from the muffin fell to the ground. Again her whole body lurched and she reached one arm across her stomach to brace it against the next attack. Her other arm she lifted so that she could cover her mouth with her hand. The retchings subsided and she used the hand to lift her head, raising it, gently forcing it back as far as it would go. She took her hand away from her mouth and let it rest against her throat. "I'm so sick," she whispered. "I'm so sick." Except for the caught breaths, she didn't move. After a moment, she said, "Do you mind if I go lie down for a while? I get so tired sometimes."

Ned was standing now and reached out his hand. "I'll help you upstairs," he said. "Or would you like to lie down on the porch for a while?"

"Upstairs. Grady can help me."

Grady put an arm around her shoulder. "I'm so sick," Claire said again, this time more in bewilderment than complaint.

Grady led her into the house and up the stairs to the bedroom. The bed was rumpled, the bottom sheet pulled loose from under the mattress, and most of the bedspread was on the floor. There was a smell in the room, too sharp to be a perfume or a flower, but Grady couldn't quite identify it. The curtains on the windows blew lightly inward, an afternoon breeze wafting the odor that filled the room.

Grady helped Claire sit on the edge of the bed, then went around to get the pillow on the far side so she could straighten it against the headboard. Claire got up and went to the dresser just a few feet from the bed. She picked up a bottle and unscrewed the top. Grady got a strong whiff of the scent she'd smelled when she first came into the room. It must be the cologne Claire used, and quite liberally.

As Grady was smoothing the blanket, she felt a few wet drops hit her arm and her ear. She looked up. Claire tilted the bottle, let some of the fluid onto her hand, then flicked it out over the bed as if sprinkling it with holy water. Grady saw the label; it was an aftershave lotion. Claire patted some of it on her cheeks and at the back of her neck, then licked the tip of her middle finger.

After Grady had lifted the bedspread onto the bed, she looked over to see if Claire was ready to lie down. Claire was staring at her, watching her with the same puzzled scrutiny that Grady had seen given before only to tree bark and flowers, to discarded beer cans and chewing-gum wrappers.

"Ready to lie down?" Grady asked.

Claire continued to study Grady's face. After a moment, she looked down at the bed. "Grady?"

"Yes?"

"May I brush your hair?"

"Brush my hair?" Grady reached up and touched the back of her head.

"Please?"

"Does it look that bad?" She tried to laugh.

"Please."

Grady shrugged. "If you want to," she said.

Claire picked up the brush from the dresser. Grady wondered for the first time if Claire's loss of hair might be contagious. Maybe Claire knew more about her plans for Ned than Grady realized and had hit upon this particular revenge, Grady gone bald. She would catch it from the hairbrush. But she reminded herself that she knew better, and besides, Claire should be allowed a few eccentricities.

They sat next to each other on the bed, Grady's back turned slightly toward Claire. Claire began to draw the brush slowly down through Grady's hair, pulling the ends lightly toward herself before letting them fall free.

Unable to stop herself, Grady looked at the dresser top and the bedside table for any evidence that might corroborate Claire's sexual claims. She was like a little girl, ignorant but curious—even suspicious—about what went on in grown-up bedrooms. The idea that she had reduced herself to a five-year-old embarrassed her and she stopped, but not before she was satisfied that she'd seen nothing particularly interesting. Surely it would require some-

thing more than a whiff of aftershave to set in motion the extrava-
gances described by Claire. But then, one never knew.

"I'm glad I'm brushing your hair," Claire finally said.

"Hmmm."

"So many times," Claire said softly, "so many times what I've
really wanted to do is pull it."

Drawing the brush out of a strand just behind Grady's left ear,
Claire, with a dreaminess that matched her movement, said,
"Like this." She took a clump of Grady's hair into her fist and
yanked it.

"Ouch!"

"Oh, did that hurt? I'm sorry." Claire took another fistful and
pulled.

"Stop it!" Grady turned and faced Claire.

"Oh, I'm sorry," her voice still dreamy and soothing. "It's just
that it's what I always wanted. I didn't mean it should hurt
though." She reached out an open hand as if she was going to
touch Grady's cheek, but when it got near, she closed it around
a thick strand of hair and pulled with all her might.

"Clair-*aire!*"

Claire let go and Grady righted her head. She thought it unfair
at best that Claire should wait until she was bald and then start
a hair-pulling contest, and Grady considered telling her exactly
that. But Claire looked so stricken, so terrified by what she'd done
that Grady could only say, "I think it's time for you to lie down
and rest."

"Oh, please. Don't go. You said I could brush your hair."

"You were not brushing my hair," Grady said evenly.

"But I will. I promise I will. See?" Claire put her hands behind
her back. "I'm not going to pull it. Just brush it."

"What you need is some rest."

"I'll rest. I promise I will. I'll even get under the covers. But
let me brush your hair. Please. Oh, Grady—!"

Grady sat down again on the bed. For a moment, nothing

happened. Then Claire resumed the brushing, slowly, gently, a light lift just before the brush let go of the last hairs at the finish of a stroke. She did this over and over and then stopped.

"There," she said. "It's all brushed."

"Thank you."

Grady thought this sounded too abrupt, maybe even a bit sarcastic, so she turned toward Claire and added, "How do I look?"

"Like you could use a shave," Claire said. She sputtered, then began to giggle. Grady watched her, Claire's body quaking, quivering with the silliness of what she'd said. Claire covered her mouth and pinched her nose. She bent over, she shook her head from side to side. The giggles wouldn't stop. She sat up straight, took her hand from her mouth and nose, looked at Grady and laughed and laughed.

"Oh, Grady," she gasped, "you're so funny. You're so *funny!*" She let her laughter subside to a panting, with a sputter now and then to help ease it out of itself. Grady waited until the breathing became slow and even, then, with a touch on Claire's shoulder, helped her get her head down onto the pillow. Grady slipped her shoes from her feet and lifted her legs up onto the bed.

Claire closed her eyes, then wearily opened them again. She strained a little up toward the middle of the pillow and straightened her arms out at her sides. She parted her lips, about to say something. Grady waited. The lips parted further, then closed. Grady waited another moment. Claire lay there, her eyes open, her body rigid as if there was something she was refusing to do. Grady started to bend over, to kiss her perhaps, but changed her mind. She stood up straight, watched the window curtains stir until they stopped, then left the room.

Outside, she saw that the picnic table had been cleared. Ned had apparently given up. He was on the tractor, already at the far side of the barnyard, headed toward the alfalfa. Grady thought she could hear Claire giggling in the room upstairs.

14

Peter jumped in first, then Royal, both of them fully clothed and still wearing the sneakers that replaced their heavy shoes when they were doing any painting. They'd been whitewashing the two-story-high corn cribs that formed the walls of the tractor shed, and were now simply reverting to a practice established earlier that summer when they'd been painting most of the other outbuildings. It was routine for them to come and wash not only their bodies but their clothes in the running stream. Splashing and dunking, they'd scrub their pants, they'd chafe their sneakers. When that was done they'd strip to their shorts to wash out any lime that might have seeped through. Then, as if they'd performed a final duty and were free at last, they'd take off their shorts, fling them onto the bank, and swim until the new energy knocked into them by the cold water had calmed itself into aimless floating and sometimes to an idle exchange of idle thoughts and random wishes.

It was during this phase of the swim that, much earlier in the summer, Peter had told Royal he'd been on the freshman basketball team but when he didn't grow enough the next summer he was thrown off the varsity after the first practice; that he'd won a spelling bee in the seventh grade but that the talent had left him; that too many stars in the sky at night made him nervous; that he liked thunder and hoped one day to be a marine biologist or a deep-sea fisherman.

Royal, had mentioned that he'd been asked to play basketball because he was so lanky, but had said no; that he expected to make a million dollars someday from inventing something; that he'd like to see a woman with long blond hair lying naked on a black silk sheet; that he had, stored in the basement at The Home, the hood of an Alfa Romeo and someday, when he got all the pieces, he'd build a whole car.

In the water now, they didn't splash at all and were less vigorous about their scrubbing. Peter had expected that they wouldn't come to the stream at all, just wash up at the farm, but it was Royal's idea and Peter had agreed. Still, it wasn't the same and Peter didn't expect it would be. Royal was Anne's friend now. Peter hadn't been taken into his bunk since the night Royal and Anne had looked at the photograph album. And Royal had gone to see her at camp twice in the past week.

Peter didn't know what he was supposed to do. He didn't know how to present himself to Royal if he wasn't trying to attract him. It had been that way from the beginning and he didn't know how to change it. He loved them both, Royal and his sister, and he didn't know what he was supposed to do now. What he and Royal had finally come to was an exchange of quiet concern, as if each were trying to coax the other out of an illness. Never had Royal been more attentive to Peter and never had he allowed Peter to be so kind to him. This had its rewards, but to be an object of comfort and sympathy was not what Peter had had in mind.

That afternoon, while they were up on the crossbeam of the tractor shed, Peter had hoped Royal would become frightened at the height, the way he had been at the gorge. Then he could help him. He could draw him to himself and whisper the way he'd whispered before, that it was Peter, that he'd never let him fall, that he had nothing to be afraid of, that he had only to hold on to him, that it was his friend Peter, that he would never let him go. But it hadn't happened. Royal had had no difficulty and they'd worked mostly in silence. And when they'd finished, Peter was quietly grateful when Royal said they would now go for their usual swim.

On their way to the river, they'd said nothing, but Peter had put his hand on Royal's shoulder, curling his fingers a little against his neck, and Royal hadn't seemed to mind.

When they had scrubbed the whitewash from their pants and washed themselves clean, they started the swim upstream to the boulder they used for diving. There were sudden springs along the way, the water colder where the underground flow erupted into the stream itself. Royal found one. "It's cold!" These were his first words since they'd come to the river.

Peter swam toward him. "Where?"

"Here, where my foot is." Royal moved away and waited for Peter to locate the spring. Peter found it.

Three more springs were discovered, two by Royal, one by Peter, and each time the cry "Cold!" was sent out into the surrounding woods. Their old enthusiasm returned. They dived, they ducked, they dunked; they jumped, they splashed, they swam. Royal found a stone made of quartz and they took turns throwing it off into the water and then diving for it, seeing who could retrieve it. Peter usually won but finally it was lost for good.

He didn't want to give up, but Royal began the slow swim back downstream and Peter followed.

On the way, Peter tried to pass again through the spring he'd found earlier. He thought it was near a birch bent out from the bank, but couldn't find it. He paddled around, reaching his foot down as deep as it would go, but no cold current cut up onto his leg or even caught his toe. He kept trying until he thought he heard Royal say something up ahead. "What?" he called.

Royal didn't answer and when Peter looked downstream he saw two girls on the bank of the river talking to Royal. Royal was swimming in a slow circle in front of them even though the water was shallow enough for him to stand up if he wanted to. Peter swam closer, then stood up, the water coming almost to his neck.

"I thought I saw one from the road and maybe it was only a crow, but it was big and if it's an owl I want Ursula to see it." One of the girls, about fifteen, squatted on the bank, scraping her hand along the earth at her side, sending bits of moss and leaves into the water. "She's never seen an owl. But it hasn't been around, huh?"

"Not that I noticed," Royal said. He turned himself toward Peter. "Is there an owl in these woods?"

"I don't know. You want to scc an owl?"

"Ursula does. She's from Albany."

Ursula was looking at Peter as if observing an uncommon but not particularly interesting species of fish. She wore a white dress with a full skirt and looked as if she was just coming from church. Except she was wearing blue running shoes and no socks. She kept wiggling her little finger into her right ear as if trying to loosen a word that had got stuck there. She had long brown hair that seemed to pick up a tinge of amber in the late afternoon light. The one talking to Royal wasn't as pretty, but she had shining blond hair brought up in a bunch on top of her head, probably to show off the back of her neck. She was wearing a pair of loose-fitting bright blue pants that could be the bottoms of her pyjamas and a yellow V-necked T-shirt that showed more of her left shoulder than her right. Because she had sandals on, Peter could see that she had a corn on the little toe of her left foot.

"Once I saw an owl looking in the window like a peeping Tom," Royal was saying, "but I don't remember too much what he looked like. I was only four and a half." He was still circling around in front of the girl, paddling his hands beneath the water so that only his head showed above the surface.

"One way to find a nest," Peter said, "is to look for bones on the ground, little bones from chipmunks and squirrels. Owls vomit after they eat." He had expected this to be disgusting enough to put an end to the conversation. He wanted the girls to leave. But Ursula found the bones and the vomiting intriguing. Examining the tip of her little finger, she said, "I'd like to see that even more than the owl. What kind of bones?"

Peter himself had never seen what he'd been describing and wasn't even sure it was true, so it gave him no trouble now to make the whole subject as uninteresting as possible. "No one knows. They're chewed too small. You probably can't even see them anyway. And I don't think we've got any owls. Maybe the Diffenderfers, the next farm over. They might have them."

"I'd like to look though," said Royal.

"Isn't it getting kind of late?" Peter asked.

Ursula pushed her hair behind her left ear, then took her hand away so it could fall right back to where it had been before. "But wouldn't that make it better so we might find it? I mean if it starts getting dark?"

"The only trouble," Peter said, "is that if you come near the bones, they attack you. The owls, I mean. It's like going too close to where they put their dead. They go right for your eyes."

Ursula turned toward her companion, who was still sending leaves down into the water. "Is that true?" she said.

The girl stopped the swinging motion and turned toward Peter. "You live here?"

"This is our stream," Peter said, hoping Royal wouldn't tell the girls he was lying. Ursula looked up at the sky through the trees as if she might find there some verification of what Peter had said. Her friend inspected the palm of her hand, then went back to raking her fingers through the moss and twigs. "Do you ever go to the Arcade?" Ursula asked Royal.

"Arcade?" Royal was still circling in front of her, an elaborate dance movement that the water made graceful. Ursula, in response, wound and unwound coils of hair through her fingers, moving her head this way and that to arrange the hair first against one shoulder, then against the other. Together, she and Royal seemed to be performing some very precise ritual whose meanings were known only to the two of them.

"The Arcade," Ursula repeated. "In the Popcorn Shop downtown Schuylerville. They got videos you never heard of if you still like that kind of thing." She then began a litany of video games and video characters.

In an effort to disrupt the continuing catalogue, Peter went to a sloped part of the bank and started to walk up out of the water. The sight of him naked would make them stop. His real hope was that they'd be frightened enough to leave. Halfway up the bank, however, he slipped and had to grab a sapling oak to keep himself from sliding back into the water. This marred the dignity of his rise, but he got his balance back and pulled himself onto the bank. Ursula stopped talking. Because he wasn't quite sure what to do next, Peter shook his head, pretending it was necessary for him to get as much water out of his hair as possible. That done, he slicked his hands down his arms.

The girls were looking at him. He wanted to dive back into the water, but forced himself to keep his fingers busy inside his hair. It was Ursula who spoke first. "If you want to go there sometime, it's where Imogene and I hang out this summer."

"You ought to come sometime." The one named Imogene had returned her attention to Royal. "You'd be good at it. The really good ones are Alison Peck and Mary Lou Moran."

"And Pat Dempsey," said Ursula.

"And Davey Barbour."

And they were off on a new litany. Peter and his nakedness had had no effect on them. He couldn't believe he was that ineffectual. Or that life in Albany was that sophisticated. He wished he had a towel to cover himself with. To get to his clothes he'd have to walk past the girls. If he did, he'd give Imogene a shove that would send her into the water. He decided to do neither.

Pretending that he'd dried himself enough, and was therefore ready to go back into the water, Peter jumped off the bank, his arms stretched out so he could make as big a splash as possible. When he surfaced, Imogene was wiping water from her arm. Peter swam up alongside Royal and splashed some more, making her jerk her head back and blink.

"You're getting me wet," she said. Still squatting on the bank, she moved backward about a foot, her hunched body set directly onto her feet, making the move look like the retreat of an annoyed buzzard.

"Then come on in, why don't you?" Peter splashed her again.

"She told you to quit it." Royal, with the heel of his hand, sent a spray right into Peter's face. Before the water could clear from his eyes, Peter felt a pull on his foot, the tug too quick to give him a chance to close his mouth. He took in a good swallow of water, then curled down toward the bottom of the stream, searching for Royal. He found an arm and used it to direct him toward the head. When he got there, he gave as heavy a push as he could, but the push wasn't weighty enough to keep the head under water. They surfaced together, aiming for each other's heads, grabbing at each other's arms, kicking with legs and feet.

Royal ducked Peter but had to submerge himself to keep him under. Peter pulled away and dived for Royal's leg. He tried to pull him toward the bottom, but found himself forced up by the lift of Royal's body. He let go and grabbed him around the waist from behind, holding him tight against him, the two of them now rolling over in the water, wrestling first toward the surface, then toward the bottom, gasping for air, then returning to the struggle.

Royal finally kicked himself free. Peter reached out to grab him again, but had lost him. He came up to the surface, but didn't see him, then dove under and searched again. When he came up for air, he saw Royal standing on the bank, looking back into the woods. His shoulders, his whole body, were heaving up and down from his exertions. He looked downstream, then again into the woods. The girls were gone.

Peter swam toward him and began moving his arms under the water, swimming in place, trying to duplicate the dance Royal had done for Imogene. Royal looked down at him at moment, then turned toward the woods.

"Aren't you coming back in?" Peter asked, the words coming with difficulty between gasps for breath. Royal shook his head. Peter pulled himself up onto the bank and went to him. "Are they gone?"

Royal nodded. "Gone." He was looking down at a small boulder. "I held you under too long," he said. "I didn't mean to. I'm sorry."

Peter moved his hand near the curve of Royal's neck. "You didn't too long. Besides, I did it too." Royal nodded, then turned and looked at Peter. "I was only talking to them," he said. "I didn't mean anything by it." He seemed to want to say more but stopped himself and looked down at the boulder instead.

Peter drew his hand away. "I just didn't want them around when we didn't have our clothes on," he said.

Again Royal nodded his agreement, then put his own hand on Peter's shoulder. "You want us to do it again, don't you?" he asked quietly. Before Peter could answer Royal said, his voice still quiet, "It's all right. We will if you want us to. But then we can't anymore." He turned a quick glance at Peter, tried to hold his gaze, but had to look again toward the woods.

Peter brought his hand up and put it back into the curve between Royal's neck and his shoulder. Without looking at Peter, Royal drew him toward himself. He waited a moment, then he whispered, "Okay?"

On the ground, Peter lay with his head turned toward the stream. Royal's mouth was close to his ear but he said nothing.

15

Martha had been waiting for the alfalfa to get taller so it would be over her head when she walked in it, but today she realized this would never happen. The alfalfa might get tall enough but it was already too thick for her to wade through. Even Raggles avoided it, too much of a tangle for her to handle. There was, of course, the corn, now over Martha's head, but that had paths between the rows, and she didn't feel in it the pleasures of concealment, of absolute solitude, that she would have found in a jungle of alfalfa. Still, it was better than nothing and on her way home she'd walk through the corn and take from its clean-floored forest what comforts she could.

Martha's main chore was to count the cows. She was on her way to do it, walking the fence path alongside the rampant alfalfa.

She would have preferred to stay in the milkhouse and help her
mother put up a new shelf, but she'd been sufficiently impressed
with the importance of her daily task to leave behind the fascina-
tions of carpentry and start for the open pasture. (That her job
was crucial to the farm's operation had been proved when Peter
and Royal took the time to teach her how to count—not just to
twenty-six, the number required for the cows—but all the way to
a hundred. It had seemed to her remarkable and right that seventy
should follow sixty, the same way that seven, earlier on, had always
followed six. There was an order to it and the repetitions had the
attraction of a refrain.)

Beyond the alfalfa was a hayfield, then the pasture where the
cows were waiting. Martha did not like the cows. They were too
big. And they resembled too closely the bull that had chased her
brother on the hill. She'd never mentioned the bull to her mother.
Instinctively, she'd known it was something secret, something
Peter shouldn't have done, and must therefore be kept safely
among the store of potential tattles for future use when and if
necessary.

It seemed odd to Martha that her mother and Peter and Royal
—and even Anne when she was home—would encourage her to
get close to the cows, to pet them and touch them. She'd been
told outright that this was preparatory to the eventual chore of
milking when she was bigger, and as much as Martha looked
forward to working as an equal with all of them, especially Peter
and Royal, she still didn't trust the assurances that the cows
wouldn't hurt her, that they liked her and were sorry when she
wouldn't come near them.

So many things that she *did* want to do were forbidden to her
that it seemed the whole organization of the world was somewhat
puzzling and, quite possibly, all wrong. She couldn't play on the
machinery; she couldn't go in the cow pond; she couldn't visit the
Ryersons on one side or the Diffenderfer farm on the other and

drink their Pepsi; she couldn't pick pears in the Colbert orchard because they were too green; she couldn't go near the stream except past the woods where it was shallow and there was clay on the banks for her to make things with; she couldn't go in other people's rooms; she couldn't try on Anne's clothes and wear her jewelry when she wasn't there; she couldn't kiss Raggles on the mouth even though Raggles always kissed *her* on the mouth; she couldn't throw pebbles at the hens to make them squawk.

Of course, Martha saw these proscriptions not as limitations but as challenges, an additional list of chores to be performed when the spirit moved her and no one was looking. Even while she feared detection and possible punishment, she took it for granted that part of life, part of living, was the circumvention of the law. It was expected of her, even demanded, and she went about her disobedience with a casual cunning and a dutiful determination.

After she'd counted the cows, she had every intention of going into Anne's room and wrapping herself in the Raggedy Ann quilt and walking around in her one pair of high-heeled shoes. It was a chore like any other and she would perform it responsibly and with the satisfaction that can only come from obstacles surmounted and tensions survived.

When she and Raggles crawled under the bottom wire of the fence that separated the alfalfa from the hay, one of the barbs caught the ring—the crown, really—of flowers she'd been wearing on her head and tore the already loosened weave so that the circle was broken and some of the daisies dropped to the ground. Martha was dismayed and Raggles sniffed the fallen flowers for a clue as to why they were there. Anne, on her last visit home, had made the crown, trying to teach Martha herself how to do it. That was three days ago and all the flowers were wilted and brown and brittle and dried, but Martha still wore it from sunup to sundown because it was, to her, the most beautiful thing in the world and because her sister, Anne, had made it.

Everything Anne did was beautiful. She and Martha had their differences and sometimes she forgot all about Anne, but nothing was allowed to obscure the perfection of everything connected with her older sister: her clothes, her face, her hands, everything. When Anne fixed Martha's hair for her, it would stay that way until Anne herself changed it. When Anne had given her a string of beads, Martha wouldn't take it off even in the bathtub or to go swimming or to bed at night. The day Anne taught her how to snap her fingers, she kept snapping them until she went to bed and then started snapping them first thing the next morning.

(Her brother Peter had a different kind of fascination. There was nothing he couldn't explain, nothing he didn't know. When Martha was puzzled by the wet grass in the morning after it hadn't even rained, it was Peter who'd told her that grass and plants, unlike people, sweat when they're cold instead of when they're hot.)

Martha combed her fingers through her hair to make sure that nothing of the crown remained. She had loved it, but now it was time for her to give it up; it ceased to be and, with the shake of her head, she let it go. She had other things to think about. By the time she reached the fence that separated the field from the pasture she'd forgotten that it had ever existed.

Most of the cows were lying down, facing the woods. They looked like heavy humpbacked clouds that had settled down in the field, resting before rising again to the sky and continuing their journey to Vermont. Martha started her count. At least today the cows weren't moving around. Today it would be easy.

Twice she found she'd stopped counting, that she was thinking of something else. But when she tried to find out what it was, all she could remember was that she'd lost her count and would have to begin again. When she reached seventeen her third time around, a thought came to her and she decided that was what had been distracting her.

There had been a thunder and lightning storm two nights

before. It had awakened her, the first time this had happened since they'd all come to the farm. She had been certain that the world was being split wide open, that she was the object of some enormous anger that only her parents could appease and control. They were her protectors and her advocates.

She'd gone down the hall to the big bedroom near the bathroom, stopping whenever the lightning cracked and the thunder crashed, putting the palm of her hand on the wall to steady herself and the house at the same time. She crawled in next to her mother, who, without waking up completely, took her into the crook of her arm and gave the pillow a punch so it would be softer under her head.

Martha listened to the storm, the lightning trying to force her to open her eyes, flashing again and again across her eyelids. But she kept them shut tight. Not all her fear had left her. This was different from all the times before, all the other storms when she'd come to her parents' bed for protection. The smells were not the same. Her father wasn't there. The warmth that seemed to pass between him and her mother, wrapping itself around her, wasn't there. Martha told herself that she was still protected, that no harm would come to her. But she wasn't sure it was true.

For the fourth time, Martha began to count the cows. To make it easier, she slipped under the fence and moved among them—something she'd never done before—and by the time she reached twenty-two, she patted Mildred's side to show herself she wasn't afraid. Mildred blinked and Martha continued her count, reasonably sure she'd dealt with her distraction. Soon she would be in Anne's room wrapped in the Raggedy Ann quilt and wearing the high-heeled shoes.

16

Grady lay on her back. The hair on Guy Duskin's arm, now damp with sweat, no longer scratched the soft flesh of her belly as he moved his hand slowly along the curve of her side. He stopped his hand and let it rest on the rise of her stomach, then lifted it a little and drew it toward himself so that only the tips of his fingers brushed gently along her skin. After a moment, he drew the hand away completely, letting his open palm press gently into her flesh. Carefully, as if he didn't want to disturb her in any way, he shifted himself onto his back. He lay still and Grady too lay still, the two of them making a silent presentation of themselves, an unspoken acceptance of what had happened between them. It was this shared consent that joined them, and Grady knew it. All that they had done achieved itself only now, as they lay at each other's side, not touching, quietly defiant of any judgment that might be made against them.

This was not what Grady had expected. The same system of communication as before had been put into operation. Grady had received in the mail a necklace of miniature brightly painted ceramic fruit, a string of pineapples, bananas, peaches, pears, oranges, and, at the center, a huge strawberry that, she supposed, was intended to suggest the shape of a heart. Today, they had met at the usual place. She had come to tell him that she wanted his attentions to stop. Considering how complicated just this brief foray into promiscuity had proved to be, Grady couldn't help wondering why it was so popular in certain quarters. It was so distracting, so intrusive. There she'd been, ready to stake the tomatoes, weed the peppers and the onions, take Martha to the mall for a new pair of shoes, and fix the screens on the back porch. Then the necklace came. It threw her off rhythm. The tomatoes, the onions, and the screens went by the board. And poor Martha was denied the ice-cream cone that was considered as integral a part of a trip to the mall as popcorn at a movie. Guy had to stop. And she intended to tell him so. There was, after all, the growing likelihood of a life with Ned. That, surely, deserved some consideration.

"You can come to my house!" he'd called to her before she'd even closed the door of her car. He spoke the words not as any alternative to their being where they were, but as a piece of unexpected news. It was neither an invitation nor a concession. It was as though a longstanding petition had finally been granted.

She was not wearing the necklace. It was in the box it came in, held in her hand. She strode toward him. His remark about coming to his house was further evidence that their friendship, fond as it may have been, must end.

"You mustn't send me things like this," she said, holding the box out to him. He laughed. She became more emphatic. "You really mustn't send me anything anymore." He laughed again as if she'd said something both witty and endearing at the same time. Grady refused to falter. "And you mustn't expect me to come here anymore." This he seemed to find hilarious.

To explain to her that her statements, appreciated as they may have been, were no longer applicable, he repeated his words, only this time with an indulgent gravity. "You can come to my house." It sounded to Grady that this was a solution that had never occurred to him before, whatever the circumstance. There was in it a note of discovery, of revelation.

"I can't go to your house," she said.

"No, no, it's all right. You can. You can come to my house." He accepted her need for reassurance; what he'd told her was obviously too good to be true. He had to be patient with her until she would be able, with his help, to realize the extent of her luck and accept the privilege being offered. He drew her toward him and enveloped her in a massive embrace.

Her struggle against him was no more than a stir, so tightly did he hold her. He apparently interpreted her movements as an attempt to get closer. He laughed affectionately into her ear to let her know he understood, then increased the pressure of his hold.

The box with the necklace was pressed into her breastbone, along with the curled hand that held it. She had to force herself a little higher, lifting herself onto her toes, just to get her nose onto his shoulder so she could breathe. This he recognized as an obvious attempt to excite him further and again he laughed, this time into her hair. He understood her needs; he would see to it that everything was taken care of.

When Grady shifted her head to get more air, her nose touched his neck. This, it seemed, was the sign he'd been waiting for. He withdrew his arms across her back so that he could hold her by the shoulders and lean her out away from him. Now she could at least catch her breath. But, seeing her draw in air with quick short gasps, his intuition or his experience told him exactly what her dazed look meant. He smiled at her with the amused sympathy one might use to reassure a child who wasn't quite sure that its wishes had been accurately read. "Follow me in your car," he whispered.

"No. Wait," Grady called, trying not to shout. "It's not far," he said. "Don't worry, we'll be there right away." He'd thought she couldn't wait, that it had to be here and now. Grady gripped the box in her hand as tight as she could, wishing she could collapse it, crumble it and the necklace too. She was tempted to throw it off into the bushes, just to get rid of it, but there was a card inside with her name on it.

Guy started his motor and waited for her to start hers. Knowing he'd sit there until he heard the sound, Grady got in, turned on the ignition and gave a few pumps to the accelerator.

She had no intention of following him. If he had misinterpreted their encounter, that was his problem. He'd pulled out to the edge of the main road and was waiting again to make sure Grady was behind him. She waved her hand through the windshield to let him know he should go ahead. It was a mistake. He waved back, then blew her a kiss, laughed, and honked his horn, three short blasts.

Grady realized she couldn't turn around and head home. He'd follow her. She had to make him understand her situation, her determinations. And she had to do it now. She would stay right where she was. If he started out, he'd see she wasn't following and come back. She'd explain everything. Twice if necessary.

He'd pulled out onto the road and stopped.again. Grady did nothing. Then his horn began to honk. She considered getting out and going to him, but that probably wouldn't work. There would simply be a rerun of the previous scene. The horn kept honking. If a car came by, it might stop to see what was wrong. Grady had no choice. She followed him.

His house was little more than a shack. It was on a sandy road that wound its way through some woods as if its original course had been set by an animal with no place in particular to go. The house itself was white clapboard raised on cinderblocks, the number of blocks varying to accommodate the uncertain level of the ground. Four steps, thick rust-colored planks, new and unpainted, led up to a door. There was no screening and the front door itself, with its porcelain knob, suggested that it had done previous service to a bathroom or a closet. The two front windows were uncurtained, but in one there was a molting pink geranium and in the other a two-foot-high plaster dog. Its breeding seemed to be a mixture of beagle, scottie, Saint Bernard and golden Lab, implying that the manufacturer had tried especially hard to please his customers, offering each a trace of his favorite. If it was intended as a watchdog it would fend off only those purists repulsed by such rampant crossbreeding.

The "front yard," the space between the road and the steps, was a sandy patch strewn with pebbles. Grady realized the site for the house had been cut from a stony hill behind. The man was living in an abandoned gravel pit, his house probably an old work shack dating back to more prosperous times. The metal stovepipe sticking out of the side of the roof suggested that even then prosperity had had its limits.

The man—Grady still couldn't identify him in her thinking as "Guy" or even "Mr. Duskin"—the man had already gone inside, leaving the front door open. She'd wait in her car, still wanting its protection when she would tell him the sad truths she'd been rehearsing during the drive. He didn't come out. She considered honking her own horn, but didn't know who might be called by the sound. There didn't seem to be neighbors, but she wasn't taking any chances. Finally she got out. She hoped that the crunch of her feet on the pebbles would at least bring him to the door. She could then talk to him from a distance that was, if not completely safe, at least beyond the reach of his arms.

He came to the doorway, filling it entirely like a huge tree blocking the entrance to a cave. For the first time since she'd met him there was a look of disappointment, even grief on his face. He was, Grady told herself, aware at last of what she'd come to tell him. Her delay had given him time to review her actions and he had finally been able to interpret them in the light—or the gloom—of reality. She was sorry for him, but she was also grateful that she'd been relieved of the necessity of telling him too explicitly what she'd come to say.

"The house," he said, "it's not as big as I thought it was. I thought when I built the new steps, that made it look different. It's not very big, is it?"

Grady could not bring herself to say that it was.

"I should have told you," he said.

It was, then, a realization about his house that had put him into mourning. His sorrow had nothing to do with what Grady intended to tell him. He had not enlightened himself about her true purpose for being there, her real reason for following him. He had seen his house through Grady's eyes. It was a shack in a gravel pit with a porcelain knob on the front door.

Grady looked at him standing in the doorway as if he hoped his bulk would shield the entire house from her gaze. He was, even in his disappointment, still its protector. He would make its shame his own, he would, with the dignity of his stand, defy its detractors. Yet, when he looked at Grady, he seemed confused as to where his first allegiance belonged. His house, he assumed, was a disappointment to her, an object unworthy of her style and social standing. And it was she whom he had hoped to please, she whom he had expected to overwhelm with its excellences. He had failed her. The house had failed him.

Grady tried not to look at the new steps, at the doomed geranium, at the plaster mongrel, but she looked anyway. Then she looked at Guy Duskin standing in his doorway. He'd started to bring one hand up to his face, but lowered it again. He made himself defenseless. He had relinquished all claims. She was free to leave.

"Don't I get to see inside?" Grady asked.

Grady, lying still, her eyes open, wondered what she should do now. The ceiling above her was blank, the wall had only a mirror that reflected the opposite wall, also blank. The window looked out on a low cliff, the remains of a hill left behind by men who had prospected for stones.

They had made love. They had been tender to each other, they had safely reached the place they'd been struggling toward. Their violent urgings, their willingness to summon new strength if the other faltered, their pleas against exhaustion had brought them at last to this moment and to this place where their solitude was given back to them. It had been sent on ahead and was waiting. Now the moment had come to take it up again and go on one's way.

Grady waited a moment, wondering if she would have thoughts of Andy, whether or not the tenderness would summon him again. She hoped so. She'd had a dream about him three nights before and she had ended it too soon. Perhaps she could end it now.

In the dream, Andy had come to the farm. He was in the living room, masked, moving in the dark, looking for something to steal. She was upstairs in her bed, but she knew what he was doing. She could even make out the shape of his body and the form of the cauled face, and he seemed to be wearing gloves.

He must not find her, he must not know that she was there. He was coming up the stairs; he was walking down the hall toward her door. It was the stretched mask she sensed more than anything. It suggested the foreskin of his penis. He was passing the bathroom, his head moving in a slow circle from side to side, up and down, so he could see through the black nylon weave.

She hadn't closed her door. She tried to wake up so she could go close it, but she couldn't make herself move. If only she could wake up. She *had* to wake up; the door *had* to be closed.

He was there, just outside, the mask shrouding his dead face come back to life. His head moved in a slow circle, up and down, from side to side. He was coming into the room. He would lift away the mask. He would show her his face. The door was opening wider, his hand pressed softly against it. Soon he would be at her bedside. The door continued to open, wider. She woke up.

She had sent him away. She shouldn't have. She should have let him lift away the mask; he should have been allowed to free himself from the caul that might now forever hide his face.

As she lay there now with Guy Duskin at her side, she tried to have thoughts of Andy. But they wouldn't materialize. What she could see instead was Royal Provo walking on his hands. Try as she might to change the picture, she couldn't. Yesterday afternoon, when she'd come around from the back of the barn after checking to see how much had been loaded into the manure spreader, there was Royal, walking on his hands in the level grass between the house and the first field. Martha, sitting on one of the stones that marked off the driveway, was watching more with interest than with pleasure. Royal's upside-down body was arched so that his heavy shoes, high in the air, seemed to be leading on the rest of him. His pants legs had fallen midway past his calves, which looked now like sticks meant mostly to present his huge shoes to the heavens.

His head was pressed back against his shoulderblades so he could see where he was going, but Raggles apparently considered the entire operation a request for a thorough face cleaning. As Royal moved forward, Raggles would back away without interrupting his assigned task, his tongue dutifully licking mostly the chin and the eyes.

Neither Royal nor Martha seemed to protest, and it then became clear to Grady that this was not an amusement but a demonstration. Martha was watching with the attention of a pupil being shown a scientific experiment, a principle of physics that might or might not convince.

After about seven paces, Royal lowered his feet in front of him until the toes of his shoes touched the grass. Then, in a single slow movement, he put his feet flat onto the ground, lifted his hands away and stood upright.

Without any reference to his presentation, he turned around and went toward the field, the direction in which his hands, a few moments before, had been taking him. Royal Provo, Grady acknowledged, was one of the most peculiar men in the world.

Guy stirred next to her and Royal was gone. It was the rasp of Guy Duskin's body against the sheets that she'd heard and now, with a graceful heave, he raised his head over her and laid it down on her stomach, facing away from her. She would let him lie there a few moments, then tell him she had to leave. Her inhalations pressed her flesh that much closer against his cheek, her exhalations a slow withdrawal. Grady too became aware of the reach of her body toward him, then its retreat, then the reach again.

"Can I come live with you?" he asked.

Grady heard the words, but wasn't sure at first who'd said them. The voice had none of the exuberance that inevitably came over Guy Duskin whenever he asked a question. Because she knew what she'd say, Grady didn't say it. She'd let him do it for her. He must know the answer as well as she. All Grady had to do was wait.

"The boy, he's my son."

The words hummed through his cheekbones and along her skin. She waited, but when he said nothing further, she spoke the name. "Royal," she said.

"Royal," he repeated. "He's my son."

Grady looked at the great head, the thick hair like black plumage. "He's a good boy," she said.

"I know." He paused, then said quietly, "He gets that from me."

To offer further identification, just to make sure they were talking about the same person, Grady said, "He knows all about machinery." When Guy gave no response, she added, "He's really a kind of genius."

Again Guy spoke quietly. "I know," he said. "He gets that from me."

It occurred to Grady to mention Royal's pale skin and red hair just to see if Guy would claim a genetic connection there too, but she had no real urge to ridicule this man. Or even to confront him with too many of the truths that his stupidity spared him. The only needed truth now was her goodbye, and in a minute she'd say it and all this would be over.

"You have to go now, don't you?" He turned his head and looked up at her, still resting on her stomach.

Grady nodded. "Yes, I really do."

He lowered his gaze to her breasts. Grady looked at him a moment, then brought her hand up from his head and, still watching him, lifted her left breast toward him. He looked at it, then slowly stretched his face upward. Grady drew her hand away and he pressed himself deep into the give of the flesh. The light tickling Grady felt near her neck was, she knew, the movement of an eyelash. He had closed his eyes.

When Grady got home it was almost dark. Before she could tell the lie she had prepared about having to stay with Claire, Peter told her that Ned had phoned. Claire had died an hour before. She was also told that Martha had eaten from the dog's dish and had claimed she could any time she wanted to because it was her dog.

17

Royal checked the milkhouse one more time to make sure he'd put everything back where it was supposed to be. As he walked the alley between the two rows of stanchioned cows, he threw a few more fistfuls of ground lime onto the cement. On his way to put the bucket back near the door, he pulled some hay out of the gutter with his foot so it made a small nesting in the alley itself. He'd noticed earlier that the cow in front of him tended to urinate in an arc out behind instead of down into the gutter, a sure sign, along with her size, that she'd calve pretty soon. Now the hay would absorb the water and keep it from running all over the alley. It would also make it easier for Ned Ryerson to clean after he'd done his milking the next morning.

Royal put the lime bucket down and surveyed the barn. Almost all of the cows were lying down by now, getting ready for the night's rest. The third from the far end on his right was eating her bedding, ignoring the grain pellets Royal had put in front of her stanchion just before he'd begun the milking. The heifers in their pen near the far end were still looking around, too young and inexperienced to realize that all the activity they'd just witnessed, the milking, the cleaning, the bedding down, meant that the day had come to an end. There'd be no more excitement until Ned himself would come in the morning to take up again the round of chores he'd set aside this one day because his wife had died and there'd been a funeral, a burial, and, even now, neighbors and relatives to feed at the trestle tables under the locust trees down in back of his house.

Royal had completed all the tasks he'd volunteered to do. He could think of nothing that would delay his approach to the table, his acceptance of the plate of food, his attempt to get Mrs. Durant away from the crowd, off by herself, so he could ask her —as he'd promised himself he'd ask her—if he could take her to see his mother's grave. It would mean a lot to him if she'd accept. The threshing machine was almost ready; soon he would be able to make it go. But his mother's grave was his greatest achievement, his proudest possession, and he would take Mrs. Durant to it and show it to her as proof of his regard. He felt that it would please her. She would recognize it as a form of tribute, an offering he wouldn't make to just anyone.

He'd taken Bob MacDonald, an older boy at The Home who'd let him work with him on an old custom Dodge; Augie Vereano, who'd been his best friend until he got adopted in the eighth grade; and Rose Albano, with whom he'd been in love. True, no one was particularly impressed and Rose Albano had even been openly scornful because of the size of the stone, but he'd always felt the mistake had been his own. He'd misjudged them. They simply weren't capable of seeing him for what he was: someone unique and not without distinction. Tony Parone had a gold watch he'd inherited from an uncle, Ida Navarre a pair of earrings from her grandmother, Wesley Throneburg a hunting knife from his father. These were more than proud possessions. They were identifying attributes. They distinguished and defined. To show them was to show oneself, a way of saying "This is who I really am."

As he was rolling the barn door closed, Royal congratulated himself on this inspiration. He was no longer hesitant about joining the feast. He wouldn't be arriving empty-handed. He had something to offer Mrs. Durant.

Because there was a pebble in the track, he had to push the door open again. Royal kicked the pebble away, then rolled the door again. The squeal sounded like a pig being poked with a stick.

The wooden handle was off the door, so he left it open wide enough for Ned Ryerson to be able in the morning to wedge himself between the jamb and the door itself for the first shove that would get it rolling. If it was closed all the way and had come the least bit off the track, it would take more tugging and pushing than there would be patience for first thing in the morning. Royal hoped Ned Ryerson would appreciate this final piece of thoughtfulness.

He hosed the rubber boots he'd brought along, then took them off. As he unbuttoned the milking coveralls he'd slipped on over his pressed chinos and his white cotton shirt, he looked down toward the backyard. Two trestle tables in addition to the regular picnic table had been set up under the trees, one of them Mrs. Durant's, dating back to the days when there had been threshing, with the thrasher going from farm to farm and everyone having to be fed just like this, under the trees, in the evening when all the work was over.

Bedsheets, one sky blue, one canary yellow, and the other just plain white, had been thrown over the tables for tablecloths, and even from where he was standing, Royal could see basins and bowls and platters of food. There seemed to be at least twenty-five guests—or mourners rather. The women were wearing dresses, bright summer colors, green and pink and blue; most of the men were wearing Sunday shirts, more blues and greens, with a few checkereds thrown in. Several had suits on with ties, those most directly involved in the funeral: Ned Ryerson himself, the pall-bearers (except for one man who'd compromised by wearing a dark check but with a tie), and a cousin of Mrs. Ryerson's from Canada.

Royal was sorry Peter wasn't there. Peter, he knew, would have liked to do the milking with him, the two of them together. And it would have cheered Peter to be at the feast, even if it was a funeral. But when Royal got the idea that he'd do Ned Ryerson's milking for him and Peter volunteered too, Mrs. Durant said one would have to stay with Martha and do the milking at home, and since Royal had spoken first, he would go to the Ryersons'. Mrs. Durant could be very firm. Still, Royal liked doing things that might help Peter feel better.

Royal was not accustomed to having the power to please. He had never had it before in all his life. Peter had given it to him. At times it confused him, mostly because of its newness, but he reveled in it. Peter's worship had given him his first notion of himself and without it he would never have had the courage to want Anne Durant. Now, with Anne, with her response to him, he was feeling almost godlike. There seemed to be nothing he couldn't do. There was no end to his power, no limit to the favors he might bestow. And from this height it was no trouble at all to rain down benefactions on poor abandoned Peter. Peter's need grieved him, but it also gave him pleasure.

Royal headed down the hill. At the table with the blue bedsheet, a man wearing a tie with a tie clip was hand-wrestling a man in a navy blue vest. Most of the mourners were standing in a semicircle at the end of the table, watching silently as if this were a continuation of the funeral rite, a competition in honor of the deceased. The man with the tie had loosened it so that it sagged down over the tie clip, but he hadn't rolled up his sleeves as the man with the vest had done.

The man in the vest, an angle of hair falling outward from his forehead, was looking not at the locked hands in front of him but at his opponent's eyes, expecting to detect there the flicker of weakness that would tell him that he could, with a quick jerk, slap his arm down onto the table.

Royal sat on a folding chair at the far end of the table and wondered if it was all right for him to go ahead and eat or if he was supposed to watch the wrestling. He was starving. A quarter of the way down from him were near-empty platters of fried chicken and cold ham. Near his elbow was a bowl with a great lump of potato salad at the bottom and Royal could see that it contained cucumbers and scallions and olives, which made it his favorite kind. Just out of reach was a big round plate with some torn tomato slices sunk down into a mess of juice and seeds. Glasses of all shapes and sizes, from stemmed goblets to cheese glasses, held the dregs of beer, wine, lemonade, or milk. Someone had had three cans of Miller Lite and had bent one can in the middle so that it looked like a crude tin hourglass. A daisy was stuck in a tall tumbler coated with milk, and a digital watch with a gold band like an expandable hat rack was set carefully in front of an emptied coffee cup, as if its owner had wanted to time himself while he drank. In the middle of the table, in a brown crock, were the remains of a bouquet of red carnations, four flowers leaning against the edge, keeping under surveillance the mustard pot just below.

Royal noticed that some of the mourners had plundered the crock; a few of the men had put carnations in their shirt pockets or buttonholes and several women were wearing the flowers in their hair. A woman they called Livia was scraping the carnation back and forth against her nostrils as if scratching an itch. Mrs. Durant had tucked one into the front of her dress, the red flower nested in the hollow of her throat. He thought of the slender stem slipped down the cleavage between her breasts, then looked at the forearm of the man with the tie. The arm was now tilted down to about a sixty-degree angle.

Royal looked again at Mrs. Durant. She wasn't watching the match. She seemed to be looking toward a window just over Royal's right shoulder. Royal heard through the window the calls and murmurs of a distant crowd, then a dialogue between two men giving each other what sounded like protracted instruction. Royal didn't want to glance back. He felt he shouldn't be tracing the line of Mrs. Durant's gaze. It might seem he was checking up on her. Obviously there was a ball game on television in the living room. The crowd in the ballpark cried out in a sudden burst of surprise and one of the men talking raised his voice and intensified his speech, determined not to be drowned out by anything that might be happening. The other voice interrupted with news that took precedence because of its superior importance. Then, as the cries of the crowd receded into a mumble, the two voices seemed to be congratulating each other for the spectacular achievement that had brought the crowd, if only momentarily, to such a frenzy.

Royal picked up a watermelon pickle. He tapped it against the side of the glass dish to shake off a few drops of brine, then put it into his mouth. After a few chews, he stopped moving his jaw, waited a moment, then turned and looked at the window. He saw an easy chair, an extra pillow punched into a corner between the back and the arm. No one was sitting there. He faced the table again, looking at the radishes, chewing the watermelon pickle again and swallowing.

Royal took a radish and popped it into his mouth, then looked up to see if Mrs. Durant had noticed that he'd come down from the barn. She was watching the woman called Livia scratch her nose with the carnation. He looked at the man in the vest who was staring patiently into the eyes of the man with the tie. Mrs. Durant was fingering the carnation at her throat, looking just past the wrestlers at a plate of half-eaten chocolate cake. Royal got up and went around the table so he could reach the fried chicken. He turned the three pieces over with his fingers, not sure which one he wanted. He wouldn't look at Mrs. Durant until he'd gone back to his chair and was eating the chicken.

As he was rubbing the tips of his fingers together to prepare them for picking up a chicken leg, he heard a thump on the table and a series of aaahhs and oohhs and a few surprised laughs. He quickly picked up the piece of chicken, then looked down at the end of the table. The wrestlers had already released their hold on each other. He wasn't sure who'd won. The man in the vest rolled down his shirt sleeve as if he'd just received an inoculation and the man with the tie unhooked his tie clip so that his tie could fall freely down over his belt buckle. Mrs. Durant was finishing a piece of chocolate cake, the plate held just beneath her flower. She was looking down at the plate to make sure she didn't cut the edge of the fork into the carnation. Royal decided now was the time to present himself. He wondered if he should bring the chicken with him or not. He decided not to. Maybe she'd offer to wait on him. Then he could tell her he'd take her to see his mother's grave.

He put the chicken back on the plate, careful to place it in just the same position as before so no one would notice he'd touched it. Again he rubbed his fingertips against each other, letting the crumbs sprinkle the piece he'd just put down. When he brought his hand away he let his fingers drag a little along the bedsheet, lightly, casually, to give them a further cleaning. He then brushed the front of his shirt. One large crumb, a cluster glued together by the batter, stuck stubbornly to one strap of his suspenders. He picked it off and set it back on the platter where it belonged, then turned to see if Mrs. Durant had noticed him yet.

She wasn't standing where she'd been. Nor was she in the group closer to the locust tree where one of the pallbearers was passing out pictures of either his grandchildren or his vacation, Royal couldn't tell except for the sounds of approval—exclamations of surprise and wonder—that sprung up from different points in the crowd as the pictures were passed along.

He looked through the screened window. She was sitting in the easy chair, but not leaning back, watching the television set. Her hands lay along the arms of the chair. The flower was gone from her throat so that she could now lower her head slightly without crushing it or having it scratch her chin.

Royal went toward the window. He'd ask her if he could bring her something, maybe some more cake or some lemonade or some wine—any offer that would get her attention. She would, of course, refuse, then get up from the chair, come out, and make sure he'd get something to eat.

When Royal got about three feet from the window, he stopped. Mrs. Durant had drawn herself up even straighter in the chair and at the same time had lowered her head so that she seemed to be looking at something on her lap. Then she lifted her head and tilted it back. Her lips were moving slightly as if she was saying something to someone perched high on the wall behind the television set. She righted her head and brought her hand up to rub her cheek. Then she looked down again at her lap, still sitting very straight. She was crying.

Royal took another step closer to the window. There was no one with her in the room. It seemed to him now that the voices on the television were accusing her of something he couldn't quite hear and that she was listening, submissive, with a mournful dignity. Then, as if to defy her accusers, she raised her head and looked directly at the set, the line of her chin straight, her lips relaxed, disdaining speech, her eyes sorrowful but unblinking, a streak of silver light—the path of a tear—marking her cheek. Royal watched the quiet face. Mrs. Durant was beautiful after all.

His hunger left him. He no longer wanted Mrs. Durant to come out and wait on him. He wanted to stand where he was and look at her. He had thought that, at this moment, she would become his mother, he her child, chosen, favored, loved. But at the transforming moment, something had intervened. What he'd thought he'd wanted more than anything in the world—Mrs. Durant for his mother—he didn't want anymore. He struggled to retrieve the need, to pluck it back before it receded beyond his reach, beyond recovery. His mother's grave. He'd take her there. He saw it stretched out at their feet, the raised mound of earth, the inadequate stone. Then he and Mrs. Durant were lying on the grave in each other's arms.

Royal stepped back from the window. Mrs. Durant had slumped back into the chair as if suddenly exhausted. Now she buried her face in her hands, sobbing. She took her hands away, then brushed her right arm across her eyes and turned her head away. She shifted her whole body and buried her face in the cushioned back of the easy chair. The move had raised the skirt of her dress higher on her right thigh. The skin was clear and white, whiter and clearer than any flesh he'd ever seen. And it was mounded in a rise perfect and graceful.

The voices on the television were now commenting on her behavior, approving of her tears, cheered by her sobs. A mocking call came from the crowd, then another. As if ready again to defend herself, Mrs. Durant quickly twisted her body around and sat up straight. But, clearly, she had been defeated. She couldn't raise her head, only reach it over and rub her nose on her right arm, then stare down at her lap. The crowd, as if finally appeased, raised a long cheer, the two voices shouting out in triumph over the tumult. Quickly, before the shouts could die down, in a clear flat voice Royal said, "I love you, Mrs. Durant."

To make sure she'd see no one if she looked toward the window, he quickly took two steps backward, then turned and headed up the hill, the overland route toward home. Before he reached the top of the rise, he remembered he'd left behind his coveralls and the boots he'd need for the morning milking. He considered leaving them there and going to get them first thing in the morning—or milking without them—but he'd already turned around and was walking back.

Standing again outside the barn, he looked down toward the house, toward the grove of locust where the tables had been set. No one was there. The tables with their blue and white and yellow sheets were still cluttered with the scraps and leavings of the feast, the plates and toppled glasses, the bowls and the emptied platters, but all the guests, the mourners, seemed to have been called away. A light wind stirred the few carnations left in the crock, nodding them up and down. Then a screen door slammed and voices were heard. A woman was laughing. They were all coming back. It occurred to Royal that they'd been summoned to witness Mrs. Durant's tears and to hear the television commentary on her sorrow, and were now ready to return to their hand-wrestling and their feasting. He didn't want to see them.

Before anyone had come into view around the side of the house, Royal was past the silo and halfway across the near field.

18

Grady was sitting on the plank steps in front of Guy's house when
he drove up. She held the key and the fine gold chain in the fist
of her right hand. A part of the chain leaked between her fingers
onto her lap. She opened her fist and, with the forefinger of her
left hand, flicked it back where it belonged and quickly closed the
fist again. She'd been tempted, when she got there, to try the key
in the front door to see if it worked, but it seemed distrustful, or
an insult to his efficiency.

He'd sent her yet another present, a key to his house on a gold
chain. The old-fashioned key had a long stem with the bit shaped
like an I; the chain wasn't long, which meant that if she'd ever
worn it, the key itself would probably rest on her breastbone like
a religious medal or a crucifix. She'd come, of course, to return

the key, and, remembering her past susceptibilities, she figured she'd better make the transaction in the open air. She also had to tell him that this would be the last time she would come to meet him. Ned was now free to marry her, and whatever her feelings about Claire's death, she was not going to let them interfere with more pressing practicalities.

It wasn't going to be that easy. At Claire's funeral, at the cemetery, Grady had become overwhelmed with the knowledge that she had hurried Claire to her grave, that she had rushed the dying woman past her final meditations, past the weeds and signs and stones where she might contemplate, probably for a final time, the shapes and colors, the curves and angles that declared the presence of the created world. One incident more than all the others haunted Grady, the time Claire had wanted to watch a particular cloud. They were on their way from the car to the door of the hospital and they were late. Claire had stopped to point at it with a barely raised index finger. "Oh look, Grady. Persia, the way it was in our geography book in the fifth grade. It's being assumed into heaven."

Grady had glanced at the sky. A cloud was moving quickly to the east, but it looked to Grady more like India or Africa. Claire was transfixed. She seemed genuinely convinced that if she'd stare long enough she'd see all of ancient Persia annexed in radiance to the heavenly kingdom.

"It's not going to heaven," Grady had said. "It's going to Vermont. And we're late."

Claire stared one more moment then lowered her head. After she'd examined the knuckles of her left hand, she straightened her head and walked firmly toward the hospital door.

If Grady had not rushed her, Claire might very well have seen the final moment when, in great and golden splendor, the heavens would have opened wide to receive the long forgotten kingdom. Grady had robbed her of the moment and Claire had given it up without complaint. It was the docile surrender that haunted Grady, Claire's quiet agreement that she should, indeed, let it go.

Standing at the side of Claire's grave, Grady knew that this was the place she'd been hurrying her to. She'd detached her, almost by force, from whatever had held her or drawn her to the earth and the sky and had guided her with a relentless step to this gaping patch of ground as if to say, "Here. This is what I want you to look at. And now you can take all the time you want."

When Guy slammed his car door, Grady moved over to one side of the step, then realized she expected him to come and sit next to her. Until that moment, it had been her thought that she'd stand up and go to him. She clenched her fist tighter, pressing the chain and the loop of the key into the flesh of her palm. The pain presented itself as a source of strength, a prop to her determination.

He didn't come to her. He went and looked at a load of boards, two-by-fours and planks, stacked next to the house. They hadn't been there the last time. She wanted to ask him now what they were for, but was afraid to discuss anything but the key. After he'd adjusted a two-by-four, making it flush with the one underneath, he started toward the steps.

He was frowning, as if something might be wrong with the wood. So far, he'd given no indication that he'd seen her. From previous experience, she'd hardly expected to be ignored in favor of a load of wood.

He came to the steps, swung his body around and sat next to her as if sitting on the steps at this hour of day were the most ordinary thing in the world. Grady wondered if, by the simple act of his giving her the key, she had been made, retroactively, a long-time tenant, a companion so familiar that greetings could now be dispensed with, that courtesies of the most common kind were no longer required. She had the impulse to punch his arm, just to let him know that she was there and didn't intend to be treated this way. But a punch might seem too domestic; it would be frankly personal, more private even than a kiss. It would be an expression of intimacy equal to his own familiarities.

"I owe you an apology," Grady said once he seemed settled down. Without her intending it, her voice had a pleased sound to it; it seemed to indicate that the recipient of the apology should be flattered to hold in debt someone so obviously superior.

But he must have heard only the words, not the voice. "I know," he said. "I thought you were going to come over right away. As soon as you got the key."

"I—I couldn't."

"I know that too. I know you have things to do."

He was smiling, almost impishly, proud of this insight and of his willingness to make concessions. But the smile changed. It was still a smile but it had become the old smile of wonder, his first amazement at the sight of her.

Grady looked down at her fist. "I hope you'll forgive me," she said quietly, "but I brought back the key. I won't need it. I mean, I can—I mean, I—I'm getting married." She blurted out this last phrase with sudden daring, surprising even herself.

He was studying her face, letting a slow gaze wander over her features, her hair, her mouth and eyes. He was studying her forehead when he said, "I don't understand."

"I can't come to see you anymore, and you mustn't send me any more presents." She paused, then said, more firmly, "I'm going to get married."

"You?" Now he was looking at her mouth. He seemed genuinely disbelieving. "Yes," she said and turned away as if she were required under the circumstances to make a chaste, retiring gesture.

"I don't understand," he repeated, shaking his head slightly as if to rearrange his impressions.

"Maybe not right away—getting married, I mean—but probably before all that long."

"You?"

"Yes. Me." He was still incredulous. His mouth was clamped shut, his eyebrows pulled down toward his eyes, his forehead creased in the perpendicular as well as the horizontal, making ridges that reached to his nose.

"You?"

"It isn't anything I can explain. It just happens to be. You'll have to take my word for it."

"I believe you. You wouldn't lie. Not to me. But—" He stopped.

"I know," Grady said. "I certainly never acted like there was another man, did I? I'm sorry about that. That's really what I should apologize for."

"No. I just—I thought I was the only one probably wanted you."

Grady stiffened slightly but laughed to make sure this was a joke. "Am I that unattractive?" she asked.

"I always thought so," he said quietly. "That's one of the reasons I liked you so much. I was so sure nobody else would."

There was so much sorrow in his voice, Grady knew he must be telling the truth. She felt she was supposed to say something like "Oh, really?" in a haughty tone, but she was too subdued by the genuineness of his disappointment to be insulted. "Well," she said quietly, "someone does."

Guy slowly shook his head. "I thought I was so smart. No more pretty women, I'd told myself. The pretty ones, they always leave you. Like they were never here. The pretty ones. The one I built this house for, she was pretty. She had this great big mouth."

"Well, we can't *all* be that pretty, can we?" Grady had decided it was all right to get a little huffy after all.

"I didn't care you weren't that pretty," he answered, still sorrowful.

"You're not very flattering, are you?"

Grady could tell that he was studying her face again, but she didn't turn toward him. "Why would I flatter you?" he asked. He leaned closer to study her even more carefully, then withdrew. "You're the best woman in the world. There's nobody else just like you." He paused to make sure he meant what he was about to say, then said it. "And maybe you're not so bad-looking after all." He paused again to question the truth of what he was saying, then continued. "I can see that now. You *are* pretty. Only I never thought so until now. I guess I shouldn't be surprised you're going off now you're pretty like the rest of them. I just didn't expect it, that's all."

"I—I'm not really *that* pretty," Grady said.

"I know. But nobody seems to see that anymore. Not even me."

Grady, still not sure if she should feel flattered or insulted, held out her closed fist as if she was going to give him a select bug or a piece of candy. Guy, in turn, held out his open hand and she dropped the key into it. He closed his fist over it, then opened it, then closed it again, then opened it like a magician trying to make it disappear.

"I thought I was making you happy," he said. "The way nobody else would. I thought I would make you so grateful you would think I was wonderful and you would belong to me for as long as I wanted." He looked out over the field on the other side of the road. "And I thought maybe that might be forever."

Grady too looked toward the field. Goldfinches darted in and out of the weeds, which meant that there were probably thistles with their seeds already rising into the air for them to feed on. On the far side were pitch pine and staghorn sumac growing from among a bramble of what seemed at the distance to be honeysuckle and raspberry with some woodbine tangling itself through. The sky had started to cloud over in the west, gray masses of sullen smoke moving east as if looking for someplace to be mean.

Grady tried to think of what she should say. Maybe she should treat him to a good dose of the truth, the same as he'd treated her. She could tell him that she'd considered him stupid to the point of retardation, that she too had felt secure in the certainty that no one else would find him acceptable, that, like himself, she had bestowed favors beyond deserving.

But she could say none of this, not because it might offend him, or even because it might expose her vanities. She couldn't say it because it might lead her to the same place his confession had led him. She too might find herself saying, "I thought I was making you happy. I thought I would make you so grateful that you would think I was wonderful and you would belong to me for as long as I wanted." And then, like him, she might go on and say, "And I thought maybe that might be—" Grady stopped herself from even thinking the absurd word. It had to end here.

She turned to Guy sitting silently next to her. He was still looking at the field, thoughtful, as if it were his most immediate concern. Grady, too, turned her gaze back toward the pitch pine and sumac. Guy lifted his right foot to the step just below the one they were sitting on and laid his forearm across his knee. "I want to buy that field someday," he said.

Grady waited a moment, then said, matter-of-factly, "You could plant something, probably."

"Yes, I could plant something," he said, but as if this were only one of more than several possibilities.

Grady waited to see if he'd elaborate, if he'd mention any of his other options, but when he didn't, she said, "The soil's not really that bad. It's not as sandy as over here."

He glanced sideways at her. He was puzzled again, surprised that he hadn't anticipated what she was going to say. "How do you know?" he asked.

"By what's growing there now," she said.

This seemed to puzzle him even more. "Nothing's growing there."

"You've got yarrow and great mullein and there's black locust and—" She stopped. What was the point? This was hardly the time to give a lecture on weeds and soil. She got up but kept looking at the field.

"I have? What are the names again?"

Grady recited her previous speech. "You've got yarrow and great mullein and black locust. For starters."

"You know all that?"

"Of course I know all that." Was she now to find out that he had thought her stupid as well as ugly? Was ignorance another of her irresistible attractions? "And you've got viper's bugloss and St. John's wort and purple loosestrife." Her voice was nice and crisp, just the way she wanted it. "The soil can handle anything from dry like great mullein right through to purple loosestrife and St. John's wort, which need it moist. Dry to moist. You can grow almost anything."

"And you know all that?"

"Yes I know all that." She was going to add "And lots more besides," but she let it go.

"You never told me you knew all that."

"Well, I do."

"Strange." He sounded as if Grady had just revealed to him some great oddity about herself.

"Not really."

"Oh, yes. Strange."

She turned to look at him. Now she would really tell him how much he had misperceived her. She'd tell him he had no idea of who she was and what she was. She was, for starters, not stupid. And she was certainly not ugly. And it was time she told him outright and no mistake about it. But when she turned toward him, she saw his look of astonishment. It was more than an amazement at her knowledge of bugloss and loosestrife. He had reverted to his original wonder that such a creature as Grady could exist. But, added to it was an additional incredulity. He had not thought her ignorant; he had thought her perfect. What she'd done, with the great mullein and the St. John's wort, was pile perfection upon perfection. He hadn't thought it possible, but she'd done it. He had indeed misperceived her: there was no end to her astonishments. It was all in the look he was giving her now. He seemed thrilled and humbled, dazed and disbelieving. He was so *proud* of her. She turned again toward the field. Never had anyone been so proud of her.

She wanted this man. She wanted to stay here with him. Her children could fend for themselves. They'd have to get along without her. Martha had Raggles, what more did she need? She had Royal Provo. *He'd* take care of her. They didn't need her, any of them. They could *have* the farm. *Anne* could marry Ned Ryerson. Maybe that would work better anyway. It would settle the problem of the fields and it would take care of the future of both farms. *Ned* could put up with Anne's moods. And Anne could put up with Ned's seriousness, his doggedness. She'd send for her things. No, she'd send for nothing. Guy Duskin would provide for her, he would give her all she needed. And he would keep her plainness a secret from her and she would keep his stupidity a secret from him.

In other words, he would become blind and she would become deaf.

It wouldn't work.

And yet. She *wasn't* ugly. In this he had indeed misperceived her. He'd even admitted as much. Which raised the question: had she in turn misperceived him? Maybe he was quite intelligent after all and she just hadn't realized it yet. Maybe he was merely idiosyncratic, maybe he had patterns of thought and reason that were entirely his own and she'd come to recognize them as time went on. It was possible.

No, it was not possible. Nothing could persuade her that Guy

Duskin was anything but stupid. No matter how hard she might try, she would always think of him as "not particularly bright." But then the idea came to her: what was wrong with that? He was a good man. He was kind; he was—God knows—thoughtful. She dared anyone to judge him inferior. She would present him to the great world, he would appear at her side, under her sponsorship and her protection. He would be the pride of her life, he would give her joy. He would be her defiance and her love.

"Do you want some wood?" she heard him say. There was neither amazement nor wonder in his tone. He spoke as if he'd come upon a solution to whatever problem either of them might have. Without waiting for her answer, he went over to the lumber stacked at the side of the house.

"What if I said I might change my mind?" Her voice was so low she wasn't sure he could hear.

He put his hand on top of the neatly stacked planks. "They're yours," he said. "I was going to build you a porch so you'd have someplace to sit and look outside. But you can have it. A wedding present." He paused, let the notion take hold, then gain force. Finally it burst out, "This is your wedding present!"

She went over to him. "But what if I told you I'd changed my mind? That I'm not getting married?"

He laughed, then shook his head. "No, you're getting married. This is your present. Even if you don't need a porch, you can have it. You can build anything you want with it. Bring the truck over. And the boy, he can come with you and the two of us, we'll load it for you." He was elated. The ideas in his mind tumbled one over the other, their energy driving him to near ecstasy. "Together. That's what this is for. For you. And for him and me to load for you." He was looking at the wood, running his hand along one of the boards. "Do you think he'd do that? The boy? Do you think he'd come here and the two of us could load it?"

"But I—"

"No! It's all settled. Just tell me when you'll be here. It's only pine, but it's good." He laughed. "I didn't know it would be a wedding present."

She stared at him. "Give me back the key," she said. "I want it back."

"No, no, no." He took her by the elbow and started leading her toward her car. "You're not that kind of woman once you're married."

"But if I don't *get* married—?"

"You'll get married. I know you better than you know yourself. I always have, from the beginning. Remember?"

She tried to free herself, but he held on. He even opened the car door for her. She turned and looked at him. He smiled and again he shook his head. She knew this meant he considered himself the wiser of the two. She was not to interrupt his moment of insight with argument or discussion. She got into the car. He closed the door after her, then stepped back. She just sat there, wondering what to do. He went back to the lumber and began moving the boards, making unneeded adjustments in the way they were stacked. He kept his back to her, shifting the planks, examining their alignments, shifting them again.

She started the car and made the turn-around. She pulled up alongside him, but he wouldn't look at her. He seemed to be counting the two-by-fours. She drove off and by the time she'd reached the highway she realized that she'd been saved from doing the dumbest thing of her life. He, of course, had been her rescuer, but she thought it better not to dwell on that. And, of course, she would never come back to get the lumber. She didn't need a porch so she'd have someplace to sit and look outside.

19

Royal had never been in Anne's room before. Part of the wallpaper between the windows had been stripped but some patches still had to be scraped off. The other walls were still covered, a pattern of white latticework with green vines that sprouted not grapes but, for some reason, strawberries. One section near the closet door had been ripped away to show the dried paste still sticking to the plaster, a design of yellowing white against tan. The bed, not much wider than his bunk, was covered with a spread that was actually a huge Raggedy Ann doll with the head raised onto the pillow. Because the pillow hadn't been plumped or straightened, it seemed now that Raggedy Ann had a collapsed cheek, one sunken eye and a half-severed head. When Anne tossed a heavy garment bag onto the bed, Royal couldn't help feeling that

Raggedy Ann had had if not the stuffing then at least the breath knocked out of her.

Royal assumed he was there to answer questions. He hadn't gone to see Anne at the camp and didn't go that morning to get her for her visit home. He'd just seen her a few moments before, sitting on a stump outside the henyard. He was on his way to wash the grease and dirt from his hands and face after an afternoon working on the threshing machine. Anne had been stroking the neck and breast of a chicken the way one would pet a cat to make it purr.

"I'm home," she'd called.

Royal went to where she was sitting. "I know," he said. "Your mother said she was going to get you. I had work I had to do."

Anne went right on stroking, but with an impatience, as if the chicken was owed a specific number of strokes and the sooner delivered the better. "I thought it'd be you came to get me."

"Like I said—"

"I know. You had work you had to do." With that, she stood up and cradled the chicken in the crook of her left arm. The chicken clucked and fluttered a few feathers, a simple request that the stroking be renewed. Anne's answer was to hold it down with her foot, pick up the butcher knife leaning against the stump, and chop off its head. Royal had never seen this done before. Anne scraped the head off onto the ground and let go of the body the way one would release a restless infant struggling to be free. "I was hoping you would have come to see me since last time." She spoke softly but didn't look at him.

The chicken, or its body rather, scurried about, protesting this betrayal of its affections, dashing itself against the stump in search of what had been taken from it, including the voice to make its protest known. It bobbed up and down as though insistent on feeding, as if going through ordinary motions would force a reversal of what had just happened. If it could only continue pecking, surely a beak would be given.

"I'm sorry," Royal said. "But I couldn't."

Anne gave this a moment's thought, then went over to a big copper pot standing on an old two-burner gas stove, the kind about eight inches high that one sets on a table or a shelf. Except here the stove was put right on the ground and there was no gas, only a wood fire underneath. Anne scooped up the chicken as if it had had enough excitement for one day. Again her touch seemed to calm it. It was completely still as she dashed it down into the steaming water. Its feathers rose all around like a final sigh, then slowly lowered themselves deep into the pot.

"But didn't you know I'd miss you?" Now Royal could see that there were tears on her right cheek.

"I guess I didn't think about it," he said.

Anne poked the chicken even deeper into the water. "How could you not think about it? I've told you how much I like it when you come to see me." The feathers had brought the chicken to the surface again; Anne gave it another poke, then quickly pulled her finger out of the scalding water. "And I thought you liked it, coming to see me." She licked her fingertip, then sniffed and rubbed the tears from her cheek with the back of her wrist.

"I did," he said. "Like it, I mean."

Anne pulled the chicken out of the water and held it away from her so it wouldn't drip all over. The blood had drained away, most of it while the chicken had been rushing around in search of its head. Anne yanked out a fistful of feathers and let them fall to her feet like the plucked petals of a huge white flower. "But you don't anymore?" she asked. "Like to see me?" She seemed genuinely bewildered that this could be possible. New tears appeared as she continued to pluck the balding chicken. The feathers stuck to her blouse, to her jeans, to her shoes, but she didn't seem to care. She tugged away, one fistful, then another.

"It's that I can't anymore."

"You mean your car doesn't work?"

"No. It works."

Anne held the chicken on the stump again and, with the ease of someone unzipping a purse, took the knife and slit it open. "Then how come you don't—" She stopped to lick a tear into her mouth with her tongue, then reached inside the chicken and turned her wrist a few times, winding clockwise, then counterclockwise. With one simple scoop she brought out the entrails, held them in her hand, picked out the liver the way one might extract a quarter from a handful of change, threw the rest toward the henyard, and plopped the liver back inside the hollowed carcass.

"I—I missed you," Anne said, her voice almost a whisper. After wiping her nose on her right arm, she picked up the butcher knife again and cut off the chicken's feet. These, too, she scraped off the stump onto the ground. One landed on top of the head, catching the eye between two of its bright yellow claws.

Anne picked up the chicken by its blunted legs and slowly examined her handiwork. "Can you come with me for a minute, or do you have more work to do? I've got something I want to show you."

"Well, I—" Royal held out his greasy hands to show how much he needed washing.

"You can do that later. Okay?"

When they passed through the kitchen on the way to her room, Anne slapped the chicken down onto the drainboard next to the sink, its legs sticking up as if it had been told to roll over and play dead.

Anne opened the garment bag. Had she brought him here just to show him a new coat or ask his opinion about something she'd just bought? He really didn't like being here with her, in her room, just the two of them. There'd been a time when this was what he would have wanted more than anything he could think of, but that time had passed.

Royal brought his hand across his forehead, then down along his right cheek. Maybe the smeared grease on his face would make him less visible, less present.

Anne was digging around at the bottom of the garment bag, and Royal couldn't help wondering if she wasn't getting dried chicken blood all over the clothes inside. She stopped her rummagings, thought a moment, then drew her arm partway out of the bag. "You have to promise not to tell anyone. I mean no one," she said.

"Tell who what?"

Without explaining, she reached back in and began bringing out brick-sized stacks of money held together with rubber bands. She tossed them onto the bed as if she was really looking for something underneath. When she'd thrown what seemed to be the last stack, she looked over the pile and let out a deep breath to let him know the job was finished. As if the structure of the heap needed an improvement in design, she picked up one bundle near the top and put it at the base. Her hand had almost no blood on it at all, just a ridge of black, crusted around the edges of her palm. She studied the pile to make sure she was satisfied with the arrangement, then put both her hands in her lap. Royal was tempted to take off his hat in the presence of so much money but thought he'd wait for certain clarifications first.

"It's yours," Anne said. "If you want it."

"Mine?"

"Yours."

"Why mine?"

"Because I'm going to give it to you."

"Why me?"

"Because I want us to go away together, just the two of us. And we'll need some money."

"We're going away?"

"Yes. The two of us. You and me." She paused, then said, "And the money."

This was the money from the holdups. Anne had it. And she was asking him to take it and go away with her. More than anything, Royal wanted to go and wash his hands and face.

"How can I go away?" he asked.

"You've got a car."

"I know, but—"

"We'll go in your car." She moved one of the bundles from the bottom of the pile to the top.

"Anne," Royal said, "I can't go away. You know that."

"Yes, you can. *We* can. Look. We have all this money." With that, she turned her face away from him as if ashamed to make the money a part of her proposal.

"I have to stay here," he said.

"But how can we be together if you stay here? I mean, really together the way we're supposed to be? Do you want us to get married and live here? Is that what you want?"

Royal rubbed his hands on his pants, smearing grease on top of grease with no noticeable effect on the hands themselves. He started to put them into his pockets but they got stuck because he was leading with his knuckles. He rubbed them across the front of his shirt, then, as if he'd cleared a space, folded his arms across his suspenders. But this didn't seem right either, so he slowly uncrossed his arms and eased them down to his sides.

"No," he said quietly. "I don't want us to get married."

"See? I told you. Then we have to go away. And we can do it with this. What's going to stop us?"

Royal moved toward the door. Anne picked up one of the bundles and stared down at it. "Is it because of you and Peter?" she asked.

"No."

"But you do it together, don't you?"

When Royal said nothing, Anne asked, "He loves you, doesn't he?"

"Yes."

Anne carefully put the bundle of money back onto the pile. "Do you love him?"

"Yes."

"Do you love me?"

Royal moved toward the door. Anne got up and stood at the side of the bed. "Do you?" she asked again. She was looking down at her hand, picking off flecks of dried chicken blood.

"Yes," he said. "But I can't do anything about it."

"Why not?"

"I just can't, is all."

"Because it hurts my brother?"

"No."

"Then why?"

Royal put his hand on the doorknob. When he tried to turn it, the grease made his hand slip. He stopped trying.

Anne had pulled her blouse out of her jeans and was taking off her shoes. After she'd slipped her feet out, she started to lift her blouse over her head but stopped when she noticed Royal hadn't made a move. "Well?" she asked. "You said you love me."

"And I said I can't."

"Yes, you can. I know you can." She pulled her blouse over her head. Before she was completely free of it, she started talking again. "I even stopped with the archery instructor, just because of you. You saw the archery instructor that time. You saw what he looks like. And I could have him instead of you, any time I want."

"I better go wash."

"No. Wait. I didn't mean that. You—you're very beautiful. I mean, when I look at you, you're beautiful. It's the truth. I really mean it."

Royal shook his head. He knew it wasn't true. She had made him believe it before, but he didn't believe it now. If he were to make himself naked, with her, he'd be too skinny, too pale, the way he'd always been. His toes would be too long, and, as if this too would be revealed by his nakedness, his ears would be too small, his eyes too narrow. He wouldn't want her to see his Adam's apple, his elbows, and his wrist bones.

He rubbed his hands again on the sides of his pants as if trying to put himself into motion. But the action ended there. If this were Mrs. Durant instead of Anne he wouldn't have minded showing himself. For Mrs. Durant he wouldn't be scrawny. The blindness attributed to love reflected back onto himself. His ardor transformed not only Mrs. Durant but himself as well. With her, his body would be supple and firm. He would be proud of his Adam's apple and his elbows. But without the transcending power of love to help it along, the metamorphosis would never take place. With Mrs. Durant he would have become a splendor to the world, sleek muscles and taut flesh. With Anne he was sticks and bones, a scarecrow with an oversized Adam's apple.

By now, Anne had taken off her clothes, showing the outline of her swimming suit, a smooth white against the tawny brown as if she had carefully preserved this paleness to match his own. "I even gave up my dad for you," she whispered. "I know I'm supposed to miss him, I know I'm supposed to think about him and wish he wasn't dead. But I don't. I think about you. I know it's wrong, but I—I—"

She sat down on the bed and bowed her head. Her hair fell straight down, almost reaching her thighs. "It's my dad's money, but you can have it. All of it. But don't go now. You're the only one I miss. It's not right. But that only makes me think about you that much more." She sprawled out onto the bed and buried her face among the bundles that lay strewn on the breast of Raggedy

Ann, the curve of her body a great white and brown hump arching over the money.

She shouldn't have taken off her clothes. She, no less then he, had become repellent. She, who Royal knew to be so beautiful, now seemed deformed and ugly. He knew he should go to her; he should try to offer her some comfort for her ugliness, but he couldn't. He didn't want to. Still, he couldn't just leave her there. He went over to the bed and sat down just below the curve of her buttocks. He reached out his hand and put it on the rounded back, onto the bones of her spine. With a single slide of her head, she put her face into his lap, then lifted herself gently, forcing him backward onto the bed. She stretched herself out next to him, straightening his legs along the bed as she moved her own into position next to his. As she kissed him, on the lips, on the eyes, on the forehead, she kept whispering, "I miss my dad. I do. I really do. I miss him."

Under them, between them, the money poked and jabbed. When Royal found himself staring into the eye of Raggedy Ann, he closed his own.

20

"Why," Grady wondered, "is there always *one* fly in here?" She was in her bedroom and the single fly was buzzing against the window, annoyed that this hard substance wasn't the air it seemed to be. It kept attacking the glass, then testing it by walking on it, then attacking it again. Grady glanced at the swatter set along the top of the radiator but figured she didn't want to take the time right now to use it. Ned had phoned. Norma had already passed her water sack and a difficult calving was expected. Could she send Royal or even Peter? No, she'd said. Peter had taken her car to drive Anne back to camp and she didn't know where Royal was. She'd come herself. Right away.

Right away, of course, did not mean she wouldn't change from her old work skirt and unironed blouse to a decent dress, the bright blue with the square neck. Grady intended this to be her last manipulation. She would settle today, once and for all, her eventual marriage to Ned Ryerson. The time for conniving was past. The time had come to simplify everything. She'd come to this decision earlier in the day, after Sunday mass.

Grady had brought along a picnic to have on the grass when church was out. It was supposed to be something of a sendoff for Martha, who would be spending a few days—a "vacation"—with her girlfriend Suzie back in Coble. And besides, it was an old custom dating back to the days when people fasted if they were going to communion and would be starved by the time mass was over. The parishioners would throw their old horse blankets down on the grass and spread before themselves a feast that would do credit to the Fourth of July. Chicken, of course. (Anne had killed this one of theirs just the day before.) Deviled eggs. Carrot cake thickly smeared with butter. Tomatoes and cucumbers. Radishes and scallions, jams and preserves, pickles and several varieties of cheese of home manufacture. Grady hadn't gotten around yet to the cheese—that would come next year—but she made up for it by bringing along the largest watermelon in her garden.

But the picnic had not gone well. The trouble began when, at the offertory collection during mass, Martha primly opened the blue plastic purse she'd gotten for her birthday, took out some money, and dropped it with great self-importance into the basket. Grady was amused and wondered who'd given it to her. Probably Royal. Then, as the basket passed back in front of her she saw that it was a fifty-dollar bill. She almost yanked it out, but the basket had already gone by. When she looked at Martha, she had retreated into her prayer book, pretending to study the picture by moving her head to show the movement of her eyes.

"Where did you get that?" Grady hissed.

Martha looked up at her and her whisper was very loud. "It was for the collection."

"I know. But where did you get it?"

"From Raggedy Ann," she said.

"You did not get it from Raggedy Ann."

"I did. I got it from Raggedy Ann."

Grady considered dragging her out of the pew and having a very serious conversation with her in the vestibule, but thought she'd better wait. She was doubly sorry for the distraction. She had to find out where the money had come from but the worry interfered with her first purpose for being at mass. She wanted to pray for Claire. She wanted to ask that Claire forgive her all her wrongs against her and that she accept her tardy love.

But that had been difficult enough even before the fifty dollars. For any prayer to have meaning surely she must make some accounting of what her life had become. Her husband was in his grave, unforgiven. Her anger at him she had translated into ruthlessness; her confusions at his death she had tried to resolve with promiscuity. How much of all this was her way of getting even with Andy and how much was a revelation of true character long suppressed she did not know. But she did know that she was no longer acceptable to herself, much less to God.

And yet to renounce her ways and correct her faults would mean giving up her campaign to marry Ned, abandoning her own farm, since she needed Ned's land to secure her own holdings. And that she would not do. Her farm was her renunciation of Andy, her dismissal of what he'd been to her, and she wouldn't give that up no matter what.

Just as she was about to formulate her own variation of the prayer of St. Augustine, to ask God to make her honest and decent and generous and forgiving—but not yet—Martha dropped the fifty dollars. And now Grady couldn't think of anything but the money passing right under her nose as if she were being told to see what it smelled like.

To convince Martha that the subject wasn't important enough

for her to lie about, Grady postponed her questions until after the picnic meal was spread. Neither Anne nor Peter, she assumed, had seen the money, since they'd had no reaction to it. They'd been particularly subdued at mass, and were, even now. But then they'd both been particularly quiet the evening before, at supper. As usual, Grady attributed this to their thoughts about their father and made no attempt to interrupt their mood.

To make conversation now, when she was passing around the chicken, Grady said, "Too bad Royal isn't here. I told him he didn't have to come to mass since he's not Catholic, but he could at least have come for the picnic. The grass isn't Catholic. The blanket isn't Catholic. The chicken isn't Catholic." She took a bite. "At least, it doesn't taste Catholic."

Nobody even smiled. Grady was about to bring up the subject of the money, but Anne spoke first. "I guess he wanted a day off."

"No," Peter said. "He has something he's working on."

"He's working too much," Grady said. "Now what's he doing?"

Peter separated a chunk of potato from a slice of cucumber, ate the potato chunk, then said, "I'm not supposed to tell."

"Not tell what?"

"I'm not supposed to tell what he's working on."

"Then I guess you'd better," Grady said cheerfully.

"I promised I wouldn't."

"He's working on that big old thing behind the pump house," said Martha. Then she stirred her finger around in the bowl of pickles.

"Martha!" Peter sounded more disappointed than surprised by his sister's revelation. Martha, for her part, simply stirred the pickles around, trying to get them all to move in the same direction.

"It was supposed to be a surprise for Mother," Anne said.

Martha, to show that she wasn't intimidated by their disapproval, added, "He said he's going to make it go."

"The old thrasher?" Grady asked.

"Ask Martha," Anne said. "She's the one knows all about it."

Grady watched Martha as she tipped a pickle up out of the bowl onto the blanket.

"He isn't going to make it go," said Martha. "It's too dirty." With that, she picked up the pickle and put it on her plate.

"He'll make it go," Peter said quietly, and Anne nodded her head. "I think so too." Her voice was quieter than Peter's.

And then nothing more was said. Everyone was silent, as if a moment were needed for all of them to think of Royal, who was absent from the feast. It was Martha who spoke first and her thoughts, too, were still on Royal. "Royal got grease and dirt all over Raggedy Ann."

This was Grady's cue to bring up the fifty dollars, and she couldn't help noting Martha's bad luck in providing an opening for her own inquisition. "Uh-huh," Grady said. "Just like Raggedy Ann gave you fifty dollars for the collection?" Anne looked over as Martha nodded her head. "It was stuck under her chin," Martha said. "And her face was dirty and she had grease all over her. From Royal."

Grady was looking at Anne, but it was Peter who began talking. "Martha," he said, "you're dribbling pickle juice all over your new dress. What's Suzie going to think when you get there and your dress is all messed up?" He reached over and with a paper napkin began rubbing the front of Martha's dress, stopping long enough to look over at Anne, his expression subdued as if he was asking a question and pleading at the same time that it not be answered. But it was answered and Grady knew what Peter knew. Anne and Royal had made love on Raggedy Ann and this was something painful to her son. And now, with his look, he was telling Anne that he forgave her the hurt.

Peter began rubbing Martha's dress even more vigorously. Anne's eyes had met his, but now she was looking down at the strawberries.

"When you eat a pickle," Peter said to Martha, "you should

lean over a little bit. Like this, see? Then you won't dribble—"
Slowly his voice trailed off as if he'd lost all interest in the subject.
He just sat there, smoothing his napkin on his knee.

"Doesn't anyone want a radish?" Grady asked. She held out the
bowl. Only Anne took one. She seemed about to take a bite but
then, as if she'd just heard what had been said, turned toward
Martha. "Did you take my fifty dollars? And you put it in the
collection? That was my pay, my money from camp." She looked
at her mother, took a bite of the radish and, while she was
chewing, said, "We'll have to ask for it back is all." She took
another bite of the radish. "And someone should teach Martha
that money isn't hers just because she sees it lying around."

"Yes," Grady said quietly. "I must remember to tell her. Martha, remind me to teach you that money isn't yours just because
it's lying around."

"Peter should fight Royal again for getting Raggedy Ann
greasy," said Martha. "He got her all dirty. He got the whole bed
full of his grease."

"All right, Martha, all right," Grady said.

"And I only took the dollar so I'd have something to go to
church!" Tears of anger came into her eyes and when Peter
touched her shoulder, she jerked herself away. "And you're not
supposed to fight without your clothes on, you and Royal. Raggles
and I see you in the woods, fighting by the river."

Anne lowered the radish from her mouth and tried to keep
looking at it, but glanced over at Peter instead. It took her only
a moment to verify what Martha had said. In a high, quiet voice,
she said to Martha, "Peter and Royal weren't fighting. They were
playing. Boys have games they play. You know that."

"They were fighting. Raggles and I saw. Because then they had
to kiss and make up."

Anne blinked as if someone had jabbed her. "That was part of
the game. And maybe you're not supposed to go looking at boys

when they go swimming and play boy games. Girls don't do that. I'm a girl and *I* don't do that."

"Raggles is a girl," Martha said, thinking this was somehow defense enough.

When no one spoke, Anne picked up the carrot cake and held it out toward Peter. "Peter?" she said softly. Peter looked at it, shook his head, then took a piece anyway.

Grady turned away from them toward the church steps. She looked up and down the church façade, the arched entry, the two gothic windows, the high-pitched roof. Then she looked at the stone bell tower just to the right, from its base to its height, where the crenelations made it look like a medieval battlement. Peter, she could see, was eating the carrot cake, examining the piece he held in his hand after each bite. Anne was searching among the strawberries. Martha bubbled the Tab in her glass with her lips so that it went up her nose.

Grady glanced from the tower to the church, from the church to the tower. For the first time in her life she realized that the church and the tower were very much like a barn and a silo. Apparently there was a constant in local architecture that needed only certain modifications to serve any and all purposes. Grady wondered why she hadn't seen this before.

She felt the dress slip down along her hips, then gave the skirt a yank at the sides to make sure it was all right in back. There was a knock at the door. Maybe it was Anne, come back to explain a few things. She'd already come earlier and brought with her a pillowcase that looked like it was stuffed with building blocks. "I don't want to talk about it," she'd said, setting the pillowcase down on her mother's bed. "There's a piece of paper inside telling you how much it is, but you'd better subtract fifty dollars. Peter's driving me back to camp in your car. I have to go now."

Saying no more, she turned and went out. When Grady looked

inside the pillowcase, there was the money Andy had stolen. And there, too, was the promised piece of paper telling her that there should be $7,142, less fifty. It was a different note Grady wanted; one that would explain what the money was for. But she found nothing.

She turned one of the bundles over and over in her hand—it seemed to be all tens—as if the heft and weight of it might give her some notion of why Andy had done what he'd done. After she dropped the money back into the pillowcase, she slumped the pillowcase against the wall next to her bed.

The knock came again. "Come in, come in." The door opened. It wasn't Anne come back for explanations. It was Royal. Before turning to look at him, she drew her right hand across her collarbone to make sure the square neck was in place.

"Mrs. Durant? Can I come in?"

"You already are." Royal was the one she was least prepared to deal with at the moment.

"Can you come see something I want to show you?" he asked.

To give herself time to think of what she was supposed to do, what she was supposed to say, Grady looked at the shoes lined along her closet floor, six pairs in all. "Come see what?" She went into the closet and picked up a pair of loafers.

"A surprise. Outside. By the old pump house."

Grady balanced on one foot, slipping the other into one of the shoes. She looked at Royal. He was scrubbed and clean. He'd taken off the fedora and was holding it in front of him. His hair was slicked back and it seemed that the pull had widened his eyes and made him unable to close his mouth. He was wearing a white shirt with the sleeves rolled down and a pair of baggy white pants of heavy cotton, almost like canvas. The shirt was bloused out by the brown twill suspenders and the pants legs crumpled themselves at the shoes, the heavy work boots she'd bought him. He passed the brim of his hat slowly through his fingers as if it were his equivalent of a rosary.

"By the old pump house?" She didn't have the heart to ruin his surprise. She already had more knowledge of his activities and his achievements than she knew what to do with and she felt she could afford to pretend ignorance in this one little instance.

"The thrasher! I made it go!" he cried. "Come see it. I made it go!"

"The thrasher?"

"The thrasher. Come see it!"

Grady slid her other foot into the left loafer and wiggled it in as deep as she could. Her foot couldn't make its way into the shoe; her heel was crushing down the counter. She raised her foot but found herself wobbling and had to put it down again. She wiggled the foot some more, scraping the shoe sideways on the floor, then lifted her foot and stuck her finger in between her heel and the back of the shoe. But before she could get the foot in securely, she began to wobble again. She even had to lift her right arm to balance herself.

Royal reached out to take hold of her hand, but then pulled it back before he'd touched her. "I can do it," he said, and before she was sure what he had in mind to do, he was kneeling in front of her, his finger easing the back of her shoe up over her heel.

"Good," she said. "Thanks." She curled and uncurled her toes inside the shoe. It was on. Royal stayed where he was, still kneeling, his head bowed. "The thrasher works just the way it used to," he said, then bent his head back and looked up at her. "The gears were all off but it'll work now. I know it will." He stopped, swallowed hard, then said, "The grain auger might need . . ." His voice trailed off as if a failure with the grain auger would be a cause for unspeakable shame. He lowered his head again.

Grady could see the back of his neck, a deep pink, more the color of scalded flesh than sunburn. The knobby bone at the top of his spine made a big lump just below the collar line. Here the skin stretching down into his shirt was white again, so white that it seemed unfinished, as if he had been too inattentive in the womb and hadn't waited to have the covering flesh completed with pigment, pores, and complexion. Instead of working on the thrasher, he would have done better to finish the making of his own body. He should not present himself in this unfinished state. It made her uneasy. He hadn't been properly prepared. It was an offense; it was an affront.

Grady backed away from where he was kneeling. She picked his hat up off the bed. It was stained and blotched with sweat, its gray felt worn through where her index finger lay across the peak of the ridge that surrounded the crown. She saw where he had pinned together the black hatband with baling wire and had tucked in a sprig of now wilted clover on the right side.

"I'd love to see it," Grady said.

"You would?"

But Grady hadn't finished saying what she'd meant to say. "Of course I would. But not right now. You can see I—"

"Oh, no," he interrupted. "It's all ready to go. You've got time."

He was indeed Guy Duskin's son. Here too an entreaty became an assurance. Here too a refusal was a goad. He was making not a plea but a promise. The expectation in the boy's eyes, the held stare, the taut hope, it was Guy Duskin all over again.

"I don't have time," she said. "I'm on my way to the Ryersons'. I mean Ned Ryerson's. Norma's having a calf that could come out hind legs first or worse." Grady noticed she'd drawn the hat toward herself and was passing the brim through her own fingers. She wanted to hold it out toward him but knew it would be rude, a dismissal too abrupt and just a little regal.

"No," he said, his voice a high-pitched whisper. "You still have time. It's something you've got to see." The boy slowly let his eyes see first her dress, then the shoes he'd helped put on. He examined the shoes for a moment, then raised one knee. He paused, looked up at her and asked, "You can't?" still not quite convinced.

"Not now I can't. I . . . I didn't even have time to . . . to change. Except my shoes." Royal stood up. Grady had started moving her hands along the hat brim again. She stopped and simply held the hat out to him. He didn't take it. Instead he looked at her with what seemed like a growing wonder, not unlike the gaze of Guy Duskin. Grady was tempted to take a step back, but stood her ground.

"I love you, Mrs. Durant."

Grady wanted to sink down onto the bed, to sit there until everything that was going to happen had happened.

"I love you, Mrs. Durant. I—" He had become too happy to speak. He looked quickly down at the floor, first to the right, then to the left of him, searching there for words he couldn't find. He fixed his eyes on her shoes and spoke rapidly, worried that the text might be removed at any moment, replaced before he'd read it through. "I love you. I didn't know that's why I was doing the thrasher, but it is. It's for you. Because I'm in love with you. And my mother's grave, I want you to come and I'll show it to you. Because I love you."

"Your mother's—"

"We can go in my car," he continued. "I'll buy the gas. I want you to see it so you'll know—"

The text seemed to have run out. He looked at the wall behind her, at the ceiling, at the dresser, at the floor again, then at her right shoulder. "Come see the thrasher? Now?"

Grady stared at him to make sure who it was standing in front of her. Then she reached over and picked up the pillowcase with the money in it. After looking down at it a moment she shoved it toward him, knocking it against his chest. "Here. Take this and go. Quick."

Royal looked at the pillowcase, then at Grady, then again at the pillowcase. With his right hand he rubbed his chest.

Grady pulled the pillowcase back toward herself, opened it, and reached inside. She took out a well-worn piece of notepaper, read it, put it back inside, and bunched the top closed again. "It's $7,142 less fifty. Take it and go. As fast as you can."

Royal backed away a step and looked at the pillowcase. Grady shoved it toward him again but when he didn't take it, she flung it onto the bed. One bundle of money came rolling out. "We're all crazy!" she said. "Didn't you know that? And we've made you crazy too. But it's not too late. You can still get away. Now take that money and run as fast as you can."

"But I—"

"I know. You love me. And you've got a thrasher that works. And your mother's grave. Forget about it. Get as far away from here as you can while you've still got an ounce of sanity left."

"But I love you."

"Good. I'm glad to hear it. And you love Anne and you love Peter. Fine. And now that that's settled, will you please go away?"

"Go?"

"Before it's too late. And don't make me explain. Just go."

The sunburn on Royal's face began to consolidate itself into splotches on his jaw, his forehead, next to his mouth, the stings and bites it seemed of something burrowed inside the skin. The hair on the back of his head had begun to spring loose from whatever he'd used to slick it down. Even as Grady stared at him, another tuft sprang up as if the brain inside the skull had lost its hold and that one by one shocks of hair would pop out like the wires of a broken toy.

"How—how can I go—"

"You've got a car? You know how to drive?"

Royal shook his head as if he didn't have a car and didn't know how to drive. Grady funbled with her hand on the dresser and picked up a hairbrush, holding it as if it were a weapon she was going to use to beat him with. She started to say something, but slammed the brush down on top of the dresser instead. Slowly she moved her head from side to side and stepped toward him. She reached out her arms and brought him slowly toward herself. Royal raised both his arms from his sides and kept them outstretched. Grady kissed his lips. As he began lowering his arms Grady stepped back.

"Yes," she said. "I could love you. I could lie down with you on that bed, the same as you lie down with Anne and with Peter."

Royal started to raise his hand as if to block off her words, but Grady went on. "But then what?"

"You—you could love me? You?"

"Yes. And then I'd despise you."

"You—?"

"I'd loathe you." Her voice was firm now. "The same as Anne will loathe you and the same as Peter will loathe you."

"Loathe? But why?"

"Never mind why. Just take the money and get out. Go. Now. Right now!"

"But you won't tell me why!"

"I did tell you. I told you we've gone crazy. That's why. I'm crazy. They're crazy. But we won't always be crazy. It'll pass. And when it's gone—"

"But I want to know why!"

"All right, then. I'll tell you. Come here. Look at yourself in the mirror. Come on. Look."

Royal stepped in front of the mirror and looked down at the knobs on the dresser drawers.

"Now look. Go ahead. Look."

Royal raised his head and looked at himself in the mirror. Grady wanted to turn away, but she forced herself to look too. Their eyes didn't meet. Royal was staring only at himself, at his face.

"We've been hysterical," Grady said. "All of us. What we think is love is really a kind of panic. And so Peter grabbed you. And Anne grabbed you. And I could do the same, I swear it."

"You're not crazy!" Royal said.

"We are! Just look at yourself. If we weren't crazy, do you think we'd fall in love with *you*? With what you see there? Look! Look at yourself. You're not blind. But we are. We're blind. But it won't last. And when we can see again, when we're not crazy any more, we'll look at you and we'll despise you because we loved you. We'll loathe the sight of you. We'll have nothing but contempt for you because you could dare aspire to our love. We love you. I love you. They love you. But we won't always. Believe me, we won't. And when we don't anymore, we'll turn on you and tear you apart the same as if we were a pack of hounds. And if you don't believe me, just keep looking at yourself until you do. And then go. Now!" She grabbed up the money from the bed, plunged the wayward bundle back inside and bunched the pillowcase closed at the top. "Take this. Take it!"

Royal was still looking at himself in the mirror. Just as he started to reach up his hand to touch his cheek, Grady turned him around and pressed the pillowcase against him. He seemed unable to do anything but blink. She took first one of his arms and put it across the money, then the other arm. "And now you have to go," she said.

Royal blinked at her a few more times, then started toward the door. "Wait," Grady said. "Your hat." He stopped but didn't turn around. She put the hat on his head for him. After a moment, he took another step toward the door. He pressed the pillowcase closer to himself, lowered his head a little to touch the top of it with his chin, then raised his head and stared at the closed door in front of him. Grady reached over and opened it; then, after he'd left, she closed it behind him.

As she went toward the gate to the tractor lane that would lead across the fields, Grady heard a great growl and whine rise into the air, a grinding and shuddering of metal as if the tin roof of the barn was having a fit. She continued toward the gate, then stopped and went past the corner of the old pump house.

The boy was standing about ten feet away from the old machine, his back to her, his arms at his sides, his head tilted upward so that his hat touched the back of his collar. At his side, leaning against his right leg, was the pillowcase. In front of him, the thrasher rattled and shook itself like an awakened locomotive trying to rouse the countryside, to warn it of its rattletrap return. It groaned and growled; it rasped and whined; it shuddered at its own strength and quivered as if to shake off the slumbers of all those years.

Grady watched, stunned, naming to herself at last all the parts her grandfather had taught her but that she'd never seen in their awakened state: the sieve pans, the knives, the grain auger, the drum and the pit, the spout, the feeder, and the whirring, slapping belt that went from the drive wheel of the tractor to the master shaft of the thrasher.

Royal was not looking; he was listening. With his gangling body, the long arms, the bloused shirt stuffed into the baggy pants, the suspenders crossing his back like a Confederate flag, he looked like the last youth left behind by all those who had come and gone before. He alone could understand the lost language the thrasher spoke; he alone could hear its complaints and its commands. He was taking to himself all the thrasher said, a great instruction that he would always heed, that he would never forget.

Grady turned and went through the gate. It wasn't until she was over the second hill beyond the end of the tractor lane and walking alongside the upland pasture that she could no longer hear the clanking and the shuddering sounds.

21

The calf, a heifer, was already born when Grady got there. It
hadn't been that difficult a birth after all. The head, apparently,
had been too far front of the forelegs but Ned said he'd reached
in and shoved the head farther back and the calf had come out
at the right time without any real trouble. It was fine; Norma was
fine. Both were on their feet. The calf was nosing away at the
cow's udder, tugging at one of the teats as if only a certain amount
of time was allotted for this particular activity and it had better
make the most of it.

Ned had done most of the cleaning up and was putting fresh
hay into the calving stall, using his foot to make the distribution
more even. His right arm was shiny with a dried slime. Seeing it,
Grady caught the sickly sweet smell that came with calving, as if

the calf, to ensure that the mother would lick it clean, had come coated in sugar syrup. "I'm due for my first in about three weeks," she said. "Mabel comes fresh about then. But I don't expect any trouble that I can see. I've felt around and the head at least seems to be where it's supposed to be."

"Well, if you need any help—" The flies had found the calf and he shooed them off her rump.

"Oh, don't worry," Grady said. "I know where to come for help." She paused so she could lower her voice and mellow it just a bit. "It makes a big difference knowing I'm not all alone out here."

"Works both ways," he said. "Everyone needs help from time to time." With the toe of his shoe he nudged some hay under the standing cow. The calf, alarmed that this might be a signal that feeding time was almost up, snorted through her snout in protest.

"We're lucky, I guess." Grady leaned forward and patted Norma's spine, then petted it with her open hand. "To have each other, I mean."

"Guess so." Ned stood out in the litter alley and surveyed the stall. Grady stepped aside so he could enjoy an unobstructed view, then looked to see if she could spot anything left undone. She felt it would verify her credentials as farmer if she could suggest some further service to the cow and to the calf. But Ned, as usual, had thought of it all, had done it all.

Still, she had to say *something*. To just stand there would mean that she wasn't interested. And she *was* interested. "It's a good calf," she said.

It was a mistake. First of all, praising someone's animals, like praising someone's children, was a sneaky and at the same time too obvious a method of ingratiation. Surely she could have done better than that.

"Well, the hind legs aren't bad," Ned conceded, "but the pasterns in front aren't so good. I'll have to keep an eye on her.

If she doesn't improve pretty fast, in a couple of weeks, well, I'll just have to wait and see."

Ned, of course, was right. Grady should know a near hobbled calf when she saw one. She looked at the pasterns, the equivalent of wrists on the human arm. They were a little turned under. It could be a temporary condition but if it didn't correct itself with exercise the calf would, in effect, be walking on her wrists.

Grady considered reversing herself as if she'd finally seen this, thanks to Ned's instruction. But such a confession of previous ignorance was not allowed. The last thing she could admit to was a need for tutelage. And besides, she'd been hypocritical enough.

"Tell me what I can do to help." Now why hadn't she said that right away? She'd been rushing herself; she'd let Royal throw her off stride. And there was no need for anxiety of any kind, not at the moment anyway. Getting it settled with Ned Ryerson that they would eventually marry was like reaching an agreement over the shared use of machinery. It made sense. The benefits were obvious. The idea was no doubt mutual. All that was needed was the open acknowledgment itself. From both of them. And a few words could take care of that.

"Nothing," he said in answer to her question. "I guess that's about it. At least until your turn in a couple of weeks. Mandy, you said?"

"Mabel. But I don't expect any problems."

"I'll be there anyway. You haven't been around this for quite a while."

"It doesn't seem so long. Not really." She hesitated, then said, "It's almost like I was never away." When Ned offered neither confirmation nor contradiction, she went on. "I'm where I belong. Finally." Again she gave him the chance to say something, but he chose instead to reach down and make an unneeded tuft of some matted hay this side of the gutter. "I probably shouldn't have left in the first place."

Saying nothing, merely nodding, Ned started down the litter alley toward the milkhouse just to the right of the barn door. Grady followed. Two of the cows turned to note their passing, then went back to their evening ruminations. In the milkhouse Ned washed his hands and arms, the sweet smell faintly rising again only to be smothered for good by the soap scent of gardenia. Grady thought she caught a suggestion of Claire's presence in the choice of soap.

Ned, washing himself, looked so obedient, always doing what he'd been taught. His Hawaiian shirt was a pattern of pink jungle flowers and huge green leaves, the flowers trumpeting a panicked call for aid, for help in freeing themselves from the monstrous growth that threatened to devour them. Grady had thought the shirts were meant to cheer Claire, that after her death he'd return to the denims and khakis he'd worn most of his life, but apparently he'd either come to like them or thought he'd wear them until they were worn out, so as not to waste the initial investment. Anyway, he could use a little excitement in his life and, as far as Grady could see, the shirts were it.

Looking at him now, Grady could almost love him. And it occurred to her that she might have if she hadn't been so intent on her manipulations. If she hadn't put the barrier of her intrigues between them, she might genuinely have reached him, touched him, and found him wonderful. If she hadn't given all her energy, all her talents, to the service of her schemes, she might have seen him differently.

And with this thought came another. Royal Provo, too, could be loved. And one didn't have to be crazy to do it. She had been wrong. She had spoken to him with a pride and an arrogance that now appalled her. In quick succession, she saw him listening to the great machine, she saw him walking on his hands, she saw him ghostlike at the top of the hill, and with tears on his cheek because Martha was afraid she'd have to go live at The Home.

Grady wanted to leave, to go and find him. She must tell him how wrong she had been. She must tell him that she loved him as she did her daughters and her son and that she would never wound him for anything in the world. She must go to him immediately.

Ned scrubbed cold water onto his face, then dried his hands by rubbing them through his sand-colored hair. Water had splashed all down the front of his shirt, making the leaves darker, more somber, and the pink flowers paler, more frail.

When Grady started to speak, to tell Ned that she was leaving, she found herself saying instead, "Of course I'm lucky." Apparently she was leading into a farewell and would get to it momentarily. But then she said, "I've got this second chance to come back and start over. Not everyone gets a second chance, but I did, didn't I?"

She had taken up again what was almost her prepared speech. Grady realized she had decided to go ahead with her original plan, then leave. It seemed to make some kind of sense. Settle with Ned what had to be settled, then go home and settle what had to be settled there. But she had to hurry.

Ned was rolling the barn door open wider. "We really should get married," she said. "Don't you think?" The door rumbled along the track. There was a momentary squeal halfway, then the only noise it made was a slight banging as it wobbled into its slot. Grady stepped outside, clear of the door. Ned slowly closed it, passing even more slowly over the place where it would squeal. It squealed anyway, and longer this time. Grady waited for the rumbling to stop, then she said, "Eventually, I mean. When it's right." She sighed a little to indicate that what she was saying was mildly boring because it was all so obvious.

"It makes sense," she said. "All the sense in the world." She began to wish he'd say something. That was one of the troubles with shy people. They made you do all the work. Well, she thought, why not. She'd taken on the responsibility and she'd see it through.

Ned had taken a few steps down toward the house, but stopped so she could come up alongside him. "At least it makes sense to me," she said. They were strolling down the slope. Ahead of them the locust trees rose to their great height like columns from an ancient ruin. Their branches seemed to spring from crevices in the cracked stone. It had always seemed strange to Grady that these oldest of trees, gaunt and gray, could send out the freshest, most delicate leaves, no bigger than her thumb, more like an outcropping from the crumbled capital than the sproutings of a living tree.

Ned, no doubt, had chosen the locust grove as the proper setting for the matter at hand. He'd always had a romantic streak in him, even when they were children, although he did his best to hide it. In times of difficulty it was his romantic side that could be reached and touched most readily. An appeal properly targeted in that direction seldom missed its mark. Grady must keep that in mind.

Ned said nothing nor did he turn to look at her. She had no intention of saying anything more until he'd said what she knew he'd say. The walk toward the house, toward the trees, had calmed her. There was no hurry. She could take her time; they could both take their time.

At the foot of the slope, only halfway to the trees, Ned stopped. Grady wondered if she should reach over and touch him, just in case he needed a little extra coaxing for what he was about to say. She decided not to.

"I know how you feel about me, Grady," he said. His voice was pitched upward as if he wanted to avoid the gravel sound that usually hoarsened his lower tones. "I know how you've always felt about me," he went on. "And you probably know how—well—how much I've thought about it."

"Yes," Grady said. "I think I know."

"I know," he continued, "that you've always been in love with me, and I know it's probably always going to be that way." Grady was stunned, too stunned to say anything. Ned continued. "I knew right away that's why you came back here after what happened to Andy. And I don't blame you for it. I've always liked you. Even if you do a lot of dumb things. Like stay in love with me like this all your life."

Grady wanted to cringe, to close in on herself. She was mortally embarrassed, but for him. He had it all wrong. *He* was the one who had always been in love with *her.* She'd never loved him. She didn't now. She never would, not in a million years.

"I know," he went on, "I know what you mean about it making sense, with the farms and all. But you should know better than to think that would work now if it never worked before. If I was going to marry you, wouldn't I have done it instead of Andy Durant?"

"Instead of Andy—?"

"Oh come on, Grady, get over it. You've loved me long enough and I've appreciated it. But I can't go on feeling sorry for you forever. And I can't let you—well—I hate to say it, but I have to—I can't keep trying to make you feel better, like that time in the barn when you first got back. I didn't mind then. I'm not without feelings. I do feel sorry for you. But you can't expect me to go on—accommodating—you with no end in sight."

Grady no longer felt herself getting smaller. On the contrary, she was growing. And she would keep on growing. She would balloon. She would expand. Soon she would tower over him. She would crush him. Like a bug, like a worm. He would be obliterated. He would be squashed into the ground with one quick grind of her foot. This puny man with the Hawaiian shirt; this runt on whom she'd spent so much pity, so much concern. He'd had his say; now it was her turn. And what she would say would be the truth. "Apparently you've made a mistake," she began.

"Oh, Grady—"

"Don't interrupt. You're wrong. Love had nothing to do with it. I never loved you. It was the farms—"

"Yes, yes, I knew you'd say that. And when I thought about it I was tempted to pretend I believed it. But we've got to face the truth."

"But I don't love you—"

"All right, all right. You don't love me. Say it if you want to. Tell me it was just common sense about the farms. If it helps you to insist on it, well, I can't stop you."

"But I never loved—"

"I told you all right. You never loved me. If that's the way you want it—"

"It's the way it is!"

"All right, all right. Whatever you say."

Grady considered punching him. Then punching him again. In the stomach, in the face, in the arm, wrestling him to the ground and pinning him there until he'd recognized and admitted the truth. But it was hopeless and she knew it. When she'd get him down on the ground he'd probably say, "See? I told you this is what you always come here for."

He was looking over toward the locust grove again, trying to remember if there was anything else he should say. He had stiffened his jaw and seemed to be holding his breath, puffing out the flesh just above his upper lip, the same expression Grady had seen on his face when they were both vaccinated. He was steeled against the moment, knowing it would pass. Finally, his face relaxed and he lowered his head. He examined a rock next to his left foot before looking again at Grady. His voice now was pitched even higher, but in an attempt to make it seem lower, he spoke in a whisper.

"And besides, I'm going under, Grady. I can't hold out. Not

anymore. I belong to the bank and they've given me one more year to play being farmer."

"You?"

"Me, you, everybody. It's all over, Grady. If you came back for anything except for sentimental reasons, a few years for old time's sake, forget it."

"But you're the best—"

"I'm finished. One more year. Two at the most. Then it'll be your turn. And don't even think you'll be able to go back to Coble. When the farms go, the small towns go. We're going to have nothing and be nowhere. So get yourself ready."

"Never. I'm debt free and I'm going to stay debt free."

"Sure you're debt free, but not for long, no matter what."

"Who says so?"

"I do. For one thing, your herd's too small to support your farm. You need more land before you can take on more animals, and where are you going to get it? Too bad you can't buy back your twenty acres. I could use the cash and you could use the fields."

"Maybe—maybe you'll lease them to me. Maybe I could afford that much."

"Sorry. For the little I'd get leasing I'm better off hanging on to it, using it for my own herd. Too bad Andy got himself killed before we closed our deal."

Ned kept right on walking, but Grady stopped. "Deal? What deal? You had a deal with Andy?"

Ned kept right on walking, so Grady followed. "Andy never told you?" he asked.

"Told me what?"

"That he planned to buy back those twenty acres. It was when he was doing those articles for the newspaper about how all the farms were going under. I was one of the first ones he talked to. I told him I wished you and he could buy back the twenty. He asked me to give him six months, he'd get the money. He actually wanted the two of you to come back and farm, he was that nutty. Even nutty enough to get himself killed trying."

Again Grady stopped. This time, Ned, after a few paces, stopped too. "You never knew?" he asked.

"I know now."

Ned started walking again, but Grady stayed where she was. "Ned?"

"Yes?"

"If I— If I was able to get the money now, would you sell?"

"Why? Have you got it after all?"

"I might be able to get it. Or most of it."

"If you're thinking about the bank, don't do it. Keep clear."

"No. Not the bank. But maybe I could still get it together. Would you sell?"

"Of course I'd sell."

"That's all I need to know." Grady turned and started toward the gate that would lead across the fields.

"Grady! Wait!"

"I can't. I have to hurry."

As she crossed the fields, Grady kept saying to herself, "Of course he'll give me back the money. I told him I was crazy, didn't I? Didn't I?"

Royal's car was gone but his clothes were still in the bunkhouse. There was no sign of the pillowcase with the money. It was when she was crossing the barnyard that Grady first noticed what seemed like soiled snow dusting the ground, tiny particles of dull silver tinged with green. She turned and went quickly behind the pump house, to the thrasher. There was the emptied pillowcase hanging limply from a stalk of ragweed. Royal had indeed made the thrasher "go." And he had found his way of testing it. It was the money she saw, cut into these dingy snowflakes, blown and scattered along the ground and in the grass.

As she stood there, a wind came up from the southwest, sending a light swirl of gray and green and silver dust playing around her feet.

It was the money Andy had died to get her. She looked from the ground to the thrasher and then out over the weeds that stretched away from the pump house.

After she picked the pillowcase from the ragweed stalk, she started toward the thrasher, stumbling twice. When she reached it, she put her forehead against the drum. And then she began to cry because her husband Andy had died and she had left him all alone.

22

As Royal walked along the shoreline of the lake, sometimes in the water up to his ankles, sometimes on a narrow sandy stretch, sometimes on the grass, the reflected glow of the amusement park behind him began to dim and he could see now the outline of the island toward the east. Twice a dog had barked. Once he thought he heard voices murmuring somewhere near a stand of willows, and about half a mile down from the park he had seen a family with two children and three grownups staring silently into the embers of a barbecue grill. He walked past a pier where a motorboat was docked and through a front yard where a small tent had been pitched under what looked, in the lights coming from the house, like a silver maple.

He was indifferent to what was about to happen. His death was

no great determination, no anguished decision. The notion had
come into his head when Mrs. Durant had refused to come and
see the thrasher. There seemed, since then, to be no quarrel
against his dying. It hadn't been the truths she'd spoken about
the eventual loathing that would be heaped upon him. With no
trouble at all he gave full assent to all she'd said. He had known
from the beginning that anything given would sooner or later be
taken away. He had long since schooled himself to that expectation. They would loathe him for his pretensions to their love, and
justly so. That much he understood. He had seen his body, this
instrument, this agent of his yearning, and he had seen as well its
pale mockery of all the splendors he was so eager to have it bestow.
And it wasn't just Mrs. Durant going to Ned Ryerson that had
brought him to the shore of the lake. It was her refusal to come
and see the thrasher. The thrasher was his gift. It would have
proclaimed his superiority over them all and this would have
sustained him through the loss of love and even through the
predicted scorn. But she had said no and it was at that moment
that the acceptance to which he had been summoned was re-
scinded, and the promised loathing began its slow, inexorable
crawl toward his helpless, transfixed body. It was as if that single
word had released in him a chemical that efficiently neutralized
all opposition to what he was about to do. It wasn't so much that
he wanted to die; he simply knew of no reason not to. Perhaps
the idea had always been with him like an incipient disease and
now his immunities had been voided. His dying was free to
advance without impediment. And so calming, so pervasive was
its presence that he could not imagine ever having known any
other resolve.

When he'd passed through the amusement park he had heard
the riders on the roller coaster screaming and shrieking at the
plunge. Their terror almost amused him now. He remembered his
own fear of heights, especially the day with Anne and Peter at the
gorge. It seemed that his reluctance to leap had been absurd. The

urge to give up all control, the lure of abandoning himself completely—he should have done it then. He would have been free, but freedom had frightened him. It didn't now. He listened for his own great cry of surrender, lessening as he fell, farther and farther from the narrow ledge, the faint echoes taken up by the rocks and stones. But he heard nothing. Everything here at the water's edge was still, and he was content at last.

Halfway into the bend of a deserted cove where some stunted trees came right down to the shore, Royal stopped and looked out toward the island. A breeze had come up and the tiniest of waves soaked into his pants just above the top of his work shoes. The water was warm in the night air. He walked out to where it touched the tips of his fingers, paused, then stepped out farther until it reached his waist. The bottom was slightly muddy but there seemed to be firm sand underneath. He raised his arms and continued until the water was up to his chest. Then, bending forward, he slipped his arms under the surface and began to swim.

His shirt and pants were sucked onto his skin and the swimming was easy. Even his work shoes didn't seem to have that much weight as he drew himself forward, his arms making long graceful reaches ahead of him. Then the water must have become deeper; it was more difficult to stay on top. To compensate, he worked his arms more, forcing them to pull harder each time he made a forward stroke. They began to feel heavy, they were harder to lift, to send up ahead of him, to draw him on, but still he insisted on their being graceful and easy.

Then he became aware of a pull from below. It was the weight of his work shoes. The shoes had made the water deeper, the shoes had tired his arms. Their pull became more insistent. This was not what he had expected. He didn't want to be dragged down, not this way. He had hoped for ease and grace and indifference. He looped down into the water to find the shoes, to untie them, to get himself free of their weight.

As if they knew he was after them, the shoes, even before he could find them, began to kick, struggling away from him. Royal too began thrashing in the water, seaching for them, trying to grab hold. His arms brushed the coarse cloth of his pants, one shoe kicked against the other leg, his head touched his knee, his hand hit against his cheek.

He thrashed even harder, but now it was no longer the shoes he was struggling against. It wasn't the shoes that were dragging him down, it wasn't the shoes that fought their way out of his grasp. It was Anne, it was Peter. They wouldn't let him untie his shoes. He struggled against them, choking, gasping. They, in turn, tugged and pulled, tangling themselves into his arms and legs, dragging him deeper. He lashed out, brutally beating the water with all the fury he could find. He hated them. Never had he hated as he hated now. A new energy was given to him by a rage he'd never known before. He had always hated, not only them but everyone, everything. Hatred had fueled his whole life; it had never been different from what it was now.

He had been betrayed. The water had betrayed him. It had delivered him to Anne and Peter and he would never be free. He looped and dived and surfaced, thrashing and twisting, but they wouldn't let go.

Could they, too, be trying to untie his shoes? Could they have come only to help? He couldn't be sure, but he begged that this be so. And it became now the one hope of all his life. He wanted not to hate them. He had loved them. He begged to be allowed to love them again. But already his rage had spilled beyond them and it seemed to have no end. He would never feel anything else, only this. With all the strength he had left, he grabbed at the water. He shoved at it with his feet. His hatred was choking him. He couldn't breathe. He gasped for air but violence rushed in, overflowing his mouth, gagging his lungs, flooding his brain until he knew his skull would burst.

Now it was not even a fight for air. His thrashings were a

struggle between his hatred and his hope. With his last strength he pulled his way to the open air. With what was left in his lungs he called for rescue. He cried out for release from the hatred that was choking him, that was dragging him down. But he screamed a word that he'd never called before, a word he hadn't even known was there. "Daddy!" It was a cry demanding and suppliant at the same time. Never before had the word come to his lips in a moment of need; it surprised him that it was there, waiting. "Daddy!" he screamed again. More violently than before he flailed the water, but now it was so that his father could see him, so that he would know where he was, so that he could be found.

He called again, but this time the word was gulped back down his throat before he could send it out into the air. He tried again but could only swallow. And when he tried once more, no word came.

And then his father heard him. Royal couldn't see him but he knew that he was there. He floated quietly to where his son was and took him into his arms. Gently he rocked him back and forth, up and down. And here Royal's struggle ended. He let himself be held; he surrendered to this tenderness. His father had come just in time. His own strength was gone. Silently his hatred was lifted from him; he was freed from all his hopes. He could feel himself enveloped in his father's hold, still slowly moving, still rocking, up and down, as together they glided, floated toward the island through the bright, bright water.

23

They buried Royal Provo in the cemetery outside Coble two days after his drowning. Grady gave him her grave, the plot next to Andy where she'd thought she herself might one day lie.

Peter he had made his heir. On the windshield of his car—which he'd left at the amusement park—was a note saying "This car and the suitcase under the bunk belong to Peter Durant," and it was signed "Royal Provo, Esq." When Peter was told about Royal's death, and the note, he went out and climbed to the roof of the bunkhouse and refused to come down. When Grady called up to him, he wouldn't answer. He wouldn't even look at her. It was only later that night, or early the next morning, when she heard him in the kitchen, that she knew he'd come down. She got out of bed, went to the kitchen door and asked if he was hungry. He said no; he was already eating some leftover green beans. He didn't want anything else. Grady left him alone but she could hear his sobs before she got back up the stairs.

Martha had been less private with her grief. She had put her head down on the kitchen table and cried. She had buried her face in the cushions of the couch and cried. She had wrapped her arms around her mother's thighs and cried into her stomach. She had hugged Raggles and cried. She had sat on the back steps, her head down on her folded arms and cried.

At first Anne refused to come home for the funeral, but she appeared at the house just before they were leaving for the service, brought by a young man she introduced as the archery instructor. It seemed the young man was going to accompany her to the funeral, but when she went back out to his car, she told him to drive himself back to the camp instead. She herself wouldn't return. She would stay home now. She then went over to Peter and asked him if he was all right. He said he was and she told him she liked his necktie.

Few people came to the funeral and even fewer to the grave. When the last prayers were being said, Grady saw Guy Duskin. He was on the ridge that ran along the edge of the cemetery, among the poplars. He stood there, more sentry than mourner, as if on guard from the heights over his son's grave. After the last words were finished, Grady reached down to the mound of earth where the undertaker had placed the flowers that had been sent to the funeral home. It was her idea to take a single flower and place it on the coffin, giving Guy time to come to the grave. She picked a peach-colored gladiolus, getting some mud on her fingers from the earth wet with the night's rain. She noticed how many flowers there were, roses and gladioli, chrysanthemums and a wreath of forget-me-nots, a heap large enough to cover the entire mound of dug earth. She realized that the undertaker, who'd buried a town supervisor earlier in the day, had appropriated some of his flowers and given them to Royal instead, so that the dirt from the opened grave could be covered completely. The phrase that came to Grady's mind was not "to bury the dead" but "to clothe the naked," and, as she placed the gladiolus on the coffin, she said a prayer, not for Royal, but for the man who had performed this final work of mercy.

Grady waited another moment, but Guy had made no move. "Go on to the car," Grady said to Peter and Anne. "I'll be right there."

"I can stay here with you," Peter said, staring at the flower his mother had set down.

"No. Go on to the car. I'll be there in a minute."

Peter turned away and Anne followed with Martha. Alone, Grady waited, wishing she could at least occupy her time with a prayer, but nothing came. When she looked up again, Guy was gone. She waited another moment, then turned and started to follow the others.

When she reached the path, everyone had already disappeared beyond the hedge that lined the road to the gate. Grady turned once more to see the grave. To her left, a gray-haired woman in yellow shorts and a black tanktop worked over the ground with a trowel, busily breaking up the clumps of earth with an impatient hand as if she was getting ready to put in radishes and onions.

On another path, a teenage boy carried a flower pot with a single geranium; he walked fast and looked from side to side as if searching for some place to dump it.

A rotating sprinkler flung out its spray like confetti, while another, a long perforated pipe, moved back and forth in a wide slow arc, bowing down first to one row of graves and then to another like a supplicant beseeching two different gods.

Guy Duskin had come to the grave. He seemed to be studying the flowers, touching them with his fingertips, rearrangeing them slightly on the mounded earth. Grady watched a moment, then lifted her eyes. She surveyed the whole expanse spread out beneath her, this planting of stones fitted into the rise and fall of a few gentle hills. The graves were marked with flags, remnants from Memorial Day last spring. A wind had come up, unfurling them so that they slapped outward again and again, trying to connect with something more substantial than air. But the flags were white. The rain, the summer sun, the weather, had done their work, fading them to these bleached banners of the dead, these signals of surrender.

Guy had moved closer to the coffin. Grady started down the incline toward him. When she was about thirty feet from him, he saw her. He jerked his body, tensing it like an animal about to flee. Grady thought she should call out to him or possibly make some motion with her hand, but before she could decide, a clump of mud hit her right shoulder. Another landed on her skirt, then one on her side. He was throwing dirt at her with all his strength.

"I never helped him," he cried. "I never did anything for him!"

Grady stopped. Now the flowers too, mixed with the mud, came at her. "He was mine," Guy called, "and I never did anything!" A chrysanthemum grazed her cheek and the thorns from a rose scratched her arm. "Nothing! Never! Never!"

Grady made no move; she neither turned nor held out her hands. With each throw now he made only a grunting sound, almost a sob, as if he were the one being hit. Some of the dirt hit her face, blinding her eyes. She raised her hand, then lowered it and let the mud fall onto her nose, onto her mouth and chin. She could see again.

He was standing about four feet from her, between herself and the grave. His face was slack, emptied of everything. His mouth was slightly open as if it had just discovered that there was no word for what it had to say. He seemed to have been caught at a moment of wounding and could now only wait dumbly for the knowledge of its cause. He took a step toward her and tried to raise his hand, but couldn't. Without turning his gaze away, in a voice low and quiet, he said, "Can't I come now, and live with you?"

Grady looked at him, then at the graves beyond. There were Andy Durant and Royal Provo, given over to the ground forever. She had loved them both and she had participated in both their deaths. Because she would not surrender herself, now or ever, to the contentments of sorrow or to the strictures of guilt, she slowly reached out her hand. Grief and remorse would be with her always, but she refused the easy solitude to which they invited her. She would take up again—and again—the chaos of all that was ignorant in her, of all that was inadequate. "Yes," she said, her voice more quiet than his, "I think you'd better come live with me."

She went to his side and took hold of his arm. A small chunk of mud fell from her shoulder onto his sleeve. Slowly she led him away as if he were a man enfeebled and confused.

At the top of the rise, she turned for one final backward glance. She saw no one cauled in black, there was no vanished hired hand come to claim his stewardship. She saw only earth and flowers and stone. But she knew that Andy was there and Royal too; she knew as well that they would be with her, in her heart, in her soul, forever, not as a benign presence but as bewildered, questioning ghosts. Still, she was grateful that they would find there a place in which to dwell.

As she and Guy continued toward the path, the flags snapped the air, clutching at them as they passed.

CRAVING THE FORBIDDEN

CRAVING THE FORBIDDEN

BY

INDIA GREY

For my blog readers
with thanks for listening, sharing
and making me smile.

CHAPTER ONE

'LADIES and gentlemen, welcome aboard the 16.22 East Coast Mainline service from King's Cross to Edinburgh. This train will be calling at Peterborough, Stevenage...'

Heart hammering against her ribs from the mad, last-minute dash down the platform carrying a bag that was about to burst at the seams, Sophie Greenham leaned against the wall of the train and let out a long exhalation of relief.

She had made it.

Of course, the relief was maybe a little misplaced given that she'd come straight from the casting session for a vampire film and was still wearing a black satin corset dress that barely covered her bottom and high-heeled black boots that were rather more vamp than vampire. But the main thing was she had caught the train and wouldn't let Jasper down. She'd just have to keep her coat on to avoid getting arrested for indecent exposure.

Not that she'd want to take it off anyway, she thought grimly, wrapping it more tightly around her as the train gave a little lurch and began to move. For weeks now the snow had kept falling from a pewter-grey sky and the news headlines had been dominated by The Big Freeze. Paris had been just as bad, although there the snow *looked* cleaner, but when Sophie had left her little rented apartment two days ago there had been a thick layer of ice on the inside of the windows.

She seemed to have been cold for an awfully long time.

It was getting dark already. The plate-glass windows of the office blocks backing onto the railway line spilled light out onto the grimy snow. The train swayed beneath her, changing tracks and catching her off guard so that she tottered on the stupid high-heeled boots and almost fell into an alarmed-looking student on his way back from the buffet car. She really should go and find a loo to change into something more respectable, but now she'd finally stopped rushing she was overwhelmed with tiredness. Picking up her bag, she hoisted it awkwardly into the nearest carriage.

Her heart sank. It was instantly obvious that every

seat was taken, and the aisle was cluttered with shopping bags and briefcases and heavy winter coats stuffed under seats. Muttering apologies as she staggered along, trying not to knock cardboard cartons of coffee out of the hands of commuters with her bag, she made her way into the next carriage.

It was just as bad as the last one. The feeling of triumph she'd had when she'd made it onto the train in time ebbed slowly away as she moved from one carriage to the next, apologising as she went, until finally she came to one that was far less crowded.

Sophie's aching shoulders dropped in relief. And tensed again as she took in the strip of plush carpet, the tiny lights on the tables, the superior upholstery with the little covers over the headrests saying 'First Class'.

Pants.

It was occupied almost entirely by businessmen who didn't bother to look up from their laptops and newspapers as she passed. Until her mobile rang. Her ringtone—'Je Ne Regrette Rien'—had seemed wittily ironic in Paris, but in the hushed carriage it lost some of its charm. Holding the handles of her bag together in one hand while she scrabbled in the pocket of her coat with the other and tried to stop it falling open to reveal the wardrobe horror beneath, she was aware of heads turning, eyes looking up at her over the tops of glasses and from behind broadsheets. In desperation she hitched her bag onto the nearest table and pulled the phone from her pocket just in time to see Jean-Claude's name on the screen.

Pants again.

A couple of months ago she would have had a very different reaction, she thought, hastily pressing the button to reject the call. But then a couple of months ago her image of Jean-Claude as a free-spirited Parisian artist had been intact. He'd seemed so aloof when she'd first seen him, delivering paintings to the set of the film she was working on. Aloof and glamorous. Not someone you could ever imagine being suffocating or possessive or…

Nope. She wasn't going to think about the disaster that had been her latest romantic adventure.

She sat down in the nearest seat, suddenly too tired to go any further. You couldn't keep moving for ever, she told herself with a stab of bleak humour. In the seat opposite there was yet another businessman, hidden behind a large newspaper that he'd thoughtfully folded so that the horoscopes were facing her.

Actually, he wasn't *entirely* hidden; she could see his hands, holding the newspaper—tanned, long-fingered, strong-looking. Not the hands of a businessman, she thought abstractly, tearing her gaze away and looking for Libra. 'Be prepared to work hard to make a good impression,' she read. 'The full moon on the 20th is a perfect opportunity to let others see you for who you really are.'

Hell. It was the twentieth today. And while she was prepared to put on an Oscar-worthy performance to impress Jasper's family, the last thing she wanted was for them to see her for who she really was.

At that moment Edith Piaf burst into song again. She groaned—why couldn't Jean-Claude take a hint? Quickly she went to shut Edith up and turn her phone off but at that moment the train swayed again and her finger accidentally hit the 'answer' button instead. A second later Jean-Claude's Merlot-marinated voice was clearly audible, to her and about fifteen businessmen.

'Sophie? Sophie, where are you—?'

She thought quickly, cutting him off before he had

a chance to get any further. 'Hello, you haf reached the voicemail service for Madame Sofia, astrologist and reader of cards,' she purred, shaking her hair back and narrowing her eyes at her own reflection in the darkening glass of the window. 'Eef you leaf your name, number and zodiac sign, I get back to you with information on what the fates haf in store for you—'

She stopped abruptly, losing her thread, a kick of electricity jolting through her as she realised she was staring straight into the reflected eyes of the man sitting opposite.

Or rather that, from behind the newspaper, *he* was staring straight into *her* eyes. His head was lowered, his face ghostly in the glass, but his dark eyes seemed to look straight into her.

For a second she was helpless to do anything but look back. Against the stark white of his shirt his skin was tanned, which seemed somehow at odds with his stern, ascetic face. It was the face of a medieval knight in a Pre-Raphaelite painting— beautiful, bloodless, remote.

In other words, absolutely not her type.

'Sophie—is zat you? I can 'ardly 'ear you. Are you

on Eurostar? Tell me what time you get in and I meet you at Gare du Nord.'

Oops, she'd forgotten all about Jean-Claude. Gathering herself, she managed to drag her gaze away from the reflection in the window and her attention back to the problem quite literally in hand. She'd better just come clean, or he'd keep ringing for the whole weekend she was staying with Jasper's family and rather ruin her portrayal of the sweet, starry-eyed girlfriend.

'I'm not on the Eurostar, no,' she said carefully. 'I'm not coming back tonight.'

'*Alors*, when?' he demanded. 'The painting—I need you here. I need to see your skin—to feel it, to capture contrast with lily petals.'

'Nude with Lilies' was the vision Jean-Claude claimed had come to him the moment he'd first noticed her in a bar in the Marais, near where they'd been filming. Jasper had been over that weekend and thought it was hilarious. Sophie, hugely flattered to be singled out and by Jean-Claude's extravagant compliments about her 'skin like lily petals' and 'hair like flames', had thought being painted would be a highly erotic experience.

The reality had turned out to be both extremely

cold and mind-numbingly boring. Although, if Jean-Claude's gaze had aroused a similar reaction to that provoked by the eyes of the man in the glass, it would have been a very different story...

'Oh, dear. Maybe you could just paint in a few more lilies to cover up the skin?' She bit back a breathless giggle and went on kindly, 'Look, I don't know when I'll be back, but what we had wasn't meant to be for ever, was it? Really, it was just sex—'

Rather fittingly, at that point the train whooshed into a tunnel and the signal was lost. Against the blackness beyond the window the reflected interior of the carriage was bright, and for the briefest moment Sophie caught the eye of the man opposite and knew he'd been looking at her again. The grey remains of the daylight made the reflection fade before she had time to read the expression on his face, but she was left in no doubt that it had been disapproving.

And in that second she was eight years old again, holding her mother's hand and aware that people were staring at them, judging them. The old humiliation flared inside her as she heard her mother's voice inside her head, strident with indignation.

Just ignore them, Summer. We have as much right to be here as anyone else...

'Sophie?'

'Yes,' she said, suddenly subdued. 'Sorry, Jean-Claude. I can't talk about this now. I'm on the train and the signal isn't very good.'

'*D'accord.* I call you later.'

'No! You can't call me *at all* this weekend. I—I'm…working, and you know I can't take my phone on set. Look, I'll call you when I get back to London on Monday. We can talk properly then.'

That was a stupid thing to say, she thought wearily as she turned her phone off. There was nothing to talk *about*. What she and Jean-Claude had shared had been fun, that was all. Fun. A romantic adventure in wintry Paris. Now it had reached its natural conclusion and it was time to move on.

Again.

Shoving her phone back into her pocket, she turned towards the window. Outside it was snowing again and, passing through some anonymous town, Sophie could see the flakes swirling fatly in the streetlamps and obliterating the footprints on the pavements, and rows of neat houses, their curtains shut against the winter evening. She imagined the people behind them; families slumped together in front of the TV, arguing cosily over the remote control, couples cuddled up on the sofa sharing a Friday evening bottle of wine, united against the cold world outside.

A blanket of depression settled on her at these mental images of comfortable domesticity. It was a bit of a sore point at the moment. Returning from Paris she'd discovered that, in her absence, her flat-mate's boyfriend had moved in and the flat had been turned into the headquarters of the Blissful Couples Society. The atmosphere of companion-able sluttishness in which she and Jess had existed, cluttering up the place with make-up and laundry and trashy magazines, had vanished. The flat was immaculate, and there were new cushions on the sofa and candles on the kitchen table.

Jasper's SOS phone call, summoning her up to his family home in Northumberland to play the part of his girlfriend for the weekend, had come as a huge relief. But this was the way it was going to be, she thought sadly as the town was left behind and the train plunged onwards into darkness again. Everyone pairing up, until she was the only single person left, the only one who actively didn't want a relationship or commitment. Even Jasper was showing worrying signs of swapping late nights and dancing for cosy evenings in as things got serious with Sergio.

But why have serious when you could have *fun*?

Getting abruptly to her feet, she picked up her bag and hoisted it onto the luggage rack above her head. It wasn't easy, and she was aware as she pushed and shoved that not only was the hateful dress riding up, but her coat had also fallen open, no doubt giving the man in the seat opposite an eyeful of straining black corset and an indecent amount of thigh. Prickling all over with embarrassment, she glanced at his reflection in the window.

He wasn't looking at her at all. His head was tipped back against the seat, his face completely blank and remote as he focused on the newspaper. Somehow his indifference felt even more hurtful than his disapproving scrutiny earlier. Pulling her coat closed, she sat down again, but as she did so her knee grazed his thigh beneath the table.

She froze, and a shower of glowing sparks shimmered through her.

'Sorry,' she muttered, yanking her legs away from his and tucking them underneath her on the seat.

Slowly the newspaper was lowered, and she found herself looking at him directly for the first time. The impact of meeting his eyes in glassy reflection had been powerful enough, but looking directly into them was like touching a live wire. They weren't brown, as she'd thought, but the grey of cold Northern seas, heavy-lidded, fringed with thick, dark lashes, compelling enough to distract her for a moment from the rest of his face.

Until he smiled.

A faint ghost of a smile that utterly failed to melt the ice in his eyes, but did draw her attention down to his mouth…

'No problem. As this is First Class you'd think there'd be enough legroom, wouldn't you?'

His voice was low and husky, and so sexy that her spirits should have leapt at the prospect of spending the next four hours in close confinement with him. However, the slightly scornful emphasis he placed on the words 'first' and 'class' and the way he was looking at her as if she were a caterpillar on the chef's salad in some swanky restaurant cancelled out his physical attractiveness.

She had issues with people who looked at her like that.

'Absolutely,' she agreed, with that upper-class self-assurance that gave the people who genuinely possessed it automatic admittance to anywhere. 'Shocking, really.' And then with what she hoped was utter insouciance she turned up the big collar of her shabby military-style coat, settled herself more comfortably in her seat and closed her eyes.

Kit Fitzroy put down the newspaper.

Usually when he was on leave he avoided reading reports about the situation he'd left behind; somehow the heat and the sand and the desperation never quite came across in columns of sterile black and white. He'd bought the newspaper to catch up on normal things like rugby scores and racing news, but had ended up reading all of it in an attempt to obliterate the image of the girl sitting opposite him, which seemed to have branded itself onto his retinas.

It hadn't worked. Even the laughably inaccurate report of counter-terrorist operations in the Middle East hadn't stopped him being aware of her.

It was hardly surprising, he thought acidly. He'd spent the last four months marooned in the desert with a company made up entirely of men, and he was still human enough to respond to a girl wearing stiletto boots and the briefest bondage dress beneath a fake army coat. Especially one with a husky nightclub singer's voice who actually seemed to be complaining to the lovesick fool on the other end of the phone that all she'd wanted was casual sex.

After the terrible sombreness of the ceremony he'd just attended her appearance was like a swift shot of something extremely potent.

He suppressed a rueful smile.

Potent, if not particularly sophisticated.

He let his gaze move back to her. She had fallen asleep as quickly and neatly as a cat, her legs tucked up beneath her, a slight smile on her raspberry-pink lips, as if she was dreaming of something amusing. She had a sweep of black eyeliner on her upper lids, flicking up at the outside edges, which must be what gave her eyes their catlike impression.

He frowned. No—it wasn't just that. It was their striking green too. He could picture their exact shade—the clear, cool green of new leaves—even now, when she was fast asleep.

If she really was asleep. When it came to deception Kit Fitzroy's radar was pretty accurate, and this girl had set it off from the moment she'd appeared. But there was something about her now that convinced him that she wasn't faking this. It wasn't just how still she was, but that the energy that had crackled around her before had vanished. It was like a light going out. Like the sun going in, leaving shadows and a sudden chill.

Sleep—the reward of the innocent. Given the shamelessness with which she'd just lied to her boyfriend it didn't seem fair, especially when it eluded him so cruelly. But it had wrapped her in a cloak of complete serenity, so that just looking at her, just watching the lock of bright coppery hair that had fallen across her face stir with each soft, steady breath made him aware of the ache of exhaustion in his own shoulders.

'Tickets, please.'

The torpor that lay over the warm carriage was disturbed by the arrival of the guard. There was a ripple of activity as people roused themselves to open briefcases and fumble in suit pockets. On the opposite side of the table the girl's sooty lashes didn't even flutter.

She was older than he'd first thought, Kit saw now, older than the ridiculous teenage get-up would suggest—in her mid-twenties perhaps? Even so, there was something curiously childlike about her. If you ignored the creamy swell of her cleavage against the laced bodice of her dress, anyway.

And he was doing his best to ignore it.

The guard reached them, his bland expression changing to one of deep discomfort when he looked down and saw her. His tongue flicked nervously across his lips and he raised his hand, shifting from foot to foot as he reached uneasily down to wake her.

'Don't.'

The guard looked round, surprised. He wasn't the only one, Kit thought. Where had that come from? He smiled blandly.

'It's OK. She's with me.'

'Sorry, sir. I didn't realise. Do you have your tickets?'

'No.' Kit flipped open his wallet. 'I—*we*—had been planning to travel north by plane.'

'Ah, I see, sir. The weather has caused quite a disruption to flights, I understand. That's why the train is so busy this evening. Is it a single or a return you want?'

'Return.' Hopefully the airports would be open

again by Sunday, but he wasn't taking any chances. The thought of being stuck indefinitely at Alnburgh with his family in residence was unbearable.

'Two returns—to Edinburgh?'

Kit nodded absently and as the guard busied himself with printing out the tickets he looked back at the sleeping girl again. He was damned certain she didn't have a first-class ticket and that, in spite of the almost-convincing posh-girl accent, she wouldn't be buying one if she was challenged. So why had he not just let the guard wake her up and move her on? It would have made the rest of the journey better for him. More legroom. More peace of mind.

Kit Fitzroy had an inherent belief in his duty to look out for people who didn't have the same privileges that he had. It was what had got him through officer training and what kept him going when he was dropping with exhaustion on patrol, or when he was walking along a deserted road to an unexploded bomb. It didn't usually compel him to buy first-class tickets for strangers on the train. And anyway, this girl looked as if she was more than capable of looking after herself.

But with her outrageous clothes and her fiery hair

and her slight air of mischief she had brightened up his journey. She'd jolted him out of the pall of gloom that hung over him after the service he'd just attended, as well as providing a distraction from thinking about the grim weekend ahead.

That had to be worth the price of a first-class ticket from London to Edinburgh. Even without the glimpse of cleavage and the brush of her leg against his, which had reminded him that, while several of the men he'd served with weren't so lucky, he at least was still alive…

That was just a bonus.

CHAPTER TWO

Sᴏᴘʜɪᴇ came to with a start, and a horrible sense that something was wrong.

She sat up, blinking beneath the bright lights as she tried to get her bearings. The seat opposite was empty. The man with the silver eyes must have got off while she was sleeping, and she was just asking herself why on earth she should feel disappointed about that when she saw him.

He was standing up, his back towards her as he lifted an expensive-looking leather bag down from the luggage rack, giving her an excellent view of his extremely broad shoulders and narrow hips encased in beautifully tailored black trousers.

Mmm… *That* was why, she thought drowsily. Because physical perfection like that wasn't something you came across every day. And although it might come in a package with industrial-strength arrogance, it certainly was nice to look at.

'I'm sorry—could you tell me where we are, please?'

Damn—she'd forgotten about the posh accent, and after being asleep for so long she sounded more like a barmaid with a sixty-a-day habit than a wholesome society girl. Not that it really mattered now, since she'd never see him again.

He shrugged on the kind of expensive reefer jacket men wore in moody black and white adverts in glossy magazines. 'Alnburgh.'

The word delivered a jolt of shock to Sophie's sleepy brain. With an abrupt curse she leapt to her feet, groping frantically for her things, but at that moment the train juddered to an abrupt halt. She lost her balance, falling straight into his arms.

At least that was how it would have happened in any one of the romantic films she'd ever worked on. In reality she didn't so much fall into his waiting, welcoming arms as against the unyielding, rock-hard wall of his chest. He caught hold of her in the second before she ricocheted off him, one arm circling her waist like a band of steel. Rushing to steady herself, Sophie automatically put the flat of her hand against his chest.

Sexual recognition leapt into life inside her, like

an alarm going off in her pelvis. He might look lean, but there was no mistaking the hard, sculpted muscle beneath the Savile Row shirt.

Wide-eyed with shock, she looked up at him, opening her mouth in an attempt to form some sort of apology. But somehow there were blank spaces in her head where the words should be and the only coherent thought in her head was how astonishing his eyes were, close up; the silvery luminescence of the irises ringed with a darker grey…

'I have to get off—now,' she croaked.

It wasn't exactly a line from the romantic epics. He let her go abruptly, turning his head away.

'It's OK. We're not in the station yet.'

As he spoke the train began to move forwards with another jolt that threatened to unbalance her again. As if she weren't unbalanced enough already, she thought shakily, trying to pull down her bulging bag from where it was wedged in the luggage rack. Glancing anxiously out of the window, she saw the lights of cars waiting at a level crossing slide past the window, a little square signal box, cosily lit inside, with a sign saying 'Alnburgh' half covered in snow. She gave another futile tug and heard an impatient sound from behind her.

'Here, let me.'

In one lithe movement he leaned over her and grasped the handle of her bag.

'No, wait—the zip—' Sophie yelped, but it was too late. There was a ripping sound as the cheap zip, already under too much pressure from the sheer volume of stuff bundled up inside, gave way and Sophie watched in frozen horror as a tangle of dresses and tights and shoes tumbled out.

And underwear, of course.

It was terrible. Awful. Like the moment in a nightmare just before you wake up. But it was also pretty funny. Clamping a hand over her open mouth, Sophie couldn't stop a bubble of hysterical laughter escaping her.

'You might want to take that back to the shop,' the man remarked sardonically, reaching up to unhook an emerald-green satin balcony bra that had got stuck on the edge of the luggage rack. 'I believe Gucci luggage carries a lifetime guarantee?'

Sophie dropped to her knees to retrieve the rest of her things. Possibly it did, but cheap designer fakes certainly didn't, as he no doubt knew very well. Getting up again, she couldn't help but be aware of the length of his legs, and had to stop herself from reaching out and grabbing hold of them to steady herself as the train finally came to a shuddering halt in the station.

'Thanks for your help,' she said with as much haughtiness as she could muster when her arms were full of knickers and tights. 'Please, don't let me hold you up any more.'

'I wouldn't, except you're blocking the way to the door.'

Sophie felt her face turn fiery. Pressing herself as hard as she could against the table, she tried to make enough space for him to pass. But he didn't. Instead he took hold of the broken bag and lifted it easily, raising one sardonic eyebrow.

'After you—if you've got everything?'

Alnburgh station consisted of a single Victorian building that had once been rather beautiful but which now had its boarded up windows covered with posters advertising family days out at the sea- side. It was snowing again as she stepped off the train, and the air felt as if it had swept straight in from Siberia. Oh, dear, she really should have got changed. Not only was her current ensemble hid- eously unsuitable for meeting Jasper's family, it was also likely to lead to hypothermia.

'There.'

Sophie had no choice but to turn and face him. Pulling her collar up around her neck, she aimed for a sort of Julie-Christie-in-Doctor-Zhivago look— determination mixed with dignity.

'You'll be OK from here?'

'Y-yes. Thank you.' Standing there with the snow settling on his shoulders and in his dark hair he looked more brooding and sexy than Omar Shariff had ever done in the film. 'And thank you for…'

Jeepers, what was the matter with her? Julie Christie would never have let her lines dry up like that.

'For what?'

'Oh, you know, carrying my bag, picking up my… things.'

'My pleasure.'

His eyes met hers and for a second their gazes held. In spite of the cold stinging her cheeks, Sophie felt a tide of heat rise up inside her.

And then the moment was over and he was turning away, his feet crunching on the gritted paving stones, sliding his hands into the pockets of his coat just as the guard blew the whistle for the train to move out of the station again.

That was what reminded her, like a bolt of lightning in her brain. Clamping her hand to her mouth, she felt horror tingle down her spine at the realisation that she hadn't bought a ticket. Letting out a yelp of horror, followed by the kind of word Julie Christie would never use, Sophie dashed forwards towards the guard, whose head was sticking out of the window of his van.

'No—wait. Please! I didn't—'

But it was too late. The train was gathering pace and her voice was lost beneath the rumble of the engine and the squealing of the metal wheels on the track. As she watched the lights of the train melt back into the winter darkness Sophie's heart was beating hard, anguish knotting inside her at what she'd inadvertently done.

Stolen something. That was what it amounted to, didn't it? Travelling on the train without buying a ticket was, in effect, committing a criminal act, as well as a dishonest one.

An act of theft.

And that was one thing she would never, *ever* do.

The clatter of the train died in the distance and Sophie was aware of the silence folding all around her. Slowly she turned to walk back to pick up her forlorn-looking bag.

'Is there a problem?'

Her stomach flipped, and then sank like a stone. Great. Captain Disapproval must have heard her shout and come back, thinking she was talking to him. The station light cast dark shadows beneath his cheekbones and made him look more remote than ever. Which was quite something.

'No, no, not at all,' she said stiffly. 'Although before you go perhaps you could tell me where I could find a taxi.'

Kit couldn't quite stop himself from letting out a bark of laughter. It wasn't kind, but the idea of a taxi waiting at Alnburgh station was amusingly preposterous.

'You're not in London now.' He glanced down the platform to where the Bentley waited, Jensen sitting impassively behind the wheel. For some reason he felt responsible—touched almost—by this girl in her outrageous clothing with the snowflakes catching in her bright hair. 'Look, you'd better come with me.'

Her chin shot up half an inch. Her eyes flashed in the station light—the dark green of the stained glass in the Fitzroy family chapel, with the light shining through it.

'No, thanks,' she said with brittle courtesy. 'I think I'd rather walk.'

That really *was* funny. 'In those boots?'

'Yes,' she said haughtily, setting off quickly, if a little unsteadily, along the icy platform. She looked around, pulling her long army overcoat more tightly across her body.

Catching up with her, Kit arched an eyebrow. 'Don't tell me,' he drawled. 'You're going to join your regiment.'

'No,' she snapped. 'I'm going to stay with my boyfriend, who lives at Alnburgh Castle. So if you could just point me in the right direction...'

Kit stopped. The laughter of a moment ago evaporated in the arctic air, like the plumes of their breaths. In the distance a sheep bleated mournfully.

'And what is the name of your...*boyfriend*?'

Something in the tone of his voice made her stop too, the metallic echo of her stiletto heels fading into silence. When she turned to face him her eyes were wide and black-centred.

'Jasper.' Her voice was shaky but defiant. 'Jasper

Fitzroy, although I don't know what it has to do with you.'

Kit smiled again, but this time it had nothing to do with amusement.

'Well, since Jasper Fitzroy is my brother, I'd say quite a lot,' he said with sinister softness. 'You'd better get in the car.'

CHAPTER THREE

INSIDE the chauffeur-driven Bentley Sophie blew her cheeks out in a long, silent whistle.

What was it that horoscope said?

The car was very warm and very comfortable, but no amount of climate control and expensive upholstery could quite thaw the glacial atmosphere. Apart from a respectfully murmured 'Good evening, Miss,' the chauffeur kept his attention very firmly focused on the road. Sophie didn't blame him. You could cut the tension in the back of the car with a knife.

Sophie sat very upright, leaving as much seat as possible between her fishnetted thigh and his long, hard flannel-covered one. She didn't dare look at Jasper's brother, but was aware of him staring, tense-jawed, out of the window. The village of Alnburgh looked like a scene from a Christmas card as they drove up the main street, past a row of stone houses with low, gabled roofs covered in a crisp meringue-topping of snow, but he didn't look very pleased to be home.

Her mind raced as crazily as the white flakes swirling past the car window, the snatches of information Jasper had imparted about his brother over the years whirling through it. Kit Fitzroy was in the army, she knew that much, and he served abroad a lot, which would account for the unseasonal tan. Oh, and Jasper had once described him as having a 'complete emotion-bypass'. She recalled the closed expression Jasper's face wore on the rare occasions he mentioned him, the bitter edge his habitual mocking sarcasm took on when he said the words 'my brother'.

She was beginning to understand why. She had only known him for a little over three hours—and most of that time she'd been asleep—but it was enough to find it impossible to believe that this man could be related to Jasper. Sweet, warm, funny Jasper, who was her best friend in the world and the closest thing she had to family.

But the man beside her was his *real* flesh and blood, so surely that meant he couldn't be all bad? It also meant that she should make some kind of effort to get on with him, for Jasper's sake. And her own, since she had to get through an entire weekend in his company.

'So, you must be Kit, then?' she offered. 'I'm Sophie. Sophie Greenham.' She laughed—a habit she had when she was nervous. 'Bizarre, isn't it? Whoever would have guessed we were going to the same place?'

Kit Fitzroy didn't bother to look at her. 'Not you, obviously. Have you known my brother long?'

OK. So she was wrong. He was every bit as bad as she'd first thought. Thinking of the horoscope, she bit back the urge to snap, *Yes, as a matter of fact. I've known your brother for the last seven years, as you would have been very well aware if you took the slightest interest in him*, and kept her voice saccharine sweet as she recited the story she and Jasper had hastily come up with last night on the phone when he'd asked her to do this.

'Just since last summer. We met on a film.'

The last bit at least was true. Jasper was an assistant director and they had met on a dismal film about the Black Death that mercifully had never seen the light of day. Sophie had spent hours in make-up having sores applied to her face and had had one line to say, but had caught Jasper's eye just as she'd been about to deliver it and noticed that he was shaking with laughter. It had set her off too, and made the next four hours and twenty-two takes extremely challenging, but it had also sealed their friendship, and set its tone. It had been the two of them, united and giggling against the world, ever since.

He turned his head slightly. 'You're an actress?'

'Yes.'

Damn, why did that come out sounding so defensive? Possibly because he said the word 'actress' in the same faintly disdainful tone as other people might say 'lap dancer' or 'shoplifter'. What would he make of the fact that even 'actress' was stretching it for the bit parts she did in films and TV series? Clamping her teeth together, she looked away—and gasped.

Up ahead, lit up in the darkness, cloaked in swirling white like a fairy castle in a child's snow globe, was Alnburgh Castle.

She'd seen pictures, obviously. But nothing had prepared her for the scale of the place, or the impact it made on the surrounding landscape. It stood on top of the cliffs, its grey stone walls seeming to rise directly out of them. This was a side of Jasper's life she knew next to nothing about, and Sophie felt her mouth fall open as she stared in amazement.

'Bloody hell,' she breathed.

It was the first genuine reaction he'd seen her display, Kit thought sardonically, watching her. And it spoke volumes.

Sympathy wasn't an emotion he was used to experiencing in relation to Jasper, but at that moment he certainly felt something like it now. His brother must be pretty keen on this girl to invite her up here for Ralph Fitzroy's seventieth birthday party, but from what Kit had seen on the train it was obvious the feeling wasn't remotely mutual.

No prizes for guessing what the attraction was for Sophie Greenham.

'Impressive, isn't it?' he remarked acidly.

In the dimly lit interior of the car her eyes gleamed darkly like moonlit pools as she turned to face him. Her voice was breathless, so that she sounded almost intimidated.

'It's incredible. I had no idea...'

'What, that your boyfriend just happened to be the son of the Earl of Hawksworth?' Kit murmured sardonically. 'Of course. You were probably too busy discussing your mutual love of art-house cinema to get round to such mundane subjects as family background.'

'Don't be ridiculous,' she snapped. 'Of course I knew about Jasper's background—*and* his family.'

She said that last bit with a kind of defiant venom that was clearly meant to let him know that Jasper hadn't given him a good press. He wondered if she thought for a moment that he'd care. It was hardly a well-kept secret that there was no love lost between him and his brother—the spoiled, pampered golden boy. Ralph's second and favourite son.

The noise of the Bentley's engine echoed off the walls of the clock tower as they passed through the arch beneath it. The headlights illuminated the stone walls, dripping with damp, the iron-studded door that led down to the former dungeon that now housed Ralph's wine cellar. Kit felt the invisible iron-hard bands of tension around his chest and his forehead tighten a couple of notches.

It was funny, he spent much of his time in the most dangerous conflict zones on the globe, but in none of them did he ever feel a fraction as isolated or exposed as he did here. When he was working he had his team behind him. Men he could trust.

Trust wasn't something he'd ever associated with

home life at Alnburgh, where people told lies and kept secrets and made promises they didn't keep.

He glanced across at the woman sitting beside him, and felt his lip curl. Jasper's new girlfriend was going to fit in very well.

Sophie didn't wait until the chauffeur came round to open the door for her. The moment the car came to a standstill she reached for the handle and threw the door open, desperate to be out of the confined space with Kit Fitzroy.

A gust of salt-scented, ice-edged wind cleared her head but nearly knocked her sideways, whipping her hair across her face. Impatiently she brushed it away again. Alnburgh Castle loomed ahead of her. And above her and around her too, she thought weakly, turning to look at the fortress-thick walls that stretched into the darkness all around her, rising into huge, imposing buildings and jagged towers.

There was nothing remotely welcoming or inviting about it. Everything about the place was designed to scare people off and keep them out.

Sophie could see that Jasper's brother would be right at home here.

'Thanks, Jensen. I can manage the bags from here.'

'If you're sure, sir...'

Sophie turned in time to see Kit take her bag from the open boot of the Bentley and turn to walk in the direction of the castle's vast, imposing doorway. One strap of the green satin bra he had picked up on the train was hanging out of the top of it.

Hastily she hurried after him, her high heels ringing off the frozen flagstones and echoing around the walls of the castle courtyard.

'Please,' Sophie persisted, not wanting him to put himself out on her account any more than he had—so unwillingly—done already. 'I'd rather take it myself.'

He stopped halfway up the steps. For a split second he paused, as if he was gathering his patience, then turned back to her. His jaw was set but his face was carefully blank.

'If you insist.'

He held it out to her. He was standing two steps higher than she was, and Sophie had to tilt her head back to look up at him. Thrown for a second by the expression in his hooded eyes, she reached out to take the bag from him but, instead of the strap, found herself grasping his hand. She snatched hers away quickly, at exactly the same time he did, and the bag fell, tumbling down the steps, scattering all her clothes into the snow.

'Oh, knickers,' she muttered, dropping to her knees as yet another giggle of horrified, slightly hysterical amusement rose up inside her. Her heart was thumping madly from the accidental contact with him. His hand had felt warm, she thought irrationally. She'd expected it to be as cold as his personality.

'Hardly,' he remarked acidly, stooping to pick up a pink thong and tossing it back into the bag. 'But clearly what passes for them in your wardrobe. You seem to have a lot of underwear and not many clothes.'

The way he said it suggested he didn't think this was a good thing.

'Yes, well,' she said loftily, 'what's the point of spending money on clothes that I'm going to get bored of after I've worn them once? Underwear is a good investment. Because it's practical,' she added defensively, seeing the faint look of scorn on his face. 'God,' she muttered crossly, grabbing a handful of clothes back from him. 'This journey's turning into one of those awful drawing-room farces.'

Straightening up, he raised an eyebrow. 'The entire weekend is a bit of a farce, wouldn't you say?'

He went up the remainder of the steps to the door. Shoving the escaped clothes back into her bag with unnecessary force, Sophie followed him and was about to apologise for having the wrong underwear and the wrong clothes and the wrong accent and occupation and attitude when she found herself inside the castle and her defiance crumbled into dust.

The stone walls rose to a vaulted ceiling what seemed like miles above her head, and every inch was covered with muskets, swords, pikes and other items of barbaric medieval weaponry that Sophie recognised from men-in-tights-with-swords films she'd worked on, but couldn't begin to name. They were arranged into intricate patterns around helmets and pieces of armour, and the light from a huge wrought-iron lantern that hung on a chain in the centre of the room glinted dully on their silvery surfaces.

'What a cosy and welcoming entrance,' she said faintly, walking over to a silver breastplate hanging in front of a pair of crossed swords. 'I bet you're not troubled by persistent double-glazing salesmen.'

He didn't smile. His eyes, she noticed, held the same dull metallic gleam as the armour. 'They're seventeenth century. Intended for invading enemies rather than double-glazing salesmen.'

'Gosh.' Sophie looked away, trailing a finger down the hammered silver of the breastplate, noticing the shining path it left through the dust. 'You Fitzroys must have a lot of enemies.'

She was aware of his eyes upon her. Who would have thought that such a cool stare could make her skin feel as if it were burning? Somewhere a clock was ticking loudly, marking out the seconds before he replied, 'Let's just say we protect our interests.'

His voice was dangerously soft. Sophie's heart gave a kick, as if the armour had given her an electric shock. Withdrawing her hand sharply, she jerked her head up to look at him. A faint, sardonic smile touched the corner of his mouth. 'And it's not just invading armies that threaten those.'

His meaning was clear, and so was the thinly veiled warning behind the words. Sophie opened her mouth to protest, but no words came—none that would be any use in defending herself against the accusation he was making anyway, and certainly none that would be acceptable to use to a man with whose family she was going to be a guest for the weekend.

'I—I'd better find Jasper,' she stammered. 'He'll be wondering where I am.'

He turned on his heel and she followed him through another huge hallway panelled in oak, her footsteps making a deafening racket on the stone-flagged floor. There were vast fireplaces at each end of the room, but both were empty, and Sophie noticed her breath made faint plumes in the icy air. This time, instead of weapons, the walls were hung with the glassy-eyed heads of various large and hapless animals. They seemed to stare balefully at Sophie as she passed, as if in warning.

This is what happens if you cross the Fitzroys.

Sophie straightened her shoulders and quickened her pace. She mustn't let Kit Fitzroy get to her. He had got entirely the wrong end of the stick. She was Jasper's friend and she'd come as a favour to him precisely *because* his family were too bigoted to accept him as he really was.

She would have loved to confront Kit Superior Fitzroy with that, but of course it was impossible.

For Jasper's sake, and also because there was something about Kit that made her lose the ability to think logically and speak articulately, damn him.

A set of double doors opened at the far end of the hallway and Jasper appeared.

'*Soph!* You're *here*!'

At least she thought it was Jasper. Gone were the layers of eccentric vintage clothing, the tattered silk-faced dinner jackets he habitually wore over T-shirts and torn drainpipe jeans. The man who came towards her, his arms outstretched, was wearing well-ironed chinos and a V-necked jumper over a button-down shirt and—Sophie's incredulous gaze moved downwards—what looked suspiciously like brogues.

Reaching her, this new Jasper took her face between his hands and kissed her far more tenderly than normal. Caught off guard by the bewildering change in him, Sophie was just about to push him away and ask what he was playing at when she remembered what she was there for. Dropping her poor, battered bag again, she wrapped her arms around his neck.

Over Jasper's shoulder, through the curtain of her hair, she was aware of Kit Fitzroy standing like some dark sentinel, watching her. The knowledge stole down inside her, making her feel hot, tingling, restless, and before she knew it she was arching her body into Jasper's, sliding her fingers into his hair.

Sophie had done enough screen and stage kisses to have mastered the art of making something completely chaste look a whole lot more X-rated than it really was. When Jasper pulled back a little a few seconds later she caught the gleam of laughter in his eyes as he leaned his forehead briefly against hers, then, stepping away, he spoke in a tone of rather forced warmth.

'You've met my big brother, Kit. I hope he's been looking after you.'

That was rather an unfortunate way of putting it, Sophie thought, an image of Kit Fitzroy, his strong hands full of her silliest knickers and bras flashing up inside her head. Oh, hell, why did she always smirk when she was embarrassed? Biting her lip, she stared down at the stone floor.

'Oh, absolutely,' she said, nodding furiously. 'And I'm afraid I needed quite a lot of looking after. If it wasn't for Kit I'd be halfway to Edinburgh now. Or at least, my underwear would.'

It might be only a few degrees warmer than the

arctic, but beneath her coat Sophie could feel the heat creeping up her cleavage and into her cheeks. The nervous smile she'd been struggling to suppress broke through as she said the word 'underwear', but one glance at Kit's glacial expression killed it instantly.

'It was a lucky coincidence that we were sitting in the same carriage. It gave us a chance to…get to know each other a little before we got here.'

Ouch.

Only Sophie could have understood the meaning behind the polite words or picked up the faint note of menace beneath the blandness of his tone.

He's really got it in for me, she realised with a shiver. Suddenly she felt very tired, very alone, and even Jasper's hand around hers couldn't dispel the chilly unease that had settled in the pit of her stomach.

'Great.' Oblivious to the tension that crackled like static in the air, Jasper pulled her impatiently forwards. 'Come and meet Ma and Pa. I haven't stopped talking about you since I got here yesterday, so they're dying to see what all the fuss is about.'

And suddenly panic swelled inside her—churning, black and horribly familiar. The fear of being looked at. Scrutinised. Judged. That people would see through the layers of her disguise, the veils of evasion, to the real girl beneath. As Jasper led her towards the doors at the far end of the hall she was shaking, assailed by the same doubts and insecurities that had paralysed her the only time she'd done live theatre, in the seconds before she went onstage. What if she couldn't do it? What if the lines wouldn't come and she was left just being herself? Acting had been a way of life long before it became a way of making a living, and playing a part was second nature to her. But now...*here*...

'Jasper,' she croaked, pulling back. 'Please— wait.'

'Sophie? What's the matter?'

His kind face was a picture of concern. The animal heads glared down at her, as well as a puffy-eyed Fitzroy ancestor with a froth of white lace around his neck.

And that was the problem. Jasper was her closest friend and she would do anything for him, but when she'd offered to help him out she hadn't reckoned on all this. Alnburgh Castle, with its history and its million symbols of wealth and status and *belonging*, was exactly the kind of place that un-nerved her most.

'I can't go in there. Not dressed like this, I mean. I—I came straight from the casting for the vampire thing and I meant to get changed on the train, but I...'

She opened her coat and Jasper gave a low whistle.

'Don't worry,' he soothed. 'Here, let me take your coat and you can put this on, otherwise you'll freeze.' Quickly he peeled off the black cashmere jumper and handed it to her, then tossed her coat over the horns of a nearby stuffed stag. 'They're going to love you whatever you're wearing. Par-ticularly Pa—you're the perfect birthday present. Come on, they're waiting in the drawing room. At least it's warm in there.'

With Kit's eyes boring into her back Sophie had no choice but to let Jasper lead her towards the huge double doors at the far end of the hall.

Vampire thing, Kit thought scornfully. Since when had the legend of the undead mentioned dressing like an escort in some private men's club? He won-dered if it was going to be the kind of film the boys in his unit sometimes brought back from leave to enjoy with a lot of beer in rest periods in camp.

The thought was oddly unsettling.

Tiredness pulled at him like lead weights. He couldn't face seeing his father and stepmother just yet. Going through the hallway in the direction of the stairs, he passed the place where the portrait of his mother used to hang, before Ralph had replaced it, appropriately, with a seven-foot-high oil of Tatiana in plunging blue satin and the Cartier diamonds he had given her on their wedding day.

Jasper was right, Kit mused. If there was anyone who would appreciate Sophie Greenham's get-up it was Ralph Fitzroy. Like vampires, his father's enthusiasm for obvious women was legendary.

Jasper's, however, was not. And that was what worried him. Even if he hadn't overheard her conversation on the phone, even if he hadn't felt himself the white-hot sexuality she exuded, you only had to look at the two of them together to know that, vampire or not, the girl was going to break the poor bastard's heart and eat it for breakfast.

The room Jasper led her into was as big as the last, but stuffed with furniture and blazing with light from silk-shaded lamps on every table, a chandelier the size of a spaceship hovering above a pair of gargantuan sofas and a fire roaring in the fireplace.

It was Ralph Fitzroy who stepped forwards first. Sophie was surprised by how old he was, which she realised was ridiculous considering the reason she had come up this weekend was to attend his seventieth birthday party. His grey hair was brushed back from a florid, fleshy face and as he took Sophie's hand his eyes almost disappeared in a fan of laughter lines as they travelled down her body. And up again, but only as far as her chest.

'Sophie. Marvellous to meet you,' he said, in the kind of upper-class accent that Sophie had thought had become extinct after the war.

'And you, sir.'

Oh, for God's sake—*sir*? Where had that come from? She'd be bobbing curtsies next. She was supposed to be playing the part of Jasper's girlfriend, not the parlourmaid in some nineteen-thirties below-stairs drama. Not that Ralph seemed to mind. He was still clasping her hand, looking at her with a kind of speculative interest, as if she were a piece of art he was thinking of buying.

Suddenly she remembered Jean-Claude's 'Nude

with Lilies' and felt pins and needles of embarrassment prickle her whole body. Luckily distraction
came in the form of a woman unfolding herself
from one of the overstuffed sofas and coming forwards. She was dressed immaculately in a clinging
off-white angora dress that was cleverly designed to
showcase her blonde hair and peachy skin, as well
as her enviable figure and the triple string of pearls
around her neck. Taking hold of Sophie's shoulders,
she leaned forwards in a waft of expensive perfume
and, in a silent and elaborate pantomime, kissed the
air beside first one cheek and then the other.

'Sophie, how good of you to come all this way to
join us. Did you have a dreadful journey?'

Her voice still bore the unmistakable traces of a
Russian accent, but her English was so precise that
Sophie felt more than ever that they were onstage
and reciting lines from a script. Tatiana Fitzroy was
playing the part of the gracious hostess, thrilled
to be meeting her adored son's girlfriend for the
first time. The problem was she wasn't that great
at acting.

'No, not at all.'

'But you came by train?' Tatiana shuddered
slightly. 'Trains are always so overcrowded these

days. They make one feel slightly grubby, don't you think?'

No, Sophie wanted to say. Trains didn't make her feel remotely grubby. However, the blatant disapproval in Kit Fitzroy's cool glare—now that had definitely left her feeling in need of a scrub down in a hot shower.

'Come on, darling,' Ralph joked. 'When was the last time you went on a train?'

'First Class isn't *too* bad,' Sophie said, attempting to sound as if she would never consider venturing into standard.

'Not really enough legroom,' said a grave voice behind her. Sophie whipped her head round. Kit was standing in the doorway, holding a bundle of envelopes, which he was scanning through as he spoke.

The fire crackled merrily away, but Sophie was aware that the temperature seemed to have fallen a couple of degrees. For a split second no one moved, but then Tatiana was moving forwards, as if the offstage prompt had just reminded her of her cue.

'Kit. Welcome back to Alnburgh.'

So, she wasn't the only one who found him impossible, Sophie thought, noticing the distinct coolness in Tatiana's tone. As she reached up to kiss his cheek Kit didn't incline his head even a fraction to make it easier for her to reach, and his inscrutable expression didn't alter at all.

'Tatiana. You're looking well,' Kit drawled, barely glancing at her as he continued to look through the sheaf of letters in his hand. He seemed to have been built on a different scale from Jasper and Ralph, Sophie thought, taking in his height and the breadth of his chest. The sleeves of his white shirt were rolled back to reveal tanned forearms, corded with muscle.

She looked resolutely away.

Ralph went over to a tray crowded with cut-glass decanters on a nearby table and sloshed some more whisky into a glass that wasn't quite empty. Sophie heard the rattle of glass against glass, but when he turned round to face his eldest son his bland smile was perfectly in place.

'Kit.'

'Father.'

Kit's voice was perfectly neutral, but Ralph seemed to flinch slightly. He covered it by taking a large slug of whisky. 'Good of you to come, what with flights being cancelled and so on. The invitation was…' he hesitated '…a courtesy. I know how busy you are. Hope you didn't feel obliged to accept.'

'Not at all.' Kit's eyes glittered, as cold as moonlight on frost. 'I've been away too long. And there are things we need to discuss.'

Ralph laughed, but Sophie could see the colour rising in his florid cheeks. It was fascinating—like being at a particularly tense tennis match.

'For God's sake, Kit, you're not still persisting with that—'

As he spoke the double doors opened and a thin, elderly man appeared between them and nodded, almost imperceptibly, at Tatiana. Swiftly she crossed the Turkish silk rug in a waft of Chanel No 5 and slipped a hand through her husband's arm, cutting him off mid-sentence.

'Thank you, Thomas. Dinner is ready. Now that everyone's here, shall we go through?'

CHAPTER FOUR

DINNER was about as enjoyable and relaxing as being stripped naked and whipped with birch twigs.

When she was little, Sophie had dreamed wistfully about being part of the kind of family who gathered around a big table to eat together every evening. If she'd known this was what it was like she would have stuck to the fantasies about having a pony or being picked to star in a new film version of *The Little House on the Prairie*.

The dining room was huge and gloomy, its high, green damask-covered walls hung with yet more Fitzroy ancestors. They were an unattractive bunch, Sophie thought with a shiver. The handsomeness so generously bestowed on Jasper and Kit must be a relatively recent addition to the gene pool. Only one—a woman in blush-pink silk with roses woven into her extravagantly piled up hair and a secretive smile on her lips—held any indication of the good looks that were the Fitzroy hallmark now.

Thomas, the butler who had announced dinner, dished up watery consommé, followed by tiny rectangles of grey fish on something that looked like spinach and smelled like boiled socks. No wonder Tatiana was so thin.

'This looks delicious,' Sophie lied brightly.

'Thank you,' Tatiana cooed, in a way that suggested she'd cooked it herself. 'It has taken years to get Mrs Daniels to cook things other than steak and kidney pudding and roast beef, but finally she seems to understand the meaning of low-fat.'

'Unfortunately,' Kit murmured.

Ignoring him, Ralph reached for the dusty bottle of Chateau Marbuzet and splashed a liberal amount into his glass before turning to fill up Sophie's.

'So, Jasper said you've been in Paris? Acting in some film or other?'

Sophie, who had just taken a mouthful of fish, could only nod.

'Fascinating,' said Tatiana doubtfully. 'What was it about?'

Sophie covered her mouth with her hand to hide the grimace as she swallowed the fish. 'It's about British Special Agents and the French Resistance in the Second World War,' she said, wondering if she could hide the rest of the fish under the spinach as she used to do at boarding school. 'It's set in Mont-martre, against a community of painters and poets.'

'And what part did you play?'

Sophie groaned inwardly. It would have to be Kit who asked that. Ever since she sat down she'd been aware of his eyes on her. More than aware of it—it felt as if there were a laser trained on her skin.

She cleared her throat. 'Just a tiny role, really,' she said with an air of finality.

'As?'

He didn't give up, did he? Why didn't he just go the whole hog and whip out a megawatt torch to shine in her face while he interrogated her? Not that those silvery eyes weren't hard enough to look into already.

'A prostitute called Claudine who inadvertently betrays her Resistance lover to the SS.'

Kit's smile was as faint as it was fleeting. He had a way of making her feel like a third year who'd been caught showing her knickers behind the bike sheds and hauled into the headmaster's office. She took a swig of wine.

'You must meet such fascinating people,' Tatiana said.

'Oh, yes. Well, I mean, sometimes. Actors can be

a pretty self-obsessed bunch. They're not always a laugh a minute to be around.'

'Not as bad as artists,' Jasper chipped in absently as he concentrated on extracting a bone from his fish. 'They hired a few painters to produce the pictures that featured in the film, and they turned out to be such prima donnas they made the actors look very down-to-earth, didn't they, Soph?'

Somewhere in the back of Sophie's mind an alarm bell had started drilling. She looked up, desperately trying to telegraph warning signals across the table to Jasper, but he was still absorbed in exhuming the skeleton of the poor fish. Sophie's lips parted in wordless panic as she desperately tried to think of something to say to steer the subject onto safer ground…

Too late.

'One of them became completely obsessed with painting Sophie,' Jasper continued. 'He came over to her in the bar one evening when I was there and spent about two hours gazing at her with his eyes narrowed as he muttered about lilies.'

Sophie felt as if she'd been struck by lightning, a terrible rictus smile still fixed to her face. She didn't dare look at Kit. She didn't need to—she could feel the disapproval and hostility radiating from him like a force field. Through her despair she was aware of the woman with the roses in her hair staring down at her from the portrait. Now the smile didn't look secretive so much as if she was trying not to laugh.

'If I thought the result would have been as lovely as that I would have accepted like a shot,' she said in a strangled voice, gesturing up at the portrait. 'Who is she?'

Ralph followed her gaze. 'Ah—that's Lady Caroline, wife of the fourth Earl and one of the more flamboyant Fitzroys. She was a girl of somewhat uncertain provenance who had been a music hall singer—definitely not countess material. Christopher Fitzroy was twenty years younger than her, but from the moment he met her he was quite besotted and, much to the horror of polite society, married her.'

'That was pretty brave of him,' Sophie said, relief at having successfully moved the conversation on clearly audible in her voice.

The sound Kit made was unmistakably derisive. 'Brave, or stupid?'

Their eyes met. Suddenly the room seemed very

quiet. The arctic air was charged with electricity, so that the candle flames flickered for a second.

'Brave,' she retorted, raising her chin a little. 'It can't have been easy, going against his family and society, but if he loved her it would have been worth the sacrifice.'

'Not if *she* wasn't worth the sacrifice.'

The candle flames danced in a halo of red mist before Sophie's eyes, and before she could stop herself she heard herself give a taut, brittle laugh and say, 'Why? Because she was too *common*?'

'Not at all.' Kit looked at her steadily, his haughty face impassive. 'She wasn't worth it because she didn't love him back.'

'How do you know she didn't?'

Oh, jeez, what was she doing? She was supposed to be here to impress Jasper's family, not pick fights with them. No matter how insufferable they were.

'Well…' Kit said thoughtfully. 'The fact that she slept with countless other men during their marriage is a bit of a clue, wouldn't you say? Her lovers included several footmen and stable lads and even the French artist who painted that portrait.'

He was still looking at her. His voice held that now-familiar note of scorn, but was so soft that for a moment Sophie was hypnotised. The candlelight cast shadows under his angular cheekbones and brought warmth to his skin, but nothing could melt the ice chips in his eyes.

Sophie jumped slightly as Ralph cut in.

'French? Thought the chap was Italian?'

Kit looked away. 'Ah, yes,' he said blandly. 'I must be getting my facts mixed up.'

Bastard, thought Sophie. He knew that all along, and he was just trying to wind her up. Raising her chin and summoning a smile to show she wouldn't be wound, she said, 'So—what happened to her?'

'She came to a sticky end, I'm afraid. Not nice,' Ralph answered, topping up his glass again and emptying the remains of the bottle into Sophie's. Despite the cold his cheeks were flushed a deep, mottled purple.

'How?' Her mind flashed back to the swords and muskets in the entrance hall, the animal heads on the wall. You messed with a Fitzroy—or his brother—and a sticky end was pretty inevitable.

'She got pregnant,' Kit said matter-of-factly, picking up the knife on his side-plate and examining the tarnished silver blade for a second before polishing it with his damask napkin. 'The Earl, poor bastard, was delighted. At last, a long-awaited heir for Alnburgh.'

Sophie took another mouthful of velvety wine, watching his mouth as he spoke. And then found that she couldn't stop watching it. And wondering what it would look like if he smiled—really smiled. Or laughed. What it would feel like if he kissed her—

No. *Stop.* She shouldn't have let Ralph give her the rest of that wine. Hastily she put her glass down and tucked her hands under her thighs.

'But of course, she knew that it was extremely unlikely the kid was his,' Kit was saying in his low, slightly scornful voice. 'And though he was too besotted to see what was going on, the rest of his family certainly weren't. She must have realised that she'd reached a dead end, and also that the child was likely to be born with the rampant syphilis that was already devouring her.'

Sophie swallowed. 'What did she do?'

Kit laid the knife down and looked straight at her. 'In the last few weeks of her pregnancy, she threw herself off the battlements in the East Tower.'

She wouldn't let him see that he'd shocked her. Wouldn't let the sickening feeling she had in the pit of her stomach show on her face. Luckily at that moment Jasper spoke, his cheerful voice breaking the tension that seemed to shiver in the icy air.

'Poor old Caroline, eh? What a price to pay for all that fun.' He leaned forwards, dropping his voice theatrically. 'It's said that on cold winter nights her ghost walks the walls, half mad with guilt. Or maybe it's the syphilis—that's supposed to make you go mad, isn't it?'

'Really, Jasper. I think we've heard enough about Fitzroys.' Tatiana laid down her napkin with a little pout as Thomas reappeared to collect up the plates. 'So, Sophie—tell us about *your* family. Where do your people come from?'

People? Her *people*? She made it sound as if everyone had estates and villages and hordes of peasants at their command. From behind Tatiana's head Caroline the feckless countess looked at Sophie with amused pity. *Get yourself out of this one*, she seemed to say.

'Oh. Um, down in the south of England,' Sophie muttered vaguely, glancing at Jasper for help. 'We travelled around a lot, actually.'

'And your parents—what do they do?'

'My mother is an astronomer.'

It was hardly a lie, more a slip of the tongue. Astronomy/astrology…people got them mixed up all the time anyway.

'And your—'

Jasper came swiftly to the rescue.

'Talking of stars, how did your big charity auction go last week, Ma? I keep meaning to ask you who won the premiere tickets I donated.'

It wasn't the most subtle of conversational diversions, but it did the trick so Sophie was too relieved to care. As the discussion moved on and Thomas reappeared to clear the table she slumped back in her chair and breathed out slowly, waiting for her heartbeat to steady and her fight-or-flight response to subside. With any luck that was the subject of her family dealt with and now she could relax for the rest of the weekend.

If it were possible to relax with Kit Fitzroy around.

Before she was aware it was happening or could stop it her gaze had slid back to where he sat, leaning back in his chair, his broad shoulders and long body making the antique rosewood look as fussy and flimsy as doll's-house furniture. His face was shuttered, his hooded eyes downcast, so that for the first time since the train she was able to look at him properly.

A shiver of sexual awareness shimmered down her spine and spread heat into her pelvis.

Sophie had an unfortunate attraction to men who were bad news. Men who didn't roll over and beg to be patted. But even she had to draw a line some-where, and 'emotion-bypass' was probably a good place. And after the carnage of her so-called casual fling with Jean-Claude, this was probably a good time.

'…really fabulous turnout. People were so gener-ous,' Tatiana was saying in her guttural purr, the diamonds in her rings glittering in the candlelight as she folded her hands together and rested her chin on them. 'And so good to catch up with all the people I don't see, stuck out here. As a matter of fact, Kit—your name came up over dinner. A girl-friend of mine said you have broken the heart of a friend of her daughter's.'

Kit looked up.

'Without the name of the friend, her daughter or her daughter's friend I can't really confirm or deny that.'

'Oh, come on,' Tatiana said with a brittle, tinkling laugh. 'How many hearts have you broken recently? I'm talking about Alexia. According to Sally Rothwell-Hyde, the poor girl is terribly upset.'

'I'm sure Sally Rothwell-Hyde is exaggerating,' Kit said in a bored voice. 'Alexia was well aware from the start it was nothing serious. It seems that Jasper will be providing Alnburgh heirs a lot sooner than I will.'

He looked across at Sophie, wondering what smart response she would think up to that, but she said nothing. She was sitting very straight, very still. Against the vivid red of her hair, her face was the same colour as the wax that had dripped onto the table in front of her.

'Something wrong?' he challenged quietly.

She looked at him, and for a second the expression in her eyes was one of blank horror. But then she blinked, and seemed to rouse herself.

'I'm sorry. What was that?' With an unsteady hand she stroked her hair back from her face. It was still as pale as milk, apart from a blossoming of red on each cheekbone.

'Soph?' Jasper got to his feet. 'Are you OK?'

'Yes. Yes, of course. I'm absolutely fine.' She made an attempt at a laugh, but Kit could hear the raw edge in it. 'Just tired, that's all. It's been a long day.'

'Then you must get to bed,' Tatiana spoke with an air of finality, as if she was dismissing her. 'Jasper, show Sophie to her room. I'm sure she'll feel much better after a good night's sleep.'

Kit watched Jasper put his arm round her and lead her to the door, remembering the two hours of catatonic sleep she'd had on the train. Picking up his wine glass, he drained it thoughtfully.

It certainly wasn't tiredness that had drained her face of colour like that, which meant it must have been the idea of producing heirs.

It looked as if she was beginning to get an idea of what she'd got herself into. And she was even flakier than he'd first thought.

CHAPTER FIVE

ROTHWELL-HYDE.

Wordlessly Sophie let Jasper lead her up the widest staircase she'd ever seen. It was probably a really common surname, she thought numbly. The phone book must contain millions of Rothwell-Hydes. Or several anyway, in smart places all over the country. Because surely no one who lived up here would send their daughter to school down in Kent?

It was a second before she realised Jasper had stopped at the foot of another small flight of stairs leading to a gloomy wood-panelled corridor with a single door at the end.

'Your room's at the end there, but let's go to mine. The fire's lit, and I've got a bottle of Smirnoff that Sergio gave me somewhere.' He took hold of her shoulders, bending his knees slightly to peer into her face. 'You look like you could do with something to revive you, angel. Are you OK?'

With some effort she gathered herself and made a stab at sounding casual and reassuring. 'I'm fine now, really. I'm so sorry, Jasper—I'm supposed to be taking the pressure off you by posing as your girlfriend, but instead your parents must be wondering why you ended up going out with such a nutter.'

'Don't be daft. You're totally charming them—or you were until you nearly fainted face down on your plate. I know the fish was revolting, but really...'

She laughed. 'It wasn't that bad.'

'What then?'

Jasper was her best friend. Over the years she'd told him lots of funny stories about her childhood, and when you'd grown up living in a converted bus painted with flowers and peace slogans, with a mother who had inch-long purple hair, had changed her name to Rainbow and given up wearing a bra, there were lots of those.

There were also lots of bits that weren't funny at all, but she kept those to herself. The years when she'd been taken in by Aunt Janet and had been sent to an exclusive girls' boarding school in the hope of 'civilising' her. Years when she'd been at the mercy of Olympia Rothwell-Hyde and her friends...

She shook her head and smiled. 'Just tired. Honest.'

'Come on, then.' He set off again along the corridor, rubbing his arms vigorously. 'God, if you stand still for a second in this place you run the risk of turning into a pillar of ice. I hope you brought your thermal underwear.'

'Please, can you not mention underwear,' Sophie said with a bleak laugh. 'The contents of my knicker drawer have played far too much of a starring role in this weekend already and I've only been here a couple of hours.' Her heart lurched as she remembered again the phone conversation Kit had overheard on the train. 'I'm afraid I got off on completely the wrong foot with your brother.'

'Half-brother,' Jasper corrected, bitterly. 'And don't worry about Kit. He doesn't approve of anyone. He just sits in judgment on the rest of us.'

'That's why I'm here, isn't it?' said Sophie. 'It's Kit's opinion you're worried about, not your parents'.'

'Are you kidding?' Jasper said ironically. 'You've met my father. He's from the generation and background that call gay men "nancy boys" and assume they all wear pink scarves and carry handbags.'

'And what's Kit's excuse?'

Pausing in front of a closed door, Jasper bowed his head. Without the hair gel and eyeliner he always wore in London his fine-boned face looked younger and oddly vulnerable.

'Kit's never liked me. I've always known that, growing up. He never said anything unkind or did anything horrible to me, but he didn't have to. I always felt this...*coldness* from him, which was almost worse.'

Sophie could identify with that.

'I don't know,' he went on, 'now I'm older I can understand that it must have been difficult for him, growing up without his mother when I still had mine.' He cast her a rueful look. 'As you'll have noticed, my mother isn't exactly cosy—I don't think she particularly went out of her way to make sure he was OK, but because I was her only child I did get rather spoiled, I guess...'

Sophie widened her eyes. 'You? Surely not!'

Jasper grinned. 'This is the part of the castle that's supposed to be haunted by the mad countess's ghost, you know, so you'd better watch it, or I'll run away and leave you here…'

'Don't you dare!'

Laughing, he opened the door. 'This is my room. Damn, the fire's gone out. Come in and shut the door to keep any lingering traces of warmth in.'

Sophie did as she was told. The room was huge, and filled with the kind of dark, heavy furniture that looked as if it had come from a giant's house. A sleigh bed roughly the size of the bus that had formed Sophie's childhood home stood in the centre of the room, piled high with several duvets. Jasper's personal stamp was evident in the tatty posters on the walls, a polystyrene reproduction of Michelangelo's *David*, which was rakishly draped in an old school tie, a silk dressing gown and a battered trilby. As he poked at the ashes in the grate Sophie picked her way through the clothes on the floor and went over to the window.

'So what happened to Kit's mother?'

Jasper piled coal into the grate. 'She left. When he was about six, I think. It's a bit of a taboo subject around here, but I gather there was no warning, no explanation, no goodbye. Of course there was a divorce eventually, and apparently Juliet's adultery was cited, but as far as I know Kit never had any contact with her again.'

Outside it had stopped snowing and the clouds had parted to show the flat disc of the full moon. From what Sophie could see, Jasper's room looked down over some kind of inner courtyard. The castle walls rose up on all sides—battlements like jagged teeth, stone walls gleaming like pewter in the cold, bluish light. She shivered, her throat constricting with reluctant compassion for the little boy whose mother had left him here in this bleak fortress of a home.

'So she abandoned him to go off with another man?'

Sophie's own upbringing had been unconventional enough for her not to be easily shocked. But a mother leaving her child...

'Pretty much. So I guess you can understand why he ended up being like he is. Ah, look—that's better.'

He stood back, hands on hips, his face bathed in orange as the flames took hold. 'Right—let's find that bottle and get under the duvet. You can tell me all about Paris and how you managed to escape the clutches of that lunatic painter, and in turn

I'm going to bore you senseless talking about Sergio. Do you know,' he sighed happily, 'he's having a tally of the days we're apart tattooed on his chest?'

The ancient stones on top of the parapet were worn smooth by salt wind and wild weather, and the moonlight turned them to beaten silver. Kit exhaled a cloud of frozen air, propping his elbows on the stone and looking out across the battlements to the empty beach beyond.

There was no point in even trying to get to sleep tonight, he knew that. His insomnia was always at its worst when he'd just come back from a period of active duty and his body hadn't learned to switch off from its state of high alert. The fact that he was also back at Alnburgh made sleep doubly unlikely.

He straightened up, shoving his frozen fingers into his pockets. The tide was out and pools of water on the sand gleamed like mercury. In the distance the moon was reflected without a ripple in the dark surface of the sea.

It was bitterly cold.

Long months in the desert halfway across the world had made him forget the aching cold here.

Sometimes, working in temperatures of fifty degrees wearing eighty pounds of explosive-proof kit, he would try to recapture the sensation, but out there cold became an abstract concept. Something you knew about in theory, but couldn't imagine actually *feeling*.

But it was real enough now, as was the complicated mix of emotions he always experienced when he returned. He did one of the most dangerous jobs on the planet without feeling anything, and yet when he came back to the place he'd grown up in it was as if he'd had a layer of skin removed. Here it was impossible to forget the mother who had left him, or forgive the studied indifference of the father who had been left to bring him up. Here everything was magnified: bitterness, anger, frustration...

Desire.

The thought crept up on him and he shoved it away. Sophie Greenham was hardly his type, although he had to admit that doing battle with her at dinner had livened up what would otherwise have been a dismal evening. And at least her presence had meant that he didn't feel like the only outsider.

It had also provided a distraction from the tension between him and his father. But only temporarily.

Ralph was right—Kit hadn't come up here because the party invitation was too thrilling to refuse, but Ralph's seventieth birthday seemed like a good time to remind his father that if he didn't transfer the ownership of Alnburgh into Kit's name soon, it would be too late. The estate couldn't possibly survive the inheritance tax that would be liable on it after Ralph's death, and would no doubt have to be sold.

Kit felt fresh anger bloom inside him. He wasn't sure why he cared—his house in Chelsea was conveniently placed for some excellent restaurants, was within easy taxi-hailing range for women he didn't want to wake up with, and came without ghosts. And yet he did care. Because of the waste and the irresponsibility and the sheer bloody shortsightedness, perhaps? Or because he could still hear his mother's voice, whispering to him down the years?

Alnburgh is yours, Kit. Don't ever forget that. Don't ever let anyone tell you it's not.

It must have been just before she left that she'd said that. When she knew she was going and wanted to assuage her guilt; to feel that she wasn't leaving him with nothing.

As if a building could make up for a mother.

Particularly a building like Alnburgh. It was an anachronism. As a home it was uncomfortable, impractical and unsustainable. It was also the place where he had been unhappiest. And yet he knew, deep down, that it mattered to him. He felt responsible for it, and he would do all he could to look after it.

And much as it surprised him to discover, that went for his brother too. Only Jasper wasn't at risk from dry rot or damp, but the attentions of a particularly brazen redhead.

Kit wondered if she'd be as difficult to get rid of.

Sophie opened her eyes.

It was cold and for a moment her sleep-slow brain groped to work out where she was. It was a familiar feeling—one she'd experienced often as a child when her mother had been in one of her restless phases, but for some reason now it was accompanied by a sinking sensation.

Putting a hand to her head, she struggled upright. In the corner of the room the television was playing quietly to itself, and Jasper's body was warm beside her, a T-shirt of Sergio's clasped in one hand, the half-empty bottle of vodka in the other. He had fallen asleep sprawled diagonally across the bed with his head thrown back, and something about the way the lamplight fell on his face—or maybe the shuttered blankness sleep had lent it—reminded her of Kit.

Fragments of the evening reassembled themselves in her aching head. She got up, rubbing a hand across her eyes, and carefully removed the bottle from Jasper's hand. Much as she loved him, right now all she wanted was a bed to herself and a few hours of peaceful oblivion.

Tiptoeing to the door, she opened it quietly. Out in the corridor the temperature was arctic and the only light came from the moon, lying in bleached slabs on the smooth oak floorboards. Shivering, Sophie hesitated, wondering whether to go back into Jasper's room after all, but the throbbing in her head was more intense now and she thought longingly of the paracetamol in her washbag.

There was nothing for it but to brave the cold and the dark.

Her heart began to pound as she slipped quickly between the squares of silver moonlight, along the corridor and down a spiralling flight of stone stairs. Shadows engulfed her. It was very quiet. Too quiet.

To Sophie, used to thin-walled apartments, bed and breakfasts, buses and camper vans on make-shift sites where someone was always strumming a guitar or playing indie-acid-trance, the silence was unnatural. Oppressive. It buzzed in her ears, filling her head with whistling, like interference on a badly tuned radio.

She stopped, her chest rising and falling rapidly as she looked around.

Passageways stretched away from her in three directions, but each looked as unfamiliar as the other. Oh, hell. She'd been so traumatised earlier that she hadn't paid attention to Jasper when he pointed out her room…

But that could be it, she thought with relief, walking quickly to a door at the end of the short landing to her left. Gingerly she turned the handle and, heart bursting, pushed open the door.

Moonlight flooded in from behind her, illuminating the ghostly outlines of shrouded furniture. The air was stale with age. The room clearly hadn't been opened in years.

This is the part of the castle that's supposed to be haunted by the mad countess's ghost, you know…

Retreating quickly, she slammed the door and

forced herself to exhale slowly. It was fine. No need to panic. Just a question of retracing her steps, thinking about it logically. A veil of cloud slipped over the moon's pale face and the darkness deepened. Icy drafts eddied around Sophie's ankles, and the edge of a curtain at one of the stone windows lifted slightly, as if brushed by invisible fingers. The whistling sound was louder now and more distinctive—a sort of keening that was almost human. She couldn't be sure it was just in her head any more and she broke into a run, glancing back over her shoulder as if she expected to see a swish of pink silk skirt disappearing around the corner.

'I'm being stupid,' she whispered desperately, fumbling at the buttons of her mobile phone to make the screen light up and act as a torch. 'There's no such thing as ghosts.' But even as the words formed themselves on her stiff lips horror prickled at the back of her neck.

Footsteps.

She clamped a hand to her mouth to stifle her moan of terror and stood perfectly still. Probably she'd imagined it—or possibly it was just the mad drumming of her heart echoing off the stone walls...

Nope. Definitely footsteps.

Definitely getting nearer.

It was impossible to tell from which direction they were coming. Or maybe if they were ghostly footsteps they weren't coming from any particular direction, except beyond the grave? It hardly mattered—the main thing was to get away from here and back to Jasper. Back to light and warmth and TV and company. Shaking with fear, she darted back along the corridor, heading for the stairs that she had come down a few moments ago.

And then she gave a whimper of horror, icy adrenaline sluicing through her veins. A dark figure loomed in front of her, only a foot or so away, too close even for her to be aware of anything beyond its height and the frightening breadth of its shoulders. She shrank backwards, bringing her hands up to her face, her mouth opening to let out the scream that was rising in her throat.

'Oh, no, you don't...'

Instantly she was pulled against the rock-hard chest and a huge hand was put across her mouth. Fury replaced fear as she realised that this was not the phantom figure of some seventeenth-century suitor looking for the countess, but the all-too-human flesh of Kit Fitzroy.

All of a sudden the idea of being assaulted by a ghost seemed relatively appealing.

'Get *off* me!' she snapped. Or tried to. The sound she actually made was a muffled, undignified squawk, but he must have understood her meaning because he let her go immediately, thrusting her away from his body as if she were contaminated. Shaking back her hair, Sophie glared at him, trying to gather some shreds of dignity. Not easy when she'd just been caught behaving like a histrionic schoolgirl because she thought he was a ghost.

'What do you think you're *doing*?' she demanded.

His arched brows rose a fraction, but other than that his stony expression didn't change. 'I'd have thought it was obvious. Stopping you from screaming and waking up the entire castle,' he drawled. 'Is Jasper aware that you're roaming around the corridors in the middle of the night?'

'Jasper's asleep.'

'Ah. Of course.' His hooded gaze didn't leave hers, but she jumped as she felt his fingers close around her wrist, like bands of iron, and he lifted the hand in which her mobile phone was clasped.

His touch was as cold and hard as his tone. 'Don't tell me, you got lost on the way to the bathroom and you were using the GPS to find it?'

'No.' Sophie spoke through clenched teeth. 'I got lost on the way to my bedroom. Now, if you'd just point me in the right—'

'*Your* bedroom?' He dropped her wrist and stepped away. 'Well, it definitely won't be here. The rooms in this part of the castle haven't been used for years. But why the hell aren't you sharing with Jasper? Or perhaps you prefer to have your own…*privacy*?'

He was so tall that she had to tilt her head back to look at his face. The place where they were standing was dark and it was half in shadow, but, even so, she didn't miss the faint sneer that accompanied the word.

'I just thought it wouldn't be appropriate to sleep with Jasper in his parents' house, that's all,' she retorted haughtily. 'It didn't feel right.'

'You do a passable impression of indignant respectability,' he said in a bored voice, turning round and beginning to walk away from her down the corridor. 'But unfortunately it's rather wasted on me. I know exactly why you want your own bedroom, and it has nothing to do with propriety and everything to do with the fact that you're far from in love with my brother.'

It was those words that did it. *My brother.* Until then she had been determined to remain calm in the face of Kit Fitzroy's towering arrogance; his misguided certainty and his infuriating, undeniable sexual magnetism. Now something snapped inside her.

'No. You're *wrong*,' she spat.

'Really?' he drawled, turning to go back along the passageway down which she'd just come.

'Yes!'

Who the hell was he to judge? If it wasn't for him Jasper wouldn't have had to ask her here in the first place, to make himself look 'acceptable' in the contemptuous eyes of his brother.

Well, she couldn't explain anything without giving Jasper away, but she didn't have to take it either. Following him she could feel the pulse jumping in her wrist, in the place where his fingers had touched her, as fresh adrenaline scorched through her veins.

'I know you think the worst of me and I can understand why, but I just want to say that it wasn't—

isn't—what you think. I would *never* hurt Jasper, or mess him around. He's the person I care most about in the world.'

He went up a short flight of steps into the corridor Sophie now remembered, and stopped in front of the door at the end.

'You have a funny way of showing it,' he said, very softly. 'By sleeping with another man.'

He opened the door and stood back for her to pass. She didn't move. 'It's not like that,' she said in a low voice. 'You don't know the whole story.'

Kit shook his head. 'I don't need to.'

Because what was there to know? He'd seen it all countless times before—men returning back to base from leave, white-lipped and silent as they pulled down pictures of smiling wives or girlfriends from their lockers. Wives they thought they could trust while they were away. Girlfriends they thought would wait for them. Behind every betrayal there was a story, but in the end it was still a betrayal.

Folding her arms tightly across her body, she walked past him into the small room and stood by the bed with her back to him. Her hair was tangled, reminding him that she'd just left his brother's bed. In the thin, cold moonlight it gleamed like hot embers beneath the ashes of a dying fire.

'Is it common practice in the army to condemn without trial and without knowing the facts?' she asked, turning round to face him. 'You barely even *know* Jasper. You did your best to deny his existence when he was growing up, and you're not exactly going out of your way to make up for it now, so please don't lecture me about not loving him.'

'That's *enough.*'

The words were raw, razor-sharp, spoken in the split second before his automatic defences kicked in and the shutters came down on his emotions. Deliberately Kit unfurled his fists and kept his breathing steady.

'If you think finding your way around the castle is confusing I wouldn't even try to unravel the relationships within this family if I were you,' he said quietly. 'Don't get involved in things you don't need to understand.'

'Why? Because I won't be around long enough?' she demanded, coming closer to him again.

Kit stiffened as he caught the scent of her again—warm, spicy, delicious. He turned away, reaching for the door handle. 'Goodnight. I hope you have everything you need.'

He shut the door and stood back from it, waiting for the adrenaline rush to subside a little. Funny how he could work a field strewn with hidden mines, approach a car loaded with explosives and not feel anything, and yet five feet five of lying redhead had almost made him lose control.

He hated deception—too much of his childhood had been spent not knowing what to believe or who to trust—and as an actress, he supposed, Sophie Greenham was quite literally a professional in the art.

But unluckily for her he was a professional too, and there was more than one way of making safe an incendiary device. Sometimes you had to approach the problem laterally. If she wouldn't admit that her feelings for Jasper were a sham, he'd just have to prove it another way.

CHAPTER SIX

SOPHIE felt as if she'd only just fallen asleep when a knock at the door jolted her awake again. Jasper appeared, grinning sheepishly and carrying a plate of toast in one hand and two mugs of coffee in the other, some of which slopped onto the carpet as he elbowed the door shut again.

'What time is it?' she moaned, dropping back onto the pillows.

Jasper put the mugs down on the bedside table and perched on the bed beside her. 'Nearly ten. Kit said he'd bumped into you in the middle of the night trying to find your room, so I thought I'd better not wake you. You've slept for Britain.'

Sophie didn't have the heart to tell him she'd been awake most of the night, partly because she'd been frozen, partly because she'd been so hyped up with indignation and fury and the after-effects of what felt like an explosion in the sexual-chemistry lab that sleep had been a very long time coming.

He picked up a mug and looked at her through the wreaths of steam that were curling through the frigid air. 'Sorry for leaving you to wander like that. Just as well you bumped into Kit.'

Sophie grunted crossly. 'Do you think so? I thought he was the ghost of the nymphomaniac countess. No such luck.'

Jasper winced. 'He didn't give you a hard time, did he?'

'He thought it was extremely odd that we weren't sharing a room.' Sophie reached for a coffee, more to warm her hands on than anything. 'I'm not exactly convincing him in my role as your girl-friend, you know. The thing is, he overheard me talking to Jean-Claude on the train and now he thinks I'm a two-timing trollop.'

'Oops.' Jasper took another sip of coffee while he digested this information. 'OK, well, that is a bit unfortunate, but don't worry—we still have time to turn it around at the party tonight. You'll be every man's idea of the perfect girlfriend.'

Sophie raised an eyebrow. 'In public? In front of your parents? From my experience of what men consider the perfect girlfriend, that wouldn't be wise.'

'Wicked girl,' Jasper scolded. 'I meant demure,

devoted, hanging on my every word—that sort of thing. What did you bring to wear?'

'My Chinese silk dress.'

With a firm shake of his head Jasper put down his mug. 'Absolutely *not*. Far too sexy. No, what we need is something a little more…understated. A little more *modest*.'

Sophie narrowed her eyes. 'You mean frumpy, don't you? Do you have something in mind?'

Getting up, Jasper went over to the window and drew back the curtains with a theatrical flourish. 'Not something, some*where*. Get up, Cinderella, and let's hit the shops of Hawksworth.'

Jasper drove Ralph's four-by-four along roads that had been turned into ice rinks. It was a deceptively beautiful day. The sun shone in a sky of bright, hard blue and made the fields and hedgerows glitter as if each twig and blade of grass was encrusted with Swarovski crystals. He had pinched a navy-blue quilted jacket of Tatiana's to lend to Sophie, instead of the military-style overcoat of which Kit had been so scathing. Squinting at her barefaced reflection in the drop-down mirror on the sun visor, she remarked that all that was missing was a silk headscarf and her new posh-girl image would be complete. Jasper leaned over and pulled one out of the glove compartment. She tied it under her chin and they roared with laughter.

They parked in the market square in the centre of a town that looked as if it hadn't altered much in the last seventy years. Crunching over gritted cobblestones, Jasper led her past greengrocers, butchers and shops selling gate hinges and sheep dip, to an ornately fronted department store. Mannequins wearing bad blonde wigs modelled twinsets and patterned shirtwaister dresses in the windows.

'Braithwaite's—the fashion centre of the North since 1908' read the painted sign above the door. Sophie wondered if it was meant to be ironic.

'After you, madam,' said Jasper with a completely straight face, holding the door open for her. 'Evening wear. First floor.'

Sophie stifled a giggle. 'I love vintage clothing, as you know, but—'

'No buts,' said Jasper airily, striding past racks of raincoats towards a sweeping staircase in the centre of the store. 'Just think of it as dressing for a part. Tonight, Ms Greenham, you are *not* going to be your gorgeous, individual but—let's face it—

slightly eccentric self. You are going to be perfect Fitzroy-fiancée material. And that means Dull.'

At the top of the creaking staircase Sophie caught sight of herself in a full-length mirror. In jeans and Tatiana's jacket, the silk scarf still knotted around her neck a lurid splash of colour against her un-made-up face, dull was exactly the word. Still, if dull was what was required to slip beneath Kit Fitzroy's radar that had to be a good thing.

Didn't it?

She hesitated for a second, staring into her own wide eyes, thinking of last night and the shower of shooting stars that had exploded inside her when he'd touched her wrist; the static that had seemed to make the air between them vibrate as they'd stood in the dark corridor. The blankness of his expression, but the way it managed to convey more vividly than a thousand well-chosen words his utter contempt...

'What do you think?'

Yes. Dull was good. The duller the better.

'Hello-*o*?'

Pasting on a smile, she turned to Jasper, who had picked out the most hideous concoction of ruffles and ruches in the kind of royal blue frequently used for school uniforms. Sophie waved her hand dismissively.

'Strictly Come Drag Queen. I thought we were going for dull—that's attention-grabbing for all the wrong reasons. No—we have to find something *really* boring…' She began rifling through rails of pastel polyester. 'We have to find the closest thing The Fashion Capital of the North has to a shroud… Here. How about this?'

Triumphantly she pulled out something in stiff black fabric—long, straight and completely un-adorned. The neck was cut straight across in a way that she could imagine would make her breasts look like a sort of solid, matronly shelf, and the price tag was testament to the garment's extreme lack of appeal. It had been marked down three times already and was now almost being given away.

'Looks good to me.' Jasper flipped the hanger around, scrutinising the dress with narrowed eyes. 'Would madam like to try it on?'

'Nope. It's my size, it's horrible and it's far too cold to get undressed. Let's just buy it and go to the pub. As your fiancée I think I deserve an enormous and extremely calorific lunch.'

Jasper grinned and kissed her swiftly on the cheek. 'You're on.'

* * *

The Bull in Hawksworth was the quintessential English pub: the walls were yellow with pre-smoking-ban nicotine, a scarred dartboard hung on the wall beside an age-spotted etching of Alnburgh Castle and horse brasses were nailed to the blackened beams. Sophie slid behind a table in the corner by the fire while Jasper went to the bar. He came back with a pint of lager and a glass of red wine, and a newspaper folded under his arm.

'Food won't be a minute,' he said, taking a sip of lager, which left a froth of white on his upper lip. 'Would you mind if I gave Sergio a quick call? I brought you this to read.' He threw down the newspaper and gave her an apologetic look as he took out his phone. 'It's just it's almost impossible to get a bloody signal at Alnburgh, and I'm always terrified of being overheard anyway.'

Sophie shrugged. 'No problem. Go ahead.'

'Is there a "but" there?'

Taking a sip of her wine, she shook her head. 'No, of course not.' She put her glass down, turning the stem between her fingers. In the warmth of the fire and Jasper's familiar company she felt herself relaxing more than she had done in the last twenty-four hours. 'Except,' she went on thoughtfully, 'perhaps that I wonder if it wouldn't be easier if you came clean about all this.'

'Came out, you mean?' Jasper said with sudden weariness. 'Well, it wouldn't. It's easier just to live my own life, far away from here, without having to deal with the fallout of knowing I've let my whole family down. My father might be seventy, but he still prides himself on the reputation as a ladies' man he's spent his entire adult life building. He sees flirting with anything in a skirt as a mark of sophisticated social interaction—as you may have noticed last night. Homosexuality is utterly alien to him, so he thinks it's unnatural full stop.' With an agitated movement of his hand he knocked his pint glass so that beer splashed onto the table. 'Honestly, it would finish him off. And as for Kit—'

'Yes, well, I don't know what gives Kit the right to go around passing judgment on everyone else, like he's something special,' Sophie snapped, un-folding the paper as she moved it away from the puddle of lager on the table. 'It's not as if he's better than you because he's straight, or me because he's posh—'

'Holy cow,' spluttered Jasper, grasping her arm.

Breaking off, she followed his astonished gaze

and felt the rest of the rant dissolve on her tongue. For there, on the front of the newspaper—in grainy black and white, but no less arresting for it—was Kit. Beneath the headline *Heroes Honoured* a photograph showed him in half profile, his expression characteristically blank above his dress uniform with its impressive line of medals.

Quickly, incredulously, Jasper began to read out the accompanying article.

'Major Kit Fitzroy, known as "the heart-throb hero", was awarded the George Medal for his "dedication to duty and calm, unflinching bravery in the face of extreme personal risk". Major Fitzroy has been responsible for making safe over 100 improvised explosive devices, potentially saving the lives of numerous troops and civilians, a feat which he describes as "nothing remarkable".'

For long moments neither of them spoke. Sophie felt as if she'd swallowed a firework, which was now fizzing inside her. The barmaid brought over plates of lasagne and chips and retreated again.

Sophie's appetite seemed to have mysteriously deserted her.

'I suppose that does give him the right to act like he's a *bit* special, and *slightly* better than you and me,' she admitted shakily. 'Did you know anything about this?'

'Not a thing.'

'But wouldn't your father want to know? Wouldn't he be pleased?'

Jasper shrugged. 'He's always been rather sneery about Kit's army career, maybe because he's of the opinion people of our class don't work, apart from in pointless, arty jobs like mine.' Picking up his pint, he frowned. 'It might also have something to do with the fact his older brother was killed in the Falklands, but I don't know. That's one of those Things We definitely Do Not Mention.'

There seemed to be quite a lot of those in the Fitzroy family, Sophie thought. She couldn't stop looking at the photograph of Kit, even though she wanted to. Or help thinking how attractive he was, even though she didn't want to.

It had been easy to write him off as an obnoxious, arrogant control-freak but what Jasper had said about his mother last night, and now this, made her see him, reluctantly, in a different light.

What was worse, it made her see herself in a different light too. Having been on the receiving end of ignorant prejudice, Sophie liked to think she would never rush to make ill-informed snap judgments about people, but she had to admit that maybe, just maybe, in this instance she had.

But so had he, she reminded herself defiantly. He had dismissed her as a shallow, tarty gold-digger when that most definitely wasn't true. The gold-digger part, anyway. Hopefully tonight, with the aid of the nunlike dress and a few pithy comments on current affairs and international politics, she'd make him see he'd been wrong about the rest too.

For Jasper's sake, obviously.

As they left she picked up the newspaper. 'Do you think they'd mind if I took this?'

'What for?' Jasper asked in surprise. 'D'you want to sleep with the heart-throb hero under your pillow?'

'No!' Annoyingly Sophie felt herself blush. 'I want to swot up on the headlines so I can make intelligent conversation tonight.'

Jasper laughed all the way back to the car.

* * *

Ralph adjusted his bow tie in the mirror above the drawing room fireplace and smoothed a hand over his brushed-back hair.

'I must say, Kit, I find your insistence on bringing up the subject of my death in rather poor taste,' he said in an aggrieved tone. 'Tonight of all nights. A milestone birthday like this is depressing enough without you reminding me constantly that the clock is ticking.'

'It's not personal,' Kit drawled, mentally noting that he'd do well to remember that himself. 'And it is boring, but the fact remains that Alnburgh won't survive the inheritance tax it'll owe on your death unless you've transferred the ownership of the estate to someone else. Seven years is the—'

Ralph cut him off with a bitter, blustering laugh. 'By someone else, I suppose you mean you? What about Jasper?'

Alnburgh is yours, Kit. Don't let anyone tell you it's not.

In the pockets of his dinner-suit trousers Kit's hands were bunched into fists. Experience had taught him that when Ralph was in this kind of punchy, belligerent mood the best way to respond was with total detachment. He wondered fleetingly if that was where he first picked up the habit.

'Jasper isn't the logical heir,' he said, very evenly.

'Oh, I don't know about that,' Ralph replied with unpleasant, mock joviality. 'Let's look at it this way—Jasper is probably going to live another sixty or seventy years, and, believe me, I have every intention of lasting a lot more than seven years. Given your job I'd say you're the one who's pushing your luck in that department, don't you think? Remember what happened to my dear brother Leo. Never came back from the Falklands. Very nasty business.'

Ralph's eyes met Kit's in the mirror and slid away. He was already well on the way to being drunk, Kit realised wearily, and that meant that any further attempt at persuasion on his part would only be counterproductive.

'Transfer it to Jasper if you want.' He shrugged, picking up the newspaper that lay folded on a coffee table. 'That would certainly be better than doing nothing, though I'm not sure he'd thank you for it since he hates being here as much as Tatiana does. It might also put him at further risk from ruthless gold-diggers like the one he's brought up this weekend.'

The medals ceremony he'd attended yesterday was front-page news. Idly he wondered whether Ralph had seen it and chosen not to say anything.

'Sophie?' Ralph turned round, putting his hands into his pockets and rocking back on the heels of his patent shoes. 'I thought she was quite charming. Gorgeous little thing, too. Good old Jasper, eh? He's got a cracker there.'

'Except for the fact that she couldn't give a toss about him,' Kit commented dryly, putting down the paper.

'Jealous, Kit?' Ralph said, and there was real malice in his tone. His eyes were narrowed, his face suddenly flushed. 'You think you're the one who should get all the good-looking girls, don't you? I'd say you want her for yourself, just like—'

At that moment the strange outburst was interrupted by Jasper coming in. Ralph broke off and turned abruptly away.

'Just like what?' Kit said softly.

'Nothing.' Ralph pulled a handkerchief from his pocket and mopped his brow. As he turned to Jasper his face lost all its hostility. 'We were just talking about you—and Sophie.'

Heading to the drinks tray, Jasper grinned. 'Gorgeous, isn't she? And really clever and talented too. Great actress.'

In his dinner suit and with his hair wet from the shower Jasper looked about fifteen, Kit thought, his heart darkening against Sophie Greenham.

'So I noticed,' he said blandly, going to the door. He turned to Ralph. 'Think about what I said about the estate transfer. Oh, and I promised Thomas I'd see to the port tonight. Any preference?'

Ralph seemed to have recovered his composure. 'There's an excellent '29. Though, on second thoughts, open some '71.' His smile held a hint of challenge. 'Let's keep the really good stuff for my hundredth, since I fully intend to be around to celebrate it.'

Crossing the portrait hall in rapid, furious strides, Kit swore with such viciousness a passing waiter shot behind a large display of flowers. So he'd failed to make Ralph see sense about the estate. He'd just have to make sure he was more successful when it came to Sophie Greenham.

* * *

It was just as well she hadn't eaten all that lasagne at lunchtime, Sophie reflected grimly, tugging at the zip on the side of the black dress. Obviously, with hindsight, trying it on in the shop would have been wise—all the croissants and baguettes in Paris must have taken more of a toll than she'd realised. Oh, well—if it didn't fit she'd just have to wear the Chinese silk that Jasper had decreed was too sexy…

Hope flared inside her. Instantly she stamped it out.

No. Tonight was not about being sexy, or having fun, she told herself sternly. Tonight was about supporting Jasper and showing Kit that she wasn't the wanton trollop he had her down as.

She thought again of the photo in the paper—unsmiling, remote, heroic—and her insides quivered a little. Because, she realised with a pang of surprise, she actually didn't want him to think that about her.

With renewed effort she gave the zip another furious tug. It shot up and she let out the lungful of air she'd been holding, looking down at the dress with a sinking heart. Her cell-like bedroom didn't boast anything as luxurious as a full-length mirror, but she didn't need to see her whole reflection to know how awful she looked. It really was the most severely unflattering garment imaginable, falling in a plain, narrow, sleeveless tube from her collarbones to her ankles. A slit up one side at least meant that she could walk without affecting tiny geishalike steps, but she felt as if she were wrapped in a roll of wartime blackout fabric.

'That's *good*,' she said out loud, giving herself a severe look in the little mirror above the sink. Her reflection stared back at her, face pale against the bright mass of her hair. She'd washed it and, gleaming under the overhead light, the colour now seemed more garish than ever. Grabbing a few pins, she stuck them in her mouth, then pulled her hair back and twisted it tightly at the back of her neck.

Standing back again, she pulled a face.

There. Disfiguring dress and headmistress hair. Jasper's dull girlfriend was ready for her public, although at least Sophie had the private satisfaction of knowing that she was also wearing very naughty underwear and what Jasper fondly called her 'shag-me' shoes. Twisting round, she tried to check the back view of the dress, and gave a snort of laughter as she noticed the price ticket hanging down between her shoulder blades.

Classy and expensive was always going to be a

hard look for the girl who used to live on a bus to pull off, as Olympia Rothwell-Hyde and her cronies had never stopped reminding her. Attempting to do it with a label on her back announcing just how little she'd paid for the blackout dress would make it damned impossible.

She gave it a yank and winced as the plastic cut into her fingers. Another try confirmed that it was definitely a job for scissors. Which she didn't have.

She bit her lip. Jasper had already gone down, telling her to join them in the drawing room as soon as she was ready, but there was no way she could face Tatiana, who would no doubt be decked out in designer finery and dripping with diamonds, with her knock-down price ticket on display. She'd just have to slip down to the kitchens and see if the terrifying Mrs Daniels—or Mrs Danvers as she'd privately named her when Jasper had introduced her this morning—had some.

The layout of the castle was more familiar now and Sophie headed for the main stairs as quickly as the narrow dress would allow. The castle felt very different this evening from the cavernous, shad-owy place at which she'd arrived last night. Now the stone walls seemed to resonate with a hum of activity as teams of caterers and waiting-on staff made final preparations in the staterooms below.

It was still freezing, though. In the portrait hall the smell of woodsmoke drifted through the air, carried on icy gusts of wind that the huge fires banked in every grate couldn't seem to thaw. It mingled with the scent of hothouse flowers, which stood on every table and window ledge.

Sophie hitched up the narrow skirt of her dress and went more carefully down the narrow back stairs to the kitchens. It was noticeably warmer down here, the vaulted ceilings holding the heat from the ovens. A central stone-flagged passage-way stretched beyond a row of Victorian windows in the kitchen wall, into the dimly lit distance. To the dungeons, Jasper had teased her earlier.

The dungeons, where Kit probably locked up two-timing girlfriends, she thought grimly, shivering in spite of the relative warmth. The noise of her heels echoed loudly off the stone walls. The glass between the corridor and the kitchen was clouded with steam, but through it Sophie could see that Mrs Daniels' domain had been taken over by legions of uniformed chefs.

Of course. Jasper had mentioned that both she

and Thomas the butler had been given the night off. Well, there was no way she was going in there. Turning on her high heel, she hitched up her skirt and was hurrying back in the direction she'd just come when a voice behind her stopped her in her tracks.

'Are you looking for something?'

Her heart leapt into her throat and she spun round. Kit had emerged from one of the many small rooms that led off the passageway, his shoulders, in a perfectly cut black dinner suit, seeming almost to fill the narrow space. Their eyes met, and in the harsh overhead bulk light Sophie saw him recoil slightly as a flicker of some emotion—shock, or was it distaste?—passed across his face.

'I was l-looking for M-Mrs Daniels,' she said in a strangled voice, feeling inexplicably as if he'd caught her doing something wrong again. God, no wonder he had risen so far up the ranks in the army. She'd bet he could reduce insubordinate squaddies to snivelling babies with a single glacial glare. She coughed, and continued more determinedly. 'I wanted to borrow some scissors.'

'That's a relief.' His smile was almost imperceptible. 'I assume it means I don't have to tell you that you have a price ticket hanging down your back.'

Heat prickled through her, rising up her neck in a tide of uncharacteristic shyness.

Quickly she cleared her throat again. 'No.'

'Perhaps I could help? Follow me.'

Sophie was glad of the ringing echo of her shoes on the stone floor as it masked the frantic thud of her heart. He had to duck his head to get through the low doorway and she followed him into a vaulted cellar, the brick walls of which were lined with racks of bottles that gleamed dully in the low light. There was a table on which more bottles stood, alongside a knife and stained cloth like a consumptive's handkerchief. Kit picked up the knife.

'Wh-what are you doing?'

Hypnotised, she watched him wipe the blade of the knife on the cloth.

'Decanting port.'

'What for?' she rasped, desperately trying to make some attempt at sensible conversation. Snatches of the article in the newspaper kept coming back to her, making it impossible to think clearly. *Heart-throb hero. Unflinching bravery. Extreme personal risk.* It was as if someone had taken her jigsaw puzzle image of him and broken it to bits, so the pieces made quite a different picture now.

His lips twitched into the faint half-smile she'd come to recognise, but his hooded eyes held her gravely. The coolness was still there, but they'd lost their sharp contempt.

'To get rid of the sediment. The bottle I've just opened last saw daylight over eighty years ago.'

Sophie gave a little laugh, squirming slightly under his scrutiny. 'Isn't it a bit past its sell-by date?'

'Like lots of things, it improves with age,' he said dryly, taking hold of her shoulders with surprising gentleness and turning her round. 'Would you like to try some?'

'Isn't it very expensive?'

What was it about an absence of hostility that actually made it feel like kindness? Sophie felt the hair rise on the back of her neck as his fingers brushed her bare skin. She held herself very rigid for a second, determined not to give in to the helpless shudder of desire that threatened to shake her whole body as he bent over her. Her breasts tingled, and beneath the severe lines of the dress her nipples pressed against the tight fabric.

'Put it this way, you could get several dresses like that for the price of a bottle,' he murmured, and Sophie could feel the warm whisper of his breath on her neck as he spoke. She closed her eyes, wanting the moment to stretch for ever, but then she heard the snap of plastic as he cut through the tag and he was pulling back, leaving her feeling shaky and on edge.

'To be honest, that doesn't say much about your port,' she joked weakly.

'No.' He went back over to the table and picked up a bottle, holding it up to the light for a second before pouring a little of the dark red liquid into a slender, teardrop-shaped decanter. 'It's a great dress. It suits you.'

His voice was offhand. So why did it make goose-bumps rise on her skin?

'It's a very *cheap* dress.' She laughed again, awkwardly, crossing her arms across her chest to hide the obvious outline of her nipples, which had to be glaringly obvious against the plainness of the dress. 'Or is that what you meant by it suiting me?'

'No.'

He turned to face her, holding the slim neck of the decanter. She couldn't take her eyes off his hands.

Against the white cuffs of his evening shirt they looked very tanned and she felt her heart twist in her chest, catching her off guard as she thought of what he had done with those hands. And what he had seen with those eyes. And now he was looking at her with that cool, dispassionate stare and she almost couldn't breathe.

'I haven't got a glass, I'm afraid.' He swirled the port around in the decanter so it gleamed like liquid rubies, and then offered it up to her lips. 'Take it slowly. Breathe it in first.'

Oh, God.

At that moment she wasn't sure she was capable of breathing at all, but it was as if he had some kind of hypnotist's hold over her and somehow she did as he said, her gaze fixed unblinkingly on his as she inhaled.

It was the scent of age and incense and reverence, and instantly she was transported back to the chapel at school, kneeling on scratchy woollen hassocks to sip communion wine and trying to ignore the whispers of Olympia Rothwell-Hyde and her friends, saying that she'd go to hell because everyone knew she hadn't even been baptised, never mind confirmed. What vicar would christen a child with a name like Summer Greenham?

She pulled away sharply just as the port touched her lips, so that it missed her mouth and dripped down her chin. Kit's reactions were like lightning— in almost the same second his hand came up to cup her face, catching the drips of priceless liquor on the palm of his hand.

'I'm sorry,' she gasped. 'I didn't mean to waste it—'

'Then let's not.'

It was just a whisper, and then he was bending his head so that, slowly, softly, his mouth grazed hers. Sophie's breathing hitched, her world stopped as his lips moved downwards to suck the drips on her chin as her lips parted helplessly and a tidal wave of lust and longing was unleashed inside her. It washed away everything, so that her head was empty of questions, doubts, uncertainties: every-thing except the dark, swirling whirlpool of need. Her body did the thinking, the deciding for her as it arched towards him, her hands coming up of their own volition to grip his rock-hard shoulders and tangle in his hair.

This was what she knew. This meeting of mouths

and bodies, this igniting of pheromones and stoking of fires—these were feelings she understood and could deal with expertly. Familiar territory.

Or, it had been.

Not now.

Not *this*…

His touch was gentle, languid, but it seared her like a blowtorch, reducing the memory of every man who'd gone before to ashes and dust. One hand rested on her hip, the other cupped her cheek as he kissed her with a skill and a kind of brooding focus that made her tremble and melt.

And want *more*.

The stiff fabric of the hateful dress felt like armour plating. She pressed herself against him, longing to be free of it, feeling the contours of the hard muscles of his chest through the layers of clothes that separated them. Her want flared, a fire doused with petrol, and as she kissed him back her fingers found the silk bow tie at his throat, tugging at the knot, working the shirt button beneath it free.

And suddenly there was nothing gentle in the way he pulled her against him, nothing languid about the pressure of his mouth or the erotic thrust and dart of his tongue. Sophie's hands were shaking as she slid them beneath his jacket. She could feel the warmth of his body, the rapid beating of his heart as he gripped her shoulders, pushing her backwards against the ancient oak barrels behind her.

Roughly she pushed his jacket off his shoulders. His hands were at her waist and she yanked at her skirt, pulling it upwards so that he could hitch her onto a barrel. She straddled its curved surface, her hips rising to press against his, her fingers twisting in his shirt front as she struggled to pull it free of his trousers.

She was disorientated with desire. Trembling, shaking, unhinged with an urgency that went beyond anything she'd known before. The need to have him against her and in her.

'Now…please…'

She gasped as he stepped backwards, tearing his mouth from hers, turning away. A physical sensation of loss swept through her as her hands, still outstretched towards him, reached to pull him back into her. Her breath was coming in ragged, thirsty gasps; she was unable to think of anything beyond satisfying the itch and burn that pulsed through her veins like heroin.

Until he turned back to face her again and her blood froze.

His shirt was open to the third button, his silk tie hanging loose around his neck in the classic, clichéd image from every red-blooded woman's slickest fantasy. But that was where the dream ended, because his face was like chiselled marble and his hooded eyes were as cold as ice.

And in that second, in a rush of horror and pain, Sophie understood what had just happened. What she had just done. He didn't need to say anything because his expression—completely deadpan apart from the slight curl of his lip as he looked at her across the space that separated them—said it all.

She didn't hesitate. Didn't think. It was pure instinct that propelled her across that space and made her raise her hand to slap his face.

But her instinct was no match for his reflexes. With no apparent effort at all he caught hold of her wrist and held it absolutely still for a heartbeat before letting go.

'You unutterable bastard,' she breathed.

She didn't wait for a response. Somehow she made her trembling legs carry her out of the wine cellar and along the corridor, while her horrified mind struggled to take in the enormity of what had just happened. She had betrayed Jasper and given herself away. She had proved Kit Fitzroy right. She had played straight into his hands and revealed herself as the faithless, worthless gold-digger he'd taken her for all along.

CHAPTER SEVEN

So in the end it hadn't even been as hard as he'd thought it would be.

With one quick, angry movement Kit speared the cork in another dusty bottle and twisted it out with far less care and respect than the vintage deserved.

He hadn't exactly anticipated she would be a challenge to seduce, but somehow he'd imagined a little more in the way of token resistance; some evidence of a battle with her conscience at least.

But she had responded instantly.

With a passion that matched his own.

His hand shook, and the port he was pouring through the muslin cloth into the decanter dripped like blood over the backs of his fingers. Giving a muttered curse, he put the bottle down and put his hand to his mouth to suck off the drops.

What the hell was the matter with him? His hands were usually steady as a rock—he and his entire team would have been blown to bits long ago if they weren't. And if he hesitated, or questioned himself as he was doing now…

He had done what he set out to do, and her reaction was exactly what he'd predicted.

But his wasn't. His wasn't at all.

Wiping her damp palms down the skirt of the horrible dress, Sophie stood in the middle of the portrait hall, halfway between the staircase and the closed doors to the drawing room. She was still shaking with horror and adrenaline and vile, unwelcome arousal and the urge to run back up to her bedroom, throw her things into her bag and slip quietly out of the servants' entrance was almost overwhelming. Wasn't that the way she'd always dealt with things—the way her mother had shown her? When the going got tough you walked away. You told yourself it didn't matter and you weren't bothered, and just to show you meant it you packed up and moved on.

The catering staff were putting the finishing touches to the buffet in the dining room, footsteps ringing on the flagstones as they brought up more champagne in ice buckets with which to greet the guests who would start arriving any minute. Sophie hesitated, biting down on her throbbing lip as for a moment she let herself imagine getting on a train and speeding through the darkness back to London, where she'd never have to see Kit Fitzroy again...

She felt a stab of pain beneath her ribs, but at that moment one of the enormous doors to the drawing room opened and Jasper appeared.

'Ah, there you are, angel! I thought you might have got lost again so I was just coming to see if I could find you.'

He started to come towards her, and Sophie saw his eyes sweep over her, widening along with his smile as he came closer.

'Saints Alive, Sophie Greenham, that *dress*...'

'I know,' Sophie croaked. 'Don't say it. It's dire.'

'It's not.' Slowly Jasper circled around her, looking her up and down as an incredulous expression spread across his face. 'How *could* we have got it so wrong? It might have been cheap as chips and looked like a shroud on the hanger, but on you it's bloody dynamite.' He gave a low whistle. 'Have you seen yourself? No red-blooded, straight male will be able to keep his hands off you.'

She gave a slightly hysterical laugh. 'Darling, don't you believe it.'

'Soph?' Jasper looked at her in concern. 'You OK?'

Oh, hell, what was she doing? She'd come here to shield him from the prejudices of his family, and so far she'd only succeeded in making things more awkward for him. The fact that his brother was the kind of cold-blooded, ruthless bastard who would stop at nothing to preserve the purity of the Fitzroy name and reputation was all the more reason she should give this her all.

'I'm fine.' Digging her nails into the palms of her hands, she raised her chin and smiled brightly. 'And you look gorgeous. There's something about a man in black tie that I find impossible to resist.'

Wasn't that the truth?

'Good.' Jasper pressed a fleeting kiss to her cheek and, taking hold of her hand, pulled her forwards. 'In that case, let's get this party started. Personally, I intend to get stuck into the champagne right now, before guests arrive and we have to share it.'

Head down, Kit walked quickly in the direction of the King's Hall—not because he was in any hurry to get there, but because he knew from long experience that looking purposeful was the best way to avoid getting trapped into conversation.

The last thing he felt like doing was talking to anyone.

As he went up the stairs the music got louder. Obviously keen to recapture his youthful prowess on the dance floor Ralph had hired a swing band, who were energetically working their way through the back catalogue of The Beatles. The strident tones of trumpet and saxophone swelled beneath the vaulted ceiling and reverberated off the walls.

Kit paused at the top of the flight of shallow steps into the huge space. The dance floor was a mass of swirling silks and velvets but even so his gaze was instantly drawn to the girl in the plain, narrow black dress in the midst of the throng. She was dancing with Ralph, Kit noticed, feeling himself tense inexplicably as he saw his father's large, practised hand splayed across the small of Sophie's back.

They suited each other very well, he thought with an inward sneer, watching the way the slit in Sophie's dress opened up as she danced to reveal a seductive glimpse of smooth, pale thigh. Ralph was a lifelong womaniser and philanderer, and Sophie Greenham seemed to be pretty indiscriminate in her favours, so there was no reason why she shouldn't make it a Fitzroy hat-trick. He turned away in disgust.

'Kit darling! I thought it must be you—not many people fill a dinner jacket that perfectly, though I must say I'm rather disappointed you're not in dress uniform tonight.'

Kit's heart sank as Sally Rothwell-Hyde grasped his shoulders and enveloped him in a cloud of asphyxiating perfume as she stretched up to kiss him on both cheeks. 'I saw the picture on the front of the paper, you dark horse,' she went on, giving him a girlish look from beneath spidery eyelashes. 'You looked utterly mouth-watering, and the medal did rather add to the heroic effect. I was hoping to see it on you.'

'Medals are only worn on uniform,' Kit remarked, trying to muster the energy to keep the impatience from his voice. 'And being in military dress uniform amongst this crowd would have had a slight fancy-dress air about it, don't you think?'

'Very dashing fancy dress, though, darling.' Leaning in close to make herself heard above the noise of the band, Sally fluttered her eyelashes, which were far too thick and lustrous to be anything but fake. 'Couldn't you have indulged us ladies?'

Kit's jaw clenched as he suppressed the urge to swear. To Sally Rothwell-Hyde and her circle of ladies who lunched, his uniform was just a prop from some clichéd fantasy, his medals were nothing more than covetable accessories. He doubted that it had crossed her mind for a moment what he had gone through to get them. The lost lives they represented.

His gaze moved over her sunbed-tanned shoulder as he looked for an escape route, but she wasn't finished with him yet. 'Such a shame about you and Alexia,' she pouted. 'Olympia said she was absolutely heartbroken, poor thing. She's taken Lexia skiing this weekend, to cheer her up. Perhaps she'll meet some hunky instructor and be swept off her skis…'

Kit understood that this comment was intended to make him wild with jealousy, but since it didn't he could think of nothing to say. Sophie was still dancing with Ralph, but more slowly now, both of his hands gripping her narrow waist while the band, ironically, played 'Can't Buy Me Love'. She had her back to Kit, so as she inclined her head to catch something his father said Kit could see the creamy skin at the nape of her neck and suddenly remembered the silky, sexy underwear that had spilled out of her broken bag yesterday. He wondered what she was wearing under that sober black dress.

'Is that her replacement?'

Sally's slightly acerbic voice cut into his thoughts, which was probably just as well. Standing beside him, she had followed the direction of his stare, and now took a swig of champagne and looked at him pointedly over the rim of her glass.

'No,' Kit replied shortly. 'That's Jasper's girl-friend.'

'Oh! *Really*?' Her ruthlessly plucked eyebrows shot up and she turned to look at Sophie again, murmuring, 'I must say I never really thought there was anything in those rumours.' Before Kit could ask her what the hell she meant her eyes had narrowed shrewdly. 'Who is she? She looks vaguely familiar from somewhere.'

'She's an actress. Maybe you've seen her in something.' His voice was perfectly steady, though his throat suddenly felt as if he'd swallowed gravel.

'An actress,' Sally repeated thoughtfully. 'Typical Jasper. So, what's she like?'

Lord, all that champagne and he didn't have a drink himself. Where the hell were the bloody waiters? Kit looked around as his mind raced, thinking of a suitable answer. *She's an unscrupulous liar and as shallow as a puddle, but on the upside she's the most alive person I've ever met and she kisses like an angel...*

'I'll get Jasper to introduce you,' he said blandly, moving away. 'You can see for yourself.'

Just as Sophie was beginning to suspect that the band were playing the Extended-Groundhog-Club-Remix version of 'Can't Buy Me Love' and that she would be locked for ever in Ralph Fitzroy's damp and rather-too-intimate clutches, the song came to a merciful end.

She'd been relieved when he'd asked her to dance as it had offered a welcome diversion from the task of Avoiding Kit, which had been the sole focus of her evening until then.

'Gosh—these shoes are murder to dance in!' she exclaimed brightly, stepping backwards and forcing Ralph to loosen his death-grip on her waist.

Ralph took a silk handkerchief from the top pocket of his dinner jacket and mopped his brow.

Sophie felt a jolt of unease at the veins standing out in his forehead, the dark red flush in his cheeks, and suddenly wondered if it was lechery that had made him cling to her so tightly, or necessity. 'Darling girl, thank you for the dance,' he wheezed. 'You've made an old man very happy on his birthday. Look—here's Jasper to reclaim you.'

Slipping through the people on the dance floor, Jasper raised his hand in greeting. 'Sorry to break you two up, but I have people demanding to meet you, Soph. Pa, you don't mind if I snatch her away, do you?'

'Be my guest. I need a—' he broke off, swaying slightly, looking around '—need to—'

Sophie watched him weave slightly unsteadily through the crowd as Jasper grabbed her hand and started to pull her forwards. 'Jasper—your father,' she hissed, casting a worried glance over her shoulder. 'Is he OK? Maybe you should go with him?'

'He's fine,' Jasper said airily. 'This is the standard Hawksworth routine. He knocks back the booze, goes and sleeps it off for half an hour, then comes back stronger than ever and out-parties everyone else. Don't worry. A friend of my mother's is dying to meet you.'

He ran lightly up the steps and stopped in front of a petite woman in a strapless dress of aquamarine chiffon that showed off both her tan and the impressive diamonds around her crêpey throat. Her eyes were the colour of Bombay Sapphire gin and they swept over Sophie in swift appraisal as Jasper introduced her.

'Sophie, this is Sally Rothwell-Hyde, bridge partner-in-crime of my mother and all round bad influence. Sally—the girl of my dreams, Sophie—'

An icy wash of panic sluiced through her.

Great. Just *perfect*. She'd thought that there was no way that an evening that had started so disastrously could get any worse, but it seemed that fate had singled her out to be the victim of not one but several humiliating practical jokes. Just as Olympia Rothwell-Hyde used to do at school.

'Pleased to meet you,' Sophie cut in quickly before Jasper said her surname.

'Sophie...'

Sally Rothwell-Hyde's face bore a look of slight puzzlement as her eyes—so horribly reminiscent of the cold, china-doll blue of her daughter's—bored into Sophie. 'I'm trying to place you. Perhaps I know your parents?'

'I don't think so.'

Damn, she'd said that far too quickly. Sweat was prickling between her shoulder blades and gathering in the small of her back, and she felt slightly sick. She moistened her lips. Think of it as being onstage, she told herself desperately as the puzzled look was replaced by one of surprise and Sally Rothwell-Hyde gave a tinkling laugh.

'Gosh—well, if it isn't that I can't think what it could be.' Her eyes narrowed. 'You must be about the same age as my daughter. You're not a friend of Olympia's, are you?'

Breathe, Sophie told herself. She just had to imagine she was in the audience, watching herself playing the part, delivering the lines. It was a fail-safe way of coping with stage fright. Distance. Calm. Step outside yourself. Inhabit the character. And above all resist the urge to shriek, *A friend of that poisonous cow? Are you insane?'*

She arranged her face into a thoughtful expression. 'Olympia Rothwell-Hyde?' She said the loathed name hesitantly, as if hearing it for the first time, then shook her head, with just a hint of apology. 'It doesn't ring any bells. Sorry. Gosh, isn't it warm in here now? I'm absolutely dying of thirst after all that dancing, so if you'll excuse me I must just go and find a drink. Isn't it ironic to be surrounded by champagne when all you want is water?'

She began to move away before she finished speaking, glancing quickly at Jasper in a silent plea for him to rein back his inbred chivalry and keep quiet. He missed it entirely.

'I'll get—'

'No, darling, please. You stay and chat. I'll be back in a moment.'

She went down the steps again and wove her way quickly through the knots of people at the edge of the dance floor. Along the length of the hall there were sets of double doors out onto the castle walls and someone had opened one of them, letting in a sharp draft of night air. Sophie's footsteps stalled and she drank it in gratefully. It was silly—she'd spent the twenty-four hours since she'd arrived at Alnburgh freezing half to death and would have found it impossible to imagine being glad of the cold.

But then she'd have found it impossible to imagine a lot of the things that had happened in the last twenty-four hours.

A waiter carrying a tray laden with full glasses was making his way gingerly along the edge of the dance floor. He glanced apologetically at Sophie as she approached. 'Sorry, madam, I'm afraid this is sparkling water. If you'd like champagne I can—'

'Nope. Water's perfect. Thank you.' She took a glass, downed it in one and took another, hoping it might ease the throbbing in her head. At the top of the steps at the other end of the hall she could see Jasper still talking to Olympia Rothwell-Hyde's mother, so she turned and kept walking in the opposite direction.

She would explain to Jasper later. Right now the only thing on her mind was escape.

Stepping outside was like slipping into still, clear, icy water. The world was blue and white, lit by a paper-lantern moon hanging high over the beach. The quiet rushed in on her, as sudden and striking an assault on her senses as the breathtaking cold.

Going forwards to lean on the wall, she took in a gulp of air. It was so cold it flayed the inside of her lungs, and she let it go again in a cloud of white as she looked down. Far, far beneath her the rocks were sharp-edged and silvered by moonlight, and she found herself remembering Kit's voice as he told her about the desperate countess, throwing herself off the walls to her death. Down there? Sophie leaned further over, trying to imagine how things could have possibly been bleak enough for her to resort to such a brutal solution.

'It's a long way down.'

Sophie jumped so violently that the glass slipped from her hand and spiralled downwards in a shower of sparkling droplets. Her hand flew to her mouth, but not before she'd sworn, savagely and succinctly. In the small silence that followed she heard the sound of the glass shattering on the rocks below.

Kit Fitzroy came forwards slowly, so she could see the sardonic arch of his dark brows. 'Sorry. I didn't mean to startle you.'

Sophie gave a slightly wild laugh. 'Really? After what happened earlier, forgive me if I don't believe that for a second and just assume that's exactly what you meant to do, probably in the hope that it might result in another "accident" like the one that befell the last unsuitable woman to be brought home by a Fitzroy.'

She was talking too fast, and her heart was still banging against her ribs like a hammer on an anvil. She couldn't be sure it was still from the fright he'd just given her, though. Kit Fitzroy just seemed to have that effect on her.

'What a creative imagination you have.'

'Somehow it doesn't take too much creativity to imagine that you'd want to get rid of me.' She turned round, looking out across the beach again, to avoid having to look at him. 'You went to quite a lot of trouble to set me up and manipulate me earlier, after all.'

He came to stand beside her, resting his forearms on the top of the wall.

'It was no trouble. You were depressingly easy to manipulate.'

His voice was soft, almost intimate, and entirely at odds with the harshness of the words. But he was right, she acknowledged despairingly. She had been a pushover.

'You put me in an impossible position.'

'It wasn't impossible at all,' he said gravely. 'It would have been extremely workable, *if* I'd ever intended to let it get that far, which I didn't. Anyway, you're right. I do want to get rid of you, but since I'd have to draw the line at murder I'm hoping you'll leave quietly.'

'Leave?' Sophie echoed stupidly. A drumbeat of

alarm had started up inside her head, in tandem with the dull throb from earlier. She hadn't seen this coming, and suddenly she didn't know what to say any more, how to play it. What had started off as being a bit of a game, a secret joke between her and Jasper, had spun out of control somewhere along the line.

'Yes. Leave Alnburgh.'

In contrast with the chaotic thoughts that were rushing through her brain, his voice was perfectly emotionless as he straightened up and turned to face her.

'I gather from Tatiana that Jasper's planning to stay on for a few days, but I think it would be best if you went back to London as soon as possible. The rail service on Sundays is minimal, but there's a train to Newcastle at about eleven in the morning and you can get a connection from there. I'll arrange for Jensen to give you a lift to the station.'

Sophie was glad she had the wall to lean on because she wasn't sure her legs would hold her up otherwise. She didn't turn to look at him, but was still aware of his height and the power contained in his lean body. It made her quail inside but it also sent a gush of hot, treacherous longing through her. She laughed awkwardly.

'Well, Major Fitzroy, you've got it all worked out, haven't you? And what about Jasper? Or have you forgotten him?'

'It's Jasper I'm thinking of.'

'Ah.' Sophie smacked herself comically on the forehead. 'Silly me, because I thought all this was for your benefit. I thought you wanted me gone because my face and my clothes and my accent don't fit and because I'm not scared of you like everyone else is. Oh, yes, and also because, no matter how much you'd like to pretend otherwise, you weren't entirely faking what happened earlier.'

For a second she wondered if she'd gone too far as some emotion she couldn't quite read flared in the icy fathoms of his eyes, but it was quickly extinguished.

'No.' His voice was ominously soft. 'I want you gone because you're dangerous.'

The anger that had fuelled her last outburst seemed suddenly to have run out. Now she felt tired and defeated, as the stags on the walls must have felt when the Fitzroy guns had appeared on the horizon.

'And what am I supposed to tell him?'

Kit shrugged. 'You'll think of something, I'm sure. Your remarkable talent for deception should make it easy for you to find a way to let him down gently. Then he can find someone who'll treat him with the respect he deserves.'

'Someone who also fits your narrow definition of suitable.' Sophie gave a painful smile, thinking of Sergio. The irony would have been funny if it hadn't all got so serious, and so horribly humiliating. 'Gosh,' she went on, 'who would have guessed that under that controlling, joyless exterior beat such a romantic heart?'

'I'm not romantic.' Kit turned towards her again, leaning one hip against the wall as he fixed her with his lazy, speculative gaze. 'I just have this peculiar aversion to unscrupulous social climbers. As things stand at the moment I'm prepared to accept that you're just a pretty girl with issues around commitment and the word "no", but if you stay I'll be forced to take a less charitable view.'

From inside came a sudden chorus of 'Happy Birthday to You.' Automatically Sophie looked through the window to where everyone had assembled to watch Ralph cut his birthday cake. The light from the huge chandeliers fell on the perma-tanned backs of the women in their evening dresses and made the diamonds at their throats glitter, while amongst them the dinner-suited men could have been the rich and the privileged from any era in the last hundred years.

I really, really do not belong here, Sophie thought.

Part of her wanted to stand up to Kit Fitzroy and challenge his casual, cruel assumptions about her, as her mother would have done, but she knew from bitter experience that there was no point. Inside, through the press of people, she could see Sally Rothwell-Hyde, all gleaming hair and expensive white teeth, as she sang, and suddenly Sophie was sixteen again, standing in the corridor at school with her packed trunk and her hockey stick beside her, watching through the glass doors of the hall as the other girls sang the school hymn and she waited for Aunt Janet to arrive.

She clenched her teeth together to stop them chattering, suddenly realising that she was frozen to the bone. Inside the rousing chorus of 'Happy Birthday' was coming to an end. If she went in now she could probably slip past unnoticed and reach the staircase while all eyes were focused on the cake.

Lifting her chin, she met Kit Fitzroy's eyes. They were as cold and silvery as the surface of the moon-lit sea.

'OK. You win. I'll go.' She faked a smile. 'But do me a favour—spend some time with Jasper when I'm gone, would you? You'll like him when you get to know him.'

She didn't wait for his reply. Turning on her heel, holding herself very upright, she walked back to the door and pulled it open, stepping into the warmth just as the party-goers finished singing and burst into a noisy round of cheering and applause. Sophie paused as her eyes adjusted to the brightness in the hall. At the top of the steps at the far end an elaborate cake made to look like Alnburgh Castle stood on a damask-covered table, the light from the candles glowing in its battlements briefly illuminating Ralph's face as he leaned forwards to blow them out.

He seemed to hesitate for a moment, his mouth opening in an O of surprise. And then he was pitching sideways, grasping the tablecloth and pulling it, and the cake, with him as he fell to the floor.

CHAPTER EIGHT

'SOMEBODY *do* something!'

Tatiana's voice, shrill with panic, echoed through the sudden silence. Before Sophie had time to process what had happened Kit was pushing past her, shrugging his jacket off as he ran across the hall towards the figure on the floor. The stunned onlookers parted to let him through, recognising by some mutual instinct that he was the person to deal with this shocking turn of events. As the crowd shifted and fell back Sophie caught a glimpse of Ralph's face. It was the colour of old parchment.

Kit dropped to his knees beside his father, undoing his silk bow tie with swift, deft fingers and working loose the button at his throat.

'Does anyone know how to do mouth-to-mouth or CPR?' he shouted.

The tense silence was broken only by the shuffling of feet as people looked around hopefully, but no one spoke. Before she could think through the wisdom of what she was doing Sophie found herself moving forwards.

'I do.'

Kit didn't speak or look up as she knelt down opposite him. Bunching up his dinner jacket, he put it beneath Ralph's feet.

'Is he breathing?' she asked in a low voice.

'No.'

Tatiana, supported now on each side by male guests, let out a wail of distress.

'Jasper,' Kit barked icily, 'take her to the drawing room. You can phone for an ambulance from there. Tell them the roads are bad and they'll need to send a helicopter. Do it *now*.'

Bastard, thought Sophie in anguish, glancing round to where Jasper was standing, his face ashen against his black dinner jacket, his eyes wide and glassy with shock. How dared Kit talk to him like that at a time like this? But his voice seemed to snap Jasper out of his trance of shock and he gathered himself, doing as he was told.

'Breathing or heart?'

He was talking to her, Sophie realised. 'Breathing,' she said quickly, and regretted it almost straight away. At the moment she could barely breathe for herself, never mind for Ralph too, but there was no time for second thoughts.

Kit had already pulled his father's shirt open and started chest compressions, his lips moving silently as he counted. Sophie's hand shook as she tilted Ralph's head back and held his jaw. His skin had a clammy chill to it that filled her with dread, but also banished any lingering uncertainty.

OK, so she'd only done this on fellow actors in a TV hospital drama, but she'd been taught the technique by the show's qualified medical advisor and right now that looked like Ralph's best hope. She had to do it. And fast.

Kit's hands stilled. 'Ready?'

For the briefest second their eyes met, and she felt an electrical current crackle through her, giving her strength. She took in a breath and bent her head, placing her mouth over Ralph's and exhaling slowly.

The seconds ticked by, measured only by the steady tide of her breath, the rhythmic movement of Kit's hands. They took it in turns, each acutely aware of the movements of the other. It was like a dance in which she let Kit lead her, watching him for cues, her eyes fixed unwaveringly on his as she waited for his signal. Fifteen rapid compressions. Two long, slow breaths.

And then wait.

Sophie lost track of time. She lost track of everything except Kit's eyes, his strong, tanned hands locked together on Ralph's grey chest...the stillness of that chest. Sometimes she thought there were signs of life—too tenuous for her to feel relief, too strong for her to give up, so again and again she bent her head and breathed for Ralph, willing the life and heat and adrenaline of her own body into the inert figure on the floor.

And then at last as she lifted her head she saw Ralph's chest convulse in a sharp, gasping breath of his own. Her gaze flew to Kit's face as he looked down at his father, pressing his fingers to Ralph's neck, waiting to see if a pulse had returned. Except for the small frown of concentration between his brows it was expressionless, but a muscle twitched in his jaw.

And then Ralph breathed again and Kit looked at her.

'Good girl.'

The sound of running feet echoed through the hall, breaking the spell. Sophie's head jerked round and she was surprised to see that the guests had all vanished and the huge room was empty now—except for the helicopter paramedics coming towards them, like orange-suited angels from some sci-fi film.

Kit got to his feet in one lithe movement and dragged a hand through his hair. For the first time Sophie saw that he was grey with exhaustion beneath his tan.

'He's been unconscious for about seventeen minutes. He's breathing again. Pulse is weak but present.'

A female paramedic carrying a defibrillator kit glanced at him, then did a classic double take. 'Well done,' she said in a tone that bordered on awestruck. 'That makes our job so much easier.'

'Come on, sweetheart. We can take over now.'

Sophie jumped. One of the other paramedics was kneeling beside her, gently edging her out of the way as he fitted an oxygen mask over Ralph's face.

'Oh, I'm so sorry,' she muttered, attempting to get to her feet. 'I was miles away...I mean, I wasn't thinking...'

Her dress was too tight and her legs were numb from kneeling, making it difficult to stand. Somehow Kit was beside her, his hand gripping her elbow as she swayed on her high heels.

'OK?'

She nodded, suddenly unable to speak for the lump of emotion that had lodged in her throat. Relief, perhaps. Delayed shock. Powerful things that made her want to collapse into his arms and sob like a little girl.

She had no idea why. Even when she was a little girl she couldn't ever remember sobbing so now was hardly the time to start. And Kit Fitzroy, who not half an hour ago had coldly ordered her to leave his family home, was definitely not the person to start on.

Raising her chin and swallowing hard, she stepped away from him, just as Jasper appeared.

'Soph—what's h—?'

He stopped, his reddened eyes widening in horror as the paramedics strapped his father's body onto the stretcher. Quickly Sophie went to his side, putting her arms around his trembling body.

'It's OK,' she soothed, suddenly poleaxed with exhaustion. 'He's alive, he's breathing and he's in the very best hands now.'

Briefly he leaned against her and she smelled the

booze on his breath and felt his shoulders shake as he sobbed. 'Sophie, thank God you were here.' He pulled away, hastily wiping his eyes. 'I should go. To the hospital, to be with Mum.'

Sophie nodded.

'I'm afraid there's only room for one person in the helicopter,' the pretty blonde paramedic apologised as they lifted the stretcher. 'The rest of the family will have to follow by car.'

Momentary panic flashed across Jasper's face as he made a mental calculation of alcohol units.

'I can't—'

'I can.' Kit stepped forwards. 'Tatiana can go in the helicopter and I'll take Jasper.' His eyes met Sophie's. 'Are you coming?'

For a long moment they looked at each other. Blood beat in Sophie's ears and her heart seemed to swell up, squeezing the air from her lungs. She shook her head.

'No. No, I'll stay and make sure everything's OK here.'

For a few minutes—seventeen apparently, who knew?—they had shared something. A connection. But it was gone again now. She might just have helped to save his father's life, but that didn't alter the fact that Kit Fitzroy had made it very clear he wanted her out of Jasper's. And his. The sooner the better.

Hours later, standing in the softly lit corridor of the private hospital, Kit rubbed a hand over his stinging eyes.

He could defuse a landmine and dismantle the most complex and dangerous IED in extreme heat and under enemy fire, but he couldn't for the life of him work out how to get a cup of instant coffee from the machine in front of him.

Stabilised by drugs and hooked up to bags of fluid, Ralph was sleeping peacefully now. The hospital staff, hearing that Lord Hawksworth was on his way, had telephoned Ralph's private physician at home. He had arranged for Ralph to be admitted to the excellently equipped private hospital in Newcastle, which looked like a hotel and had facilities for relatives to stay too. Once she was reassured that her husband wasn't in any immediate danger Tatiana, claiming exhaustion, had accepted the sleeping pill the nurse offered and retired to the room adjoining Ralph's. Jasper, who had obviously knocked back enough champagne to float half the

British Navy, didn't need medication to help him sleep and was now snoring softly in the chair beside Ralph's bed.

Which just left Kit.

He was used to being awake when everyone else was asleep. The silence and stillness of the small hours of the morning were tediously familiar to him, but he had found that the only way of coping with insomnia was to accept it. To relax, even if sleep itself was elusive.

He groaned inwardly. Tonight even that was out of the question.

Back in Ralph's room a small light was on over the bed, by which Kit could see his father's skin had lost its bluish tinge. An image floated in front of his eyes of Sophie, lowering her head, her mouth opening to fill Ralph's lungs with oxygen, again and again.

He closed his eyes momentarily. Details he'd been too focused to take in at the time rising to the surface of his mind. The bumps of her spine standing out beneath the pale skin at the base of her neck. Her green gaze fixing on his in a way that shut out the rest of the world. In a way that showed that she trusted him.

He winced. In view of everything that had taken place between them that evening, that was something of a surprise.

But then there was quite a lot about Sophie Greenham that surprised him, such as her ability to make a cheap dress look like something from a Bond Street boutique. The way she'd stood up to him. Fought back. The fact that she could give the kiss of life well enough to make a dead man breathe again.

And another one feel again.

Rotating his aching shoulders, he paced restlessly over to the window, willing away the throb of arousal that had instantly started up inside him again.

The incident in the wine cellar seemed like days rather than hours ago, and thinking about it now he felt a wave of self-disgust. He had told himself he was acting in Jasper's best interests, that somehow he was deliberately seducing his brother's girlfriend *for his benefit*.

Locking his fingers behind his neck, Kit exhaled deeply and made himself confront the unwelcome truth Sophie had flung at him earlier. He had done it to prove himself right, to get some small, petty revenge on his father and score a private victory over the girl who had so unsettled him from the moment he'd first laid eyes on her. He had barely thought of Jasper at all.

But he forced himself to look at him now. Slumped in the chair, Jasper slept on, his cheek resting on one hand, his closed eyelids red and puffy from crying. He looked very young and absurdly fragile.

A pickaxe of guilt smashed through Kit's head.

Always look out for your weakest man—his army training overruled the natural inclination forged by his family circumstances. *Never exploit that weakness, or take risks with it.* Even when it had irritated the hell out of you for as long as you could remember.

Jasper might lack the steel Kit was used to in the men he served with, but that didn't give Kit the right to kiss his girlfriend, just to show that he could. And to enjoy kissing her, so much that he had spent the evening thinking of nothing else but kissing her again. Right up until the moment he'd ordered her to leave.

Horrified realisation jolted through him. He swore sharply.

'Are you OK there?'

Kit spun round.

A plump, homely-looking nurse had appeared on silent feet and was checking the bag of fluid that was dripping into Ralph's arm. She glanced at Kit.

'Can I get you anything—coffee perhaps?'

'No, thanks.' Picking up his car keys, he headed for the door, his need for caffeine paling into insignificance in the light of this new imperative. To get back to Alnburgh and make sure that Sophie Greenham was still there. And that she would stay. For as long as Jasper needed her.

The red tail lights of the last catering van had disappeared under the archway and the sound of the engines faded into a thick silence that was broken only by the distant hiss of the sea. Shivering with cold and fear, Sophie turned and went back inside, shutting the massive oak door with a creaking sound that came straight from *The Crypt* and sliding the bolts across with clumsy, frozen fingers.

She still felt weak with shock and there was a part of her that wished she were in one of those vans, sweeping down the drive to civilisation and a warm bed in a centrally heated home. Going through the hallway beneath the rows of glassy eyes, she hummed the opening lines of 'My Favourite Things', but if anything the eerie echo of her voice through the empty rooms made her feel more freaked out than ever. She shut up again.

Her mind would insist on replaying events from the moment she'd seen Ralph fall, like one of those annoying TV adverts that seemed to be on twice in every break. She found herself hanging on to the memory of Kit's strength and assurance, his control of the situation. And the way, when her resolve was faltering, he'd wrapped her in his gaze and said 'good girl'.

Good girl.

He'd also said an awful lot of other things to her tonight, she reminded herself with a sniff, so it was completely illogical that those two should have made such an impression. But he was the kind of stern, upright person from whom you couldn't help but crave approval, that was why it was such a big deal. And that was the biggest irony of all. Because he was also the kind of person who would never in a million years approve of someone like her.

Miserably she switched the lights out and went into the portrait hall.

Not just the person he thought she was—Jasper's

two-timing girlfriend—but the real Sophie Green-ham, the girl who had been haphazardly brought up on a bus, surrounded by an assortment of hippies and dropouts. The girl who had no qualifications, and who'd blown her chance to get any by being expelled from school. The girl whose family tree didn't even stretch back as far as her own father, and whose surname came—not from William the Conqueror—but from the peace camp where her mother had discovered feminism, cannabis and self-empowerment.

In her gilded frame opposite the staircase the superior expression on Tatiana's painted face said it all.

Sophie flicked off the light above the portrait and trailed disconsolately into the King's Hall. The chandeliers still blazed extravagantly, but it was like looking at an empty stage after the play had finished and the actors had gone home. She had to steel herself to look at the place where Ralph had collapsed, but the caterers had cleaned up so that no evidence remained of the drama that had taken place there only a few hours earlier. She was just switching the lights off when she noticed something lying on the steps. Her pulse quickened a little as she went over to pick it up.

Kit's jacket.

She stood for a second, biting her lip as she held it. It *was* very cold, and there was absolutely no way she was going to go upstairs along all those dark passageways where the countess's ghost walked to get a jumper. Quickly she closed her eyes and slid it across her shoulders. Pulling it close around her, she breathed in the scent of him and revelled in the memory of his kiss…

A kiss that should never have happened, she told herself crossly, opening her eyes. A kiss that in the entire history of disastrous, mistaken, ill-advised kisses would undoubtedly make the top ten. She had to stop this sudden, stupid crush in its tracks; it was doomed from the outset, which of course was why it felt so powerful. Didn't she always want what she knew would never be hers?

In the drawing room the fire had burned down to ashes. There was no way she was going to brave the ice-breathed darkness upstairs, so she piled logs on, hoping there was enough heat left for them to catch.

In the meantime she would keep the jacket on, though...

It was going to be a long, cold night.

Perched on its platform of rock above the sea, Alnburgh Castle was visible for ten miles away on the coast road, so by the time Kit pulled into the courtyard he already knew that it was entirely in darkness.

Lowering his head against the sabre-toothed wind, he let himself in through the kitchen door, remembering how he'd often done the same thing when he came home from boarding school for the holidays and found the place deserted because Ralph and Tatiana were at a party, or had gone away. He'd never been particularly bothered to find the castle empty back then, but now...

Lord, she'd better still be here.

His footsteps sounded as loud as gunshots as he walked through the silent rooms. Passing the foot of the stairs, he glanced at the grandfather clock and felt a sudden beat of hope. It was half past three in the morning—of course—she'd be in bed, wouldn't she?

He took the stairs two at a time, aware that his

heart was beating hard and unevenly. Outside the door to her room he tipped his head back and inhaled deeply, clenching his hand into a fist and holding it there for a second before knocking very softly. There was no answer, so, hardly breathing, he opened the door.

It was immediately obvious the room was empty. The curtains were undrawn, the moonlight falling on a neatly made bed, an uncluttered chest of drawers.

She might be in bed, he thought savagely. The question was, whose?

Adrenaline was circulating like neat alcohol through his bloodstream as he went back down the stairs. How the hell was he going to break the news to Jasper that she'd gone?

And that it was all his fault?

He headed for the drawing room, suddenly in desperate need of a drink. Pushing open the door, he was surprised to see that the fire was hissing softly in the grate, spilling out a halo of rosy light into the empty room. He strode over to the table where the drinks tray was and was just about to turn on the light beside it when he stopped dead.

Sophie was lying on the rug in front of the fire,

hidden from view by the sofa when he'd first come into the room. Her head was resting on one out-stretched arm, and she'd pulled the pins from her hair so that it fell, gleaming, over the white skin of her wrist like a pool of warm, spilled syrup. She was lying on her side, wearing a man's dinner jacket, but even though it was miles too big for her it couldn't quite disguise the swooping contours of her hip and waist.

He let out a long, slow breath, unaware until that moment that he'd been holding it in. Tearing his gaze away from her with physical effort, he reached for a glass and splashed a couple of inches of brandy into it, then walked slowly around the sofa to stand over her.

If the impact of seeing her from behind had made him forget to breathe, the front view was even more disturbing. Her face was flushed from the warmth, and the firelight made exaggerated shadows be-neath the dark lashes fanning over her cheeks and the hollow above the cupid's bow of her top lip. Tilting his head, he let his eyes move over her, inch by inch, adjusting his jaded perception of her to fit the firelit vision before him.

She looked...

He took a swallow of brandy, hoping it might wash away some of the less noble adjectives that arrived in his head, courtesy of six months spent in the company of a regiment of sex-starved men. *Vulnerable*, that was it, he thought with a pang. He remembered watching her sleep on the train and being struck by her self-containment. He frowned. Looking at her now, it appeared to him more like self-protection, as if she had retreated into some private space where she was safe and untouchable.

He felt a sudden jolt pass through him, like a tiny electric shock, and realised that her eyes had opened and she was looking up at him. Like a cat she raised herself into a sitting position, flexing the arm she'd been sleeping on, arching her spine.

'You're back,' she said in a voice that was breathy with sleep.

He took another mouthful of brandy, registering for the first time the sheer relief he'd felt when he saw her, which had got rather subsumed by other, more urgent sensations.

'I thought you'd gone.'

It was as if he'd dropped an ice cube down her back. Getting to her feet, she turned away from him, smoothing the wrinkled dress down over her hips. He could see now that jacket she was wearing was his, and a fresh pulse of desire went through him.

'Sorry. Obviously I would have, but I didn't think there would be any trains in the middle of the night.' There was a slight hint of sarcasm in her voice, but it was a pale echo of her earlier bravado. 'And I didn't want to leave until I knew how Ralph was. Is he—?'

'He's the same. Stable.'

'Oh.' She turned to him then, her face full of tentative hope in the firelight. 'That's good, isn't it?'

Kit exhaled heavily, remembering the quiet de-termination with which she'd kept fighting to keep Ralph alive, reluctant to take the hope away. 'I don't know. It might be.'

'Oh.' She nodded once, quickly, and he knew she understood. 'How's Tatiana? And Jasper?'

'Both asleep when I left. They gave Tatiana a sleeping pill.' He couldn't keep the cynicism from his tone. 'Unsurprisingly Jasper didn't need one.'

Sophie's laugh had a break in it. 'Oh, God. He'll be unconscious until mid-morning. I hope the nurses have a megaphone and a bucket of iced water.'

Kit didn't smile. He came towards the sofa and leaned against the arm, swilling the last mouthful of brandy around his glass so that it glinted like molten sunlight. Warily, Sophie watched him, hardly able to breathe. The fire held both of them in an intimate circle, sealed together against the darkness of the room, the castle, the frozen world beyond.

'He was very emotional. I know he's had a lot to drink, but even so...'

Sophie sat down on the edge of a velvet armchair. 'That's Jasper. He can't help it. He wears his heart on his sleeve. It's one of the things I love most about him.'

'It's one of the things that irritate me most about him,' Kit said tersely. 'He was in bits all the way to the hospital—sobbing like a baby and saying over and over again that there was so much he still needed to say.'

Bloody hell, Jasper, Sophie thought desperately. Coming out to his family was one thing. Getting drunk and dropping heavy hints so they guessed enough to ask her was quite another. 'He was upset, that's all,' she said quickly, unable to keep the defensiveness from her tone. 'There's nothing wrong with showing emotion—some people might regard it as being normal, in fact. He'd just seen his father collapse in front of him and stop breathing—'

'Even so. This is just the beginning. If he can't cope now—'

'What do you mean, this is just the beginning?'

Kit got up and went to stand in front of the fire, looking into the flames. 'Who knows how long this will go on for? The doctors are saying he's stable, which Tatiana and Jasper seem to think is just a stage on the way back to complete recovery.'

'And you think differently,' Sophie croaked. Oh, dear. Something about the sight of his wide shoulders silhouetted against the firelight had made it hard to speak. She tucked her legs up beneath her, her whole body tightening around the fizz of arousal at its core.

'He was without oxygen for a long time,' Kit said flatly.

'Oh.' Sophie felt the air rush from her lungs and felt powerless to take in any more to replace it. She had tried. She had tried so hard, but it hadn't been enough.

'So what are you saying?'

'I'm saying it's highly likely he won't come out of this. That at some point in the next few days Jasper's going to have to deal with Ralph's death.'

'Oh. I see,' she said faintly. 'That soon?' Something about the way he was talking set alarm bells off in some distant part of her brain. He's going to tell me he wants me to leave now, she thought in panic. Tonight, before Jasper gets back…

'I think so.' His voice was low and emotionless. 'And if I'm right, I think it would be better if he didn't also have to deal with the girl he's crazy about running out on him.'

Steeling herself as if against a blow, Sophie blinked in confusion. 'But…I don't understand. You asked me to go…'

Kit turned around to look at her. The firelight gilded his cheekbones and brought an artificial warmth to his cold silver eyes. 'Things have changed,' he drawled softly, giving her an ironic smile. 'And now I'm asking you to stay. You've played the part of Jasper's doting girlfriend for two days. I'm afraid you'll just have to play it a bit longer.'

CHAPTER NINE

KIT was used to action. He was used to giving an order and having it obeyed, working out what needed to be done and doing it, and in the days that followed trying to penetrate the dense forest of bureaucracy that choked the Alnburgh estate tested his patience to the limit.

He spent most of his time in the library, which was one of the few staterooms at Alnburgh to have escaped the attention of Tatiana's interior designer. A huge oriel window overlooked the beach, and on a day like today, when sea, sky and sand were a Rothko study of greys, the bleakness of the view made the inside seem warm by comparison.

Putting the phone down after yet another frustrating conversation with the Inland Revenue, Kit glanced along the beach, subconsciously looking for the slender figure, bright hair whipped by the wind, who had made it so bloody difficult to concentrate yesterday. But apart from a couple of dog walkers the long crescent of sand was deserted.

He turned away, irritation mixing with relief.

It had been three days since Ralph's heart attack, three days since he'd asked Sophie to stay on at Alnburgh, and things had settled into a routine of sorts. Every morning he drove a pale, shaken Jasper and a tight-lipped Tatiana to the hospital in Newcastle to sit at Ralph's bedside, though Ralph remained unconscious and unaware of their vigil. He stayed long enough to have a brief consultation with one of the team of medical staff and then returned to Alnburgh to avoid Sophie and begin to work his way through the landslide of overdue bills, complaints from estate tenants and un-followed-up quotes from builders and surveyors about the urgent work the castle required.

It was a futile task, of that he was certain. Often, as he came across yet another invoice from Ralph's wine merchant or Tatiana's interior designer, he remembered Ralph saying, *I have every intention of lasting a lot more than seven years.*

Now it looked as if he wouldn't make it to seven days, and his inexplicable refusal to acknowledge the existence of British inheritance tax probably meant that the Alnburgh estate was doomed. It would be sold off in lots and the castle would be turned into a hotel, or one of those awful conference centres where businessmen came for team-building weekends and bonding exercises.

Ironically, because in thirty-four years there Kit hadn't formed any kind of bond with the rest of his family.

He walked back to the desk, leaning on it for a moment with his arms braced and his head lowered, refusing to yield to the avalanche of anger and bitterness and sheer bloody frustration that threatened to bury him.

There's nothing wrong with showing emotion— some people might regard it as being normal.

Sophie's voice drifted through his head, and he straightened up, letting out a long, ragged breath. It was something that had happened with ridiculous regularity these last few days, when time and time again he'd found himself replaying conversations he'd had with her, thinking about things she'd said, and wondering what she'd say about other stuff.

It made him uncomfortable to suspect that a lot of the time she'd talked a lot of sense. He'd wanted to write her off as a lightweight. An airhead actress who was easy on the eye, and in other respects too, but who wasn't big on insight.

But if that was the case, why did he find himself wanting to talk to her so badly now?

Because Jasper was either drunk or hungover and Tatiana was—well, Tatiana, he thought wearily. Sophie was the only other person who hadn't lost the plot.

An outsider, just like him.

Sophie dreamed that she was being pulled apart by rough hands. She curled up tightly into a ball, hugging her knees to her chest, trying to stop shivering, trying to stop the hurting deep inside and calling out to Kit because he was the only one who could help her. She needed his strong, big hands to press down and stop the blood from coming.

She awoke to see a thin light breaking through the gap in the curtains. Her body was stiff with cold, and from the cramped position that she'd slept in, but as she unfurled her legs she felt a familiar spasm of pain in her stomach and let out a groan of dismay.

Her mind spooled backwards. Had it really been a month since that December night in Paris? Jean-

Claude had called at the apartment in the early hours, reeking of wine and sweat and cigarettes, almost combusting with lust after an evening working on 'Nude with Lilies'. Bent double with period pain, Sophie had only gone down to let him in because she'd known he'd wake the whole street if she didn't. That might have been preferable to the unpleasant little scene that had followed. Jean-Claude had been unwilling to take no for an answer, and it was only thanks to the amount of booze he'd sunk that Sophie had been able to fend him off. He'd fallen asleep, snoring at ear-splitting volume, sprawled across the bed, and Sophie had spent the rest of the night sitting on a hard kitchen chair, curled around a hot-water bottle, deliberately not thinking of anything but the pain blossoming inside her.

Tentatively she sat up now, wincing as the fist in her belly tightened and twisted. Since she was thirteen she'd suffered seven kinds of hell every month with her period. The cramps always came first, but it wouldn't be long before the bleeding started. Which meant she'd better get herself to a chemist pretty quickly, since she hadn't come prepared and neither Tatiana nor Mrs Daniels were the kind of cosy, down-to-earth women she could ask for help. Just the thought of saying the words 'sanitary protection' to either of them brought her out in a cold sweat.

She got out of bed, stooping slightly with the pain, and reached for her clothes.

It was the coldest winter in forty years. The temperature in the castle hardly seemed to struggle above freezing, and Sophie was forced to abandon all ambitions of style in favour of the more immediate need to ward off death by hypothermia. This had meant plundering Jasper's wardrobe to supplement her own, and she'd taken to sleeping in his old school rugby shirt, which was made to keep out the chill of a games field in the depths of winter and was therefore just about suitable for the bedrooms at Alnburgh. She couldn't bear the thought of exposing any flesh to the icy air so pulled her jeans on with it, zipping them up with difficulty over her tender, swollen stomach, and grabbed her purse.

Going down the stairs, clutching the banister for support, she glanced at the grandfather clock in the hall below. Knickers, she'd slept late—Jasper would have gone to the hospital ages ago.

She felt a twist of anguish as she wondered if he'd

been hungover again this morning. Sergio had been putting pressure on Jasper to let him come up and be with him through all this, and Jasper was finding it increasingly hard to deal with his divided loyalties. Sophie didn't blame him for trying, though. Kit had given her a hard enough time—what would he do to flamboyant, eccentric drama-queen Sergio?

Not kiss him, presumably…

'Morning. Just about.'

Talk of the devil. His sardonic, mocking voice startled her. That was why her mouth was suddenly dry and her heart had sped up ridiculously.

'Morning.'

She attempted to sound aloof and distracted, but as she hadn't spoken a word since she'd woken up she just sounded bad-tempered. He was wearing a dark blue cashmere sweater and in the defeated grey light of the bitter morning he looked tanned and incongruously handsome, like some modern-day heart-throb superimposed on a black and white background. Maybe that accounted for the bad-tempered tone slightly as well.

His deadpan gaze swept over her, one arched brow rising. 'Off to rugby training?'

She was confused for a second, until she remembered she was wearing Jasper's rugby shirt.

She faked an airy smile. 'I thought I'd give it a miss today and have a cigarette behind the bike sheds instead. To be honest, I'm not sure it's really my game.'

'Oh, I don't know,' he drawled quietly with the faintest smile. 'I think you'd make a pretty good hooker.'

'Very funny.' She kept going, forcing herself to hold herself more upright in spite of the feeling of having been kicked in the stomach by a horse. 'I'm going to the village shop. I need to pick up a few things.'

'Things?'

Bloody hell, why did she always feel the need to explain herself to him? If she hadn't said anything she wouldn't have put herself in the position of having to lie. Again.

'I'm coming down with a cold. Tissues, aspirin—that sort of thing.'

'I'm sure Mrs Daniels would be able to help you out with all that,' he said blandly. 'Would you like me to ask her?'

'No, thank you,' she snapped. The kicked-by-a-horse feeling was getting harder to ignore. She paused on the bottom step, clinging to the newel post as nausea rose inside her. The pain used to make her sick when she was younger and, though it hadn't happened for a few years, her body seemed to have developed a keen sense of comedy timing whenever Kit Fitzroy was around. 'I'll go myself, if that's OK? I wasn't aware I was under house arrest?'

From where she was standing his hooded eyes were on a level with hers. 'You're not.'

Sophie gave a brittle little laugh. 'Then why are you treating me like a criminal?'

He waited a moment before replying, looking at her steadily with those cold, opaque eyes. A muscle was flickering slightly in his taut, tanned cheek. 'I suppose,' he said with sinister softness, 'because I find it hard to believe that you've suddenly been struck with an urgent desire to go shopping when it's minus five outside and you're only half dressed.'

'I don't have time for this,' she muttered, going to move past him, desperate to escape the scrutiny of his gaze. Desperate for fresh air, even if it was of the Siberian variety. 'I'm dressed perfectly adequately.'

'I suppose it depends what for,' he said gravely as she passed him. 'Since you're clearly not wearing a bra.'

With a little gasp of outrage, Sophie looked down and saw that the neck of the rugby shirt was open wide enough to reveal a deep ravine of cleavage. Jasper's fourteen-year-old chest was obviously considerably smaller than hers. She snatched the collar and wrenched it together.

'Because I've just got out of bed.'

'And you're just about to rush into someone else's while Jasper's not here?' Kit suggested acidly.

That did it. The contempt in his voice, combined with another wringing cramp, made her lose her temper. 'No,' she cried, hands clenched into fists at her sides, cheeks flaming. 'I really *am* rushing to the village shop. In minus five temperatures and with stomach cramps that possibly register on the Richter scale, not because I *want* to, but because I'm about to start the period from hell and I am completely unprepared for it. So now perhaps you'll just let me go before it all gets messy.'

For a moment there was silence. Complete. Total. Kit took a step backwards, out of the orbit of her anger, and Sophie saw the spark of surprise in his eyes. And then the shutters went down and he was back in control.

'In that case you're not going anywhere,' he said with a faint, ironic smile. 'Or only as far as the library anyway—at least you won't freeze to death in there. Leave it to me. I'll be back as soon as I can.'

Sitting in the car and waiting for the fan to thaw the ice on the windscreen, Kit dropped his head into his hands.

He had always thought of himself as level-headed. Rational. Fair. A man who was ruled by sense rather than feeling. So in that encounter how come he'd emerged as some kind of bullying jailer?

Because there was something about this girl that made him lose reason. Something about her smile and her eyes and the way she tried to look haughty but could never quite pull it off that made him *feel* far too much. And still want to feel more.

Her body, for a start. All of it. Without clothes.

He started the engine with an unnecessary roar and shot forwards in a screech of tyres. Lord, no matter how incredible he found it, she was his younger brother's girlfriend and the only reason she was still here was because he'd ordered her to stay. That made two good reasons why he should be civil to her, so he'd better start by behaving less like a fascist dictator and more like a decent human being.

After that he could have a look through his address book and find someone who would be happy to supply him with the sexual release he so obviously needed before going back to his unit and channelling his energy into the blessedly absorbing task of staying alive.

Sophie managed to wait until Kit had left the library and shut the door before putting her hands over her burning cheeks and letting out a low moan of mortification.

Saints in heaven, why had she blurted all that out? She was supposed to be an *actress*. Why couldn't she ever manage to act mysterious, or poised, or *elegant*?

Especially around Kit Fitzroy, who must be used to silken officer's-wife types, with perfect hair and manners to match. Women who would never do anything as vulgar as swear or menstruate. Or lose their temper. Or kiss someone without realising they were being set up, or put themselves in a position where someone would want to set them up in the first place...

Women with class, in other words.

She let her hands drop again and looked up, noticing the room properly for the first time. Even seen through a fog of humiliation she could see straight away that it was different from the other rooms she'd been in at Alnburgh. There was none of the blowsy ostentation of the drawing room with its raw-silk swagged curtains and designer wallpaper, nor the comfortless, neglected air of upstairs. In here everything was faded, used and cherished, from the desk piled with papers in the window to the enormous velvet Knole sofa in front of the fire.

But it was the books that jolted her out of her self-pity. Thousands of them, in shelves stretching up to the high ceiling, with a narrow galleried walkway halfway up. Where she had grown up the only books were the few tattered self-help manuals that the women at the peace camp had circulated between themselves, with titles like *Freeing the Warrior Woman Within* and *The Harmonious Vegan*, and even when Sophie had managed to get hold of a book of her own from a second hand shop or jumble sale there had never been anywhere quiet to read it. She had always dreamed of a room like this.

Almost reverentially she walked along the bookcases, trailing her finger along the spines of the books. They were mostly old, faded to a uniform brown, the gold titles almost unreadable, but in the last section, by the window, there were some more modern paperbacks—Dick Francis, Agatha Christie and—joy—a handful of Georgette Heyer. Moving the faded curtain aside, Sophie gave a little squeak of delight as she spotted *Devil's Cub*, and felt a new respect for Tatiana. Maybe they did have something in common after all.

In her embarrassment she'd temporarily forgotten about the pain in her tummy, but the dragging feeling was back again now so she took Georgette over to the sofa and sank down gratefully. At the age of fourteen she'd fallen spectacularly in love with Vidal, and known with fervent adolescent certainty that she would never find a man who could match him in real life.

Her mouth twisted into an ironic smile. At fourteen everything seemed so black and white. At twenty-five, it was all infinitely more complicated.

Her teenage self had never considered the possibility that she might meet her Vidal, only for him to dismiss her as…

Her thoughts stalled as a piece of paper slid out of the book onto her knee.

Unfolding it, she saw straight away that it was a letter and felt a frisson of excitement. The date at the top was thirty years ago, the writing untidy, masculine and difficult to read, but she had no trouble making out the first line.

My Darling—

Technically Sophie was well aware that it was wrong to read other people's letters, but surely there was some kind of time limit on that rule? And anyway, any letter that began so romantically and was found in a Georgette Heyer novel was begging to be read. With a sense of delicious guilt she tucked her knees up tighter and scanned the lines.

It's late and the heat is just about bearable now the sun has gone down. I'm sitting on the roof terrace with the remains of the bottle of gin I brought back from England—I'd rather like to finish it all right now, but I couldn't bear the thought of Marie throwing the bottle away in the morning. It was the one we bought in London, that you held underneath your coat when we ran back to the hotel in the rain. How can I throw anything away that's been so close to your body?

Oh, how gorgeous! Sophie thought delightedly, trying to imagine Ralph writing something so intimate. Or doing anything as romantic as dashing through the rain to ravish the woman he loved in a hotel room.

Thank you, my love, for sending the photograph of K in your last letter. He's growing up so quickly—what happened to the plump baby I held in my arms on my last visit to Alnburgh? He is a boy now—a person in his own right, with a real character emerging—such fearless determination! Saying goodbye to him was so much harder this time. I never thought that anything would come close to the pain of leaving you, but at least your letters keep me going, and

the memories of our time together. Leaving my
son felt like cutting out a piece of myself.

Sophie's heart lurched and the written lines
jumped before her eyes. Was K referring to Kit?
Thirty years ago he must have been a small boy of
three or four. Breathlessly she read on.

I suppose I've learned to accept sharing you
with Ralph because I know you don't belong to
him in any real sense, but the fact that K will
grow up thinking of R as his father makes me
rage against the injustice of everything.
Why couldn't I have found you first?

Her mouth had fallen open. Incredulously she
read the lines again. After thirty years the sense of
despair in them was still raw enough to make her
throat close, but her brain couldn't quite accept the
enormity of what she was reading.

Ralph Fitzroy wasn't Kit's father?

The sound of the door opening behind her made
her jump about a mile in the air. Hastily, with trembling, nerveless fingers, she slid the letter back be-

tween the pages of Georgette Heyer and opened it randomly, pretending to read.

'Th-that was quick,' she stammered, turning round to see Kit come into the room carrying a bulging carrier bag. He was wearing the dark blue reefer jacket she remembered from the train and above the upturned collar his olive tan glowed with the cold. As he moved around the sofa he brought with him a sharp breath of outside—of frost and pine and ozone.

'I sensed that there was a certain amount of urgency involved.'

He put the bag down on the other end of the sofa and pulled out a huge box of tampons, which he tossed gently to her. Catching it, she couldn't meet his eye. The embarrassment of having him buy her sanitary products had paled into near-insignificance by the enormity of the discovery she'd just made.

'Thanks,' she muttered, looking round for her purse.

Taking off his jacket, he looked at her, slightly guarded. 'You're welcome. It's the least I could do for being so—' a frown appeared between his dark brows '—controlling. I'm sorry.'

'Oh, please—don't be,' Sophie said quickly. She

meant it. The last thing she needed now was him standing here looking like the beautiful hero from an art-house film and being *nice*, wrenching open the huge crack that had appeared in her Kit-Fitzroy-proof armour after reading the letter.

He glanced at her in obvious surprise. 'I anticipated you'd be harder to make up to,' he said, delving back into the bag, pulling out the most enormous bar of chocolate. 'I thought this might be needed, at least. And possibly even this.' He held up a bottle.

'Gin?' Sophie laughed, though her heart gave another flip as she thought of the letter, and Kit's mother and her unknown lover drinking gin in bed while it poured down outside.

Oh, dear. Best not to think of bed.

Kit took the bottle over to a curved-fronted cupboard in the corner of the room behind the desk. 'Mrs Watts in the village shop, who under different circumstances would have had a brilliant career in the CID, looked at the other things I was buying and suggested that gin was very good for period pains.'

'Oh, God—I'm so sorry—how embarrassing for you.'

'Not at all, though I can't comment on the reliability of Mrs Watts's information.'

'Well, gin is a new one on me, but to be honest if someone suggested drinking bat's blood or performing naked yoga on the fourth plinth, I'd try it.'

'Is it that bad?' he said tonelessly, opening the cupboard and taking down a can of tonic water. Sophie watched the movements of his long fingers as he pulled the ring and unscrewed the gin bottle.

'N-not too bad this time. But sometimes it's horrendous. I mean, not compared to lots of things,' she added hastily, suddenly remembering that he was used to working in war zones, dealing with the aftermath of bombings. 'On a bad month it just makes it, you know…difficult.'

'There's some ibuprofen in the bag.' He sloshed gin into a glass. 'What does the doctor say?'

'I haven't seen one.' She wasn't even registered with one. She'd never really been in the same place for long enough, and Rainbow had always been a firm believer in remedies involving nettles and class B drugs. 'I looked it up on the Internet and I think it might be something called endometriosis. Either that, or one of twenty-five different kinds of terminal cancer—unlikely since I've had it for the last twelve years—appendicitis—ditto—or arsenic poisoning. I decided to stop looking after that.'

Kit came towards her, holding out a large glass, frosted with cold and clinking with ice cubes. 'You should see a doctor. But in the meantime try a bit of self-medicating.'

There was something about the sternness of his voice when combined with the faintest of smiles that made her feel as if she'd had a couple of strong gins already. Reaching up to take it from him, she felt herself blushing all over again.

'I don't have many unbreakable rules, but drinking hard spirits, on my own, in the middle of the morning is actually one I try to stick to. Aren't you having one too?' she said, then, realising that now he'd fulfilled his obligation he might be wanting to escape, added quickly, 'Unless you have something else you need to do, of course.'

'Not really. Nothing that won't keep anyway.' He turned away, picking up another log from the huge basket by the fireplace and dropping it into the glowing grate before going to pour another gin and tonic. 'I'm trying to go through some of the paperwork for the estate. It's in a hell of a mess. My father isn't exactly one for organisation. The whole place has been run on the ostrich principle for decades.'

'So Jasper gets his tendency to bury his head in the sand from Ralph?'

'I'm afraid so.' He sat down at the other end of the massive sofa, angling his body so he was facing her. 'And his tendency to drink too much and rely on charm to get him out of the more unpleasant aspects of life.' He broke off to take a large swig of his drink and shook his head. 'Sorry, I shouldn't be talking about him like that to you. To be fair, the womanising gene seems to have passed him by.'

'Yes.' Sophie's laugh went on a little too long. If only Kit knew the truth behind that statement. 'You're right, though. He and Ralph are astonishingly alike in lots of ways.'

She took a quick sip of her drink, aware that she was straying into dangerous territory. Part of her wanted desperately to ask him about the letter, or more specifically the shattering information it contained, but the rest of her knew she would never dare make such a personal assault on Kit Fitzroy's defences.

Silver eyes narrowed, he looked at her over the rim of his glass.

'Whereas I'm not like him at all.'

It was as if he had read her thoughts. For a

moment she didn't know what to say, so she took another mouthful of gin and, nearly choking on it, managed to croak, 'Sorry. It's none of my business. I didn't—'

'It's fine.' Leaning back on the huge sofa, he tipped his head back wearily for a moment. 'It's no secret that my father and I don't get on. That's why I don't feel the need to spend every minute at his bedside.'

The room was very quiet. The only sounds were the hissing of the logs in the grate and the clink of ice in Sophie's glass as the hand that held it shook. Largely with the effort of stopping it reaching out and touching him

'Why?' she asked in a slightly strangled voice. 'Why don't you get on with him?'

He shrugged. 'It's always been like that. I don't remember having much to do with him before my mother left, and after she went you'd have thought we would have been closer.'

'Weren't you?'

'Exactly the opposite. Maybe he blamed me.' Kit held up his glass, looking through it dispassionately. The fire turned the gin the colour of brandy. 'Maybe he didn't, and just took it out on me, but what had previously been indifference became outright hostility. He sent me to boarding school at the soonest possible opportunity.'

'Oh, God, you poor thing.' Just thinking of her own brief boarding school experience made Sophie's scalp prickle with horror.

'God, no. I loved it. I was the only kid in the dorm who used to dread holidays.' He took a mouthful of gin, his face deadpan as he went on, 'He used to call me into the drawing room on my first evening home and go through my report, seizing on anything he could—a mark dropped here, a team captaincy missed there—and commenting on it in this strange, sarcastic way. Unsurprisingly it made me more determined to try harder and do better.' He smiled wryly. 'So then he'd mock me for being too clever and on too many teams.'

Sophie's heart turned over. She could feel it beating against her ribs with a rapid, jerky rhythm. The book, with its outrageous secret folded between the pages, stuck up slightly from the sofa cushions just inches from her right hip.

'Why would he do that?'

'I have no idea,' Kit drawled softly. 'It would be nice to think that he just wasn't someone who liked children, or could relate to them, but his unbridledjoywhenJaspercamealongkindofdisproves that. Anyway, it hasn't scarred me for life or anything, and I gave up trying to work it out a long time ago.'

'But you keep coming back here,' Sophie murmured. 'I'm not sure I would.' She looked down at the crescent of lemon stranded on the ice cubes in the bottom of her glass, letting her hair fall over her face in case it gave away how much of a howling understatement that was.

'I come back because of Alnburgh,' he said simply. 'It might sound mad but the place itself is part of my family as much as the people who live in it. And Ralph's approach to looking after the castle has been similar to the way he looked after his sons.'

She lifted her head. 'What do you mean?'

'All or nothing—five thousand pounds for new curtains in the drawing room, while the roof goes unmaintained.'

Their eyes met. He gave her that familiar brief, cool smile, but his eyes, she noticed, were bleak. Compassion beat through her, mixing uneasily with the longing churning in her tender stomach. *I know why it is*, she wanted to blurt out. *I know why he was always vile to you, and it isn't your fault.*

The moment stretched. Their gazes stayed locked together. Sophie felt helpless with yearning. The heat from the fire seemed to be concentrated in her cheeks, her lips…

She jumped out of her skin as the phone rang.

Kit moved quickly. He got to his feet to answer it so he didn't have to lean across her.

'Alnburgh.' His voice was like ground glass.

Sophie's hands flew to her face, pressing against her burning cheeks with fingers splayed. Her heart was galloping. From miles away, his voice reduced to a tinny echo, she could just make out that it was Jasper on the phone.

'That's good,' said Kit tonelessly. Then, after a pause, 'Ask her yourself.'

He held out the phone. Sophie couldn't look at him as she took it.

'Soph, it's good news.' Jasper's voice was jubilant. 'Dad's regained consciousness. He's groggy and a bit breathless but he's talking, and even managed a smile at the pretty blonde nurse.'

'Jasper, that's wonderful!' Sophie spoke with as much warmth as possible, given what she'd just found out about Ralph Fitzroy. 'Darling, I'm so pleased.'

'Yes. Look, the thing is, neither Ma nor I want to leave him while he's like this, so I was wondering if you'd mind very much if we didn't come back for dinner? Will you be OK on your own?'

'Of course.' Unconsciously she found her gaze moving back to Kit. He was standing in front of the fire, head bent, shoulders tensed. 'Don't worry. I'll be fine.'

'The other thing is,' Jasper said apologetically, 'Ma gave Mrs Daniels the day off…'

Sophie laughed. 'Believe it or not, some of us have evolved to the stage where we can survive without staff. Now, go and give Ralph…my regards.'

Her smile faded quickly as she put the phone down. The room was quiet again, as if it were waiting.

'They're not coming back,' she said, trying to sound casual. 'He just wanted to check we'd be OK, since it's Mrs Daniels' day off and I'm not known for my culinary skills.' She gave a nervous laugh. 'Where's the nearest Indian takeaway?'

'Hawksworth.' Kit turned round. His face was blank. 'But forget takeaway. I don't know about you but I need to get away from here. Let's go out.'

CHAPTER TEN

It's not a date, it's not a date, it's not a date.

Sophie looked at herself sternly in the mirror as she yanked a comb roughly through her wet hair. After a walk on the beach this afternoon it had needed washing anyway. She wasn't making any special effort because she was going out for dinner with Kit.

Her stomach dipped. *Period pain*, she told herself.

It would be rude not to make a little bit of effort, and, after being shut up at Alnburgh for days without seeing a soul apart from the odd dog walker on the beach, it was actually pretty good to have an excuse to liven up her corpselike pallor with blusher and put on something that wasn't chosen solely for its insulating properties.

But what?

She stopped combing, and stood still, her mind running over the possibilities. She was sick and tired of jeans, but discounting them only left the black shroud, the vampire corset thing or the Chinese silk dress Jasper had ruled out for Ralph's party on the grounds that it was too sexy. Tapping a finger against her lip, she considered.

It's not a date...

Absolutely not. But she wasn't wearing the shroud. And the corset would look as if a she were meeting a client and charging for it. The Chinese silk it would have to be.

A wave of undeniable nervousness rolled through her and she had to sit down on the edge of the bed. She was being ridiculous, getting dressed up and wound up about a dinner arrangement that was based purely on practical and logical reasons. Jasper wasn't coming back, Mrs Daniels was away, neither of them could cook and they were both going stir-crazy from being cooped up in the castle for too long. Unlike every other dinner invitation she'd ever had, this one very definitely wasn't the opening move in a game that would finish up in bed.

No matter how fantastic she sensed going to bed with Kit Fitzroy would be.

Stop it, she told herself crossly, getting up and slapping foundation onto her flushed cheeks. This was nothing to do with sex. That look that had passed between them in the library earlier had *not* been the precursor to a kiss…a kiss that would have led to who-knew-what if the phone hadn't rung. *No.* It was about finally, miraculously putting their differences behind them. Talking. About her being there at a rare moment when he had needed to offload.

She sighed. The trouble was, in a lot of ways that felt a whole lot more special and intimate than sex.

Her hands were shaking so much it took three goes to get her trademark eyeliner flick right. Then there was nothing else to do but put on the Chinese silk dress. She shivered as the thick crimson silk slid over her body, pulling tight as she did up the zip.

'*It's not a date,*' she muttered one more time, pulling a severe face at her reflection in the little mirror above the sink. But her eyes still glittered with excitement.

In the library Kit put down the folder of Inland Revenue correspondence he'd been going through and looked at his watch. Seven o'clock—his lip curled slightly—about three minutes later than the last time he'd checked.

He got up, stretching his aching back and feeling fleetingly glad that he didn't have a desk job. He felt stiff and tired and restless; frustrated from being inside all day and surrounded by papers. That was all it was. Nothing to do with the persistent throb of desire that had made concentrating on tax impossible, or the fact that his mind kept going back to that moment on the sofa just before the phone rang.

The moment when he had been about to kiss her. Again. Only this time it wouldn't have been because he was trying to prove anything or score points or catch her out, but because he wanted to. *Needed* to.

Letting out a ragged sigh, he ran his hands through his hair and down over his face.

What the hell was he doing asking her out to dinner?

He was looking after her for Jasper, that was all. Trying to make up a little for the unrelenting misery of her visit, and for boring her with his life story earlier.

Especially for that.

It wasn't a *date* or anything.

Grimly he turned the lights out in the library and strode through into the hall, rubbing a hand across his chin and feeling the rasp of stubble. As he went into the portrait hall he heard footsteps echoing on the stone stairs and looked up.

His throat closed and his heart sank. He had to clench his teeth together to stop himself from swearing.

Because she was beautiful. Undeniably, obviously, hit-you-between-the-eyes beautiful, and it was going to be impossible to sit across a table from her all evening and not be aware of that for every minute. She was wearing a dress of Chinese silk that hugged her body like a second skin, but was high-necked and low-hemmed enough to look oddly demure.

Her footsteps slowed. She was looking at him, her expression uncertain, and it struck him that she was waiting for his reaction.

Swiftly he cleared his throat, rubbing his jaw again to unclench it. 'You look…great,' he said gruffly. He'd been about to say beautiful, but stopped himself at the last minute. It seemed too intimate.

'I'm way overdressed.' She'd come to a standstill halfway down the stairs and turned around, preparing to bolt back up again. 'I didn't really have anything else, but I can put on jeans—'

'No.'

The word came out more forcefully than he'd meant and echoed off the stone walls. Her eyes widened with shock, but she didn't move.

'You're fine as you are, and I'm starving. Let's just go, shall we?'

He took her to a restaurant in Hawksworth. Tucked away in a small courtyard off the market square, it had a low-beamed ceiling, a stone-flagged floor and fires burning in each of its two rooms. Candles stuck into old wine bottles flickered on every table, throwing uneven shadows on the rough stone walls. Thanks to these it was mercifully dark and Sophie felt able to relax a little bit in her too-smart dress.

'You were right,' she said brightly, studying the menu without taking in a single thing on it. 'It is good to be away from the castle. And it's good to be warm, too.'

The maître d', recognising Kit, had shown them to the best table in a quiet corner of the far room, next to the fire. Its warmth stole into Sophie's body, but somehow she couldn't stop herself from shivering.

'Alnburgh hasn't quite lived up to your expectations, then?' Kit asked dryly as he studied the wine list, and Sophie remembered that journey from the station in the back of the Bentley when she'd seen the castle for the first time.

'Let's just say I'm a big fan of central heating. When I was little I used to think that I wouldn't mind where I lived as long as it was warm.'

Oh, dear, that was a stupid thing to say. She looked down, picking bits of fossilised wax off the wine bottle candle-holder with a fingernail and hoping he wouldn't pick up the subject of when she was little. The last thing she wanted to talk about was her childhood.

Actually, come to think of it, there were quite a lot of things she didn't want to talk about. Or couldn't. She'd better not drink too much or she'd be letting skeletons, and Jasper, out of the closet by dessert time.

'So where *do* you live?' he asked, putting the menu down and looking at her directly.

'Crouch End.' Beneath his gaze she felt ridiculously shy. 'I share a flat with a girl called Jess. Or I did, but then I went to Paris for two months for the Resistance film and when I got back her boyfriend had moved in. I guess it might be time to look for somewhere else.'

'Would you move in with Jasper?'

She shook her head, suppressing a rueful smile as she imagined Sergio's reaction if she did. 'I love Jasper, but it's not—'

She stopped as the waitress appeared; a slim, dark-skinned girl who slid a pencil out of her casually piled up hair to take their order. Sophie, who couldn't remember a single thing from the menu, spotted linguine on the specials board behind Kit and ordered that, cursing herself almost instantly for choosing something so inelegant to eat.

No sooner had the waitress sauntered off with catwalk grace than the maître d' brought a dish of olives and the wine, pouring it into glasses the size of goldfish bowls with a great deal of theatre. Sophie's pulse went into overdrive as the incident in the wine cellar came rushing back to her. Looking away, she felt her cheeks flame and wondered if Kit was remembering the same thing.

When they were alone again he raised his glass and said, 'Go on.'

She made a dismissive gesture, deliberately choosing to misremember where she'd got up to. Jasper was probably one of the subjects best placed on the 'Avoid' list.

'So anyway, I'll probably be flat-hunting when I get back to London, unless I stick it out at Love Central until I find out if I've got the vampire film role, because that'll involve about four weeks' filming in Romania...' She picked up her glass and took a huge mouthful, just to shut herself up. The glass was even bigger than she thought and some of the wine dripped down her chin, reminding her even more painfully of the port.

'Is it a big part?'

Kit's voice was low. In contrast to her he was utterly relaxed, his face impassive in the firelight. But why wouldn't he be relaxed? she thought despairingly. He didn't have a thumping great crush to hide, as well as most of the truth about himself.

'No. Lots of scenes but not many lines, which is perfect—' She looked up at him from under her lashes with a grimace of embarrassment. 'The only downside is the costume. My agent is always sending me scripts for bigger parts, but I don't want to go down that route. I'm quite neurotic enough as it is.'

Aware that she was babbling again, she picked up an olive, putting it in her mouth and sucking the salty oil off her fingers while she steadied herself to continue. 'I love what I do now,' she said more slowly. 'It's fun and there's no pressure. I'm not trained or anything and I just fell into it by chance, but it means I get to travel and do interesting things, and pick up the odd useful skill too.'

The waitress arrived and set plates down between them before sauntering off again.

'Such as?'

Kit's eyes were heavy-lidded, dark-lashed, gleaming.

Sophie looked down, knowing for certain there was no way she was going to be able to eat linguine when her stomach was already in knots. She picked up her fork anyway.

'Let me see… Archery. You never know when you might have to face an invading army with only a bow and arrow—especially at Alnburgh. Milking a cow. Pole dancing. Artificial respiration.'

Kit looked up at her in surprise. 'You learned that through acting?'

'I did a season in a TV hospital drama series.' She wound ribbons of pasta around her fork, assuming a lofty tone. 'I'm surprised you don't remember it actually—it was the highlight of my career, until the scriptwriters decided to kill me off in a clifftop rescue scene in the Christmas episode instead of letting me go on to marry the consultant and do another series.'

His smile was sudden and devastating. The firelight had softened his face, smoothing away the lines of tension and disapproval, making him look less intimidating and simply very, very sexy.

'Were you disappointed?'

She shook her head. 'Not really. It was good money but too much like commitment.'

'What, marrying the consultant or doing another series?'

The low, husky pitch of his voice seemed to resonate somewhere inside her, down in the region of her pelvis.

'Both.'

The place had emptied and the waitress was looking bored and sulky by the time Kit eventually stood up, stooping slightly to avoid the low beams as he went to sort out the bill.

Sophie watched him, her mouth dry, her trembling hands tucked beneath her thighs on the wooden bench. The gaps in the conversation had got longer and more loaded, the undercurrents of meaning stronger. Or so it had felt to her. Maybe he had just run out of things to say to her?

They drove back in silence. The sky was moonless, and veils of mist swathed the castle like chiffon scarves, making it look oddly romantic. Sophie's hands were folded in her lap and she held herself very stiffly, as if she were physically braced against the waves of longing that were battering at her. In the light of the dashboard Kit's face was tense and unsmiling. She gave an inward moan of despair as she wondered if he'd been totally bored by the whole evening.

He pulled into the courtyard and got out of the car immediately, as if he was at pains to avoid drawing the evening out a moment longer than he had to. Sophie followed, misery and disappointment hitting her more forcefully than the cold. For all her self-lecturing earlier, she had secretly longed to break through the barriers of Kit's reserve and rekindle the spark of intimacy that had glowed so briefly between them.

She caught up with him at the top of the steps as he keyed in the number.

'Thank you for a lovely evening,' she said in an oddly subdued voice. 'It seems awful to have had such a good time when Jasper and Tatiana are at the hospital. I hope Ralph is OK.'

'Given the mess Alnburgh's finances are going to be in if he dies, I do too,' Kit said sardonically as he opened the door. Standing back to let her through, he rubbed a hand across his forehead. 'Sorry. I didn't mean it to sound like that.'

'I know.'

She stopped in front of him, instinctively reaching up to touch the side of his face.

He stiffened, and for a moment she felt a jolt of horror at the thought that she'd got it badly wrong *again*. But then he dropped his hand and looked at her, and in the split second before their mouths met she saw desire and despair there that matched her own. She let out a moan of relief as his lips touched hers, angling her head back and parting her lips as he took her face between his hands and kissed her.

It was as though he was doing something that

hurt him. The kiss was hard but gentle at the same time, and the expression on his face as he pulled away was resigned—almost defeated. Arrows of anguish pierced Sophie's heart and she slid her hand round his neck, tangling her fingers in his hair as she pulled his head down again.

The door swung shut behind them, giving a bang that echoed through the empty halls. They fell back against it, Sophie pressing her shoulders against the ancient wood as her hips rose up to meet his. Her hands slid over the sinews of his back, feeling them move as their bodies pressed together and their mouths devoured each other in short, staccato bursts of longing.

'Soph? Soph, darling, is that you?'

'Jasper,' she whimpered.

Kit pulled away, jerking his head back as if he'd been struck. They could hear footsteps approaching across the stone flags of the hall. Beneath the light of the vast lantern high above, Kit's face looked as if it had been carved from ice.

Helplessly Sophie watched him turn away, then, smoothing her skirt down, she went forwards, will-ing her voice not to give her away.

'Yes, it's me. We didn't expect you back so…'

Her words trailed off as Jasper appeared in the doorway. His face was swollen and blotched from crying, and tears still slid from his reddened eyes.

'Oh, my darling—' she gasped.

Jasper raised his hands in a gesture of hopelessness. 'He died.'

And in an instant Sophie was beside him, taking him into her arms, stroking his hair as he laid his head on her shoulder and sobbed, murmuring to him in a voice that ached with love.

Over his shoulder she watched Kit walk away. She willed him to turn round, to look back and catch her eye and understand.

He didn't.

CHAPTER ELEVEN

AND so, not quite a week after Ralph's lavish birthday party, preparations were made at Alnburgh for his funeral.

Kit returned to London the morning following Ralph's death. Sophie didn't see him before he left and though Thomas murmured something about appointments with the bank, Sophie, rigid with misery she couldn't express, wondered if he'd gone deliberately early to avoid her.

She was on edge the whole time. It felt as if her heart had been replaced with an alarm clock, like the crocodile in *Peter Pan*, making her painfully aware of every passing second. The smallest thing seemed to set her alarm bells jangling.

The bitter weather continued. The snow kept falling; brief, frequent flurries of tiny flakes that were almost invisible against the dead sky. Pipes in an unused bathroom burst, making water cascade through the ceiling in a corner of the armoury hall and giving the pewter breastplates their first clean in half a century. Thomas, who since Ralph's death seemed to have aged ten years, shuffled around helplessly, replacing buckets.

After that time in the hall Sophie didn't see Jasper cry again, but his grief seemed to turn in on itself and, without the daily focus of sitting at Ralph's bedside and the hope of his recovery to cling to, he quietly went to pieces. He was haunted by regret that he hadn't had the courage to come out about his sexuality to his father, driven to despair by the knowledge that now it was too late.

Sophie's nerves were not improved by a lonely, insecure Sergio ringing the castle at odd hours of the day and night and demanding to speak to Jasper. She fielded as many of the calls as possible. Now was not the time for the truth, but the charade had come to seem pointless and the main difficulty in Jasper and Sergio's relationship was not that it was homosexual but that Sergio was such an almighty, selfish prima donna.

On the occasions when Jasper did speak to Sergio he came off the phone with hollow eyes and a clenched jaw, and proceeded to get drunk. That was something else Sophie was worried about. It was becoming harder to ignore the fact that as the days wore on he was waking up later and making his first visit to the drinks tray in the library earlier.

But there was no one she could talk to about it. Tatiana barely emerged from her room, and Sophie sensed that speaking to Mrs Daniels or Thomas, as staff, would break some important social taboo. Of course, it was Kit that she really longed to talk to, but even if he had been there what could she say? Unless she was prepared to break Jasper's confidence, any concerns she expressed about his welfare would only serve to make Kit think more badly of her. Who could blame Jasper for drinking too much when his girlfriend had been about to leap into bed with his brother, while he was with his dying father?

As the week dragged on she missed him more and more. She even found herself counting the days to the funeral, where she knew she would see him again.

Looking forwards to a funeral, she told herself bleakly, was a mark of a truly bad person.

The day before the funeral Sophie was perched on top of a stepladder in the armoury hall. Taking down the antique pistols that had got soaked in the burst-pipe deluge, she dried them, one by one, as Thomas was anxious that, left alone, the mechanisms would rust. Sophie was very glad to have something to occupy her while Jasper huddled on the drawing room sofa, mindlessly watching horseracing.

Her roots were beginning to come through, and what she would really have liked to do was disappear into the bathroom with a packet of hair dye, but there was a line of shallowness that even she couldn't bring herself to cross. Anyway, the pistol-cleaning was curiously therapeutic. Close up, many of them were very beautiful, with delicate filigree patterns engraved into their silver barrels. She held one up to the light of the wrought-iron lantern, feeling the weight of it in her hand and wondering under what circumstances it had last been fired. A duel, perhaps, between two Fitzroy brothers, fighting over some ravishing aristocratic virgin.

The despair that was never far away descended on her again, faster than the winter twilight. If she was ravishing, or aristocratic—or a virgin for that matter—would Kit feel enough for her to want to fight for her?

Theatrically she pressed the barrel of the gun to her ribs, just below her breasts. Closing her eyes, she imagined him standing in front of her, in tight breeches and a ruffled white muslin shirt, his face tormented with silent anguish as he begged…

'Don't do it.'

Her eyes flew open. Kit was standing in the doorway, his face not tormented so much as exhausted. Longing hit her first—the forked lightning before the rumble of scarlet embarrassment that followed.

'Tell me,' he drawled coolly, picking up the stack of letters that had come in the last few days, 'had you considered suicide before, or is it being here that's driven you to make two attempts in the last week?'

Sophie made an attempt at a laugh, but it dried up in her throat and came out as a sort of bitter rasp. 'It must be. I was perfectly well adjusted before. How was your trip?'

'Frustrating.'

He didn't look up from the envelopes he was sifting through. Sophie averted her eyes in an attempt not to notice how sexy he looked, especially from her vantage point where she could see the breadth of his shoulders and the way his hair curled into the back of his neck, however, her nipples tingled in treacherous recognition. She stared at the pistol in her hand, polishing the barrel with brisk strokes of the cloth.

'I expect you'll be going back to London yourself when the funeral's over,' he said absently, as if it were of no consequence to him.

'Oh.' The idea had come out of the blue and she felt suddenly disorientated, and a little dizzy up there on the ladder. She took a quick breath, polishing harder. 'Yes. I expect so. I hadn't really thought. Are you going to be staying here for a while?'

He took one letter from the pile and threw the rest down again. 'No. I'm going back.'

'To London?'

To give her an excuse not to look at him she put the gun back on its hooks on the wall, but her hands were shaking and it slipped from her fingers. She gave a cry of horror, but with lightning reactions Kit had stepped forwards and caught it.

'Careful. There's a possibility that some of these guns might still be loaded,' he said blandly, handing it back to her. 'No. Not London. Back to my unit.'

For a moment the pain in Sophie's chest felt as if the gun *had* gone off.

'Oh. So soon?'

'There's not much I can do here.' For the first time their eyes met and he gave a brief, bitter smile. 'And at least it's a hell of a lot warmer out there.'

Sophie's heart was thumping hard enough to shake the stepladder. She could tell from his off-hand tone and his abstracted expression that he was about to walk away, and she didn't know when she would see him alone again, or get the chance to say any of the millions of things that flooded her restless head at night when sleep wouldn't come and she lay awake burning for him.

'I only came back to pick this up.' He held up the letter. 'I have an appointment with Ralph's solicitor in Hawksworth, so—'

'Kit—wait.' She jumped down from the stepladder, which was a bit higher than she thought, and landed unsteadily in front of him so he had to reach out a hand to grab her arm. He withdrew it again immediately.

Sophie's cheeks flamed. 'The other night—' she began miserably, unable to raise her head. 'I just wanted you to know that it wasn't a mistake. I knew what I was doing, and I—'

His eyes held a sinister glitter, like the frost outside. Beautiful but treacherous. 'Is that supposed to make it better?'

She shook her head, aware that it was coming out wrong. 'I'm trying to explain,' she said desperately. 'I don't want you to think that Jasper and I— It's not—we're not—'

Kit's mouth twisted into a smile of weary contempt. 'I'm not blaming *you* for what happened—it was just as much my fault. But I don't think either of us can really pretend it wasn't wrong.' Moving past her, he went to the huge arched door and put his hand on the iron latch. 'Like you, I don't have that many unbreakable rules but I wasn't aware until recently that one of them is that you don't touch your brother's woman. Under any circumstances.'

'But—'

'Particularly not just because you're both bored and available.'

The cruelty of his words made her incapable of reply. The door gave its graveyard creak as he opened it and went out, leaving nothing but an icy blast of winter in his wake.

The windscreen wipers beat in time to the throbbing in Kit's head, swiping the snow from in front of his eyes. But only for a minute. No sooner was the glass clear than more snow fell, obscuring everything again.

It seemed hideously symbolic of everything else in his life right now.

In London, trying to make some sense of Alnburgh's nightmarishly complicated legal and financial position, he had come up against nothing but locked doors and dead ends. But at least there he had had some perspective on the situation with Sophie.

Being back within touching distance of her had blown it all out of the water again.

Was it her acting ability or the way she looked up at him from under her eyelashes, or the fact that watching her rub the barrel of that gun had almost made him pull her down off the ladder and take her right there, against the door, that made him want to believe her? Wanted to make him accept it without question when she said that a little thing *like being*

Jasper's girlfriend was no obstacle to them sleeping together?

He pulled up in the market square and switched the car engine off. For a moment he just sat there, staring straight ahead without seeing the lit-up shops, the few pedestrians, bundled up against the weather as they picked their way carefully over the snowy pavements.

Since his mother had left when he was six years old, Kit had lived without love. He didn't trust it. He had come to realise that he certainly didn't need it. Instead he had built his life on principles. Values. Moral codes. They were what informed his choices, not *feelings*.

And they were what he had to hold on to.

He got out of the car and slammed the door with unnecessary force and headed for the offices of Baines and Stanton.

The Bull was beginning to fill up with after-work drinkers when Kit came out of his meeting with the solicitor. He knocked back his first whisky in a single mouthful standing at the bar, and ordered another, which he took to a table in the corner.

He intended to be there for a while; he might as

well make himself comfortable. And inconspicuous. On the wall opposite he noticed the Victorian etching of Alnburgh Castle. It looked exactly the same now as it had done a hundred years ago, he thought dully. Nothing had changed at all.

Apart from the fact it was no longer anything to do with him because *Ralph Fitzroy wasn't his father.*

It was funny, he thought, frowning down into the amber depths of his glass, several whiskies later. He was a bomb-disposal expert, for God's sake. He was trained to locate explosives and disarm them before they did any damage, and all the time he'd been completely oblivious to the great big unexploded bombshell in the centre of his own life.

It explained everything, he mused as the whisky gave a sort of warm clarity to his thoughts. It explained why Ralph had been such a spiteful *bastard* when he was growing up. And why he had always refused to discuss the future of the estate. It explained…

He scowled, struggling to fit in the fact that his mother had left him with a man who wasn't his father, and failing.

Oh, well, it explained some things. But it changed everything.

Everything.

He stood up, his chest suddenly tight, his breath clogging in his throat. Then, draining his whisky in one mouthful, left the bar.

Wrapped in a towel, still damp from the bath, Sophie put her bag on the bed and surveyed the contents in growing dismay.

Out of long habit she hadn't ever bothered to unpack, so she couldn't, even for a moment, enjoy a glimmer of hope that there might be something she'd temporarily forgotten about hanging in the wardrobe. Something smart. And black. And suitable for a funeral.

Black she could do, she thought, rifling through the contents of her case, which was like a Goth's dressing up box. It was smart and suitable where she fell down.

Knickers.

How could she have been so stupid as to spend most of the day looking for displacement activities and polishing pistols when she could have nipped out to The Fashion Capital of the North, which must surely do an extensive range of funeral attire? But it was way too late now. And she was pretty much left with one option.

She'd balled her last unlucky purchase from Braithwaite's in the bottom of the bag, from whence she'd planned to take it straight to the nearest charity shop when she got back to London, but she pulled it out again now and regarded it balefully. It was too long obviously, but if she cut it off at the knee and wore it with her black blazer, it might just do…

Rubbing herself dry, she hastily slipped on an oversized grey jumper of Jasper's and some thick hiking socks and set off downstairs. It was late. Tatiana had retired to her room ages ago and had supper on a tray, Thomas had long since gone back to his flat in the gatehouse and Sophie had helped a staggering, slightly incoherent Jasper to bed a good hour ago, after he had fallen asleep on the sofa watching *The Wizard of Oz*. However, the fact that all the lights were still on downstairs suggested Kit hadn't come back yet.

Her heart gave an uneven thud of alarm. Passing through the portrait hall, she looked at the grandfather clock. It was almost midnight. Kit had said something about him going to see the solicitor—surely he should have been back hours ago?

Visions of icy roads, twisted metal, blue lights zigzagged through her head, filling her with anguish. How ridiculous, she told herself grimly, switching the light on to go down the kitchen steps. It was far more likely that he'd met some old flame and had gone back to her place.

The anguish of that more realistic possibility was almost worse.

She switched the kitchen light on. On the long table in the centre of the room a roast ham and roast joint of beef stood under net domes, waiting to be sliced up for the buffet at the funeral tomorrow. After that she'd be going back to London, and Kit would be leaving for some dusty camp somewhere in the Middle East.

Sophie felt her throat constrict painfully.

She'd probably never see him again. After all, she'd been friends with Jasper all these years without meeting him. She remembered the photo in the paper and wondered if she'd catch glimpses of him on the news from time to time. A horrible thought struck her: please, God, not in one of those reports about casualties—

She jumped as she heard a noise from the corridor behind her. It was a sort of rusty grating; metal against metal: the noise made by an old-fashioned key being turned in a lock—yet another piece from Alnburgh's archive of horror-film sound effects. Sophie turned around, pressing herself back against the worktop, the scissors held aloft in her hand—as if that would help.

In the dark corridor the basement door burst open.

Kit stood there, silhouetted against the blue ice-light outside. He was swaying slightly.

'Kit.' Dropping the scissors, Sophie went towards him, concern quickening inside her. 'Kit, what happened? Are you OK?'

'I'm fine.'

His voice was harsh; as bleak and cold and empty as the frozen sky behind him.

'Where's the car?' Her heart was pumping adrenaline through her, making her movements abrupt and shaky as she stepped past him and slammed the door. In the light from the kitchen his face was ashen, his lips white, but his eyes were glittering pools of darkness.

'In town. Parked in the square outside the solicitor's office. I walked back.'

'Why?'

'Because I was well over the limit to drive.'

He didn't feel it. No gentle, welcome oblivion for him. The six-mile walk home had just served to sharpen his senses and give a steel-edged sharpness to every thought in his head.

And every step of the way he'd been aware of the castle, black and hulking against the skyline, and he'd known how every potential intruder, every would-be enemy invader, every outsider, for God's sake, for the last thousand years had felt when confronted with that fortified mass of rock.

One thought had kept him going forwards. The knowledge that the six-foot-thick walls and turrets and battlements contained Sophie. Her bright hair. Her quick smile. Her irreverence and her humour. Her sweet, willing body…

'What happened?'

She was standing in front of him now, trembling slightly. Or maybe shivering with the cold. She was always cold. He frowned down at her. She appeared to be wearing a large sweater and nothing else. Except thick woollen socks, which only seemed to make her long, slender legs look even more delicious. They were bare from mid-thigh downwards, which made it hard to think clearly about the question she'd just asked, or want to take the trouble to reply.

'Kit? Was it something the solicitor said?'

She touched his hand. Her skin was actually warm for once. He longed to feel it against his.

'Ralph wasn't my father.'

He heard his own voice say the words. It was hard and maybe, just maybe a tiny bit bitter. Damn. He didn't want to be bitter.

'Oh, Kit—'

'None of this is mine,' he said, more matter-of-factly now, walking away from her into the kitchen. He turned slowly, looking around him as if seeing it all for the first time.

'It all belongs to Jasper, I suppose. The castle, the estate, the title...'

She had come to stand in the doorway, her arms folded tightly across her chest. She was looking up at him, and her eyes were liquid with compassion and understanding and...

'I don't.'

Her voice low and breathless and vibrating with emotion as she came towards him. 'I want you to know that I don't belong to Jasper. I don't belong to *anyone.*'

'And I don't have a brother any more.'

For a moment they stared at each other wordlessly. And then he caught her warm hand in his and pulled her forwards, giving way to the onslaught of want that had battered at his defences since she'd sat down opposite him on the train.

Together they ran up the stairs, pausing halfway up at the turn of the staircase to find each other's mouths. Kit's face was frozen beneath Sophie's palms and she kissed him as if the heat of her longing could bring the warmth back into his body. His jaw was rough with stubble, his mouth tasted of whisky and as he slid his hands up beneath the sweater she gasped at the chill of his hands on her bare breasts while almost boiling over with need.

'God, Sophie…'

'Come on.'

Seizing his hand, she ran onwards, up the rest of the stairs. Desire made her disorientated, and at the top she turned right instead of left, just as she had that first night. Realising her mistake, she stopped, but before she could say anything he had taken her face in his hands and was pushing her up against the panelled wall, kissing her until she didn't care where they were, just so long as she could have him soon.

Her hips ground helplessly against him, so she could feel the hardness of his erection beneath his clothes.

'My room,' she moaned. 'It's the other way—'

'Plenty more.' He growled against her mouth and, without taking his lips from hers, felt along the panelling for the handle of the door a few feet away. As it opened he levered himself away from the wall and stooped to hoist her up against him. She wrapped her legs tightly around his waist as he carried her forwards.

Sophie wasn't sure if this was the same room she'd stumbled into on her first night, or another one where the air was damp and the furniture draped in dust sheets. The window was tall, arched, uncurtained, and the blue light coming through it gleamed dully on the carved oak posts of an enormous bed.

As he headed towards it her insides turned liquid with lust. The room was freezing, but his breath was warm against her breasts, making her nipples harden and fizz. He was still dressed, the wool of his jacket rough and damp against her thighs. As she slid out of his arms and onto the hard, high bed she pulled it off his shoulders.

She was on her knees on the slippery damask bedspread and he stood in front of her. His face was bleached of colour, its hard contours thrown into sharp relief, his heavy-lidded eyes black and fathomless.

He was so beautiful.

Her breath caught. Her hands were shaking as she reached out to undo the buttons of his shirt. He closed his eyes, tipping his head back, and Sophie could see the muscles quilt in his jaw as he fought to keep control.

It was one battle he wasn't going to win.

Gently now, she slid her hands beneath his open shirt, feeling him flinch with his own raw need. His skin still felt chilled. Tenderness bloomed and ached inside her, giving her desire a poignancy that scared her. She felt as if she were dancing, barefoot, free, but right on the edge of a precipice.

His shirt fell away and quickly she peeled off her jumper. Slowly, tightly, she wrapped her arms around him, pressing her warm, naked body against his cold one, cradling his head, kissing his mouth, his cheekbones, his eyes, his jaw as he lowered her onto the bed.

His heartbeat was strong against her breasts. Their ribs ground together as he undid his jeans with one hand and kicked them off. Sophie reached up and yanked at the damask cover so she could pull it over them, to warm him again. She was distantly aware of its musty smell, but she couldn't have cared less because he was cupping her cheek, trailing the backs of his fingers with exquisite, maddening lightness over her breast until her nerves screamed with desperation.

Reality blurred into a dreamlike haze where she was aware of nothing but his skin against hers, his breath in her ear, his lips on her neck. She kept her eyes fixed on his, swimming in their gleaming depths as beneath the sheets his hands discovered her body.

And with each stroke of his palm, each well-placed brush of his fingers she was discovering herself. Sex was something she was relaxed about, comfortable with. She knew what she was doing, and she enjoyed it. It was *fun*.

And this was as far removed from anything she'd ever felt before as silk was from sackcloth. This wasn't fun, it was essential. As he entered her, gently, deeply, she wasn't sure if it was more like dying or being born again.

Her cry of need hung in the frigid air.

She had never known anything more perfect. For a moment they were both still, adjusting to the new bliss of being joined together, and, looking into his eyes, she wanted to make it last for ever.

But it was impossible. Her body was already crying out for more, her hips beginning to move of their own accord, picking up their rhythm from him. His thumb brushed over her lips, and she caught it between her teeth as with the other hand he found her clitoris, moving his fingertip over it with every slow, powerful thrust.

The thick, ages-old silence of the room pooled around them again. The massive bed was too strong to creak as their bodies moved. Sophie wanted to look at him for ever. She wanted to hold for a lifetime the image of his perfect face, close to hers, as she spiralled helplessly into the most profound chasm of sensation. Their legs were entwined, his muscles hard against hers, and she didn't know where he ended and she began.

She didn't know anything any more. As a second

cry—her high, broken sob of release—shattered the stillness she could only feel that everything she'd ever thought she believed was ashes and dust.

Kit slept.

Whether it was the whisky or the six-mile walk or the shattering, deathlike orgasm he didn't know, but for the first time in years he slept like the angels.

He woke as the sun was coming up, streaking the sky with rose-pink ribbons and filling the room with the melting light of dawn. In his arms Sophie slept on, her back pressed against his chest, her bottom warm and deliciously soft against his thighs.

Or, more specifically, against his erection.

Gritting his teeth, he willed it away as remorse began to ebb through him, dissolving the haze of repletion and leaving him staring reality in the face. He closed his eyes again, not wanting to look at reality, or at Sophie, whose vibrant beauty had an ethereal quality in the pink half-light. As a way of blotting out the anger and the hurt and the shock of his discovery, last night had been perfect—more than he could have hoped for, and certainly more than he deserved. But it was a one-off. It couldn't happen again.

Sophie stirred in his arms, moving her hips a fraction, pressing herself harder against the ache of his erection. He bit back a moan, dragging his mind back from the memories of her unbuttoning his shirt, wrapping her arms around him and holding him when he most needed to be held, folding herself around him as he entered her...

The whisky might have blunted the pain and temporarily short-circuited his sense of honour, but it hadn't dulled his memory. Every detail was there, stored and ready for instant replay in the back of his head. A fact that he suspected was going to prove extremely inconvenient in the nights ahead when he was alone in a narrow bunk, separated from the rest of his men by the thinnest of makeshift walls.

Rolling out of bed, he picked his jeans up from the floor and pulled them on. The pink light carried an illusion of warmth, but the room was like a fridge and he had to clench his teeth together to stop them chattering as he reached into the sleep-warm depths of the bed and slid his arms under her.

She sighed as he gathered her up as gently as possible, but she didn't wake. Kit found himself fighting the urge to smile as he recalled the swiftness with which she'd fallen asleep on the train the first time he'd seen her, and the way it had both intrigued and irritated him. But, looking down into her face as he carried her down the shadowy corridor to her own room, the smile faded again. She was like no woman he'd ever known before. She'd appeared from nowhere, defiant, elusive, contradictory, and somehow managed to slip beneath his defences when he'd wanted only to push her away.

How had she done that?

With one shoulder he nudged open the door to her room. The window faced north, so no dawn sunlight penetrated here, and it was even colder, if that were possible, than the room they'd just left. It was also incredibly neat, he noticed with a flash of surprise, as if she was ready to leave at any moment. Her hair was fragrant and silken against his bare chest as he laid her gently down on the bed, rolling her sideways a little so he could pull back the covers and ease them over her.

Her eyes half opened as he tucked her in and she gazed up at him for a moment, her lips curving into a sleepy smile as she reached out and stroked the back of her hand down his midriff.

'It's cold without you,' she murmured. 'Come back.'

'I can't.' His voice was like sandpaper and he grasped her hand before it went any lower, his fingers tightening around hers for a moment as he laid it back on the bed. 'It's morning.'

She rolled onto her back and gave a little sighing laugh. 'It's over, you mean.'

'It has to be.' He pushed the heels of his hands into his eyes, physically stopping himself from looking at her as he spoke so his resolve wouldn't weaken. 'We can't change what we did last night, but we can't repeat it either. We just need to get through today without giving Jasper any reason to suspect.'

Against the pillow her face was still and composed, her hair spilling around it and emphasising its pallor. She closed her eyes.

'OK.'

The small, resigned word wasn't what he had expected and it pushed knives of guilt into his gut. Why was she making him feel as if this were his fault? Last night they had both been reckless but the result was just the logical conclusion to everything that had happened between them since the moment they'd met. It had felt inevitable somehow, but nonetheless forbidden.

Kit turned away and walked to the door, bracing his arm against the frame before he opened it and saying with great weariness, 'Sophie, what did you expect?'

Her eyes opened slowly, and the smile she gave him was infinitely sad.

'Nothing,' she said softly. 'Nothing.'

After he'd gone Sophie rolled over and let the tears spill down her cheeks.

He had slept with her because he'd finally found a get-out clause in his moral rule book. He no longer had a duty to Jasper, and that made it OK for him. But what about her?

Last night she thought he understood, without making her spell it out, that she wasn't betraying Jasper by sleeping with him.

It seemed he didn't.

She hadn't expected for ever. She hadn't expected declarations of undying love. Only for him to trust her.

CHAPTER TWELVE

'THE cars are here, madam.'

Thomas appeared in the hallway, his face rigidly blank as he made his announcement. But Sophie heard the slight break in his voice and felt the lump of emotion in her throat swell a little.

She mustn't cry. Not when Tatiana was holding herself together with such dignity. Getting into the gleaming black Bentley, she was the picture of sober elegance in a narrow-fitting black skirt and jacket, her eyes hidden by a hat with a tiny black net veil. Jasper got in beside her. He was grey-faced, hollow-cheeked, a ghost of the languid, laughing boy she knew in London. She noticed his throat working as he glanced at the hearse in front, where Ralph's polished coffin lay decked in white flowers, and as he settled himself in the back of the car he had to twist his hands together to stop them shaking.

Poor Jasper. She had to stay strong for him. Today was going to be such an ordeal, and his grief was so much more profound than anything she'd ever experienced. She dug her nails into her palm. And anyway, what did she have to cry about? She'd hardly known Ralph. And it was stupid, *stupid* to be upset over a one-night stand with a man she wasn't going to see again after today.

'After you.'

She looked up and felt her knees buckle a little. Kit was standing behind her on the steps to the castle, his perfectly tailored black suit and tie cruelly highlighting his austere beauty. His face was completely expressionless, and his silver eyes barely flickered over her as he spoke.

His indifference was like knives in her flesh. It was as if last night had never happened.

'Oh. I'm not sure I should go in the official car,' she stammered, looking down at her shoes. 'I'm not family or anything.'

'That makes two of us,' he murmured acidly. 'You're Jasper's girlfriend, that's close enough. Just get in—unless you're planning to walk in those heels.'

She did as she was told, but without any of the grace with which Tatiana had performed the manoeuvre, and was aware that Kit would have got a very unflattering view of her bottom in the tight black dress. She wondered if he'd seen that the hem was stuck up with Sellotape where she'd hurriedly cut it off at the knee this morning and hadn't had time to sew it.

Further evidence of her lack of class. Another reason for him to put her in the category of 'Women to Sleep With' (subsection: Once) rather than 'Women to Date'.

He got in beside her and an undertaker with a permanent expression of compassionate respect shut the door. Sophie found herself huddling close to Jasper so she could leave an inch of cream leather seat between her leg and Kit's. As the car moved silently beneath the arched gateway she bit her lip and kept her head turned away from him, her gaze fixed out of the window. But she could still catch the faint dry, delicious scent of his skin and that was enough to make the memories of last night come flooding back. She wished she could switch them off, as Thomas had switched off the water supply when the pipe had burst. But even if she could, she thought sadly, her body would still remember and still throb with longing for him.

* * *

The rose-pink sunrise had delivered a beautiful winter's day for Ralph's send-off—crisp, cold and glittering, just like the day of his party. The leaden clouds of the last grim week had lifted to reveal a sky of clean, clear blue.

Outside the church of St John the Baptist people stood in groups, stamping their feet to keep warm as they talked. Some were smartly dressed in black, but most of them wore everyday outdoor gear, and Sophie realised they must be local people, drawn by the social spectacle rather than grief. They fell silent and turned sombre, curious faces towards them as the cars turned into the churchyard.

'I forgot to bring the monkey nuts,' muttered Jasper with uncharacteristic bitchiness.

'People are curious,' said Tatiana in a flat, cold voice. 'They want to see if we feel things differently from them. We don't, of course. The difference is we don't show our feelings.'

Sophie bit her lip. She was one of those people, with her cheap dress and her Sellotaped hem. She wasn't part of the 'we' that Tatiana talked about. She wasn't even Jasper's girlfriend, for pity's sake. As they got out of the car and Jasper took his mother's arm to escort her into the church, Sophie tried to slip to the back, looking for Thomas and Mrs Daniels to sit with. A firm hand gripped her arm.

'Oh, no, you don't,' said Kit grimly.

He kept hold of her arm as they progressed slowly down the aisle of the packed church, behind Tatiana and Jasper and the coffin. Torn between heaven and hell at his closeness, Sophie was aware of people's heads turning, curious eyes sweeping over her beneath the brims of countless black hats, no doubt wondering who she was and what right she had to be there. She felt a barb of anguish as she realised people must think she was with Kit.

If only.

'I am the resurrection and the life…'

Beside her Kit's hands were perfectly steady as he held his service sheet without looking at it. Sophie didn't allow herself to glance at him, but even so she knew that his gaze was fixed straight ahead and that his silver eyes would be hard and dry, because it was as if she had developed some supernatural power that made her absolutely instinctively aware of everything about him.

Was that what loving someone did to you?

She lifted her head and looked up at the stained-glass window above the altar. The winter sunlight was shining through it, illuminating the jewel-bright colours and making the saints' faces positively glow with righteousness. She smiled weakly to herself. It's divine retribution, isn't it? she thought. My punishment for playing fast and loose with the affections of Jean-Claude and countless others. For thinking I was above it all and being scornful about love…

There was a shuffling of feet as the organ started and the congregation stood up. Sophie hastily followed suit, turning over her service sheet and trying to work out where the words to the hymn were. She was aware of Kit, towering above her like some dark angel, as he handed her an open hymn book, tapping the right page with a finger.

'I vow to thee my country…'

It was a hymn about sacrifice. Numbly Kit registered the familiar lines about laying down your life for your nation and wondered what the hell Ralph knew about any of that. As far as Kit knew, Ralph had never put his own needs, his own desires anything but first. He had lived for pleasure. He had died, the centre of attention at his own lavish party, not alone and thousands of miles from home on some hot, dusty roadside.

He would never have sacrificed his happiness for the sake of his brother.

Was that yet another item on his list of character flaws, or evidence that he was a hell of a lot cleverer than Kit after all?

Kit let the hymn book in his hands drop and closed his eyes as the hymn reached its stirring climax. Everyone sat down again, and as Sophie moved beside him he caught a breath of her perfume and the warmth of her body on the arctic air.

Want whiplashed through him, so that he had to grip the back of the pew in front to steady himself. Kit had attended too many funerals, carried too many flag-draped coffins onto bleak airfields to be unaware that life was short. Rules and principles didn't help when you were dead.

Joy should be seized. Nights like the one he'd just spent with Sophie should be celebrated.

Shouldn't they?

In the elaborately carved pulpit supplied by another long-gone Fitzroy, the vicar cleared his throat and prepared to start his address. Kit forced himself to drag his attention away from Sophie's hands, resting in her lap. The skin was translucent pale against her black dress. They looked cold.

He wanted to warm them, as she'd warmed him last night.

'We come together today to celebrate the life of Ralph Fitzroy, who to those gathered here was not just the Earl of Hawksworth, but a husband, father and friend.'

It was just sex. That was what she'd said on the phone the first time he'd seen her, wasn't it? Just sex. He had to forget it. Especially now, in the middle of a funeral…

'Let's just take a few moments of silent reflection,' the vicar encouraged, 'to enjoy some personal memories of Lord Fitzroy, and reflect on the many ways in which he touched our lives…'

Ye Gods, thought Kit despairingly, rubbing at the tense muscles across his forehead. In his case, remembering the ways in which Ralph had touched his life really wasn't such a good idea. All around him he was aware of people reaching for tissues, sliding arms around each other in mutual support while he sat locked in the private dungeon of his own bitterness. Alone.

And then, very gently Sophie put her hand over his, lacing her cold fingers through his, caressing the back of his hand with her thumb with a touch that had nothing to do with sex, but was about comfort and understanding.

And he wasn't alone any more.

'Lovely service,' people murmured, dabbing their eyes as they filed out into the sharp sunlight to the strains of The Beatles singing 'In My Life'. That had been Jasper's idea.

'You OK?' Sophie asked him, slipping her arm through his as Tatiana was swept up in a subdued round of air-kissing and clashing hat brims.

'Bearing up.' He gave her a bleak smile. 'I need a drink.'

'What happens now?'

'We go back for the interment.' He shuddered. 'There's a Fitzroy family vault at Alnburgh, below the old chapel in the North Gate. It's tiny, and just like the location for a low-budget horror film, so I'll spare you that grisly little scene. Mum and I, and the vicar—and Kit too, I suppose—will do the honours, by which time everyone should have made their way back up to the castle for the drinks. Would you mind staying here and sort of shepherding them in the right direction?'

In spite of the sunshine the wind sweeping the

exposed clifftop was like sharpened razor blades. Jasper was rigid with cold and spoke through clenched teeth to stop them chattering. Weight had dropped off him in the last week, Sophie noticed, but whether it was from pining for his father or for Sergio she wasn't sure. Reaching up, she pressed a kiss on his frozen cheek.

'Of course I will. Go and say your goodbyes.'

He got into the car beside Tatiana. 'Save a drink for me,' he said dismally. 'Don't let the hordes drink us dry.'

Sophie bent to look at him through the open door. 'Of course I will.'

She turned round. Kit was standing behind her, obviously waiting to get into the car, his eyes fixed on some point in the far distance rather than at her rear.

'Sorry.' Hastily Sophie stepped out of the way. 'Are you going to the interment too?' she added in a low voice.

A muscle twitched in his cheek. 'Yes. For appearance's sake. At some point Jasper and I need to have a proper talk, but today isn't the right time.' He looked at her, almost reluctantly, with eyes that were as bleak as the snow-covered Cheviots stretching away behind him. 'At some point you and I should probably talk too.'

An icy gust of wind whipped a strand of hair across Sophie's face. Moving her head to flick it out of the way again, a movement in the distance caught her eye. Someone was vaulting over the low wall that separated the graveyard from the road, loping towards them between the frosty headstones.

Oh, no... Oh, please, no... Not now...

Sophie felt the blood drain from her head. It was a familiar enough figure, although incongruous in this setting. A bottle of vodka swung from one hand.

'Today might not be the best time for that either,' she said, folding her arms across her chest to steady herself. 'You should go—I think they're waiting.'

It was an answer of sorts, Kit thought blackly as he lowered himself into the Bentley and slammed the door. Just not the one he'd hoped for.

As the car began to move slowly away in the wake of the hearse Kit watched her take a few steps backwards, and then turn and slip into the cluster of people left behind outside the church. He lost sight of her for a few seconds, but then caught a glimpse of her hair, fiery against the monochrome landscape. She was hurrying in the direction of someone walking through the churchyard.

'Such a lot of people,' said Tatiana vaguely, pulling her black gloves off. 'Your father had so many friends.'

Jasper put an arm around her. 'It was a great service. Even Dad, who hated church, would have enjoyed it.'

Kit turned his face to the window.

The man's clothes marked him out as being separate from the funeral-goers. He was dressed neither as a mourner nor in the waterproofs and walking boots of the locals, but in skintight jeans, some kind of on-trend, tailored jacket with his shirt tails hanging down beneath it. Urban clothes. There was a kind of defiant swagger to the man's posture and movements, as if he was doing something reckless but didn't care, and as the car waited to pull out onto the main road Kit watched in the wing mirror as Sophie approached him, shaking her head. It looked as if she was pleading with him.

The car moved again, and for a few seconds the view in the wing mirror was a blur of hedge and empty sky. Kit stared straight ahead. His hands were clenched into fists, his heart beating heavily in his chest.

He waited, counting the beats. And then, just before the bend in the road when the church would be out of sight, he turned and looked back in time to see her put her arms around him.

When she'd taken his hand in church like that, it had changed something. Or maybe that was wrong—maybe it hadn't changed, so much as shown him what was there before that he hadn't wanted to admit.

That possibly what he wanted from her—with her—wasn't just sex. And the hope that, at some point, when she had settled things with Jasper, she might want that too.

It looked as if he'd been wrong.

'Please, Sergio. It won't be for long. A couple of hours—maybe three, just until the funeral is over.'

Sergio twitched impatiently out of her embrace. 'Three hours,' he sneered. 'You make it sound like nothing, but every hour is like a month. I've waited over a week already and I've just spent all day on a stupid train. I *need* him, Sophie. And he needs me.'

'I know, I know,' Sophie soothed, glancing back

at the church with its dwindling crowd of mourners, and sending up a silent prayer for patience. Or, failing that, forgiveness for putting her hands round Sergio's elegant, self-absorbed neck and killing him.

What had Kit meant, they needed to talk? And why did bloody Sergio have to choose the very moment when she could have asked him to stage his ridiculous, melodramatic appearance?

'You don't,' Sergio moaned theatrically. 'Nobody knows.'

'I know that Jasper's in despair without you,' Sophie said with exaggerated patience. 'I know he misses you every second, but I also know that his mother needs him right now. And he needs to get closure on this before he can be with you properly.'

It was the right thing to say. 'Closure' was the kind of psychological pseudoscience that Sergio lapped up.

'Do you think so?'

'Uh-huh.' Sensing victory, Sophie took the bottle out of his hand and began to lead him through the gravestones back in the direction from which he'd just come. 'And I also think that you're tired. You've had a horrible week and an exhausting journey. The pub in the village has rooms—why don't we see if they have anything available and I'll tell Jasper to join you there as soon as he can? It would be better than staying at the castle, just for now.'

Sergio cast a wistful glance up at Alnburgh Castle, its turrets and battlements gilded by the low winter sun. Sophie sensed rebellion brewing and increased her pace, which wasn't easy with her heels snagging into the frosty grass. 'Here—I'll come with you and make sure you're settled,' she said firmly. 'And then I'll go to Jasper and tell him where you are.'

Sergio took her arm and gave it a brief, hard squeeze, in the manner of a doomed character in a war film. His blue eyes were soulful. 'Thank you, Sophie, I do as you say. I *trust* you.'

The hallway was filled with the sound of voices and a throng of black-clad people, many of whom had been here only a week earlier for Ralph's party. After the surreal awfulness of the little scene in the Alnburgh vault Kit felt in desperate need of a stiff drink, but he couldn't go more than a couple of paces without someone else waylaying him to offer condolences, usually followed by congratulations on the medal.

His replies were bland and automatic, and all the time he was aware of his heart beating slightly too fast and his body vibrating with tension as he surreptitiously looked around for Sophie.

'Your father must have been immensely proud of you,' said an elderly cousin of Ralph's in an even more elderly fur coat. The statement was wrong in so many ways that for a moment Kit couldn't think what could have prompted her to make it. 'For the George Medal,' she prompted, taking a sip of sherry and looking at him expectantly.

It was far too much trouble to explain that such was his father's indifference that he hadn't told him. Oh, and that he wasn't actually his father either. Instead he gave a neutral smile and made a polite reply before excusing himself and moving away.

Conversation was impossible when there was so much that he couldn't say. To anyone except Sophie.

He had to find her.

'Kit.'

The voice was familiar, but unexpected. Feeling a hand on his arm, Kit looked around to see a large black hat and, beneath it, looking tanned, beautiful but distinctly uneasy, was Alexia.

'Darling, I'm so sorry,' she murmured, holding on to her hat with one hand as she reached to kiss each of his cheeks. 'Such a shock. You must all be devastated.'

'Something like that. I wasn't expecting to see you here.'

Kit knew that his voice suggested that the surprise wasn't entirely a pleasant one, and mentally berated himself. It wasn't Alexia's fault he'd seen Sophie falling into the arms of some tosser in a girl's jacket amongst the headstones, or that she'd subsequently disappeared.

'Olympia and I were in St Moritz last weekend, but when her mother told us what happened I just wanted to be here. For you, really. I know I wasn't lucky enough to know your father well, but...' Beneath her skiing tan her cheeks were pink. 'I wanted to make sure you're OK. I still care about you, you know...'

'Thanks.'

She bent her head slightly, so the brim of her hat hid her face, and said quietly, 'Kit—it must be a horrible time. Don't be alone.'

Kit felt a great wave of despair wash over him. What was this, International Irony Day? For just about the first time in his life he didn't *want* to be alone, but the only person he wanted to be with didn't seem to share the feeling.

'I'll bear that in mind,' he said wearily, preparing to make his escape. And no doubt he would, but not in the way she meant.

'Hello, Kit—so sorry about your father.'

If they were standing in the armoury hall, Kit reflected, at this point he would have had difficulty stopping himself grabbing one of the pistols so thoroughly polished by Sophie and putting it against his head. As it was he was left with no choice but to submit to Olympia Rothwell-Hyde's over-scented embrace and muster a death-row smile.

'Olympia.'

'Ma said you were an absolute *god* at the party, when it happened,' she said, blue eyes wide with what possibly passed for sincerity in the circles she moved in. 'Real heroic stuff.'

'Obviously not,' Kit said coolly, glancing round, 'since we find ourselves here…'

Olympia, obviously unaware that it was International Irony Day, wasn't thrown off her stride for a second. Leaning forwards, sheltering beneath the brim of Alexia's hat like a spy in an Inspector Clousseau film, she lowered her voice to an excited whisper.

'Darling, I have to ask… That redhead you sat next to in church. She looks terribly like a girl we used to know at school called Summer Greenham, but it *can't* be—'

Electricity snapped through him, jolting him out of his apathy.

'Sophie. She's called *Sophie* Greenham.'

'Then it *is* her!' Olympia's upper-crust voice held a mixture of incredulity and triumph as she looked at Alexia. 'Who can blame her for ditching that embarrassing drippy hippy name? She should have changed her surname too—apparently it came from the lesbian peace camp place. Anyway, darling, none of that explains what she's *doing* here. Does she work here, because if so I would *so* keep an eye on the family silver—'

'She's Jasper's girlfriend.' Maybe if he said it often enough he'd accept it.

'No way. No. *Way!* Seriously? Ohmigod!'

Kit stood completely still while this pantomime of disbelief was going on, but beneath his implacable exterior icy bursts of adrenaline were pumping through his veins.

'Meaning?'

Beside Olympia, Alexia shifted uneasily on her designer heels. Olympia ploughed on, too caught up in the thrill of gossip to notice the tension that suddenly seemed to crackle in the air.

'She came to our school from some filthy traveller camp—an aunt took pity on her and wanted to civilise her before it was too late, or something. Whatevs.' She waved a dismissive hand. 'Total waste of money as she was expelled in the end, for stealing.' She took a sip of champagne before continuing in her confident, bitchy drawl. 'It was just before the school prom and a friend of ours had been sent some money by her mother to buy a dress. Well, the cash disappeared from the dorm and suddenly—by astonishing coincidence—Miss Greenham-Extremely-Common, who had previously rocked the jumble-sale-reject look, appears with a *very* nice new dress.'

A pulse was throbbing in Kit's temple. 'And you put two and two together,' he said icily.

Olympia looked surprised and slightly indignant. 'And reached a very obvious four. Her aunt admitted she hadn't given her any money—I think the fees were quite enough of a stretch for her—and the only explanation Summer could give was that her mother had bought it for her. Her mother who lived on a *bus*, and hadn't been seen for, like, a *year* or something and so was conveniently unavailable for comment, having nothing as modern as a *telephone*...'

Looking down at the floor, Kit shook his head and gave a soft, humourless laugh. 'And therefore unavailable to back her up either.'

'Oh, come on, Kit,' said Olympia, in the kind of jolly, dismissive tone that suggested they were having a huge joke and he was spoiling it. 'Sometimes you don't need *evidence* because the truth is so obvious that everyone can see it. And anyway—' she gave him a sly smirk from beneath her blonde flicky fringe '—if she's Jasper's girlfriend, why would she have just been checking into a room in the pub in the village with some bloke? Alexia and I went for a quick drinkie to warm ourselves up after the service and saw her.' The smirk hardened into a look of grim triumph. 'Room three, if you don't believe me.'

* * *

If Sophie had known she was going to walk back from the village to the castle in the snow, she would have left the shag-me shoes at home and worn something more sensible.

It was just as well her toes were frozen, since she suspected they'd be even more painful if they weren't. Unfortunately even the cold couldn't anaesthetise the raw blisters on her heels and it was only the thought of finding Kit, hearing what it was he had to say that kept her going.

She also had to find Jasper and break the news to him that Sergio had turned up. Having ordered an enormous breakfast for him to mop up some of the vodka and waited to make sure he ate it, she had finally left him crashed out on the bed. He shouldn't be any trouble for the next hour or so, but now the formal part of the funeral was over she knew that Jasper wouldn't want to wait to go and see him. And also she was guiltily keen to pass over the responsibility for him to Jasper as soon as possible. Sitting and listening to him endlessly talking about his emotions, analysing every thought that had flickered across his butterfly brain in the last week had made her want to start on the vodka herself. She had found herself thinking wistfully of Kit's reserve. His understatement. His emotional integrity.

Gritting her teeth against the pain, she quickened her steps.

The drive up to the castle was choked with cars. People had obviously decided they were staying for a while, and parked in solid rows, making it impossible for anyone to leave. Weaving through them, Sophie could hear the sound of voices spilling out through the open door and carrying on the frosty air.

Her heart was beating rapidly as she went up the steps, and it was nothing to do with the brisk walk. She paused in the armoury hall, tugging down her jacket and smoothing her skirt with trembling hands, noticing abstractedly that the Sellotaped hem was coming down.

'Is everything all right, Miss Greenham?'

Thomas was standing in the archway, holding a tray of champagne, looking at her with some concern. Sophie realised what a sight she must look in her sawn-off dress with her face scarlet from cold and exertion, clashing madly with her hair.

'Oh, yes, thank you. I just walked up from the village, that's all. Do you know where Jasper is?'

'Master Jasper went up to his room when he got back from the interment,' said Thomas, lowering his voice respectfully. 'I don't think he's come down yet.'

'OK. Thanks. I'll go up and see if he's all right.' She hesitated, feeling a warm blush gather in her already fiery cheeks. 'Oh, and I don't suppose you know where I could find Kit, do you?'

'I believe he's here somewhere,' Thomas said, turning round creakily, putting the champagne glasses in peril as he surveyed the packed room behind him. 'I saw him come in a little while ago. Ah, yes—there he is, talking to the young lady in the large hat.'

Of course, he was so much taller than everyone else so it wasn't too hard to spot him. He was standing with his back half to her, so she couldn't see his face properly, only the scimitar curve of one hard cheekbone. A cloud of butterflies rose in her stomach.

And then she saw who he was talking to. And they turned into a writhing mass of snakes.

CHAPTER THIRTEEN

A CHILDHOOD spent moving around, living in cramped spaces with barely any room for personal possessions, being ready to move on at a moment's notice, had left its mark on Sophie in many ways. One of them was that she travelled light and rarely unpacked.

Once she'd seen Jasper it didn't take her long to get her few things together. It took a little longer to get herself together, but after a while she felt strong enough to say goodbye to her little room and slip along the corridor to the back staircase.

It came out in the armoury hall. As she went down the sound of voices rose up to meet her— less subdued and funereal now as champagne was consumed, interspersed with laughter. She found herself listening out for Kit's voice amongst the others, and realised with a tearing sensation in her side that she'd never heard him laugh. Not really laugh, without irony or bitterness or cynicism.

But maybe he would be laughing now, with Olympia.

She came down the last step. The door was ahead of her, half-open and letting in arctic air and winter sunshine. Determined not to look round in case she lost her nerve, Sophie kept her head down and walked quickly towards it.

The cold air hit her as she stepped outside, making her gasp and bringing a rush of tears to her eyes. She sniffed hard, and brushed them impatiently away with the sleeve of her faithful old coat.

'So you're leaving.'

She whirled round. Kit was standing at the top of the steps, in the open doorway. His hands were in his pockets, his top button undone and his tie pulled loose, but despite all that there was still something sinister in his stillness, the rigid blankness of his face.

The last glowing embers of hope in Sophie's heart went out.

'Yes.' She nodded, and even managed a brief smile although meeting his eye was too much to attempt. 'I saw you talking to Olympia. It's a small world. I suppose she told you everything.'

'Yes. Not that it makes any difference. So now

you're going—just like that. Were you going to say goodbye?'

Sophie kept her eyes fixed on the ivy growing up the wall by the steps, twining itself around an old cast-iron downpipe. Of course it didn't make any difference, she told herself numbly. He already knew she was nothing. Her voice seemed to come from very far away. 'I'll write to Tatiana. She's surrounded by friends at the moment—I don't want to barge in.'

'It was Jasper I was thinking of. What about him?'

Sophie moved her bag from one hand to the other. She was conscious of holding herself very upright, placing her feet carefully together, almost as if if she didn't take care to do this she might just collapse. She still couldn't bring herself to look at him.

'He'll be OK now. He doesn't need me.'

At the top of the steps Kit made some sudden movement. For a moment she thought he had turned and was going to go inside, but instead he dragged a hand through his hair and swung back to face her again. This time there was no disguising the blistering anger on his face.

'So, who is he? I mean, he's obviously pretty special that he's come all this way to claim you and you can't even wait until the funeral is over before you go and fall into bed with him. Is it the same one I heard you talking to on the train, or someone else?'

After a moment of confusion it dawned on Sophie that he must have seen her with Sergio. And jumped, instantly, to the wrong conclusion.

Except there wasn't really such a thing as a wrong conclusion. In her experience 'wrong conclusion' tended to mean the same thing as 'confirmation of existing prejudice', and she had learned long ago that no amount of logical explanations could alter people's prejudices. That had to come from within themselves.

'Someone else.'

'Do you love him?' Suddenly the anger that had gripped him seemed to vanish and he just sounded very tired. Defeated almost.

Sophie shook her head. Her knees were shaking, her chest burning with the effort of holding back the sobs that threatened to tear her apart.

'No.'

'Then why? Why are you going to him?'

'Because he'd fight for me.' She took a deep

breath and lifted her head. In a voice that was completely calm, completely steady she said, 'Because he trusts me.'

And then she turned and began to walk away.

Blindly Kit shouldered his way through the people standing in the hall. Seeing his ashen face and the stricken expression on it, some of them exchanged loaded glances and murmured about grief striking even the strongest.

Reaching the library, he shut the door and leaned against it, breathing hard and fast.

Trust. That was the last thing he'd expected her to say.

He brought his hands up to his head, sliding his fingers into his hair as his mind raced. He had learned very early on in life that few people could be trusted, and since then he had almost prided himself on his cynicism. It meant he was one step ahead of the game and gave him immunity from the emotional disasters that felled others.

It also meant he had just had to watch the only woman he wanted to be with walk away from him, right into the arms of someone else. Someone who wore designer clothes and left his shirt tails trailing and *trusted* her. Someone who would fight for her.

Well, trust might not be his strong suit, but fighting was something he could do.

He threw open the door, and almost ran straight into the person who was standing right on the other side of it.

'Alexia, what the—?'

'I wanted to talk.' She recovered from her obvious fright pretty quickly, following him as he kept on walking towards the noise of the party. 'There's something I need to tell you.'

'Now isn't a good time,' he said, moving through the groups of people still standing in the portrait hall, gritting his teeth against the need to be far more brutally honest.

'I know. I'm sorry, but it's bothered me all these years.' She caught up with him as he went through the archway into the armoury hall and moved in front of him as he reached the door. 'That thing that happened at school. It wasn't Summer, it was Olympia. She set it all up. I mean, Summer— Sophie—did have the dress and I don't know how she got the money to pay for it, but it certainly wasn't by stealing it from the dorm. Olympia just said it was.'

'I know,' Kit said wearily. 'I never doubted that bit.'

'Oh.' Alexia had taken her hat off now, and with-

out it she looked oddly exposed and slightly crest-
fallen. 'I know it's ages ago and it was just some
silly schoolgirl prank, but hearing Olympia say it
again like that, I didn't like it. We're adults now. I
just wanted to make sure you knew the truth.'

'The truth is slightly irrelevant really. It's what
we're prepared to believe that matters.' He hesitated,
his throat suddenly feeling as if he'd swallowed
arsenic. 'The other thing—about her checking into
the hotel with a man. Was that one of Olympia's
fabrications too?'

'No, that was true.' Alexia was looking at him
almost imploringly. 'Kit—are you really OK? Can
I help?'

From a great distance he recognised her pain as
being similar to his own. It made him speak gently
to her.

'No, I'm not. But you have already.'

He wove his way through the parked cars jam-
ming the courtyard and broke into a run as he
reached the tower gate. At the sides of the driveway
the snow was still crisp and unmarked, but as he
ran down he noticed the prints Sophie's high-heeled
shoes had made and they made her feel closer—as
if she hadn't really gone. When he reached the road

through the village they were lost amongst everyone else's.

The King's Arms was in the mid-afternoon lull between lunchtime and evening drinkers. The landlord sat behind the bar reading the *Racing Times*, but he got to his feet as Kit appeared.

'Major Fitzroy. I mean Lord Fitzr—'

Kit cut straight through the etiquette confusion. 'I'm looking for someone,' he said harshly. 'Someone staying here. Room three I believe? I'll see myself up.'

Without giving the flustered landlord time to respond he headed for the stairs, taking them two at a time. Room three was at the end of the short corridor. An empty vodka bottle stood outside it. Kit hammered on the door.

'Sophie!'

Kit listened hard, but the only sounds were muted voices from a television somewhere and the ragged rasp of his own breathing. His tortured mind conjured an image of the man he'd seen earlier pausing as he unzipped Sophie's dress and her whispering, *Don't worry—he'll go away...*

But he wouldn't. Not until he'd seen her.

'Sophie!'

Clenching his hand into a fist, he was just about to beat on the door again when it opened an inch. A face—puffy-eyed, swarthy, unshaven—peered out at him.

'She's not here.'

With a curse of pure rage, Kit put his shoulder to the door. Whoever it was on the other side didn't put up much resistance and the door opened easily. Glancing at him only long enough to register that he was naked except for a small white towel slung around his hips, Kit pushed past and strode into the room.

In a heartbeat he took in the clothes scattered over the floor—black clothes, like puddles of tar on the cream carpet—the wide bed with its passion-tumbled covers and the room darkened, and he thought he might black out.

'Kit—' Jasper leapt out of the bed, dragging the rumpled sheet and pulling it around himself. Blinking, Kit shook his head, trying to reconcile what he was actually seeing with what he had expected.

'Jasper?'

'Look, I didn't want you to find out like this.' Jasper paused and ducked his head for a moment, but then gathered himself and raised his head again, looking Kit squarely in the eye while the man in the white towel went to his side. 'But it's probably time you knew anyway. I can't go on hiding who I really am just because it doesn't fit the Fitzroy mould. I love Sergio. And I know what you're going to say but—'

Kit gave a short, incredulous laugh as relief burst through him. 'It's the best news I've had for a long time. Really. I can't tell you how pleased I am.' He turned and shook hands with the bewildered man in the white towel, and then went over to Jasper and embraced him briefly, hard. 'Now please—if Sophie's not here, where the hell is she?'

The smile faded from Jasper's face. 'She's gone. She's getting the train back to London. Kit, did something happen between you, because—?'

Kit turned away, putting his hands to his head as despair sucked him down. He swore savagely. Twice. And then strode to the door.

'Yes, something happened between us,' he said, turning back to Jasper with a suicidal smile. 'I was just too stupid to understand exactly what it was.'

The good news was that Sophie didn't have to wait long for a train to come. The bad news was that there was only one straight-through express service to London every day, and that was long gone. The one she boarded was a small, clanking local train that stopped at every miniature village station all along the line and terminated at Newcastle.

The train was warm and virtually empty. Sophie slunk to a seat in the corner and sat with her eyes closed so she didn't have to look at Alnburgh, transformed by the sinking sun into a golden fairy tale castle from an old-fashioned storybook, get swallowed up by the blue haze.

She was used to this, she told herself over and over. Moving on was what she did best. Hadn't she always felt panicked by the thought of permanence? She was good at new starts. Reinventing herself.

But until now she hadn't really known who 'herself' was. Sophie Greenham was a construction; a sort of patchwork of bits borrowed from films and books and other people, fragments of fact layered up with wistful half-truths and shameless lies, all carried off with enough chutzpah to make them seem credible.

Beneath Kit's cool, incisive gaze all the joins had dissolved and the pieces had fallen away. She was left just being herself. A person she didn't really know, who felt things she didn't usually feel and needed things she didn't understand.

As she got further away from Alnburgh her phone came back into signal range and texts began to come in with teeth-grating regularity. Biting her cheeks against each sledgehammer blow of disappointment, Sophie couldn't stop herself checking every time to see if any were from Kit.

They weren't.

There were several from her agent. The vampire film people wanted to see her again. The outfit had impressed *them*, at least.

'Tickets from Alnburgh.'

She opened her eyes. The guard was making his way along the swaying carriage towards her. She sat up, fumbling in her broken bag for her purse as she blinked away the stinging in her eyes.

'A single to London, please.'

The guard punched numbers into his ticket machine with pudgy fingers. 'Change at Newcastle,' he said without looking at her. 'The London train goes from platform two. It's a bit of a distance so you'll need to hurry.'

'Thank you,' Sophie muttered, trying to fix those details in her head. Until then she'd only thought as far as getting on this train. Arriving at Newcastle, getting off and taking herself forwards from there felt like stepping into a void.

She dug her nails into her palms and looked unseeingly out of the window as a wave of panic washed over her. Out of nowhere a thought occurred to her.

'Actually—can you make that two tickets?'

'Are you with someone?'

For the first time the guard looked at her properly; a glare delivered over the top of his glasses that suggested she was doing something underhand. The reality was she was just trying to put something right.

'No.' Sophie heard the break in her voice. 'No, I'm alone. But let's just say I had a debt to pay.'

The station at Alnburgh was, unsurprisingly, empty. Kit stood for a moment on the bleak platform, breathing hard from running and looking desperately around, as if in some part of his mind he still thought there was a chance she would be there.

She wasn't. Of course she wasn't. She had left, with infinite dignity, and for good.

He tipped his head back and breathed in, feeling

the throb of blood in his temples, waiting until the urge to punch something had passed.

'Missed your train?'

Kit looked round. A man wearing overalls and a yellow high-vis jacket had appeared, carrying a spade.

'Something like that. When's the next one to London?'

The man went over to the grit bin at the end of the platform and thrust the spade into it.

'London? The only straight-through London train from here is the 11.07 in the morning. If you need to get one before that you'll have to get to Newcastle.' He threw the spadeful of grit across the compacted snow.

Hopelessness engulfed Kit. Numbly he started walking away. If he caught a train from Newcastle, by the time he'd got to London she'd be long gone and he'd have no way of finding her. Unless…

Unless…

He spun round. 'Wait a minute. Did you say the only straight-through train was this morning? So the one that just left…'

'Was the local service to Newcastle. That's right.'

'Thanks.'

Kit broke into a run. He didn't stop until he reached the tower gate, and remembered the cars. The party was evidently still going on, and the courtyard was still rammed with vehicles. Kit stopped. Bracing his arms against the shiny black bonnet of the one nearest to him, letting his head drop as ragged breaths were torn from his heaving chest, almost like sobs.

She had gone. And he couldn't even go after her.

'Sir?'

Dimly he was aware of the car door opening and a figure getting out. Until that point he hadn't registered which car he was leaning against, or that there was anyone in it, but now he saw that it was the funeral car and the grey-haired man who had just got out was the undertaker.

'I was going to ask if you were all right, but clearly that would be a daft question,' he said, abandoning the stiff formality of his role. 'A better question would be, is there anything I can do to help?'

'Yes,' Kit rasped. 'Yes, there is.'

Sophie stood on the platform and looked around in confusion.

Newcastle Central Station was a magnificent example of Victorian design and engineering. With its iron-boned canopy arching above her, Sophie felt as if she were standing in the belly of a vast whale.

Apart from the noise, and the crowds, maybe. Being inside a whale would probably be a blissfully quiet experience compared to this. People pushed past her, shouting into mobile phones to make themselves heard above the echoing announcement system and the noise of diesel engines.

Amongst them, Sophie felt tiny. Invisible.

It had been just a week and a half since she'd dashed onto the 16.22 from King's Cross but now the girl with the stiletto boots and a corset dress and the who-cares attitude could barely bring herself to walk away from the little train that had brought her from Alnburgh. After the space and silence of the last ten days it felt as if the crowds were pressing in on her and that she might simply be swept away, or trampled underfoot. And that no one would notice.

But the guard had said she needed to hurry if she was going to catch the London connection. Adjusting her grip on her broken bag, holding it awkwardly to make sure it didn't spill its contents, she forced herself to move forwards.

Platform two. Where was platform two? Her eyes

scanned the bewildering array of signs, but somehow none of the words made sense to her. Except one, high up on the lit-up board of train departures.

Alnburgh.

Sophie had never been homesick in her life, probably because she'd never really had a home to be sick for, but she thought the feeling might be something like the anguish that hollowed out her insides and filled her lungs with cement as she stared at the word.

She looked away. She didn't belong there—hadn't she told herself that countless times during the last ten days? The girl from nowhere with the made-up name and the made-up past didn't belong in a castle, or in a family with a thousand years of history.

So where did she belong?

Panic was rising inside her. Standing in the middle of the swarming station concourse, she suddenly felt as if she were falling, or disappearing, and there was nothing there to anchor her. She turned round, desperately searching for something familiar…

And then she saw him.

Pushing his way through the crowds of commuters, head and shoulders above everyone else, his face tense and ashen but so beautiful that for a moment Sophie couldn't breathe. She stood, not wanting to take her eyes off him in case he disappeared again, unable to speak.

'Kit.'

It was a whisper. A whimper. So quiet she barely heard it herself. But at that moment he turned his head and looked straight at her.

His footsteps slowed, and for a second the expression on his face was one she hadn't seen before. Uncertainty. Fear. The same things she was feeling—or had been until she saw him. And then it was gone—replaced by a sort of scowling ferocity as he crossed the distance between them with long, rapid strides. Gathering her into his arms, he kissed her, hungrily and hard.

There were tears running down Sophie's face when she finally pulled away. She felt tender and torn with emotions she couldn't begin to unravel— gratitude and joy and relief, undercut with the terrible anguish she was beginning to realise went with loving someone.

'My train…' she croaked, steeling herself for the possibility that he'd just come to say goodbye.

Slowly he shook his head. His eyes didn't leave hers. 'Don't get on it.'

'Why not?'

He took her face between his hands, drawing her close to him so that in the middle of the crowd they were in their own private universe. Under his silver gaze Sophie felt as if she were bathed in moonlight.

'Because then I would have to get on it too,' he murmured gravely, 'and I'd have to sit opposite you for the next two and a half hours, looking at you, breathing in your scent and wanting to take your clothes off and make love to you on the table.' He gave her a rueful smile that made her heart turn over. 'I've done that once before, so I know how hard it is. And because I hijacked a hearse and committed several civil and traffic offences to find you, and now I have I don't want to let you go again. Not until I've said what I have to say. Starting with sorry.'

Tears were still spilling down her cheeks. 'Kit, you don't have to—'

'I've been rehearsing this all the way from Alnburgh,' he said, brushing the tears away with his thumbs, 'so if you could listen without interrupting that would be good. I saw Jasper.'

'Oh! And—'

He frowned. 'I'm horrified…'

Sophie's mouth opened in protest, but before she could say anything he kissed her into silence and continued softly, '…that he ever thought I wouldn't *approve*. Lord, am I such a judgmental bastard?'

Sophie gave a hiccupping laugh that was half sob. 'I think you're asking the wrong person.'

He let her go then, dropping his hands to his sides and looking down at her with an expression of abject desolation. 'God, Sophie, I'm so sorry. I've spent my whole miserable life not trusting anyone so it had become something of a habit. Until Olympia told me what she did to you at school and I wanted to wring her neck, and it made me realise that I trusted you absolutely.'

'But what about with Sergio—you thought—'

Out of his arms, without his touch Sophie felt as if she were breaking up again. The crowed swelled and jostled around them. A commuter banged her leg with his briefcase.

'No.' It was a groan of surrender. An admission of defeat. He pulled her back into his arms and held her against him so that she could feel the beat of his heart. 'I was too bloody deranged with jealousy to think at all. I just wanted to tear him limb from limb. I know it's not big or clever, but I can't help it. I just want you for myself.'

Tentatively she lifted her head to look up at him, her vision blurred by wonder and tears.

'Really?'

In reply he kissed her again, this time so tenderly that she felt as if he were caressing her soul.

'It'll never work,' she murmured against his mouth. 'I'm not good enough for you.'

'I think…' he kissed the corner of her mouth, her jaw '…we've already established that you're far too good for me.'

She closed her eyes as rapture spiralled through her. 'Socially I mean. I'm nobody.'

His lips brushed her ear lobe. 'So am I, remember?'

It was getting harder to concentrate. Harder to think of reasons why she shouldn't just give in to the rising tide of longing inside her. Harder to keep her knees from buckling. 'I'd be disastrous for your career,' she breathed. 'Amongst all those officers' wives—'

He lifted his head and gazed at her with eyes that were lit by some inner light. 'You'll outshine them all,' he said softly, simply. 'They'll want to hate you for being so beautiful but they won't be able to. Now, have you any more objections?'

'No.'

He seized her hand. 'Then for God's sake let's go and find the nearest hotel.'

Still Sophie held back. 'But I thought you had to report back for duty...'

'I called in some favours.' Gently he took her face between his hands and kissed her again. 'I have three weeks' compassionate leave following my father's death. But since Ralph wasn't actually my father I think we can just call it passionate leave. I intend to make the most of every second.'

EPILOGUE

IT WAS just a tiny piece in the property section of one of the Sunday papers. Eating brioche spread thickly with raspberry jam in the crumpled ruins of the bed that had become their world for the last three weeks, Sophie gave a little squeal.

'Listen to this!

'Unexpected Twist to Fitzroy Inheritance.
'Following the recent death of Ralph Fitzroy, eighth Earl of Hawksworth and owner of the Alnburgh estate, it has come to light that the expected heir is not, in fact, set to inherit. Sources close to the family have confirmed that the estate, which includes Alnburgh Castle and five hundred acres of land in Northumberland as well as a sizeable slice of premium real estate in Chelsea, will pass to Jasper Fitzroy, the Earl's younger son from his second marriage, rather than his older brother, Major Kit Fitzroy.'

Putting the last bit of brioche in her mouth, she continued,

'Major Fitzroy, a serving member of the armed forces, was recently awarded the George Medal for bravery. However, it's possible that his courage failed him when it came to taking on Alnburgh. According to locals, maintenance of the estate has been severely neglected in recent years, leaving the next owner with a heavy financial burden to bear. While Kit Fitzroy is rumoured to have considerable personal wealth, perhaps this is one rescue mission he just doesn't want to take on...'

She tossed the newspaper aside and, licking jam off her fingers, cast Kit a sideways glance from under her lashes.

'"Considerable personal wealth"?' She wriggled down beneath the covers, smiling as she kissed his shoulder. 'I like the sound of that.'

Kit, still surfacing from the depths of the sleep he'd been blessed with since he'd had Sophie in his bed, arched an eyebrow.

'I thought as much,' he sighed, turning over and

looking straight into her sparkling, beautiful eyes. 'You're nothing but a shallow, cynical gold-digger.'

'You're right.' Sophie nodded seriously, pressing her lips together to stop herself from smiling. 'To be honest, I'm really only interested in your money, and your exceptionally gorgeous Chelsea house.' The sweeping gesture she made with her arm took in the bedroom with its view of the garden square outside. 'It's why I've decided to put up with your boring personality and frankly quite average looks. Not to mention your disappointing performance in bed—'

She broke off with a squeal as, beneath the sheets, he slid a languid hand between her thighs.

'Sorry, what was that?' he murmured gravely.

'I said...' she gasped '...that I was only interested in your...money.' He watched her eyes darken as he moved his hand higher. 'I've always wanted to be a rich man's plaything.'

He propped himself up on one elbow, so he could see her better. Her hair was spilling over the pillow—a gentler red than when he'd first seen her that day on the train—the colour of horse chestnuts rather than holly berries—and her face was bare of make-up. She had never looked more beautiful.

'Not a rich man's wife?' he asked idly, leaning down to kiss the hollow above her collarbone.

'Oh, no. If we're talking marriage I'd be looking for a title as well as a fortune.' Her voice turned husky as his lips moved to the base of her throat. 'And a sizeable estate to go with it...'

He smiled, taking his time, breathing in the scent of her skin. 'OK, that's good to know. Since I'm fresh out of titles and estates there's probably no point in asking.'

He felt her stiffen, heard her little gasp of shock and excitement. 'Well, there might be some room for negotiation,' she said breathlessly. 'And I'd say that right now you're in a pretty good bargaining position...'

'Sophie Greenham,' he said gravely, 'I love you because you are beautiful and clever and honest and loyal...'

'Flattery will get you a very long way,' she sighed, closing her eyes as his fingertips trailed rapture over the quivering skin on the inside of her thighs. 'And *that* will probably do the rest...'

His chest tightened as he looked down at her. 'I love you because you think underwear is a better investment than clothes, and because you're brave and funny and sexy, and I was wondering if you'd possibly consider marrying me?'

Her eyes opened and met his. The smile that spread slowly across her face was one of pure, incredulous happiness. It felt like watching the sun rise.

'Yes,' she whispered, gazing up at him with dazed, brilliant eyes. 'Yes, please.'

'I feel it's only fair to warn you that I've been disowned by my family...'

Serene, she took his face in her hands. 'We can make our own family.'

He frowned, smoothing a strand of hair from her cheek, suddenly finding it difficult to speak for the lump of emotion in his throat. 'And I have no title, no castle and no lands to offer you.'

She laughed, pulling him down into her arms. 'Believe me, I absolutely wouldn't have it any other way...'

* * * * *

THE MOST COVETED PRIZE
Penny Jordan

THE COSTARELLA CONQUEST
Emma Darcy

THE NIGHT THAT CHANGED EVERYTHING
Anne McAllister

CRAVING THE FORBIDDEN
India Grey

HER ITALIAN SOLDIER
Rebecca Winters

THE LONESOME RANCHER
Patricia Thayer

NIKKI AND THE LONE WOLF
Marion Lennox

MARDIE AND THE CITY SURGEON
Marion Lennox

Mills & Boon® Large Print
March 2012

THE POWER OF VASILII
Penny Jordan

THE REAL RIO D'AQUILA
Sandra Marton

A SHAMEFUL CONSEQUENCE
Carol Marinelli

A DANGEROUS INFATUATION
Chantelle Shaw

HOW A COWBOY STOLE HER HEART
Donna Alward

TALL, DARK, TEXAS RANGER
Patricia Thayer

THE BOY IS BACK IN TOWN
Nina Harrington

JUST AN ORDINARY GIRL?
Jackie Braun

0212 Rom LP